D1462792

FLATHEAD POST

MILK RIVER
MARIAS R.
TETON R.
MISSOURI R.
FORT McKENZIE
GREAT FALLS

COLUMBIA RIVER

YELLO

THREE FORKS

JEFFERSON R.
MADISON R.
GALLATIN R.

WILLAMETTE R.

SNAKE R.

YELLOWSTONE LAKE
BIG HORN RIVER

FORT BOISE

JACKSON LAKE
JACKSON HOLE

SNAKE R.

MALADE R.

WIND R.

SWEETWATER R.

GREAT
SALT LAKE

SEEDS-KEE-DEE OR GREEN R.

FORT
BRIDGER

COLORADO R.

PACIFIC
OCEAN

▼ Site of the *Mandan* Massacre   △ Upper Teton Valley

♠ Rendezvous of 1837   ◆ Northern Pass over the Divide

palacios

the big sky

A. B. Guthrie, Jr. **the**

With an Introduction by

big sky

Walter Van Tilburg Clark

TIME Reading Program Special Edition
Time-Life Books Inc., Alexandria, Virginia

Time-Life Books Inc.
is a wholly owned subsidiary of
TIME INCORPORATED

TIME Reading Program: *Editor*, Max Gissen

For information about any Time-Life book, please write:
Reader Information, Time-Life Books,
541 North Fairbanks Court, Chicago, Illinois 60611.

editors' preface

The town of Choteau, Montana, is 80 miles south of the Canadian border. In 1901, when Alfred Bertram Guthrie, the author of *The Big Sky*, was six months old, his father moved the family from southern Indiana to Choteau, which was about as close to the edge of the settled area of the United States as it was possible to reach and still find schools and newspapers.

The elder Guthrie went to Choteau to become principal of the Teton County Free High School. His son began his own career as a printer's devil on the weekly Choteau *Acantha*. Choteau was then a cattle town, built where Deep Creek flows into the Teton River and was headquarters for the big cattle ranches thereabouts. The Teton River valley forms part of the setting for *The Big Sky*, and a sense of the wilderness wealth and the immense distances of the Rockies helps give the book its lasting quality. Peaks like Rocky Mountain (9,392 feet) and Silvertip (8,890) may have been among the first snowcapped mountains that the explorers Lewis and Clark saw when they came through the valley in 1805. The Rockies are awesome mountains ("We all believe that we are about to enter on the most perilous and dificuelt part of our Voyage," Clark wrote), and few books had ever succeeded in coming to grips with their grandeur until this one was published in the spring of 1947.

The Big Sky was greeted with what may have been the most uniformly enthusiastic press in the history of American fiction— and much of the praise made the same point: for the first time a novelist had captured the feeling of the Rockies in understandable terms. Ever since Lewis and Clark, writers had tried to describe the mountain world, its lonely expanse, its mystery and enchantment, its magnetic attraction and the lurking sense of fear that it generated. But the weakness of all this writing was that the most extravagant accounts fell far short of the astounding reality. The writers invariably lapsed into purple prose: the literature of the Rockies dwindles away into monotonous references to sublime vistas, grand and majestic panoramas, sunsets beyond compare and sunrises touching the distant peaks with unearthly beauty. Adding to the frustration of the reader was the traditional and unreal nobility with which such writers endowed the mountain dwellers.

In *The Big Sky* the Rockies emerge in all their majesty and the people in all their humanity. They were a hardened, cold and brutal people, and their heroism was hidden within tedious, dirty, dangerous or even squalid events. For years there had been a current in critical writing directed toward the forming of a native American school of realistic Western fiction, as opposed to the stereotyped Hollywood variety. It was led by the late Bernard De Voto, an impassioned enthusiast who, as one reviewer put it, usually delivered his critical judgments as if he were calling on the author to surrender in the name of the great Jehovah and the Continental Congress. De Voto saw *The Big Sky* as the culmination of his long years of effort to convince writers of the wealth of material in the West—in its real history, rather than in the melodramas that stemmed from dime novels and expanded into Western movies. "The book is so extraordinary that I find it hard to express the full measure of my admiration without being extravagant," De Voto wrote of the Guthrie novel. "It is an exceedingly distinguished book, an unusually original work, and one of the most thoroughly wrought acts of the imagination I have ever read." It was also, he noted with satisfaction, one of the most authentic novels of the West ever written.

Walter Van Tilburg Clark in his new introduction to this special edition has given eloquent testimony of Guthrie's path-breaking achievement in writing of the heroism of the mountain men. This portion of the work is carefully drawn from historical sources.

Guthrie has said that he used Osborne Russell's *Journal of a Trapper, or, Nine Years in the Rocky Mountains, 1834-1843*, and that he drew heavily on the works of Francis Parkman. Indeed, the lives and legends of such famous mountain men as Jim Bridger, Kit Carson, Hugh Glass, Thomas Fitzpatrick, Andrew Henry and Jedediah Smith are familiar to the expert, and the journals and diaries exist in such numbers that creative invention is all but unnecessary in writing about them: the boldest imagination could never keep up with their actual exploits. Hugh Glass, clawed by a grizzly so badly that he was left for dead, crawled 60 miles or more until he came to a fortified post, where he eventually recovered. Jedediah Smith in a little over two years made his way from Salt Lake to the Gulf of California, over the deserts to San Diego, back to the Colorado, north through Oregon, and then up the Columbia and the Kootenay almost to the Canadian border, then back to Wyoming, in a series of trips so extensive, through so much country completely unknown, that the imagination can scarcely envision the difficulties he must have encountered.

It is an irony of history that the end result of all this striving was the manufacture of hats. The fortunes of the mountain men rose and fell with the price of beaver skins, which in turn fluctuated according to the fashions in men's hats. It was highest, of course, when the beaver hat was in style.

But though trapping beaver was in itself an unheroic matter, the heroism of the mountain men is beyond dispute. No one at all familiar with the source works for *The Big Sky* can feel that Guthrie overstressed the hazards: Indians, grizzlies, weather, distance, whiskey, traders—and other trappers. Years after the period depicted in this novel, Francis Parkman reported with awe on the life of the average trapper he met on the journey that gave him *The Oregon Trail:* "Frequently he must content himself with devouring his evening meal uncooked, lest the light of his fire should attract the eyes of some wandering Indian; and sometimes having made his rude repast, he must leave his fire still blazing and withdraw to distance under cover of the darkness, that his disappointed enemy, drawn thither by the light, may find his victim gone and be unable to trace his footsteps in the gloom. This is the life led by scores of men among the Rocky Mountains. I once met a trapper whose breast was marked with the scars of six bullets and arrows, one of his arms broken by a shot and one of his knees shattered; yet still, with the mettle of New England whence he had come, he continued to follow his perilous calling."

In its fidelity to the historical records, *The Big Sky* is a genuine historical novel, as true a synthesis of the mountain men as we have. But that is not all it is. *The Big Sky* is, in addition, a searching and perceptive psychological study of its central character, Boone Caudill. Caudill is a violent, inarticulate, uneducated man whose simplicity of action is combined with psychological subtlety. He bears a certain resemblance to some of William Faulkner's characters. Like Faulkner's backwoods Mississippi farmers, he is at war with the civilized world. The event that starts him on his way West from Kentucky at age 17 is a scene of pure Faulknerian melodrama. Turning on his drunken and brutal father for the first time, he does too workmanlike a job of it, pasting the old man with a stick of stovewood. Has he killed him? As Boone is preparing to run away, his mother shows concern about his father's whereabouts. Boone says nothing. His brother answers, "He's lyin' out there with the rain beatin' on him and he don't even know it"—a superb line straight out of Faulkner, perhaps even better than Faulkner would have done with it.

The first part of the novel deals with Boone's flight before he starts for the mountains. Wary as a wild animal, he moves along the ridges parallel to the roads, sleeps in cow barns, steals a boat, steals horses, endures a beating. At the climax of the story he is running from a crowd in a flight that seems nightmarishly protracted and oddly static, broken with talks and discussions within earshot of the sounds of a pursuit that never seems to get nearer. In the second part of the book, Boone finds sanctuary in the Western mountain country, hunting for a time with scout Dick Summers, and after that living with the Piegan Indians. It is an idyllic life, which is finally ended by the arrival of the inevitable settler.

It is in part the two sides of Guthrie's novel—the contrast between the unspoiled wilderness of the Rockies and the meanness and pettiness of the human conflicts—that give the book its peculiar flavor. For in both the story of Dick Summers and the mountain men, and in the story of Boone Caudill seeking an end to his torment among them, the persistent element is the freshness and wonder of the mountain wilderness. The winds from the west blowing along the Gallatin, the mountains in great peaks and bulges of rocks, the lakes with little circles from the rising trout, are all fragments of a new world:

> The sun was gone, and the dark was beginning to creep on the wooded slopes beyond the lake, but the sky was clear and light yet and the lake lay bright against its edging of earth and timber, like a piece fallen from above. To the east the sun lingered on the very tops of the mountains. ... Overhead, from somewhere or everywhere, there was a high, fine singing. Only when a man was quiet did he hear it, but there it was then, thin and coming on and fading and coming on again, and it might have been the high pines talking, or the mountains, or time humming, far off and old ... the sound of a grazing horse, but that was all, except for the thin singing.

Clearly, no man could write of the mountains with such familiarity except one who had spent considerable time in them. Guthrie has said that in his early years he fished and hunted a good deal, and now that he is older he is content to enjoy the outdoors for its own sake. He graduated from the Teton County Free High School, studied at the University of Washington and graduated from the University of Montana in 1923. He worked on an engineering project in Lower California, served in the Forest Service, knocked around the West with his brother and became a reporter on the *Leader* in Lexington, Kentucky, where an uncle lived. He made his home thereafter in Lexington, but his summers were spent in Montana.

Guthrie's first book, a mystery story with a Western background called *Murders at Moon Dance*, was published in 1943; it was rather coldly received, when it was mentioned at all, and he has said that he himself has an unfavorable opinion of the book. In 1944, as an editorial writer on the *Leader*, Guthrie was awarded a Nieman Fellowship at Harvard. During the year of freedom from professional duties the fellowship gave him, he had time to work on *The Big Sky*. Much of the book was written under the supervision of Professor Theodore Morison, who went over the chapters, week by week, as they were completed. Guthrie was further inspired by Harvard Professor Frederick Merk, the grand old man among historians of the frontier.

Following the success of *The Big Sky*, Guthrie wrote another novel, *The Way West* (in which mountain man Dick Summers again appears, guiding an emigrant train to Oregon); it was the Pulitzer Prize novel of 1950 and, like *The Big Sky*, was made into a movie. Guthrie found movie work appealing. He became a Hollywood scriptwriter, his best-known work being the script for the movie *Shane*, and his later stories and novels strongly reflected the influence of movie technique and attitudes.

But *The Big Sky* remains unique in his own writing as well as in the literature of the Rocky Mountains—a solitary and independent sort of masterpiece, standing entirely alone among contemporary American works of fiction, as apart in its own way as the people it deals with were apart from the life of their time.

—THE EDITORS

introduction

This is a book about a mountain man, and if American mythmaking had followed anything like the true ancient pattern, the mountain man would certainly be our number one Hero by now. Our tendency toward urban uniformity, with its multiplication of human frustrations, our high degree of literacy, and the presence of movies, radios and TV sets have already made his time, the time of the great westering, into a kind of American golden age. And that is exactly the sort of remote, enviable but not quite believable morning of the world in which heroes (with a small "h") have always been freed of their too-literal being and become Heroes, representative figures capable of performing legendary deeds.

The process has taken place, in our case, with alarming rapidity. It is only a little more than 50 years since the end of the westering, and a little more than a hundred since the end of the mountain man's part in it. But it has taken place, no question about that. Just think of the books that have been written about the westering; just look at the number of movies and TV shows which have drawn upon it. If you have always worked in a New York office, or a Chicago factory or even a San Francisco store, you do not really believe in cowboys—not in the profane, grimy, mustached variety which actually drove longhorns over the Chisholm Trail, at any rate—let alone in mountain men. In fact you may find it hard to believe in the country they lived in, even if you take a summer tour into those parts of the West which can still suggest to your eyes what they must have seen: the inner parks of the Rockies, the Blackfoot plains country of upper Montana, the long, shining valleys of the Missouri headwaters, the Jefferson, the Madison and the Gallatin. You are likely, if you have never looked at actual Western landscapes before, to find those regions not only unbelievable, but also a little dismaying.

Indeed, even if you live in those parts of the West which have not yet been littered beyond recognition with the advantages of civilization (and the mountain states haven't), it still isn't altogether easy to imagine them as the Indian and the mountain man saw them (or even as the border cavalryman, or those early litterbugs, the covered-wagon pioneers and the overland forty-niners, saw them): utterly townless, fenceless and abounding in wildlife. It is even something of a problem to visualize such people and their way of life. It helps a little to visit the remains or reconstructions of some of the old forts—Laramie and Bridger on the Oregon Trail, Sutter's Fort in Sacramento, the spooky, adobe vestiges of Fort Churchill near the Carson River in Nevada. It helps a little, too, to visit the lonesome, barren site of the legendary Battle of the Little Bighorn, or the Indian pueblos of the Colorado, which still have a life of their own, or the Spanish towns of Taos and Santa Fe, where many of the mountain men wintered, or old mining towns which still suggest their past, towns such as Leadville, Colorado, and Virginia City, Nevada. It helps also to go out and look at the buffalo and the elk in Yellowstone Park, the legitimate Indian, cowboy and cavalry paintings of Charles Russell and Frederic Remington, and the exhibits in the Museum of the American Indian in New York. But there you are, you see. It takes people and things to bring us close to belief now. The world of the westering, and particularly the almost unpeopled, thing-free, game-abounding world of its early years, has certainly become our mythical world.

So, to get back to the point, the mountain man should just as certainly have become our most important Hero. He was the first of all our possible Heroes to enter that world. (Excepting the Indian, of course, but the Indian was a candidate for Worthy Foe, and even the worthiest foe cannot be Hero.) He had it all to himself in its cleanest and most spacious time, and then, as scout and guide he led the missionary, the pioneer settler and the forty-niner across it;

and all the rest—the border cavalryman, the stagecoach driver, the pony-express rider, the buffalo skinner, the cowboy, the prairie sodbuster, the railroad engineer and gandy dancer and the lumber jack —trooped after.

He had a legitimate claim by ancestry too, this mountain man. He was the direct descendant of the backwoods leatherstocking, the Daniel Boone, who was the only earlier candidate for the pantheon, and he was a more complete representative of the type, because he moved in a much vaster and even more dangerous wilderness, and separated himself much more completely from every manifestation of unheroic civilization.

Finally, and most importantly, he actually possessed all the true, ancient heroic virtues—courage, strength, endurance, wiliness, pride, resourcefulness, intimacy with nature—to a considerably greater degree than any of those who followed him. He had to, in order to survive.

Something must have gone radically wrong, then, with the American mythmaking process. All those later travelers have already made their way into the pantheon. Even such unexpected and minor hangers-on as the bartender, the gambler and the cancan girl have found places by way of amusing old melodramas, fiction all the way from Bret Harte to yesterday, and movies and TV shows which have made them as familiar as the next-door neighbor. The lumberjack, in a tall-story, American way, has become a true mythical figure, Paul Bunyan. And, needless to say, that johnny-come-lately in the real procession, the cowboy, has become *the* American Hero. He has become more than that. He is Mr. Old West, the demigod.

Meanwhile the poor mountain man is still sitting by the river in a tiny, shadowy St. Louis which isn't there any longer, waiting for a ghostly keelboat which never comes, with all his second westering before him. He has no known folk songs or folk tales of his own. His monuments and memorials are very few and his relics are to be found only in obscure and shadowy corners of Indian museums. He has made no memorable dramatic appearance on stage, screen or TV. The factual literature about him is meager compared with that which attends every other major figure in the group. And there are only three noteworthy novels about him: *The Long Rifle*, by Stewart Edward White, *Lord Grizzly*, by Frederick Manfred, and the book you are about to read, *The Big Sky*, by A. B. Guthrie. This last is the only full-length portrait, factual or fictional, of the mountain man, the only account of how he came to be, how he lived and what for, and how and why he passed.

Since Mr. Guthrie himself will give you the complete mountain man in an imaginative resurrection of the first order—and his world too, in its last and bitterest phase—it may be that the best service we can render him here is simply to try to answer the question we have already raised at such length: Why has the mountain man, apparently America's most natural candidate for Hero, failed completely, so far, to stir the popular imagination? Nobody could hope to answer such a question completely, but even a partial answer should go far toward suggesting what a formidable task Mr. Guthrie undertook—and undertook quite knowingly too; his Boone Caudill is no lucky find, no Hero by chance—when he decided to launch the mountain man upon his second westering himself.

Part of the answer, of course, has already been implied in the discussion of how the westering became our golden age. We are much more fact-minded these days than the ancient mythmakers were, and our world has been changing much more rapidly than theirs ever did. As a result, we cannot visualize our golden age nearly as clearly as they did theirs, and the partial disbelief which makes myth tends to become complete disbelief, which never made anything.

This tendency to complete disbelief has been increased, in the case of the mountain man, because he was a unique and short-lived figure. There was never anybody quite like him before he appeared; he lasted, in his full being, only about one short generation; and there has never been anybody in the least like him since. More than that, the last of his breed, the real breed, was dead before anybody now alive was even born. Such complete disconnection could never have occurred in the ages of true mythmaking.

And finally, the mountain man himself lived in an unprecedented isolation, so that, as we've already seen, nobody else could record him to any extent, and never was there another being since the cave man, unless it was the Indian, who was so reluctant to record himself. Silence was the first rule of survival in his world, both as hunter and as hunted. And silence gets to be a habit. (It will be very much worth your while to watch Boone Caudill learning the use of his senses as he goes—another department in which contemporary man has lost a great deal—and becoming indifferent to talk as he does so, and finally even contemptuous of it.) More often than not he was completely illiterate, and he didn't care much for writing when he wasn't. He carried his maps in his head, as the Indian did, and very precise ones too, except when, for immediate purposes, he drew them in the sand with a twig or a finger, and then he erased all traces of them when the lesson had been taught, as he erased all signs of his caches of supplies and furs. It was not in his nature, in short, to leave tracks of any kind behind him. In his world that could get to be a habit too, and it was very likely to be a fatal one.

So, for our fact-hunting minds, his personal record is not very suggestive. In the main he has to be made out indirectly, by way of company account books or the official journals of expeditions which entered his country, and the popular imagination is not stirred by that kind of reading.

Not all of that put together, however, seems nearly enough to explain why the mountain man has been so completely excluded from the roster of Heroes. No, there is something else at work against the mountain man, and much more importantly at work. It is nothing very obscure, unfortunately, or very interesting either, but it needs to be pointed out again. It can be, quite briefly, by way of one summary glance at a typical letter about *The Big Sky*, and another at the cowboy on the mountain man's pedestal.

The letter was written by a lady, to use that appellation in its least winning sense. It complained that *The Big Sky* should never have been allowed to get into print at all because it made Boone Caudill out to be a thief, a gambler, a liar, a blasphemer, a roistering drunk, a man who indulged in illicit sex, and with Indian women at that, and a murderer of so low a sort that he would kill his best friend without giving him a chance to prove his innocence or to defend himself. (She overlooked the fact that he also bathed rarely, wiped bloody hands on his shirt, ate without a knife and fork, and seldom shaved or cut his hair.) It should not be possible, she felt, for any decent adult or innocent child to find such a book lying about, especially when it made a hero of that sort of man. None of our brave, pioneer ancestors, she intimated, ever behaved like that. Mr. Guthrie himself, then, was responsible for the entire awfulness. He was trying to capitalize upon sensationalism of the most disgusting kind.

We all know the cowboy on the pedestal already. Suffice it to say that he is the complete antithesis of Boone Caudill. He is freshly shaven, his shirt is clean, his Stetson is newly pipestoned, he never swears at all, seldom drinks and but little then, and he wouldn't dream of gambling, lying or stealing. He must shoot at somebody once in a while, of course, or where is the drama, but the target is always his alter ego, the badman, who good and well deserves shooting several times over, and it is always the badman who starts the shooting too. Above all, this Hero is invariably fond of children, anybody's children, kind to animals (nobody has ever found out what he does with all those shorthorns that keep going by) and polite to a downright courtly degree, not only to true ladies, but even to women who could scarcely be called that. It would never occur to him to approach the woman more closely than that under any circumstances, or the lady either, except in true love, and after marriage, and after the show too.

The short road to a place in the American pantheon, a high place, at least, apparently takes the candidate, hat in one hand and lollipop in the other, through ladies' drawing rooms and children's hours. Unless he is content to become Unworthy Foe.

That state of things can't last. Children aren't that foolish, for one thing. There are changes going on already, even in the cowboy Hero. Only Heroes born in verity can give a nation a soul, and only Heroes who give a nation a soul can find a place in its enduring pantheon. Even so, it is going to be a long, slow second-westering for Boone Caudill, though he is already a little more than mortal as he starts, drunk and grieving blindly over his losses, the loss of his love, the loss of his friend, the loss of his world, "weaving big and dark into the darkness."

—WALTER VAN TILBURG CLARK

To My Father

contents

Editors' Preface   v

TIME Reading Program Introduction   xi

Part One   **1830**   3

Part Two   **1830**   63

Part Three   **1837**   163

Part Four   **1842-1843**   251

Part Five   **1843**   335

PART I

1

Serena Caudill heard a step outside and then the squeak of the cabin door and knew that John was coming in. She kept poking at the fireplace, in which a hen was browning. "Where's Boone?"

"Around, I reckon." She looked up then and saw him shut the door against the rain, saw him shut it behind him without turning while his eyes took in the murky kitchen. He limped to the wall, making an uneven thump on the puncheon floor, started to hang his coat on its peg, thought better of it and hunched it back around his neck. In the warmth of the room the smells of cow and sweat and drink and wet woolens flowed from him.

"A body kin tell when it's rainin' just by the sound of your feet," she said, while her gaze followed him.

"You said that aplenty of times." He stood facing the window, as if he could see out of the oiled paper that did for glass. "You'd sing different if you had a ball in your leg."

"I ain't belittlin' it," she said, and tried the hen with a fork. In her mind's eye she was seeing him, that day when he got back from Tippecanoe with a ball in his thigh and the bloody hide of an Indian in his knapsack. He had kept the scalp and tanned the skin and made himself a razor strop out of it. It was a time ago, a right smart time, for a man still to have misery from a wound.

He swung around. "I said, where's Boone?"

She could keep her mouth shut, but her head bobbed as if he had pushed it, pointing in the direction of the dog trot that led to the cabin they slept in.

His voice filled the room. "Boone! You Boone!"

Steps sounded on the dog trot, above the busy whisper of the rain. The door swung open. Boone stood just outside, letting the rain fall on him. "What you want?"

"Come in!"

"What you want, Pap?" Boone sidled in, leaving the door open.

"You been to the store ag'in, drinkin' liquor and raisin' sand, just like you was growed up."

Serena tried to keep the quaver out of her voice. "If he did, he come by it honest."

"It ain't for the calf to beller like the bull. You keep your long nose out of this, old woman."

His eyes went back to the boy. "You prit' near killed Mose Napier."

"He deviled me."

"He'll devil ye more. Ambrose Napier's swore to a warrant."

"Ambrose went to the law?" Serena asked.

"Goddam it, will you keep your mouth shut! Yes, he taken out a warrant." To Boone he said, "Git on out."

"You ain't goin' to whale me ag'in, Pap."

"So?"

"I come seventeen last month, and I don't figger to take no more."

"You can figger for your own self when the law says you be old enough."

"I ain't takin' no more, I said. I'll stand up to you."

Pap caught Boone's arm and pushed him toward the door. "You ain't man enough for your pap yit."

"I'll leave this here place. For good, too. I ain't held here."

Serena said, "He means it, Pap. Can't you tell? And us standin' in need of him like we do."

"I told you onc't to hush, but no, by God, you got to have your say! I ain't just tellin' you ag'in." Pap gave Boone a shove. "If'n you leave, the law'll draw you back. Git outside!"

Serena watched them go out. For height they were almost of a size, but Pap's heft made Boone look skinny. She turned back to the fireplace and with the fork she had forgotten in her hand stabbed again at the hen.

Boone heard Pap following close on his heels as he stepped beyond the door. He caught the strong whiff of whisky that had staled in the stomach. He heard the door pull to and felt the beat of the small rain on his hair.

Pap's voice surprised him, sounding changed now and friendly. "Boone. Oh, Boone."

Boone turned his head, and then Pap struck. His fist caught Boone high on the cheek. Boone staggered ahead and fell in the mud. Above the pounding in his head he heard Pap's voice. "Goddam you! Think you can match me!" Pap's boot swung back for a kick. Boone rolled away from it, got his knees under him and scuttled ahead, until at last he found his feet and began to run.

Pap came after him, his boots slapping against the wet earth like those of a man with two good legs. The woodpile lay ahead. A stick stuck up from it as if waiting to be grabbed. It pulled out easy. Turning with the swing of it, Boone had one glimpse of Pap's scared face. The smack of the stick against it was like a lick on a punkin. Pap took a couple of crazy steps and fell full length and lay still.

Boone said "There!" and let the stick fall. Now he had quit running he could feel the blood pumping in his ears.

Out of the shadows around the Caudills' old barn Dan came slipping. "Godamighty, Boone!" he said, bending down to look at Pap. "I been hidin' out, knowin' Pap was on the warpath. He'll kill you now, if he ain't dead hisself."

"Not me, he won't."

"Won't?"

"I'm leavin'."

"Leavin'?"

"You want to come with me?"

"I reckon not, Boone. Anyways, Pap ain't mad at me."

"I knew you wouldn't."

"Where you goin' to?"

"Ain't sayin'." Boone turned and made for the cabin, from which came the gleam of a new-lit candle. Before he got to the door, Dan came running up and pushed ahead of him into the kitchen.

Ma was taking the bird from its spit.

"Boone done for Pap, most likely," Dan told her.

She had started for the table with the bird. The words stopped her. Her eyes turned to Boone.

"Goddam him!" he said.

"What?"

"I hit him a lick with a club."

Dan added, "He's lyin' out there with the rain beatin' on him and he don't even know it."

Ma put on a bonnet and started to pull on the rag of a coat. Boone asked, "Wait'll I git gone?"

"Gone?" She stood again without moving, as if letting thought sink into her. "You ain't really leavin', Boone? He'll put the law after you."

Boone walked across the kitchen and out the door to the dog trot and went into the other cabin and took a hickory shirt and cotton underwear and hand-knit socks from a chest. Back in the kitchen, he spread the shirt on the floor and dropped the other things on it and rolled them up.

Serena watched him. From underneath the water shelf she dug out a small sack and handed it to him without speaking.

Dan said, "You sure fotched him a dandy, Boone."

"You go see about your pap," Ma told him. "I'll be there in a shake." Dan shuffled toward the door. To Boone she said, "I do' know why you want that there strop, nor the hair, neither."

Boone held up the strop and scalp that Pap had got in the fight with the Prophet. The strop was a muddy brown and had commenced to crumble at the edges, but it was an honest-to-God Indian-skin strop all the same. The hair on the scalp had lost its shine, and the little patch of skin that held it together had shriveled and curled and lay lost in the hair like a bur in a dog's coat.

"I know," answered Dan. "He wants to make a show of 'em, like Pap always done." He snickered. "I reckon he'll favor a leg, too."

Boone said, "I don't hanker to be like Pap, and I won't take much off'n you, neither, Dan. Hear?" He unrolled the shirt and put the strop and scalp with the rest and rolled the bundle tight again, dropping it into the bag Ma had given him. He looked about the room afterward, moving to the corner by the door as his eye fell upon Pap's rifle with its powder horn and pouch.

"I don't know what your pap'll do without that there rifle gun," Ma said.

"If'n you didn't kill him with the club, you'll kill him by takin' Old Sure Shot," Dan put in.

Boone slung the horn and pouch from his shoulder and picked up his rifle and bundle. He looked at Dan and then at Ma.

"Best hurry, Boone," Dan said, looking at the door. "Can't tell when Pap'll come to hisself." Underneath his funning and his go-easy way Dan was a good-enough boy.

Serena turned from Boone and all at once seemed to see the hen lying forgotten on the table. She picked it up and rolled it in a rag and handed it to Boone. Her eyes wouldn't come level with his; they fixed themselves on his chest. Of a sudden he saw that she looked like a tired, sad rabbit, her eyes round and watery and her nose twitching. He felt his face twist suddenly and his throat knot and the tears about to come. He said, "Goodbye."

Her voice was a rusty whisper. "Good luck to ye, Boone."

Dan followed him to the door. Night had closed down outside, so wet and black a body felt almost like drawing back. Dan spoke just with his breath. "To St. Louis?"

Through the murmur of the rain there came to them the beat of a horse's hoofs. The Caudills' old dog began to bark. "You shut your mouth!" Boone said, and stepped into the dark.

2

All night Boone walked through the rain, feeling the steady drip of it on his head and shoulders while his eye poked for the dark trail among the trees and his mind kept going over the fight at the store and the later trouble with Pap. He reckoned he'd broke Mose Napier's face all right. He could see him, with his open jaw skewed over and his eyes rolling as he lay in the dirt. It was all right, too. It was what Mose had asked for. Mose was older than him, by two year anyway, and a sight too big for his breeches. A body could take so much and then, if he was a man, he didn't take any more, leastwise as long as he could hit back.

He figured he might have done for Pap, too. It was a keen lick he'd fotched him. And, like with Mose, it was all right. It pleasured Pap to beat on somebody, especially when he was mean with liquor. It didn't seem like liquor acted on Pap the way it did on others. It didn't make him laugh and feel big. He just got meaner and meaner and his face screwed down like a crazy man's, and, when he came home, everybody better act like he was God Almighty or Pap would whop him. Like as not he would anyway, far as that went.

Boone figured he hadn't done anything that a true man wasn't bound to do. A man couldn't look himself in the face if he let people make little of him. What if he did have some store liquor in him when he tackled Mose? It was still right, and it settled things man to man, like they ought to be settled. And still the Napiers had gone to law and put the high sheriff after him. And it would be like Pap to get the law on his side, being he couldn't do for himself. It wasn't fair, bringing in the sheriff, just because a body did what he had to. It wasn't right to set the law on a man, making him feel small and alone, making him run away. It wasn't right, all taking sides against one and the one not in the wrong.

It was like people and things were all banded against him, the trail losing itself in the dark and the trees hunched close around him and the night dripping wet and maybe unfriendly eyes watching from it, laughing when he stumbled. It was enough to put a lonesome fright in the heart and a lump in the throat.

Pap would know where to look for him. Dan would tell, if Pap pushed him. Dan knew as well as anybody that he'd strike for St. Louis, aiming to move into Injun country from there and so, maybe, to meet up with Uncle Zeb Calloway. Uncle Zeb was Ma's brother and had lit out ten years before to trap varmints in the west. He had fought with the Injuns and killed buffalo and made many a far journey into country where you mightn't see another man for a year, unless it was an Injun and you dropped to the ground and bellied up and leveled on him. That one time when Uncle Zeb came back to Kentucky for a visit, he wore buckskins that were black from grease and blood and camp fire, and he smelled of smoke and musk and liquor, and when he told about where he had been it was almost like a speechmaking. He spoke in a big voice and waved his arms and talked about being free like it was something you could heft.

Pap sat around and drank and watched Uncle Zeb when he was talking, and as the drink took hold and his face got darker, he tried to make out that the west wasn't so much, after all, but Uncle Zeb looked at him, like you'd look at something too small to take notice of. And sometimes Uncle Zeb went quiet, looking away like he didn't see, and Dan put questions to him to get him started again.

Daylight came slow and gloomy, but the rain had fallen off to a drizzle and the drizzle by and by dried up in the cold air. The sky was still gray, though, and low, and when Boone paused on a ridge to look back the distances were shut off by mist. He moved off the trail anyhow, now that day had come, and in a close grove of black oak unwrapped the hen and tore a leg-and-thigh off. It wasn't much more than a bite, hungry as he was, but when he had sucked the bones clean he wound the rag back around the rest of the hen and stuffed it in the sack and set about charging Old Sure Shot, the long-barreled Kentucky rifle that Pap had set such store by. Pap would hardly let a body look at it, he prided it that much. The feel of the smooth steel and dressed sugar wood was good to the hand.

The loading done, Boone settled his shoulders against the base of a tree, feeling his muscles melt. He would get up in a shake and go on, he told himself, and fell asleep at once. He woke up worried and stiff with chill. By the looks of the sunless sky he figured the time to be high noon. He got up, anxious with the feeling that he had wasted time that might go against him, and set off again.

He kept to the side of the trail now, in the cover of the wooded ridges, and scanned the back track when the view opened behind him. The going was rough, this way, but safer, and for mile after mile he climbed and dipped and wound through the timber, until dark began to settle again and he stood high above the valley of the Kentucky river, and through the thickening dusk saw below him a spread of buildings that he took for Frankfort.

He stood still, and felt tiredness on him like a weight, pulling at his muscles, trying to drag him down to earth. As he halted there on the height where the rolling Blue Grass fell away toward the river, he began to shake with cold. Even yet there was a dampness in his clothes which went chill against his skin as the wind blew up the river, driving through his homespun coat and worn jeans. Little riffles ran across the muscles of his chest and back, and, unless he kept his jaw clenched, his teeth set up a fine clicking.

There was no help for it, though. He hadn't thought to bring flint and steel, and though he had heard that a man could get himself a fire by shooting at close range into powder sprinkled over lighters he shied from the risk of both shot and blaze. He might go down into the town, of course, and ask for a place to sleep, but there was no telling what people were like, living crowded up that way. Probably there was more law there than a man could believe, and a peck of rules to go by or run into trouble. Anyhow, it was too close to home. Maybe someone there would know him. Maybe they already had heard the law was after him.

He started angling down the long slope, aiming to the right, away from the town. It was dark when he reached the river, but a light shone from a window downstream and he went toward it, walking soft, letting the noise of his steps lose itself in the sound of the heavy water by his side. He tripped and picked himself up, and then laid down his sack and groped backward until his hand closed on a rope. He followed it down, until it ended at the nose of a boat. His hand went out and explored her bottom and found it dry, and on the gunwales felt the oars shipped in their locks as if the owner had left her against a quick return. He stowed his rifle in her, and his bag, and then, following the rope back up the bank, untied it from the tree and pushed off.

He wasn't a knowing hand with a boat, and the stream was high and strong, but by and by he got her nosed well into the current and felt her push ahead as he put his back to the oars. The shore faded to a dark rim, far and dim as a cloud in a night sky, and now there was only the river running black beneath him and the pull of it against the boat and the busy whisper of the water. The light ashore fell back and was gone, leaving no point by which he could judge his drift, but he felt the stronger muscle of the current as he came into the channel and knew that he was being carried far downstream. He kept at his oars, bending far forward and coming back with all the power of legs and back and arms, feeling the shuddering give of the blades as he brought them through. A second light peeped at him, distant on the other bank, and he took it for his guide and bent harder to the oars until the current let up and the shore rose like a wall before his eye. He eased her in, then, and pulled her up and tied her and, taking his rifle and bag, set out toward the light.

He tried to go quiet in the dark, feeling ahead with his feet before he let them down, but a tangle of short growth on the slope crackled under his softest step. From the direction of the house a dog began to bark.

Boone stopped and waited, hitching the rifle closer in the crook of his arm. He was trembling again, now that the hard work of rowing was over, but the cold didn't seem to touch him close. It was as if his body was numb, being too tired and hungry to feel. The dog kept barking, coming on as the silence made him braver. Boone leaned his rifle against a tree and from his bag took the one-legged carcass of the hen. He tore off the other leg, rewrapped the bird and put it back, and then stepped forward with his hand out while he whispered, "Here, boy! Here, boy!"

He felt the dog before he could see him, felt the cold nose and the food taken from his hand and heard the bones snapping. He stooped. "All right, boy." The dog's head came under his fingers. He scratched it around the ears. "Hush now!"

A square of light appeared ahead, and a man's figure lined itself in it and stood there silent for a moment. Then a voice said, "He's just barkin' a coon," and afterward it rose in a call, "Here, Blackie! Here!" The dog slipped from under Boone's hand and grew to be one with the darkness. The square of light narrowed to a ribbon and went out.

Boone hunched down, shivering, until after the gleam in the window itself had died. Then he edged ahead like a hunter and came to a small farmyard and made out the house and, to his right, the outline of a barn. He stole to the barn and felt for the door and let himself in.

The warm odor of cow came to his nose. He heard a soft breathing. "Saw, Boss!" he said under his breath, closing the door behind him. He stood without moving, letting the animal warmth of the place get to his skin, then shifted his bag to the arm that held his rifle and stepped forward, saying, "Saw! Saw!" His hand groped ahead, meeting nothing, and he wondered where the cow was, until his foot touched the soft hide and he realized she was lying down.

"Saw!" he said, expecting her to rise. "Saw!" But she lay there, and he thrust his hand down to the warm hide, wondering at her gentleness. He felt in the straw at her side to see that it was dry, and brought himself around and eased down on his butt in the soft litter and snuggled his back against her.

He put his rifle down close to hand and opened his bag, taking out what was left of the hen. He ate it all, ending by crunching up the softer bones and sucking out the pockets of lights while the cow chewed on her cud and let him take of her warmth. Then he squirmed closer, pillowing his head on her flank, and with the familiar odor of the barn strong in his nostrils closed his eyes.

Out of the tired cloud of his mind Ma's face appeared, the dark and watery eyes, the broad nose, the pinched mouth, the sad look of having given up to work and worry and Pap. He saw Dan going to the barn and the woodpile doing chores—Dan who could get around Pap, but hadn't the spunk to face him. He saw the shagbark hickory back of the cabin, the worm fence, the smoke trailing from the chimney. Before he could stop it, a sob broke in his throat. He turned his face against the flank of the cow and let himself cry. "Good luck to you, too, Ma," he said.

After a while he sat up and gouged the tears from his eyes, feeling ashamed but relieved, too, and slowly almost cozy, safe and unseen in the dark barn with the gentle cow for company. He settled back against her.

3

The movement of the cow roused him. She came over on her belly and with a grunting sigh got her back legs under her and heaved her hindquarters up. He was wide awake at once, but cold and stiff clear to his bones. Still, he felt rested, and anxious to get on while the world still slept. He stood and gave himself time to stretch. He wondered how long it was until sunup. Three hours, he reckoned. Anyhow, he best be moving. First, though, he felt for his rifle and went over it with the sack that had held the hen. There was enough grease in the cloth to hold off rust. Afterwards he emptied the bullet pouch and counted the balls as he dropped them back, stuffed his bundle of clothes into the sack, and then found his way to the door and went out.

It had turned off clear. The stars were out, small and frosty. Almost straight overhead he could make out the Big Dipper lying upside down. A light streak showed along the eastern sky line. From somewhere came the thin chirp of a bird. In another hour it would be light.

Home would be to the east and north, to the left of the coming sun. He faced that way, seeing the cabin in his mind and the shagbark and the smoke trailing from the chimney. Inside, Ma was readying for breakfast, cooking side meat and eggs and hot bread. It could be he wouldn't see Ma again or ever eat her cooking. Maybe he would only remember, seeing her face always sad and tired, tasting her soup and sweetening and cuts of meat only by recollecting. She would be thinking and worrying about him now, most likely, but not saying much as long as Pap was around. He wished he could look at her just once more. Such a weakness came on him that he thought, for a little, he couldn't make himself go on. It was Pap that stiffened him, the thought of Pap mad as any bull, and of the unfair lick he'd hit and of the whoppings he had given before just for the fun he got. Probably Pap already was on his trail with the law along to help.

Boone moved off stiffly, less careful about noise now he was leaving, pointing back upstream to reach the turnpike that led from Frankfort to Louisville. When he found it, he turned and followed it to the right and buckled to the long, stiff rise out of the valley.

By the time he got to the top he was warm again and panting from the climb, and as he stopped to blow he looked back over the dark bowl of the town. It was beginning to stir. Here and there a light showed. In the stillness he caught the small echo of a voice and the measured knock of an ax against wood. In the east the streak of light had broadened to a band. The stars were winking out.

He brought his rifle to the crook of his arm, lifted his bag, and set out again, walking in the middle of the wet and rutted road. It was early yet for travel, and now that he had crossed the river, he felt safer, though less at home. It was all strange country ahead;

but somewhere to the west where the road led lay Louisville, and beyond it Greenville, Paoli, Vincennes, Carlyle, Lebanon, and St. Louis. He could hear Uncle Zeb calling out the names, going on west in his mind like a man with a spell on him.

There wasn't any cause to leave the road yet, he decided, thinking maybe he would be safe to stay to it all day, except when he came to towns and tollhouses. He'd circle around them. And if he saw any travelers, he'd just cut out into the woods like a man hunting.

He wished he had something to eat. Corn bread and sorghum and salt pork, like his ma would give him if he was still home, or anything fit to put his teeth to. He had an empty ache in his stomach, and the spit came into his mouth just from thinking.

He kept walking while the sky paled and the naked trees along the way stood black against the cold gray of morning. The sun edged up and looked over the rim of the world like a careful eye from behind a wall.

Glancing back, Boone saw a stage coming and so left the road and screened himself in the trees. He watched it go by, the four horses spanking along as the driver flicked them, the polished metal gleaming in the sun, the body swaying in its thorough-braces as the wheels rose and fell in the rough trail. When it had gone from sight, he came back to the road and from a hill saw a settlement in the distance. The driver's trumpet sounded ahead, telling the townsmen the stage was coming in.

Boone cut around the town and circled back to the trail a half mile beyond it, having waited on a ridge until the coach had rolled on ahead.

As far as he could see, the road lay clear. He hitched up his jeans and took the rifle from under his arm and rested it on his shoulder and fell into stride again. He wondered how far it was to Louisville. He wondered whether Pap or the law was on that stage. He wished he had something to eat.

Wondering and wishing, he didn't hear the traveler behind him until it was too late.

"Where you headin'?" asked a friendly voice.

Boone's hand tightened on the butt of his rifle as he turned. The voice came from on top an old work wagon drawn by two sad mules.

"Down the road a piece."

"Hop up."

The driver had an open, friendly face, not old, twenty-five or thirty, maybe, but colored and lined by the weather as a man's face ought to be. He had an eye as bright blue as a summer sky. From underneath his worn cap a lock of red hair fell.

Boone got in.

"Goin' to Louisville myself," the driver said. "Wisht I could make her afore night, but it ain't no use. Time don't mean nothin' to a dead man, no more'n to a hog, but seems like it means a heap to his kin." He jerked his thumb toward the back of the wagon, and Boone, looking over his shoulder, saw a plank box there.

"Name's Deakins," said the man. "Jim Deakins. Live just several hollers from here."

The blue eyes asked a question. After a little Boone answered, "Zeb Calloway."

Deakins put out his hand. "Pleased to run into you, Zeb. Now, you take some fellers, it don't make ary difference if their company's dead or alive, but me, I can't get no pleasure out of a corpse."

He looked at Boone for a "Me, neither."

"They just lay back quiet," he went on, "never sayin' a word, and by and by you shut your mouth yourself, feelin' oneasy like as if what you said would be turned against you, in heaven or hell, one." He added, "A dead body's like someone sittin' in judgment."

He caught Boone's eye on the basket that stuck out from under the seat.

"Have an apple," he said, and reached down and got one for him.

"Reckon you been workin' with cows?" he asked, while his nose opened and his eyes went over Boone. His hand went out and flicked a piece of manure from Boone's sleeve.

"Uh-huh."

"You can nigh always tell what a man is by lookin' at him," said Deakins. "Now you take the old gentleman there in the box. He's got four women dead. Four. And a fifth one still livin' on the farm. And young! God Almighty! He's got chirren beyond countin'."

He paused and gave Boone a solemn look. "And what would you say he ought to take after, with all them wives and a passel of young?"

When Boone didn't speak, he answered his own question. "He ought to look like a goat, I figger. And that's just what the old gentleman looks like. Got white whiskers that'll reach to his belly button.

"Me," he went on, "I got nary woman and nary a young'n—to tell about, leastways—so I keep the brush down pretty short. That, and my whiskers is kind of a dirty brindle. Have another apple."

Farther on a tollhouse came into sight.

"You'll get jolted around some," Deakins said, pulling his team out of the road. "At what I took this job for I can't be payin' no tolls, savin' one I can't get out of. Must be six or seven of 'em 'twixt here and Louisville, and it's twenty up to twenty-five cents every time. It don't take long to eat up three dollars."

Boone asked, "Why you takin' the dead man to Louisville?"

"When a feller's had a bunch of wives, he's sure enough got trouble, even after he can't hear 'em no more. The one that's livin' wanted to bury the old gentleman on the farm, but the chirren by the other wives wouldn't hear to it. They live at Louisville mostly, and when they hearn he was gone they come to the farm and give notice to the widder woman that he had to be put down proper, at Louisville. So they rastled around for two-three days, yellin' Pa would want this and Pa would want that. When Louisville won out, I got the job of haulin' his body in."

They jolted through the open fields, skirting the tolltaker's land. The wagon rocked and bumped and squeaked as the mules lagged ahead. The plank coffin screeched, sliding on the wagon bed.

"Got to take 'er slow on these here shun-pikes," Deakins explained. "Not that it hurts the old gentleman, but I can't deliver him bruised up too much. How would he feel, when they open the lid for a last look, if he had a couple of black eyes?" He grinned at Boone. "Don't hang back on them apples. That's what God made 'em for, to eat."

They came back to the road. Swinging an already frayed-out switch, Deakins got the mules to step a little faster. "They say a mule'll always get you there," he said, beating on their rumps, "but time he does, like as not you don't want to go."

They came after a while to another tollgate and circled it and later to another that Deakins let the mules head for. "There's a crick tears through here," he explained, "and she's steep on both sides, and this here body will sure enough come out, whiskers and all, if we don't cross the bridge."

The tollkeeper came out of the house and stretched out his hand. "Two bits."

Deakins dug in his pocket, bringing out a thin handful of cut money. He offered a ragged, pie-shaped piece.

The tolltaker eyed it.

"She's cut finer'n a frog hair," Deakins said. "Quarter of a silver dollar, exact."

The man looked as if he had his doubts, but he motioned them on.

"It wasn't so short at that," Deakins told Boone when they were under way again. "Not more'n two-three cents. I had to cut 'er with a chisel, which ain't as close as shears."

The afternoon dragged on and the winter sky came down. Darkness lay like a fog on the ridges.

"I'd love to get shet of this here body." Deakins' voice sounded uneasy. "Maybe we could get there afore mornin' if we kep' goin' and the mules held out."

"Got to git him there tonight?"

"No. Tomorrow'll do, long as it's cold like this. I got feed for the mules and a bedroll and some beans and side meat cooked up and a piece of corn bread. But I'd just as leave not spend the night with a corpse." Deakins' eyes of a sudden were hopeful. "It's best to stop, though. Would you keer to stay with me?"

"I was fixin' to say I would." Just the name of food made Boone's stomach hurt. He was dizzy and weak for want of it, and windy with the apples he had eaten.

Deakins pulled the team over and, while Boone gathered wood, unhooked and fed the mules, tying them to the wagon wheels.

When they had eaten the pan of corn bread and warmed-up beans and fat meat, Deakins lifted out the bedroll and spread it on the ground. Taking off their boots, they lay down, drawing the thin cover over them. Boone stowed his rifle under the blanket at his side.

Deakins lay on his back, his eyes open and blinking at the sky. "Here we are," he said, "a-lookin' up at the stars and feelin' good with food in our belly and talkin'. Makes a body wonder where the old gentleman's went to. Makes a body wonder what he's seein' and feelin' and doin'. Reckon he's up there listenin' to us, knowin' all that goes on? Reckon his dead women is there, or did God give him a new one? Or you reckon he's still in the box, waitin' his turn to go up, or maybe down?"

He was silent for a breath or so, and then he asked, "Zeb, don't it make you feel kind of techy?"

Boone was so tired he could barely keep track of the talk. His muscles had flattened out. When he closed his eyes, his mind went drifting off.

Deakins' voice came again. "Don't it?"

"He's dead, ain't he?"

"That's what they say."

"Let's git on to sleep, then. A dead dog never bit nobody."

Even then, though, Deakins didn't sleep right away. Through a dream Boone heard him ask, "I reckon there ain't much that skeers you, be there, Zeb?"

4

ouisville was busy as an anthill and bigger than all the places, put together, that Boone had ever seen. Even on the fringe of the town, where a man could still look off and mark where the river ran, the houses squatted pretty near elbow to elbow, and farther on the buildings looked to be pushing for room, trying to keep from being pinched. It put him in mind of the time he and Dan and Pap and Ma all slept in one bed after Pap had come in drunk and set fire to the other bed with his pipe. In and out of the buildings men and women, whites and niggers, kept popping. They made a stream along both sides of the street. Wagons loaded with lumber and ropes and hides, and carriages drawn by high-stepping horses with heads strapped back rolled east and west and crosswise. A canvas-topped wagon rattled across the street in front of them, showing the faces of three children who stared from its tail with solemn, wondering eyes. There were chimneys everywhere, all breathing out a slow, black smoke that came down in a regular fog, except that it bit at a man's lungs and set his nose to running.

"Godamighty!" said Boone.

"She's big," agreed Deakins, and spit over the wheel. "Twenty thousand, last count." He thought for a moment, then added, "I can't figger why folks'll do it, less'n they don't know no better."

Boone shook his head. "I don't hanker to live in no anthill."

"Me neither."

"I aim to go west into Injun country and trap me some beaver."

"Sure enough?" asked Deakins, his face lighting. "Now, that there is what I call man's talk. Leave the piss ants swarm!" He sobered and fell silent, studying the rumps of his mules while the wagon creaked ahead.

Boone stole a long look at him. There was nothing to shy away from in the mild and open face, he decided, but a talker like Deakins could get a man into trouble.

"All I got's these here mules," Deakins observed, as if to himself. "Them and maybe a couple dollars' worth of meal and salt meat." His glance came to Boone. "I reckon they'd look pretty piddlin' once a man got hisself out there."

"I reckon."

"There ain't nobody to keer. Not even a dog. Ol' Rip got tore up in a fight and bled hisself to death."

Boone asked, "You thinkin' about going your own self?"

"Well," Deakins answered, talking slow now that the question had been put, "I do' know. All I got's these here mules, and a man don't learn no love for a mule."

Boone broke a long silence. "I wouldn't raise no holler at company, I reckon, if it was company a body could trust."

"Meanin'?"

"He would have to stand by a man, come whatever."

Deakins' inquiring blue gaze went again to the rumps of his mules. "I ain't no half-horse, half-alligator. I been whopped, plenty of times, and I reckon I will be ag'in. But I never laid down yit on a friend, regardless."

"He would have to know to keep his tongue."

There was a stiffness in Deakins' manner when he answered. "I ain't askin' to go—with you, anyways." He clucked to the team.

"Would you, Jim?"

"Are you askin'?"

"I'm askin'."

Deakins' sorrel beard riffled to his grin. "Wrap 'er up and charge 'er down, then," he said. "Zeb, I'm your parcel. I been lookin' for someone p'inted west myself, and you suit me, longways and sidewise."

"My name ain't Zeb Calloway."

"The handle don't matter."

"It's Boone. Boone Caudill."

"Pleased to meetcha."

"I'm runnin' away from Pap. That's why I said a man would have to keep his tongue."

Deakins nodded. "A pry pole couldn't git it out." He added abruptly, "Here we are." He reined the mules to the side. "I'll pull over and find someone to help me tote the old gentleman in. You watch the mules. They ain't used to city life." He jumped from the wagon and headed for the undertaker's door.

Boone waited, holding the reins while his thoughts ran ahead. He would be safe before night, safe across the state line, beyond the river. The Ohio would lie yonder, and across it was country a man could get his breath in. They figured wrong if they thought they'd lock him up for the lick he had given Mose Napier, even if it killed him. He would go over the river and laugh at them, him and Jim Deakins would, taking their time, then, to St. Louis. It was a right smart of a river, though, wide and deep. They would have to find a way to cross it.

While his mind ran on, he studied the people that thumped up and down the board walk, the city men walking duck-footed with their bellies out, the women snugged up at the waist like a sack with a rope around it. There was a man had got himself a knock, with the towel wrapped around his head. A fat man walked with him, a man as fat as Mr. Harrison Combs, the high sheriff. The bandaged head tilted back. The eyes under the bandage looked at Boone, and a flash came into the dark face.

Boone's hand grabbed for his rifle and bag. His legs shot him over the off wheel. The bag caught on the wheel and pulled out of his hand, the bag with his clothing in it and the Indian-skin strop and the scalp that he had aimed to prove himself by. "Stop! You're under arrest!" He landed running, bowling over a fat woman in a checkered bonnet as he rounded the corner and made in the direction of the river. Behind him he heard the mules snort, heard the wagon clatter and the coffin scrape on the floor boards as the team leaped. He heard voices crying "Whoa! Whoa! Halt!" Above all came Pap's hoarse "Stop him!" and then the sound of running feet, few at first, just a patter of them, but growing with each stride of his own, as if he shook them from the buildings and doorways and walks, out of the quiet tap of business into the pound of the chase.

He slanted from the sidewalk into the street, hearing the footfalls change behind him, clattering on the boards and fading off into a dull thumping against earth as they slanted after him. Up a cross street he caught sight of the mules swinging into a turn, coming toward him now, the old work wagon flying behind them. A little more and they would have cut him off. A carriage came toward him and rolled on by, moving smartly while the man on the seat leaned out and peered at him and the horses arched their heads and snorted.

It must be a far piece to the river, farther than he had thought. The rifle jolted in his hand; the pouch and horn flapped against him. The air burned his throat as he sucked it in. Pap kept shouting, "Ketch 'im! Ketch 'im!" He looked back and saw them, a half a hundred men on his trail, and he knew how an old coon felt with the hounds singing after him. They would catch him yet, without he dropped Old Sure Shot. They were at the cross street now, along with the carriage that had passed him. While he looked the mules charged out of the cross street.

He caught one glimpse of them, running hard and wild at the crowd, and heard the crowd's first shrill cries. He brought his eyes around to get his bearings and saw a heavy man in a red shirt jump from a doorway ahead of him and run into the street and stand ready for him, his hands up for the catch. Boone kicked him in the groin, and found his stride again and went on.

The street crossing behind him was a whirl of animals and men. He saw the mules, lunging away from the hands that reached for their heads. The carriage lay on its side with one wheel off. The men were shouting, darting in to hold the teams. Nearer, the man Boone had kicked was jacknifed, his hands clutching his crotch. Pap appeared out of the crowd, his toweled head shining white. His arms made motions, and his hoarse voice rose. He was running again, and part of the crowd fell in with him, taking up the chase. Boone made himself look away from them, made himself look ahead, made his legs work, striding long and hard while his breath whistled in his throat. He might make it yet, thanks to the mules.

And then before him lay the Ohio, wide as an ocean. God, what a river! Under his feet the ground went wet and sticky, though the river was still a rifle shot away. Wreckage streamed past him, shaken by his stride, a storehouse tilting crazily, a flatboat overturned and gaping at the seams, drift lodged against the fronts of buildings, in and out of which men moved carrying buckets of mud. A load of new lumber came toward him and ran on by, shining in the sun, glimmering at the pound of his feet, and then the gleaming skeleton of a building going up, from which came the busy beat of hammers, until the workmen heard the crowd's cries and saw him going by with mud flying from his feet.

He looked at the river again. Not a craft rode it. Out on the bosom of the stream the drift swept along. It was a flood, a flood going down but still too much for a boat. No one would put out in that current, unless to save his hide. Over on the other side, upstream, he saw the ferry, moored high and idle by the rank of buildings that was now the shore line.

He cut left, around the corner of a house that barely cleared the flood, and a stone's throw farther on saw a round man sitting on a broken porch eying the sweep of water. On the edge of the box on which he sat a long piece of punk smoked. Below him, tied to the porch's slanting upright, a rowboat rocked to the lap of the water.

The round man raised his eyes, on his face an asking look, as Boone came running through the mud. He put his hand to his side and got his stick of punk and held it to his pipe while his mouth worked at the stem.

"Acrost!" Boone said.

The man's glance lifted from the bowl of his pipe, to come to sudden point as Boone brought the rifle up. He took the pipe from his mouth and laid down his piece of punk. "Son," he said, "if I'm bound to die one way or t'other I'll take 'er right here, warm and nice and sudden."

Boone was working at the rope on the upright, his rifle in the crook of his arm. The man sat quiet, puffing. His head turned as the crowd rounded the corner and the voices came into full cry as if a door had opened.

Boone had the knot untied at last. He jumped into the boat. The front of the pack charged up like a wave above him and threatened to break over. Pap grabbed the upright and leaned out, circling it with one arm while he shook the fist on the other. As if from a distance, while he bent to his oars, Boone heard Pap's "Come back, you tarnal fool!" It rose above the cries of the others, strained and sharp, and after it came another voice like a war whoop. "See you in St. Louis. Wait thar for me!" On the edge of the porch, waving his arms like a rooster, stood Jim Deakins, bareheaded, his sorrel hair whipping in the breeze.

The boat pulled like a mule, trying to get her head around and to run with the current. He fought her with all his strength, straining at the right-hand oar to keep her nosed up. He saw the shore backing away and realized the crowd had fallen silent and stood watchful and expecting. Deakins' voice floated out, "Take 'er easy! Watch you don't git rammed!"

The watchers lost outline, fading to a jerky shimmer of color as the stream caught him and bore him down. A half mile up the river they were now, though he was still within easy holler of the shore. The bank streamed past him and edged away by inches.

He felt the scrape of it on her side before it hit. The nose of the boat rose, slow at first, and then the whole craft pitched over. From the tail of his eye, as he snatched for his rifle, he glimpsed the log that had run him down. He came up gasping and kicked out, still headed for the farther shore. The boat was below him, turning bottom side up as it ran with the stream.

The water pulled at him. He felt the power of it from ankle to neck as he flattened and began to stroke, felt the pressure of it, the heavy, brute force of it all about him. The rifle was like a great sinker in his hand, but he hung to it, fighting with his other hand to keep up and going. The quick waves lapped at his face and head.

The bigger ones washed over him. His pouch and horn trailed like an anchor under his belly. He strangled and went under and came up coughing water, thrashing out with his free arm. The hand struck something, struck and held while his nails bit for a hold. He pulled up and rested, riding a soggy timber that floated low in the water. He brought his rifle to it and managed to lift it and work it onto the timber. Keeping the butt under one hand while the other clutched the far side of his raft, he started kicking again for the shore.

The river came out of its heavy flow and began to race. The timber swung around, and around again. Water swam in his sight, and the two shores and quick patches of sky before the timber settled again to the current like a mule to a lead rope.

Boone kept kicking, trying to keep pointed right, trying to push beyond the hold of the channel. It was a time before he realized that the current had changed and was washing over toward the Indiana shore. He locked his chin on the timber and hung there, numb, and after a while made his feet kick again, seeing only the rifle shining wet and dark on the wood and the water moving around him.

He knew when an Indiana farmer fished him out and got his arms around him from behind and dragged him to his cabin. He heard the man grunting over him. "Let 'er go, sonny! Your rifle will be safe as anything. Let 'er go!"

5

The river lay behind him, the river and the Indiana farmer who had put him up and had given him flint and steel, a horn of powder, a little poke of coarse meal, and a chunk of salt meat. "If you kin use that there rifle like she was made to be used, you'll make out," the farmer had said, and Boone had thanked him while he scuffed the ground with the toe of his boot. "Maybe it'll be turn about one day," he muttered. The farmer smiled and waved away the idea, and Boone turned and headed west out of the valley.

The land was flattening out. Back of him when the trees

thinned he still could see the dark arches of the hills that flanked the river, but ahead the way was leveling, broken by low rolls covered with oak and maple and hackberry, and sycamore whose trunks stood out white and naked from the rest.

The air was heavy, the sky gray and cold like a winter's pond. The bare branches of the trees veined themselves against it, forking darkly down to the trunks.

Boone wondered how soon he could reach St. Louis. "Take a man a full week, likely, if he kep' at it," he said to himself, thinking ahead to beaver and buffalo and the free plains. The road was good. Once in a while he saw a cabin at the base of a hill or the edge of a grove and felt better for its company. Sometimes he met horsemen, and once a Conestoga wagon, crowded to the canvas, rolling on west.

"We'd lift ye, boy," the driver said through a mat of whiskers as the wagon drew abreast, "but we're so jam-packed we hadda make the bedbugs git out and walk." He added, "They're gonna be some sore-footed chinches, time we get to Marthasville." The faces of a woman and two children, crowded to his left, made stiff smiles and sobered again as the driver swung his whip.

As it drew on toward dusk, Boone kept an eye out for game. He had seen a turkey earlier, and deer tracks at the side of the trail, but now the way was empty of game or sign of it. Overhead a V of wild geese drove to the north, high-flying and silent except for one inquiring honk that found no answer below. Then a rabbit bounced from roadside to bush and settled, its lines and color melting into the brown tangle of twig and blade and only the dark ball of its eye showing clear.

It was poor game, but Boone came up slow with his rifle so as not to scare it, remembering Pap's brag that if a man was sharp-eyed and steady he could knock out a possum's eye with Old Sure Shot, far as he could see it. The gun cracked, and the rabbit leaped as if jerked from above and came down kicking. Boone patted the butt of his weapon and, bringing the piece into the crook of his arm, went over and stood above the stilling body as he reloaded.

The air was thickening with dusk, with the wet, sad dusk of early spring. The sun that had ridden all day behind a veil whitened the sky line ahead. It was getting colder.

Boone picked up the rabbit and started on, looking for a place to spend the night. No house was in sight, and no light, but a little farther on, just off the road, he found a smooth and level spot among the trees, at the side of which a slow branch flowed.

He piled dead wood at the edge of his camp site and built a fire, sprinkling gunpowder over a handful of dry rot, lighting it with a spark from his flint and feeding the flame with twigs. When he had it going well he stepped to the stream and skinned and gutted the rabbit. He found a flat rock at the edge of the creek and angled it up from the fire, then went to the bank again and with his bloody hands molded four balls of meal and water. He cut the carcass of the rabbit into small pieces and with the ball of his thumb tagged them onto the angled stone, which he moved closer to the fire. The cakes he dropped into the coals. It wasn't much meal for a hungry man, he thought, and so cut two slices from his piece of salt meat. He dangled them in his poke of meal and laid them on the rock beside the rabbit's flesh, which already was drawing with the heat.

He sat back to wait, the knife held in his hand, hearing the creek moving, the breeze singing in the bare tree tops, and fire hissing at a wet spot in the wood. The heat on his face and chest was good. He nodded in it.

"Evenin', sir," said a soft voice. It went on quickly, "No harm intended," for Boone had scrambled up and seized his rifle from the tree against which he had leaned it. He swung around in a half crouch.

"The night caught us," the voice explained, "and I hanker for company." In the dark Boone made out the outlines of a horse and rider. The horse let out a quivering snort.

"Git down, then," said Boone, "and come where I kin see you."

"Sure," the man said amiably and swung from his horse. "Here I am," he continued, holding his arms wide under the cape of a dove greatcoat. He took off his high white beaver hat and came toward the fire. "Friend, tell me if I qualify." He stood silent, making a figure in his greatcoat and the cutaway beneath it, in the trousers that hugged his thighs and calves and were held snug by straps that looped under his boots. As he waited, his long nose caught the smell of the roasting meat, and he let out a sigh that stank the air with alcohol. His gaze ran everywhere, to Boone, to the fire, to the slanted stone, to the trees about them, to the gun that Boone held at ready. "A beautiful iron," he said, as if the eye of the rifle wasn't fixed on him. "On my saddle," he said when Boone did not speak, "I have a jug of very fine Monongahela. Would you care for a swallow before your meal?" He did not wait for an answer. The jug gurgled as he brought it forward.

"A part of it is gone," he said. "A small part. But enough is left for two." He held out the jug. After a long look Boone rested his rifle on his shoulder. He strangled a little as his throat tightened against the bite of the liquor. He squeezed out "Thank ye" and returned the jug, which the other upended. "My name," the man said as he brought the back of his hand across his mouth, "is Jonathan Bedwell, late of New Orleans."

Boone made a little gesture toward the fire. "It's no more'n a rabbit. I didn't see nothin' better, but I can put some more side meat on." As the man looked at him he added, "There's johnny-cakes."

The fire flared up, lighting Bedwell's face. He smiled a wide, long smile. "Why, we'll make out, friend." He patted the jug and motioned toward the fire. "Between this and that. Have another."

"Thanks again, mister."

Bedwell drank and put the jug on the ground. "I'll unsaddle my horse and picket him." He turned and went back. He and his horse were shadows moving at the edge of darkness. Boone put his rifle back against the tree and cut more meat. He turned the slices already on the stone. They were done when Bedwell returned carrying his rigging. Bedwell picked up the jug and offered it again.

After their meal they built up the fire and gathered more wood and settled on the ground. Bedwell's eyes were busy again. They gleamed wetly in the fire light. "I'm glad to see one man," he said, "that knows a cap and ball is better than a flintlock." He picked up the jug.

"Pap says so."

"Funny. The cap and ball was hit on more than twenty years ago—by a preacher, so they say. But I suppose there's still more flintlocks. The old boys argue that this kind jumps off the mark."

"It ain't so—with this rifle, anyhow."

"No. I say again, it's a beautiful piece."

"Old Ben Mills made it hisself, at Harrodsburg. She's true as could be. That rabbit, I took the eye right out of him. I reckon you heard of old Ben Mills?"

Bedwell turned his face toward Boone. It was a sharp face, lined around the eyes and mouth, as if smiles had worn creases in it. "I reckon I have! So Mills made it! Mills himself!"

"Yep, it's a Mills." Boone took the jug that Bedwell held out to him.

"You ought to take good care of it, friend. You ought to keep it cleaned and shined up and be careful nobody steals it. There's men would give a pretty lot for that rifle."

Boone said, "I watch over it, all right."

Bedwell had taken off his dove coat and let it lie back of him. Boone saw its lining lift and flutter raggedly as the breeze touched it. His gaze swam forward to the beaver hat which Bedwell had placed between his feet, and saw that it was worn and soiled. Bedwell sat with his knees up, the tails of his cutaway spread back from his rump. His legs in their snug casings seemed spindly for the rest of him.

"So," Bedwell said, "you're bound west."

"To St. Louis first, and then on."

"Here's to good luck!" The jug gurgled as Boone took it.

"I aim to trap beaver and shoot buffalo and fight Injuns, maybe. I kin shoot, all right."

"I'd take you for a marksman." The bare head moved and the creases deepened into a smile.

"I taken the eye right out of that rabbit."

"Light was bad, too, huh?"

"Dark-like. But I got him through the eye."

"You'll do." Bedwell got up and put more wood on the fire. "You'll make a mountain man."

The night closed in. There was the point of fire and Bedwell vague and swimming in its flicker, and close about them the wall of darkness. Boone let himself back and put his head on his arm.

"Haven't you got a blanket, friend?"

"No," Boone heard himself say, "nary blanket." He heard the whisper of the tight legs, heard the boots cracking the twigs, heard the small noises of movement. The earth swung with him. Then there were the noises again, the whisper, the crackling, and Bedwell's voice. "You use my blanket." Boone felt it fan the air against his cheek. It settled over him. "I'll keep the fire going. With it and my coat I'll be warm aplenty. Here's your rifle, friend. Best to keep it by your side. How about a nightcap?"

Boone awakened sick and trembling with cold in the first flush of the morning. He felt for the blanket and, not finding it, sat up slowly. The fire was a gray ash, in which the cook-rock had fallen and lay half buried. The breeze rolled a tuft of rabbit hair across it. He tasted his mouth and made a face and brought his fingers to his eyes to rub the film away. He looked around for Bedwell. He must have gone to see about his horse, he thought. His hand felt at his side, felt and reached out and felt again. Each finger carried its small sharp message to him. Without looking, he knew that Old Sure Shot was gone.

6

Boone got up quickly. The earth tilted and fell back and tilted again, and he bent over and put his hands to his head and closed his eyes to steady himself. He went over the ground, from creek to campfire to bedding spot, and finally to the place where Bedwell had picketed his horse. He found rope marks on a small elm there and saw the grass trampled by hoofs and flattened where the horse had lain. From a pile of manure a faint steam lifted.

He went back to the stream and lay down and drank, feeling the cool touch of the water to the pit of his stomach. He got up slowly, keeping his uneasy balance with the earth, and suddenly his stomach tightened like a squeezed bag. Holding to a bush, he hung over and vomited. The night's whisky was foul in his mouth. He rubbed the tears from his cheeks and picked up his poke of meal, dropping the bit of meat into it. "Goddam him!" he said aloud.

The morning mists were rising. Above the knobs to the east the sun appeared, its shine spread out and heatless. A lean hog nosed into the clearing and halted, its round snoot twitching as it sampled the air. "Git!" said the boy, and it gave a grunt and lumbered off.

Boone lagged to the trail and stopped and looked back. Home seemed a far piece now, beyond the knobs, beyond the great river, through the hills. His ma would be wondering about him, he reckoned. Maybe she grieved, hearing from Pap that the river must have got him. Maybe she said, "Boone! Boone!" to herself while her wet eyes leaked over. Of a sudden, weakness came on him again, taking the strength out of him and the grit. It wasn't any use trying to run away. Everywhere people picked on a boy, chasing after him like they'd chase a wild brute, or playing friendly and stealing from him. Better to go back to Ma and let Pap beat on him. Better to have something to eat and a home to lie in. Only, the law was after him now, and maybe home would be the jailhouse, and Pap would want to kill him, or come nigh to it. He straightened. Anyhow, he'd even things with Bedwell. He aimed to get Old Sure Shot back one way or another. He turned around and started west again, his head pounding to his step, his eyes following the horse tracks on the trail.

Boone wondered about Jim Deakins. Had Jim crossed the river? Would he really come? He saw the open, friendly face, the sorrel beard sprouting, the mild blue eyes. A man got lonesome, all by himself in a strange country. When Boone saw a gristmill, though, and the miller busy with his sacks, he put his head down and passed on, only muttering to the friendly hail. The few houses along the road he passed by, too, indrawn and distrustful. A lean brown and white dog ran out from one of them, nagging at his heels, and he turned and kicked at it, ignoring the promise of a man at the door who called, "He won't bite ye, boy."

He was in country different from home. The hills were smaller and more rounded, and there were more oaks and beech groves, but there were hickories, too, and walnuts, elms, wild cherries, and a few pines. In the smaller growth he made out dogwood, pawpaws, thorns, and persimmons. If it happened to be fall, now, he could find ripe pawpaws aplenty and shake himself down a bellyful of persimmons. He had ought to eat, regardless. Pap always said food was good for whisky fever. Not pawpaws or persimmons, though. They gagged a man, just thinking about them. Ham and parched corn and shucky beans would go better, and fresh meat better yet. If he had Old Sure Shot he could get himself some meat. Just having Old Sure Shot, without the meat, would make him feel tolerable—just having it, without the horn and pouch that Bedwell had stolen, too.

It was still early when he caught sight of a town and stopped to consider. If he circled it he might lose Jonathan Bedwell's trail, might pass him by while he was tied up at an inn. But he pulled away from the thought of entering the place, of being looked at and questioned and circled around with strangers' ways. He would eat first, anyway. Maybe eating would take the ache out of his head. Behind a small growth that screened him from the trail he built a fire and made more journey cakes and warmed two slices of his fat meat and choked the food down, against the uneasy turning of his stomach. When he got up he struck in an arc around the town.

Beyond it the road was marked more by hoofs and wheels. No longer could he feel sure that it was the tracks of Bedwell's horse he saw. There were a half-dozen sets of fresh tracks, now separate, now mixed, now blurred by the ribbon marks of tires. Boone faced toward the town, thinking again that he ought to go into it and shrinking from it again.

He traveled all day, walking even-timed, thinking now about Ma and now about Deakins and now about Bedwell and always about his stolen rifle. It hung in his mind, pulling him on. Somewhere he would come up on Bedwell. Some way he would get his gun back. The sun let itself down from overhead and looked him in the face and went on, sliding behind the far hills. He passed a two-story log house set back from the trail, and beyond it saw a lone hen pecking in the road. He looked back to see if anybody watched, then reached into his poke and drew out a handful of meal. He moved off the trail, to a tree that hid him from the house, and began scattering his hand of bait, singing a soft "Here, chuck, chuck, chuckie! Here, chuck, chuck, chuckie!" Twenty feet away, the hen canted her head and fixed one bright eye on him. She came over, waddling and suspicious, and took a long-necked peck at the nearest fleck of corn. Boone swung his hand slowly, letting the meal sift from his fingers. She tilted her head at him again, studying him for danger. He fanned out another pinch. The eye left him and fixed on the ground and the head went down with a jerk and the beak picked up another crumb, and another, and another. The neck stretched for more, and one foot moved the hungry beak ahead. "Chuck, chuckie!" The other foot moved, and then the first, while the beak did its tiny beat. Boone fell forward, smothering the bird in his arms. She started a wild outcry, but his quick fist choked it off, and she stared at him, silent and lidless and fearful, as he brought her under his arm.

He scanned the back trail again and struck off to the right toward a bunch of locusts. Through the trees he saw a sinkhole, and in the steep and rocky farther side a black triangle that he took to be the entrance to a cave. He let himself down into the sinkhole, skirted the puddle at its bottom, and climbed the small bluff and looked in. At its beginning the cave was big enough to hold a man, standing or lying. He squinted into it, and as his eyes widened saw that it choked off into two small tunnels. The place had the rank, sour smell of vixens and pups, but the floor was smooth, and the walls and roof would protect him from the night's wet chill.

Boone climbed down, took the hen from under his arm and tore her head off. While she fluttered he gathered firewood and placed it inside the cave. He kindled a small fire just inside the entrance, watching with satisfaction as the slow breath of the cavern carried the smoke outside.

At the edge of the puddle he dressed his hen and ran her through with a length of green sapling. Back at the fire he rested the sapling in the forks of two sticks raised at the sides of the blaze and made solid with stones. He went into the cave and sat down to wait, eased by the warmth that had begun to creep inside. It was good to rest, to let his muscles hang loose and aimless, to feel hunger in his stomach again, to be shut of the dizzy ache in his head. There seemed nothing so bad with him now that getting his gun back wouldn't fix it. He turned the bird on its spit.

He ate half the half-raw hen. Afterwards he restrung the carcass on the sapling and leaned the sapling against the side of the cave. He renewed his fire and lay down, and a dead sleep closed on him.

Morning came wet and dismal. He sat up and rubbed his eyes and squirmed the crimps from his muscles. He could hear rain on the stones, dropping from ledge to ledge. He looked out and saw the sky close and gray, with tatters of rain clouds beating low before the breeze. Inside the cave it was dry and windless. He felt a small, quick pleasure at being there. It would be good to stay, safe and sheltered, while the day made its gloomy turn.

He took the body of the hen from its stick and began to wrench at it with his teeth. There wasn't much left, even for a fox, when he got through. He picked up his poke and set out, hunched against the rain. By the time he hit the road he was wet to the skin but warm from moving. Ahead of him the way ran, to Paoli, Vincennes, St. Louis. He walked at its side, out of the mud, studying the tracks for some sign that Bedwell had gone before him. After a while the sun came out.

The day was drawing on to noon when he spied the man in the black coat. The man was sitting a horse which he had pulled up at the top of a rise, sitting there motionless, looking off to the north, thinking, or watching something, or waiting for somebody. While Boone paused, the man's hand went inside his coat and came out with a pistol. Boone slipped to one side of the trail behind a tree. Still holding the pistol, the man got off his horse and tied it up. While his back was squarely turned Boone sneaked closer, watching through a screen of brush. The man picked a dead leaf from the ground and walked over to a tree and stuck the leaf against it, behind a finger of bark. He walked back about twenty steps, then leveled at the leaf and fired. Bark flew from the tree, almost a full hand above the leaf. The man shook his head and began reloading.

Boone slipped deeper into the woods and edged around behind him, keeping trees and bushes between them, planning to ease by and go on. It wouldn't do to let himself be seen spying. It made a body feel small, being caught that way. Besides, he didn't know about the man. You couldn't tell about strangers. Maybe, seeing him, this one would up and shoot. Or ask questions. Or take him into a town. If Boone had his own rifle, now, he might feel different. He could drill that leaf plumb center with Sure Shot.

Despite his care the man saw him, just as he was about to get out of sight. The man shouted, "Hey, boy!" Boone made out not to hear. "Hey, you! What you running fer?" But now he was out of sight, and he stopped and waited, his breath light and quick in his throat, asking himself why he ran and whether he should run again if the man chased him. He hadn't done anything—in Indiana, anyway—to make him shy away from people this way, unless it was to steal a hen. After while he heard the pop of the pistol and knew the man had gone back to his practice.

He listened as he went on, and watched the back trail, ready to slip into the woods and hide, and before he had gone a mile he caught a glimpse of movement behind him. A horseshoe rang against rock. The woods were thin here, but off to the left a thick stump squatted. He ran to it and threw himself down behind it, watching through a fringe of grass, hearing a long outward snuffle of the horse before he could see it. From behind a cluster of trees rode a dove great coat and a white beaver hat, and under it a sharp, lined face. Boone saw Old Sure Shot, tied to the saddle. He lay there until the horse and man had passed him and lost themselves in the woods ahead, reminding himself as they went by that a man couldn't outrun a horse or go up against a rifle unarmed, either. Then he got up and set out after them, trotting to keep close.

He came on Bedwell suddenly an hour later. Making a turn at the edge of a grove that had hidden the way, he saw the horse drinking at a creek that crossed the road, and Bedwell on the ground with his back toward him, flicking his snug leg with the switch he carried in his hand. They were no more than a stone's throw away. While Boone watched, Bedwell opened his breeches and made water, buttoning up slowly afterwards.

Now was the time, Boone told himself, but careful, careful! His hand dropped the poke. He felt his legs running under him and a breeze fanning his face. His feet kicked up a noise in the road. Bedwell straightened his trousers and turned and saw him and set himself, waiting, not trying to get the rifle from the saddle. He stood there and met the charge, and they went down, rolling into the little stream and out of it. Boone heard the horse snort and saw the hoofs dance away. He felt the man's hand slip under his cap and clamp on his hair. The other hand came up and the thumb of it found Boone's eye, and now the two hands worked together, the one holding his head while the thumb of the second pushed into the socket. Pain was like a knife turning in his skull. The eye started from its hole. He let go of Bedwell's throat and tore himself free and scrambled to his feet. Bedwell stood blurred before him, stood dripping, his lips a little open, not saying anything, the lines making small half circles at the corners of his mouth. His eyes studied Boone. Boone lunged in, swinging at the face. Bedwell's knee jerked up, and his hands pushed Boone away as if the last lick had been struck. Boone doubled and stumbled back. A straining noise came out of his throat. He tried to straighten against the fierce pain in his groin.

"Well?" asked Bedwell. His hand brushed at the mud on his coat.

"You taken my rifle!"

"So?"

"I aim to git it back."

"Aim ahead."

"I ain't through yit."

Bedwell's eyes slid off Boone, looking over his shoulder, and a sudden glint came into them that Boone did not understand. He was smiling now, smiling on one side of his face. "Afraid, aren't you, pup?"

Boone's shoulder caught him in the chest. The man went over, easy this time, with Boone on top of him. The strength seemed to have drained out of Bedwell. He tried to squirm from under and fell back, grunting. His hands fluttered, fending Boone's thumbs from his eyes. He was yelling, making a roar in Boone's ears. "Help! Help!" Boone got his hand beneath the flutter. His thumb poked for an eye. It had just found it when a voice like a horn sounded. "Stop it, damn you! Stop it!"

A hand grabbed Boone's shoulder and jerked him loose. The man in the black coat stood over him, and now Boone saw there was a star on the coat. "I'm the sheriff."

"Thank God, sheriff!" It was Bedwell speaking. He got to his feet and picked his white hat from the water and brushed at it. "He would have killed me." He pointed at Boone. "Must be crazy."

The sheriff's gaze went to Boone. "I seen him afore, sneakin' through the woods."

"He slipped up on me. I was letting my horse drink, and he charged me from behind."

"What's the idee, boy?" the sheriff asked, and answered his own question. "Robbery, that's what." His eyes went to Bedwell's horse, standing hip-shot across the creek. "Wanted to get the gentleman's horse and rifle and outfit, didn't you?"

"No."

Bedwell was nodding his head. "I hadn't thought of that, sheriff."

The sheriff went on, "I bet you'd've jumped me, only you seen my pistol."

"He stoled my gun. I aimed to git it back," Boone said.

The sheriff's voice was a pounding in Boone's ears. "That why you got to go sneakin' through the woods like a varmint?"

"He stoled it."

"What you doin' "—the sheriff's eyes went over Boone's dirty homespun—"with a handsome piece like that?"

"He stoled it, I said."

Bedwell gave the sheriff a small smile. "Poor excuse."

"Worser than none. Come along, both of you."

7

The sheriff's thumb signaled the direction. "March!" he said. "No funny business, now." He had his pistol in his hand. To Bedwell he said, "You climb your horse and go ahead. We'll keep him 'twixt us." He strode back, keeping his eyes fixed over his shoulder on Boone, and caught up his own horse. Bedwell grinned at Boone. He said softly, "Looks like you won't get to St. Louis for a spell." They set off, Bedwell and the sheriff, mounted, at head and tail of the line and Boone, afoot, between them.

They came into a town a mile farther on. Boone took it for Paoli. Alongside Louisville it was a little place, but it was still big enough, and it was all eyes and moving lips. The eyes looked at Boone from windows and doorways and the lips said things, and people closed the doors and walked over to fall in with the sheriff, and he could feel their eyes boring at his back and hear their lips talking.

"What is it, sheriff?"

"That young'n there."

"Looks rough, sure enough."

"Is there gonna be a trial?"

The sheriff's big voice said, "Could be."

"The jury ain't been excused, from yesterday."

"The president judge went off to Corydon, but the side judges are around."

"All side and no judges."

The voices cackled. They were making fun behind him, like going to a quilting or a bee. Bedwell seemed to like it. He squirmed around on his horse, smiled at the men following, and said to the sheriff, "I hope we can get this over with quick. I got to get on."

The courthouse was a long, low building, made of logs. "Tie up here," the sheriff said to Bedwell, and hitched his own horse at the rack. "I'll take the rifle, and your horn and pouch." He motioned them inside. "Git the coroner for me, will you?" he asked one of the men before he went in.

Boone found himself in that part of the room meant for judges and lawyers and the jury and people who were lawing. At the front of it were a platform and a high bench, and behind the high bench was another bench, with a back to it, to sit on. Out from the platform were three tables and some chairs, and at the side of it were places for the jury to sit. The section was separated from the rest of the room by a pole which ran from side to side and was tied to the walls. Beyond the pole were hewn benches for those who wanted to watch and listen. A few people already sat there, and more were coming, entering through a door at the other side of the pole. The sheriff motioned, "Set down." A dark little man with eyes like wet acorns touched the sheriff on the arm. The sheriff said, "Hello, Charlie. We got to get set. Seen Eggleston and the judges?"

"They're across, havin' one."

The sheriff took Bedwell by the arm. "Watch this here boy, will you, Charlie?" he said to the dark little man. The man sat down. The sheriff and Bedwell went out.

The section beyond the pole was filling. The voices made a single, steady noise in the room, a noise without words, rising and falling but still steady, coming at a man like waves and washing up on him. The people stopped and looked up front as they came in and then went and sat down and looked up again and began to talk, their voices going into the wave.

After while the door beside Boone opened to let in the sheriff and Bedwell and half a dozen other men. Two of them stepped up on the judges' platform and sat down and waited there, quiet and open-eyed, like owls in the light. One of them had a body like an egg, and a red face and eyes with little rivers of blood running in them. The other was pale and had eyes like a sick hound. He slumped back when he sat down and didn't make a motion, letting his eyes go over everything as if nothing mattered. A third man went to a little table and put a big book on it and sat down behind it and got out a pen. The sheriff nudged Boone to his feet and pushed him over in front of the judges. The red-veined eyes fastened on him. "What's your name, boy?"

"Boone Caudill."

"You are charged with assault and battery. Guilty or not guilty?"

"I ain't done nothin'."

"Not guilty, then. Ready to stand trial?"

When Boone didn't answer the red eyes flicked impatiently. "Here, this boy needs counsel." The eyes picked out a man. "Squire Beecher."

One of the half-dozen men who had just come in stepped forward. "Yes, your honor." He wore a brown coat with a rolling collar and underneath it a lighter-colored vest. His hair was thick and straw-colored, and at the nape of his neck it flowed into a queue, tied with some kind of skin, which reached to his tail. He looked to be twenty-five or twenty-six years old.

"Can you take the defense? The court doubts if there's a fee in it." The man nodded slowly, and the judge went on, "Eggleston says the state's ready. We got a jury, from yesterday."

"Give me a minute," asked Squire Beecher.

"Sure thing. Take the defendant into the grand jury room. Then we'll git on."

"Suppose you tell me all about it," said Squire Beecher after they had sat down in the other room. There was a table in it, and twelve chairs, and five or six spittoons that reared up, wide-mouthed, as if begging for a squirt. "Well?" prompted Beecher.

"That gun, he stoled it from me."

"How?"

"He just taken it, and I was aimin' to git it back."

"That's why you tackled him?"

"To git it back."

The squire hitched himself in his chair. "Look, boy! I'm on your side, but unless you tell me the facts of the case I can't help you. Start at the first now, and tell the whole story."

"Ain't nothin' to tell, savin' he came up on me two nights ago and gave me his name and took supper with me."

"Where?"

"Two days away, yonder."

"Then what?"

"He sneaked off in the night, takin' my gun and my horn and bullet pouch."

"When he came up on you, do you mean it was at your house?"

"Outside."

"How did you happen to be outside?"

Squire Beecher waited for an answer. "You mean you were traveling?"

"To St. Louis."

"From where?"

Again the squire waited. "Is this all you're going to tell me, just that his man Bedwell came up on you while you were camping out, and shared your supper and later stole off with your gun while you slept?"

Boone said, "That's all there is."

Squire Beecher bent his head and brought his queue around in front and fingered it while he thought. It was eelskin, likely, it was tied by. Beecher said, "You don't give yourself much chance. How do you happen to be tramping through Indiana with no money? You haven't any money, have you? No food? No horse?"

The sheriff's horn of a voice came into the room. "Court's ready, Beecher." While Beecher looked at him Boone said, "It don't matter. He stoled my rifle, I told you." The young lawyer got up, a frown wrinkling his smooth face. "Come on, then."

"Ready?" asked the red-faced judge. Squire Beecher nodded. "Ready as can be, Judge Test." To the sheriff the judge said, "Summon the jury." The sheriff strode to the door and bellowed "Jury!" like a man calling hogs. Afterward he came back and pounded on a table. "Oyez! Oyez!" There was a scuffling of feet as everybody stood. The voice boomed around the room. Beecher motioned Boone toward one of the tables. They sat down by it. Bedwell was seated at the other, and with him was a lean-faced man who kept fiddling with his chin. The man's eyes were so gray they were almost white, like glass, and, like glass, they looked hard and cool.

The fat man called Judge Test sat forward on his seat, his arms crossed on the bench in front of him. The other judge stayed slumped back, looking tired. Judge Test had his hand up and was saying something to the jurymen, seated over to the right against the side wall. Boone wondered if the pale judge was as sick as he looked. Beecher and the cold-eyed man were putting questions to the jury. A man might get as white as that if he never let the weather touch him. The red-veined eyes swung around. "Let the witnesses be sworn. Stand up! Hold up your hand there, boy!"

". . . sweart'ell the truth, the whole truth and nothing but the truth, s'helpyouGod?"

As the judge said "God" a queer look flashed over his face. His eyes flicked wide, as if he had been poked in the behind, and his jaw fell down and his mouth made a round hole in his face. His hands fluttered. There was the sound of wood splintering. Boone just caught a glimpse of the wide eyes and open mouth and the hands grabbing, and then the judge's face dropped out of sight behind the bench as if he were playing fort and had ducked a rock. Boone heard his rump thump on the platform. The pale judge seized the bench in front of him and held himself up while the other end of the seat beneath him went down. Judge Test got up, blowing and redder than ever. He said, "Dammit!" and looked at the sheriff. "It's the sheriff's job to see that this here courtroom is kept in repair."

The sheriff said something that Boone couldn't hear because people had begun to laugh. Judge Test pounded for silence. The cold-eyed man at the other table nodded wisely. He muttered, "It appears that this is a mighty weak bench."

They hollered then, the people at the other side of the pole did, and slapped each other and whooped while Judge Test pounded. The judge's eyes flashed redly, but the cold-eyed man just grinned at him and by and by the judge swallowed and made himself grin, too. A man brought in a block of wood, and they set the end of the bench on it, and Judge Test lowered himself slowly, trying it out.

"All right, Eggleston," he said, "if you're through with your funnin'," and the cold-eyed man said, "Come around, sheriff."

The sheriff handed Old Sure Shot to another man and came over and sat down in a chair beside the judges' bench, facing the crowd.

Eggleston asked, "You are Mark York, sheriff of Orange county?"

"Sure."

A thumb motioned toward Boone. "Ever see this defendant before?"

"Sure."

"When and where?"

"First time, he went sneakin' around me, on the Greenville road. That was about noon."

"What were you doing there?"

"Matt Elliott got a cow stole. I was coming from there."

"What do you mean when you say he sneaked around you?"

"He left the road and circled behind me. I just got a flash of him makin' off."

"Do you know any reason why he would want to sneak by you?"

Squire Beecher jumped up. "Objection!"

Eggleston said, "Oh, all right," and went on. "When did you see him for the second time?"

"Up the road a piece. He had this here gentleman down and was gougin' him."

"They were fighting?"

"Sure."

"Who would you say was the aggressor?"

"This young feller here was on top."

Squire Beecher cried "Objection!" again. Judge Test looked at him, then said, "This court isn't going to tie itself up with a lot of fiddle-faddle. It's the truth we want. Go ahead, Eggleston."

"And you brought them in?"

"Sure." He pointed at Boone. "He was fixin' to get the gentleman's horse and outfit."

"Objection!"

Eggleston turned his white eyes on Squire Beecher. "Pass the witness."

The squire said, "Sheriff, so far as you know, the man Bedwell might have started the fight, might he not?"

"Could be."

"Actually, you couldn't tell who the aggressor was?"

"This one was on top."

"But that doesn't prove anything?"

"Proves he was gettin' the best of it."

The answer set people to nudging one another and giggling and talking at the corners of their lips. The sheriff grinned back at them and made a slow wink. Judge Test rapped.

"That's all."

The sheriff got up and walked over to the side and took Old Sure Shot from the man he had handed it to.

"Bedwell."

The dove greatcoat switched, the tight breeches scissored, the white hat swung from one hand.

The prosecutor looked at his papers. "You are Jonathan Bedwell, of New Orleans?"

"The same."

"You know the defendant here?"

"I saw him, just the once."

"Tell the court about it."

"He attacked me."

"Go on."

"It was about noon today. I had stopped and got off my horse while I let him drink."

"Where?"

"On the Greenville road, a mile or so out."

"Yes?"

"I heard someone running, and turned around, and it was this man, charging me."

"Ever see him before?"

"No."

"Why would he attack you?"

"I object," called Beecher. Except for one flicker of the veined eyes, Judge Test gave him no notice.

"I don't know. The sheriff said it was robbery, but I don't know."

The lean face of the prosecutor turned on Boone. "He looks like he needed something of everything, all right." People smiled at that, and some of them cackled while Beecher objected and Judge Test pounded on the bench. There was just one man who didn't smile. He was an Indian in the first row beyond the pole, sitting straight and unmoving, his hands holding a pair of quilled moccasins which he had brought to town to sell, likely. The pale judge came out of his slump and fixed his sad eyes on the prosecutor. "That ain't law, Eggleston, and you know it."

Eggleston went on. "At any rate, he charged you and knocked you down and was trying to do you bodily injury when the sheriff happened on the scene."

"He would have killed me, I think."

"You have a horse?"

"A good one."

"And a rifle?"

"A good one, but a little light."

It wasn't light, either, Boone said to himself, but heavy enough for even b'ar or buffler.

"I guess any robber—" the cold eyes were on Boone—"would be glad to get them."

"I suppose so."

"I object." It was Beecher again, standing and shaking his head so that the queue swung behind his back. Judge Test moved one finger. "No fiddle-faddle."

"You can have him," said Eggleston to Squire Beecher.

Beecher asked, "Did you say you had never seen this boy before?"

"Never."

Beecher aimed a finger at Bedwell. "But, as a matter of fact, you shared his supper with him night before last, didn't you?"

"No."

"You shared his supper with him and spent the night at his campfire, and you got up early, while the boy still slept, and made off with his rifle and horn and pouch, didn't you?"

"No. I did not."

Eggleston interrupted. "The state objects to this line of questioning."

"Go on," said Judge Test to Beecher.

"And the boy attacked you just in the hope of getting his rifle back?"

"It wasn't his rifle."

The questions went on. Through a window Boone could see a tavern across the street and, at the side of it and farther on, the wooded knobs lifting to the horizon. He thought of the cave where he had spent the night, and the rain whispering on the rocks while he stayed dry inside.

"That's all," said Beecher. Bedwell started to get up, but Eggleston motioned him back. Eggleston's thin mouth worked carefully. "Just a minute. Can you identify the rifle?"

"Of course. It was made by old Ben Mills at Harrodsburg, Kentucky. I bought it from him."

"Sheriff," Eggleston asked, "bring the rifle around, will you?" He looked at the piece, held it for Beecher's inspection and then handed it to the jurymen. It made the rounds among them while they nodded their heads. The prosecutor let himself smile.

Squire Beecher was on his feet. "Wait! Wait!" His finger leveled at Bedwell. "You could have memorized the name of the maker after you had stolen the rifle, couldn't you?"

"Yes," said Bedwell. "If I had stolen it."

"As a matter of fact, that would probably be the first thing you would do, wouldn't it?" asked Beecher, his eyes going from one juror to another. They looked at him and looked away, as if they couldn't be jarred loose from an idea.

Bedwell said, "Probably. If I had stolen it."

Eggleston pointed his lean face at the bench. "That's the case."

Squire Beecher turned to Boone. "All right," he said. His finger showed the way to the witness stand.

Boone got up and went over and sat down. At one side of him were the jurors, at the other the judges' bench. In front of him were the attorneys and Bedwell and the clerk with his big book and pen, and beyond them the townspeople, staring at him, turning to talk behind shielding hands out of eager, curling mouths. The eyes came together on him, as if everything was just one big eye and he was all there was to see. Only the Indian sat quiet, looking at him out of eyes that caught a gleam from the window, his hands idle in his lap, holding the moccasins. He wouldn't be a real western Indian, but a Miami, or maybe a Pottawatomi. Far back in the room a man was smiling at Boone, like a body would smile at a friend. In the whole passel of faces his was the only friendly one, unless it would be the Indian's.

"What is your name?" asked Beecher.

"Boone Caudill."

"In your own words," said Beecher quietly, "will you tell the court about your fight this morning and the circumstances surrounding it?"

"It's my gun. He stoled it."

"Wait a minute, now. Start at the first."

"I was fixin' my supper——"

"When and where?"

"Night before yistiddy. Down the road a piece."

"The other side of Greenville?"

"I reckon so."

"Go on."

Boone made a little gesture at Bedwell. "He came ridin' up."

"Yes?"

"He gave me his name and asked if he could put up, too."

"Yes?"

"Come mornin', he was gone, and the rifle to boot."

"And so," said Squire Beecher, "when you came upon him today you tried to get your rifle back?"

"Yes."

Eggleston barked, "Objection!"

"Quit coachin' him," ordered Judge Test.

"That's the way it was," Boone said.

"Can you identify the rifle?"

"Ben Mills made it, at Harrodsburg."

Squire Beecher got up. "Your honors," he said, while a frown wrinkled his face, "we believe a motion for dismissal is in order. As to the identification of the gun, the court simply has a contradiction, without supporting evidence on either side. Neither does the charge of assault and battery stand up. There again the court has a contradiction, and the testimony of the sheriff on the one side does nothing to enforce the accusation. The sheriff simply saw the men fighting. Any conclusion he has drawn or implied is pure assumption, without weight before the law. The only thing of actual proof is that a fight took place."

Eggleston had arisen, protesting. "We want to cross-examine the witness."

Judge Test waved them both back. "Go on, then," he said to the prosecutor, but Squire Beecher said, "Wait, your honor. We're not through." His eyes came back to Boone. "Have you any other way of identifying the rifle? Are there any other marks on it, or scratches that would identify it?"

"It's got nary scratch on it."

Squire Beecher rested his chin on his fist. His eyes studied the table in front of him. "Maybe," he said after a pause, "you can establish your claim to the rifle through the horn or pouch." His head came up. "How many bullets in the pouch?"

"There was eleven, and I shot a rabbit. Ten, there would be."

Beecher motioned, and the sheriff brought over the pouch. Eggleston came and stood over Beecher as Beecher emptied the pouch on the table. "One, two, three . . ."

Eggleston broke in, "There's eight. Just eight."

Beecher's hand fumbled in the pouch and came out empty. "Of course," he said to Boone, "anyone who stole it could have fired it a couple of times, couldn't he?"

Eggleston looked down at Beecher, grinning, and said, "I ought to object. You're coaching him again." He went back over to his seat, still grinning.

Beecher said, "That's all."

Judge Test's red face turned on Eggleston. "Go on."

Eggleston leaned forward toward Boone, like a snake with a stand on a bird. "How long have you owned this rifle?"

"A spell."

"How long?"

Boone heard the pen scratching as the man at the little table wrote in the big book. It scratched and stopped, and he saw the pen raised, waiting. From the back of the room the man still smiled at him, like someone who was on his side.

"I asked how long. Good Lord, boy, if the rifle is yours you must know how long you've owned it."

"I couldn't rightly say as to that."

"Oh, you couldn't rightly say. Where did you get the rifle, anyway? Is it really yours?"

The pen was scratching again, and stopping again. Boone felt his hands knotted between his knees. His tongue came out and wet his lips.

Eggleston yelled, "Is it?" and pounded on the table with his fist.

"Your honors," Squire Beecher complained, "we object that the questioning amounts to abuse."

"He won't answer."

The judge's red eyes rested on Boone. "Boy, a defendant can't be made to incriminate himself—but I'll have to warn ye, if you don't answer, the jury's most likely to hold it against you."

Boone said, "My pap gave it to me."

The prosecutor's hand fiddled with his chin. After a silence he said, "How old are you, boy?"

"Comin' eighteen."

"You're seventeen then." Eggleston's light eyes studied him. "You're a runaway, aren't you?"

Boone heard Beecher cry "Objection!" and Judge Test answer, "He's cross-examinin'."

"Where you from?"

Boone brought his hands from between his knees and took hold of the bottom of his chair. "St. Louis."

"What are you doing here?"

"Goin' back."

"From where?"

"Around."

"Just around, eh?"

"Reckon so."

The prosecutor looked at the judges, his eyebrows up, making wrinkles in his forehead. "He ought to be held for investigation. Probably a bound boy."

Squire Beecher came forward, and again the yellow queue swung. "The charge is assault and battery. No other accusation is before the court."

"Let's git on with it, first," Judge Test said to Eggleston. "Ready for pleadin'?" There was a little buzz of whispers in the crowd and a shifting of butts on the benches. They sat forward, as if this was what they had been waiting for. While Boone looked, the man in the back nodded his head, as if to say everything would be all right.

"You can come here," Squire Beecher said, not unkindly, and Boone left the witness chair and sat at the table by him.

Beecher got up and stepped over in front of the jury and began to talk. His voice, lighter than Eggleston's, seemed to turn on and off like a spigot as he faced one way and then another. It was a sight, the way his pigtail joggled. Beyond him, through the window, was the tavern and, farther on, the woods against the sky and the sky itself clear and blue as water. Boone made out a bird against it, probably just a buzzard, but sailing free and easy like keeping up was no trick at all. The spigot turned on and off. "Only one man's word . . . No case has been proved . . . All that has been shown, all you can be sure of, is that a fight took place . . . In the circumstances you must resolve the doubt in favor of the defendant. . ." Out beyond the pole everybody was looking at Beecher, except when he pointed, and then the eyes all moved over, as if they were on a string, and bored at Boone. And everybody was listening, too, and sometimes smiling and sometimes frowning, and whispering once in a while. Maybe a man would find it easy enough to listen, to keep his mind to what was being said, if he was out there. Maybe it was right pleasant, watching and listening and not having fingers aimed at you and eyes putting holes through you, knowing you could get up and go any time you wanted to, to St. Louis or wherever. ". . . this innocent and friendless boy . . ." He didn't want anyone to be friends, unless it was Jim Deakins. And he wasn't a boy, but a man, growed and out on his own. ". . . ask the jury in its wisdom and mercy to return a verdict of acquittal."

Beecher was sweating when he sat down.

Eggleston lifted himself from his chair and went over toward the jury with his hands in his pockets and his head down. When he got there, though, the hands came out and the head lifted. His voice was loud, so that Boone could hear it plain, if he set himself to listening, no matter how Eggleston faced. Eggleston marched back and forth in front of the jurymen, his arms swinging. Once in a while he turned and pointed and fixed Boone with his whitish eyes, and, when he did, his voice boomed in Boone's ears, saying "ragged rascal" and "plain piece of banditry" and "murderous tramp." When he turned back his words hit the wall first and seemed to run like echoes in the room. Beyond him, way beyond him, the buzzard was still circling, light as a feather, not moving its wings but just tilting, round and round, with the wind. Words came at Boone again, like rocks being pitched. He felt the eyes on him and his skin trying to be small inside his clothes. "I submit, gentlemen, that you can come to only one verdict, and that is the verdict of guilt." The arm swung over, like a loose limb in the wind. "Look at him! Look him over well! Ask yourselves what a man like this—" a finger pecked at his clothes—"would be doing with a piece like that." Then it was the echo again, bouncing from the wall. "The penalty, gentlemen, I leave to your good judgment."

Eggleston turned around and went to his seat, giving Squire Beecher a smile on the way. Boone reckoned they were pretty good friends outside of court.

Judge Test rapped once. "The jury can retire." They got up, stretching, and filed out. Through the window Boone could see them cross the street and go into the tavern. The crowd began to shuffle out, most of them making for the tavern, too. The Indian arose, his dark face still as set as a picture, and got his blanket closer around his neck and went through the door, letting the moccasins dangle from his hand. The smiling man in the back was among the last to go out. Watching him, Boone saw that he was crippled. One shoulder was withered, and one leg dragged on the floor. He was still smiling as he drew closer, but smiling a fool's smile, Boone could see now, smiling without meaning, out of an idiot's face. Before he passed through the door he turned and stuck his tongue out at Boone. Bedwell tidied his beaver and after a final look around left the courtroom. Judge Test came down from the bench and cut himself a chew of tobacco. He and the sheriff began to chaff.

After while the sheriff said, "This was just a one-drink case." He motioned out the window, to the jury coming from the tavern. Beecher shook his head but didn't say anything.

The jurymen lagged in. Judge Test lifted himself back on the platform and sat at the bench pulling at his dewlaps. The pale judge sat with his jaw in his hand. His eyes opened slowly as the jury tramped by him. The clerk came and sat down before his book.

"Gentlemen, have you come to a decision?"

One of the jurors got up and stood framed in the window, shutting out the woods and the sky and the bird soaring. "We have."

"Let the court hear it."

"Judge, your honor, we say the boy's guilty, but not too orful guilty."

The judge pursed his lips while his red eyes waited on the speaker.

"We figger," said the juror, "that he'll have to work it out, if'n you fine him, so we say about five dollars, or seven days."

Judge Test whispered to the pale judge and they both nodded, and Judge Test said, "Let it be seven days." The clerk's pen scratched in his book. To Eggleston Judge Test added, "That'll give you time enough to run him down."

Boone felt the hand of the sheriff on his arm. "Come along!" Eggleston looked up as they were about to pass him. "Maybe you can get something out of him, sheriff." One cold eye winked. The sheriff said, "Sure." As he passed out the door he said to the little man named Charlie, "Git Little Betsy, will you?"

The jail was a log cabin with a heavy oak door. The sheriff sprang the lock with a rusty key. It was a big lock, as big as a terrapin. For a minute Boone couldn't make things out after he had got inside. Then he saw a plank bunk with a ragged cover on it, and a broken table, on which a half-burned candle was stuck.

A voice outside said, "Here's Betsy." The sheriff said, "Thanks. Watch the door." The door whined as it closed.

The sheriff was a big man, tall and bony, with a look of power about him. Boone hadn't noticed before how stiff his face could be. It was like a rock face, like Pap's when the devil got in him.

"Time we get well acquainted," said the sheriff, "maybe you'll feel more like talkin'." The right hand came away from his side, holding something that for a minute dragged on the floor. "Turn around!"

Boone cried, "You ain't going to whale me, mister!"

Before he had finished, the whip whistled.

8

Giddap, old boy, giddap, giddap."

Jim Deakins timed his words to the pace of the horse under him, kicking the horse's belly when he got too poky. He was over the river at last, after waiting two days for the water to go down and the ferryman's courage to rise. Even then he had had to pay an extra dollar to get the ferryman to put out. His two mules were gone, and the old work wagon. In their place he had a horse and a bit of money in his pocket. "Giddap, giddap."

He hadn't found any trace of Boone yet. No one had seen him. A tall, dark boy? No. Carrying a rifle? No. Seventeen or eighteen, going to St. Louis? Nope. Nope. Ain't seed such a boy. He wondered if the river had got Boone after all. From the shore they had seen the boat turn over and the head bob and then go out of sight, but a man's head was a little thing to see in the water such a piece away. Boone looked strong, and stout-winded as a pup. He was a good swimmer, likely.

Jim had bought his horse after the ferry had put him off, and had ridden down the Indiana shore, looking, but there wasn't anyone to home at the one likely place, and instead of waiting he had returned to the road and struck out, figuring if Boone had got across he was already on his way to St. Louis.

"Seed a boy go by here, mister, last two or three days, goin' west, afoot?"

The man at the cabin dumped his bucket of slop water and stood straight. "Don't reckon I have."

"Alf, we did so, don't you recollect?" There was a woman at the door, talking shrill. The baby in her arms began to cry. Alf scratched his head.

"When might it be, Missus?"

Before she answered, she brought out a breast and gave it to the baby, saying, "There, will you quit your squallin'?" She wiped the hair from her eyes. "Lemme see. Was it yesterday or day before, Alf? I swear, a body gets mixed up on time. What was it, Alf?"

"Time don't matter so much, just so's he went by."

"He did that, didn't he, Alf? You recollect?" She looked at Jim. "He's awful forgetful, but he seed him all right."

Alf said, "A boy, afoot? He don't come to mind." He put the bucket down and looked up and down the road, as if he might see Boone now. "Reckon Ma's right. She's mighty noticin'."

"I'm obliged to ye." Jim kicked the old horse.

It was a cold day, cold and unfriendly, with a little wind that worried at a man and let him be and then came back and worried him again, as if it couldn't put him out of its mind.

Jim came to a mill, lying silent except for the gurgle of water by its side. It was streaked where the rain had washed channels in the dust. "Hello, the mill." He heard footsteps inside. A man came to the door and looked out and slapped his legs and stomach, sending out puffs of dust. His eyes peered out from whitened lashes for the bag that a farmer would carry on his saddle.

"It ain't business."

The man leaned against the side of the doorway. "Mean day."

"Looked this morning like it was fixin' to fair off."

"Signs lie, just like everybody. You can't put no trust in signs."

Jim brought one leg over and sat sidewise in his saddle. "Reckon not. I got me once right spang at the end of a rainbow, but there wasn't nothin' there but me. You taken any notice of a boy goin' by here afoot, last day or two?"

The miller chewed on a grain of corn. "A lean boy? Tall?"

"That's him."

"A plain-dressed boy?"

"Uh-huh."

"A sull young'n?"

"Quiet-like, anyways."

"Sull is what I said."

"When was it?"

"I hollered at him, friendly, but he went by with his eyes down like he was deaf. Young'ns got no manners these days. You got to beat manners in a boy. No beatin', no manners."

"When'd you say it was?"

The miller put another grain in his mouth and tried it with his teeth. "Yesterday."

"What time o' day?"

"Round about this time. No, come to think on it, it was earlier." The miller spit out a husk. "Runaway?"

Jim shook his head. "He's my brother. I'm just tryin' to catch up. This the road to Paoli?"

"One of 'em."

Jim grinned at him. "One at a time is a plenty. Obliged." The miller stood in the doorway, chewing on his corn, as the horse plodded away.

Farther on, a dog ran out from a house and planted himself with his legs wide apart, barking. "Anyone to home?" The door of a shed whined open. A man came out and leaned on a manure fork. He'd seen a boy, yesterday, a mean boy who kicked at his dog and went on without a how-de-do. Rifle? No, he didn't have a rifle, just a little sack. It wasn't until Jim rode away that it occurred to him Boone wouldn't have his rifle. A man couldn't swim carrying a gun.

Jim bought himself a bite to eat at the store in Greenville. The storekeeper hadn't seen a tall, dark, plain-dressed boy? The man rested his hands on the counter and shook his head while his mouth came out like a snout. 'Course, he could have missed him. A store job was half bending over, lifting and opening. A lot of folks went by a body didn't see.

At the tavern across the road they hadn't seen Boone either. He hadn't been in there, hadn't passed by, far as they knew.

Jim went to the hitch rack and untied his horse and mounted and rode on, wondering. There wasn't any place for a man to lose himself between the mill and town.

He put up at a farmhouse that night and rode on the next morning in the rain. The farmer had given him a square of canvas to drape across his back, and the rain pattered on it and ran down and wet the saddle and the saddle wet his breeches. He would be something to see when he got off the horse, with his seat sopping as a baby's.

Along toward the middle of the day the rain let up, and the sun got itself from behind the clouds. Jim heard a redbird whistle. It was a prime day for going west, after all, he decided. If only he could find Boone, everything would be slick. Anyone taken notice of a boy, hoofin' it? Could be they missed him. Could be he went by early, or after dark. Giddap! Giddap!

It was growing dark when he arrived at Paoli. He reined up to a tavern and hitched his horse next to a chestnut standing with his head down. Under an antlered skull wired to a board above the door a sign said "White Stag Tavern." There was a bar inside, and a fireplace and tables and chairs, and a little white-haired man with a stomach like a melon who came from behind the bar, his eyes saying, "Well?"

"Kin you put me up?"

"Supper, breakfast, bed, one dollar, hard money."

"I got a horse outside."

"Twenty-five cents more. Hay and a feed of corn."

Jim got out his money. "When's supper?"

"Directly. Your room's first door to the right, upstairs. There's a place to wash in back. You can see the backhouse from there. Make yourself to home."

Jim looked around. An old man sat in a chair by the fireplace, holding a paper that trembled in his hand. His cane was angled against the chair.

The little man went back behind the bar and started to wrestle with a keg.

"I better have a drink," Jim said.

"Whisky? Common, rectified, or Monongahela?"

"Common'll do." Jim leaned against the bar, picked up his whisky and tasted it while his eyes held the little man's attention. "Been a boy by here, last day or two, seventeen-eighteen year old?"

The little man stood still. His hands settled on the bar, and his eyes went blank as a dead fish's, as if he were waiting. "Might be," he said.

The old man in the chair rustled his paper. " 'Course we seen such a boy, Shorty," he said in a voice sharp and high with age. "He's the one in the jailhouse. Where's your mind gone?"

Jim turned half around. The old man's eyes looked at him over the edge of his paper. The old man's voice asked, "You run into trouble, too?"

Jim said, "No. No trouble."

"What might the boy be like?" Shorty asked.

"You seen him, Shorty," the old man persisted. "Tall, he is, and got a deep, mean look in his eye."

Jim shook his head and sipped again at his whisky. "Mine's middlin'." Shorty was looking at the old man. "Middlin', with a blue eye, and like as not whistlin'. He whistles all the time, like a bird."

The old man said, " 'Tain't this 'un, by a damn sight. This 'un tried to rob a man. Went after his horse and rifle. He pounded him around some, too."

"So?"

"That's a fact. There's the rifle, standin' in the corner."

Jim took his glass and walked over to the corner. His eyes went to the gun, studied it, slid to the little man, and came back to the rifle again.

"What did the boy allow?"

The old man answered. "Said the rifle was his'n. Said the man snitched it. He was lyin'."

"What might be the name of the boy you're lookin' for?" Shorty asked.

Jim drained his glass before he answered. "William. Bill Williams. Give me another, will you, mister? He'll be along. He's around somewheres, askin' about mules."

"Mules?"

"Mules." Jim nodded his head and kept his eyes on his refilled glass while Shorty's gaze questioned him. Finally Shorty said, "No mules for sale around here. None that I know of." He turned and gave his attention to the keg again.

"That's the man's horse, outside," the old man volunteered.

"So? Reckon they'll put the boy away for a spell."

"Court's already sat. Seven days. They think he's a runaway. That'll give 'em time to see." The old man's head went behind his paper.

Shorty had the keg in its standard now, and the spigot driven in. He looked up as the door creaked open. "Evenin'. See the door's closed, will you? Damn that dog!"

"Whisky, Shorty."

The customer lifted his drink and looked at it and downed it all at once, with a snap of his head. He paid for it and went out, giving no attention to the dog that had followed him in.

The dog sniffed at the corner of the bar, and the little man called Shorty leaned over and yelled, "No, you don't! Goddam you, Curly Locks, git away from there!" It was a big brown dog, furred

56

from toenails to topknot with long, slim rings of hair that joggled when he walked.

Jim said, "I never seed a dog like that."

"Never will another time," Shorty promised. "That there's a piss hound."

"Never heerd of such."

"He's the only one. He ain't mine, but he comes in here a hunderd times a day, and, first off, he makes for the corner there and gives it a smell, and up comes his leg."

"So?"

"Look!" said the little man. "He kin come in here and sprinkle and I put him out, and directly someone lets him in, and what you think?"

Jim shook his head.

"By God, he goes right there and smells again, and don't even recognize hisself, from just a wink before. So up his leg comes. . . ." The little man trailed off.

"Why'n't you knock him one on the head?"

"He belongs to the sheriff."

The old man rustled his paper. From behind it he said, "And the sheriff leaves money aplenty here."

Shorty came from behind the bar and put the dog out. "Take a chair. Time Ma had supper ready." He went through a door. Jim heard him say, "Ready, Ma? Good God, what you been doin'?"

A woman's voice answered, hot and high-pitched. "You git back in there, Shorty Carey. I been workin', that's what, workin' and wearin' my fingers to a nub while you're in there drammin'. Supper'll be ready when it's suppertime."

Shorty came back, shaking his head. "Maybe you want to wash first. There's time to put up your horse. You'll see the barn. Take the third stall."

"I'll let the horse go for a spell. Reckon I could stand a wash, though."

When Jim came back, a table had been set and bowls of food were sending up little clouds of vapor. Three men were at the table. One of them had on a black coat on which a metal star shone. The other wore a cutaway and had dropped a gray greatcoat over the back of his chair. The third was the old man who had been reading a paper. His hand shook with age as it carried food to his mouth. Shorty motioned Jim to a chair at the table. "Set up and eat." A woman in an apron came from the kitchen, carrying more food.

The men looked at Jim as he sat down. "Evenin'," he said. The sheriff had a bruise under one eye, which would get black, likely. The man in the cutaway said, "Good evening."

Jim realized, when the sheriff turned to speak to him, that the man had some drinks under his belt. "I don't recollect seein' you around before."

"First time."

"Passin' through?" The sheriff's eyes questioned him.

Jim asked, "Heerd what St. Louis's offerin' for mules?"

The old man said, "Plenty. Got some?"

"I know where some are, anyways. If it was me, I'd have a piece of meat on that there eye, sheriff."

"Don't amount to nothin'." He said to his companion, "That boy fit, Bedwell, like a b'ar, as I been tellin' you. Jesus!"

They were quiet for a while, and then the sheriff added, "He ain't going to feel so pert tomorrow. Second day's the worst, by a whole lot."

"Get anything from him?" Bedwell asked.

"Not more'n two or three words, and they was cuss words. A little more leather'll loosen his tongue."

The sheriff pushed his plate away from him. His voice rolled out strong as any hound's. "Bring a *bottle* over, Shorty. I can spit more'n your glasses hold."

Shorty filled a bottle from a keg. He brought it over, and two glasses with it. "Drink?" the sheriff asked of Jim, as if he didn't mean it. "Not now. Obliged." The old man got up, clearing his throat, and went back to his chair by the fireplace.

As the sheriff poured the drinks Bedwell said, "I got no business idlin' here thisaway, sheriff. It's the company, I reckon."

The door at the front opened, and Curly Locks came in behind the man who had opened it. The dog eased over to the corner of the bar. Shorty came from the kitchen just then and said "Git!" and made as if to kick him, and Curly Locks dropped his leg and backed up. He padded over to Jim, his tongue rolling out of the side of his mouth, and stopped while Jim's hand rubbed his ears.

"Shorty's awful damn particular," the sheriff said, refilling the glasses. "Won't let my dog piss on his bar, but what he sells you out of his bar'ls is the same stuff."

Shorty grunted.

Bedwell got out a pipe and puffed on it slow and deep. Jim leaned over and talked to the dog while he scratched the furry head. The sheriff, by littles, was getting quiet with the drink in him. His eyes were unwinking and fixed, and Jim could tell he wasn't seeing anything, except what was in his mind. He just grunted and went on drinking and staring when two more men came in and walked over to him. One of them said, "Hear you're still champeen, sheriff." When he didn't answer they went to the bar.

By and by the sheriff said, "I ought to take some supper to that there boy." His hand reached into the pocket of his black coat and came out with a key through which a whang was looped. It was a long, rusty key, which the sheriff kept turning under his thumbs, looking at it but not really seeing it. "Serve him right if I left him empty." He put down the key and lifted his glass, and then put the glass down and picked the key up and fiddled with it some more.

"Why not?" asked Bedwell.

"Got to keep him strong, so's he can work on the road."

It was a big key, too big to hide easy, even if a man could sneak it off the table. Jim's hand explored Curly Locks' head.

"I ought to take him some victuals." The sheriff didn't move, except to fill his glass.

Might be a man could slip the whang around the dog's neck and make an excuse to go out, whispering Curly Locks out with him. But it was risky. Like as not someone would see the key dangling. Jim's hand pulled a curl out to its full length. The key would show some, for all that hair.

The sheriff felt of his eye again. Jim could see his eyeballs were getting red. Bedwell was humming a little song to himself. The key was out on the table, the whang lying in a circle from it. Wouldn't do to ask about the key. Wouldn't do to eye it too much.

Jim got up and strolled to the bar and bought himself a drink, and then went out to the backhouse. Sometimes a man could think best when his breeches were down, he reflected as he lowered himself. What if he started a blaze in the privy and went running in yelling fire? No good. A man didn't have no excuse for firing a privy. What if he touched off the tavern? Jesus, they'd lock a man away for a coon's age if they caught him.

He went back in the tavern. The sheriff was still slouched in his chair, looking sleepy and kind of loose. There was the key on the table, caught in its circle of thong. Bedwell was at the bar, talking with three men. Curly Locks came over and smelled of Jim when he came in and followed along to a chair, holding his head up to be scratched. The circle would go over the big head all right, and nice and snug, too. It would be a little thing to slip it on.

The sheriff belched and stirred and filled his glass, spilling a little down his chin when he drank. His eyes held Jim. "Don't recollect seein' you around before."

"First time."

"I recollect," the sheriff said. "You're buyin' mules." He slumped back. There was the key and here the dog, and the sheriff's eyes half-closed and maybe unseeing.

Jim's hand was easing out when he heard running footsteps outside. The door of the tavern burst open. "Sheriff!" The man who had entered looked around, spotted the sheriff, and strode over to him. "Matt Elliott's comin' in. He searched out his cow. The one that was stole."

The sheriff's eyes lifted and came to focus. The men at the bar had turned, looking and listening.

The man blurted, "He's got the feller what stole her, too. In his wagon, with his tail full of lead. I ran ahead, soon's I learned."

The sheriff got up, pulled himself together, and made for the door. The men at the bar trooped out after him. Shorty was at the door, looking out. Jim's eyes ran around the room. There wasn't anybody, except Curly Locks, and there was the key, lying on the table. His hand went out and took it in and tucked it in his pocket. He got up, feeling his heart thumping in his throat. "Reckon I'll put my horse up," he said as he edged past the tavern keeper.

This must be the jail all right. With the key Jim poked for the keyhole. The lock screeched as he turned. He loosened the hasp from the staple and gave the door a little push and whispered,

"Boone! Boone!" It was a time before he got an answer. "It's me, Jim Deakins."

He heard a voice then, just a blurt of sound like a man surprised, and heard Boone's feet, moving slow and uneven. "Jim!"

"Don't ask no questions. Git on the horse. Quick! We'll ride double."

Even in the dark Jim could see that Boone moved like an old man, an old man just getting out of a chair and waiting for his joints to ease. "Hurry up, Boone!"

Jim wouldn't have known Boone's voice. "Goddam 'em! Goddam 'em! I'll kill 'em." Boone wasn't even fixing to get on the horse.

"You'll get kilt. Come on, Boone! They'll be on to us in a shake."

"He whopped me! He whopped me till I was near dead." Boone's voice broke. "I'll kill him, I tell you." He jerked his arm loose from Jim's grasp and faced toward the town. "Stoled my gun, too!"

"You want to go to St. Louis, don't you, Boone? That's what counts. Not this here. You want to trap beaver and fight Injuns and live like a natural man."

"Not yit, I don't."

"Shhh! You want to get 'em down on us! Come on, now. We got to hurry. Bedwell's horse's at the rack, and the sheriff's, too. Won't take 'em long to ketch us if we don't get goin'."

"You see my gun?"

"You ain't got a chanct to git it, Boone. Not a chanct. Climb on, now."

"It's mine, all the same."

"Sure it's yours. Sure it is. I'll help you get it, some time, come a chanct. I promise. Git on!"

"I'm bound to get even," Boone said, letting himself be urged toward the horse. "You can't talk me out'n it."

"Sure. But not now. Some time."

Boone's hand felt for the neck of the horse, and his foot lifted and fell back. "It ain't no use. I can't git on, Jim, I'm that stove up."

"Here. I'll help. Easy now. I'll ride behind. Rein him around, Boone. Hear? You're bound smack back into town. Turn him! Godamighty, Boone! The other way! Are you crazy?"

Boone sat stiff as a pole. There was no give-in to his voice. "I told you I was bound to get even. I'll keep to the shadders. If it's so's it can be, Goddam 'em, me and you's both going to have a horse."

It seemed to Jim that the little whinings of the saddle and the creak of the horse's joints and the soft thump of its hoofs could be heard as plain as any shout. The dark wasn't so thick but that an eye could see them, looming big and sneaky. From down the road came the sound of voices and of turning wheels.

Boone pulled up across the road from the tavern and handed the reins back to Jim. Not speaking, he tried to get off. Jim moved back on the horse to give Boone's stiff leg room to come over.

Jim could make out the horses tied at the rack. Down the road the sounds were getting louder. Nothing was in sight, though. Night hid the sheriff and the men and Matt Elliott and the thief with the lead in his tail. Boone limped across the road as if he didn't give a damn who saw him. Light from the tavern made a shadow out of him, a shadow moving by the big shadows that were the horses. After what seemed like a year, the little shadow moved away from the rack and a big one followed it. They came straight across to Jim, seeming to make loud noises as they moved, seeming to make an easy sight of themselves.

"There, by God!" Boone said, and got his foot up and pulled himself into the saddle.

"Best walk soft for a ways," Jim said under his breath. The sounds down the road were so close now he expected any time to hear a voice cry out, telling that a horse had been stolen. "Easy, Boone, I tell you."

The voices faded as they walked the horses along. After a while they were no more than far echoes. Dim ahead of them, like a swath through the trees, the road opened, leading to Vincennes, leading to St. Louis.

"Now we can git," Jim said, and kicked his horse into a run. Already Boone was galloping ahead.

PART II

1830

9

The camp was silent, except now and then for the mutter of one man to another and the clink of spoons against metal plates. The fire around which they were circled glowed and died and glowed again as the breeze played with it. Against the river the keelboat *Mandan* was a black shape, raising a slim finger into the sky.

Boone sopped up the bean juice with a piece of corn bread and swallowed the last of his bitter coffee. The food tasted better than city fare, for all that it was plain. The three weeks he had passed in St. Louis waiting for a chance to go west would do him for a time. It didn't suit him to be where people were so thick, though he had got himself a good-enough job working in a livery stable, where he fed and brushed down horses and cleaned carriages and tidied up the stalls. Jim, having more learning and more liking for folks, had found work in a store, where he got to parcel out beans and meal and copperas.

Summers, the hunter, got up and looked at the men about the fire. His eye fixed on the patron. As if to break a spell he said, "I be dogged, Jourdonnais, keep feedin' us them bastardly white beans and I do believe we'll blow your boat to the Roche Jaune." The men looked at him unsmiling, their eyes catching glints from the fire.

"It is the gran' idea," Jourdonnais answered. He brought his feet up in a cross-legged squat and spread his hands. "If only the res' could make the wind like you."

The cook arose and stirred the pot that hung over the fire. The rushes that the men had tramped down to make a camping place squeaked under his step. "We maybe need that wind," he said while he screwed his face against the heat. "Ten days from St. Louis, and already two men down."

"We will eat the meat," the patron continued, "when Monsieur Summers shoots it."

The hunter's lean face grinned at Boone. In the firelight his buckskins looked ghostly. "Jourdonnais would like a milk cow. He would now." To Jourdonnais he said, "You'll have meat aplenty when we hit meat country." He moved off toward the bank where the boat lay. Boone rolled over on his side and watched him, saw him walk up the plank angled against her side, and disappear in the bow.

Jim Deakins was lying on his belly. He reached out and put a hand on Boone's arm. "Which you rather do, tow or pole or row?"

"I'd rather set and let the wind work."

"If it just would." Jim brought his hand before his face and spread the fingers wide. "That towline like to wore me to the bone. I pret' near hope we have to pole tomorrow. Or get stuck."

"It don't seem to bother the French."

"God, no! And it don't gall a woodchuck to dig a hole or a hound to run. They don't know no better. They don't know nothin' but workin' a boat up this river."

Summers was a white shadow against the black of the cargo box. He came back without a sound and stood while the eyes of the men questioned him. Jourdonnais looked up. Summers' face made a little sidewise move as if the news was bad.

"It is the bellyache, no more," said Jourdonnais, and gave his gaze back to the fire. "Tomorrow, all right. Better, at the least."

The men around the fire looked at one another and at the hunter again. "Zephyr got down a dose of honey and whisky."

"Good. With the calomel he be all right."

The bosseman got up, moving with a sort of heavy care, as if he still held in his hands the pole he plied from the bow of the *Mandan*. To Boone, his chest looked as deep as a horse's. "Holy Jesus," he said, "how they die sometimes!"

With one hand the patron pushed his black mustaches up from his mouth, as if to clear the way for his words. His voice was sharp. "Must you see death always, Romaine? It is the bellyache, for women to worry of."

Romaine muttered, "Brain fever, black tongue, lung fever, bellyache, it is sickness."

Like a hand on him, Boone felt the silence. Against it there was only the busy lipping of the water and the whisper of the wind in the walnuts. A half-moon, clear and bold, mounted the eastern sky. A raw chill was in the air that crept through the clothes and drew up the skin.

The cook fed the fire, fixing food against tomorrow. It crackled and sent a flame at the black underbulge of the pot. The cook said, "In sickness whisky is good. Much whisky."

Jourdonnais didn't answer. Summers lighted his pipe with a brand. His voice was light and joking. "You'll get plenty of whisky, all the Injuns can't drink."

"If there are any to swallow it."

"*Très bien*," conceded Jourdonnais. "Morning and night, whisky for all, until the bellyache is gone."

The hunter sat down at Boone's side. He and Deakins and Boone made a little group by themselves. "How long since you seed Uncle Zeb?" Boone asked.

"Well, now, it's a spell. Five or six year, I'm thinking. Me and him been on many a spree, like I told you. Could be we'll run into him. That hoss is somewheres around, if he ain't gone under."

Boone studied the hunter's face. It was a face that a body took to, a lined, lean, humorous face with a long chin. Boone felt good, deep down in him, that Summers acted so friendly to Jim and him. Like as not, that was because of Uncle Zeb.

Summers was looking around at the men. "When the French don't sing they ain't right."

"Sure enough?"

"They're skeered of the boat now, and the sick. Time we get up river where the Injuns are bad they'll be wantin' to sleep on board, I'm thinking, and to anchor out from shore to boot."

Boone hitched himself closer. "It's fair country up there, I reckon."

Summers looked at him, and his mouth made a small smile. "Wild. Wild and purty, like a virgin woman. Whatever a man does he feels like he's the first one done it." He halted and was silent for a long time, his gaze on the fire.

Boone wondered whether he was thinking of the upcountry or of a woman. It wouldn't be a woman like the one he had bedded with on the night before they put out, a smelly woman in a crib who demanded a dollar first and answered to it like a man setting out to do a job of work.

He could feel her squirm under him. Her breath blew against his ear. "Not so damn rough, honey. Christ, you kids are just like mountaineers the first night back!" It was a tired and whiny voice, and his ears told him, better than his eyes could, that she was old. Her perfume made a sick fog around him. Beneath it he smelled the animal of her. He rolled from the bunk when he had done and put on his boots. Her voice followed him into the street. "Don't forget me, honey." Forget? He'd remember a sight too well to come back. Jim had stood outside, licking his mouth like a dog after a feed. "God, you're poky!" he said. "Yours good, too?"

The hunter's voice picked up the thread of his thought. "I seen most of it. Colter's Hell and the Seeds-kee-dee and the Tetons standin' higher'n clouds, and north and south from Nez Perce to Comanche, but God Almighty, there's nothin' richer'n the upper Missouri. Or purtier. I seen the Great Falls and traveled Maria's River, dodgin' the Blackfeet, makin' cold camps and sometimes thinkin' my time was up, and all the time livin' wonderful, loose and free's ary animal. That's some, that is."

"Lord God!"

"A man gets a taste for it."

The hunter filled his pipe. His eye went around the camp site. Most of the men were down, but not yet asleep. An uneasy murmur came from them. "Git the French away from water and they ain't worth a damn, but they shine with a boat."

Jourdonnais came over to them and sat down sighing, as if he had a weight of trouble on him. "*Sacré crapaud!*" he said softly. "Sickness, and so soon."

"No cause to worry about these two," answered Summers between puffs on his pipe. "They'll stick, I'm bettin'."

Jourdonnais looked at Jim and then at Boone.

"We aim to go where the boat goes," Jim said, "long as you're payin' us."

"And you, Caudill?"

"I come a right smart piece a'ready. I ain't turnin' back."

"You are signed," said Jourdonnais, as if to clinch the matter. "The deserter 'ave hard time."

He got out a cigar and lit it from Summers' pipe. When he drew on it the small red glow spread to his face. "She's a long night."

The hunter knocked the heel from his pipe. "How's Romaine?"

"Ah! All right. He complain, but he stick. He is with me a long time, and always faithful."

"That makes three of us, for watches."

"*Oui*. We watch."

"B'God, we better, if we want a crew. It'll be better, away from the settlements. That is, if we git by Leavenworth."

"Pouff! They find no whisky on the *Mandan*, except what is permit' the crew."

"We got to be slick."

"A good wind, and night. Pouff!"

"Take away the whisky and we won't have but a smidgen of goods to trade with."

The patron stroked his black mustache. Under it his mouth eased into a grin. "Six cats, too."

"How much you figger for them?"

Jourdonnais shrugged. "One plew, two each. Maybe more if the mice are enough."

They talked quietly, like men spending time speaking of little things while a bigger one was in their thoughts. They reminded Boone of people around a body waiting for the preacher to get started.

"And you'd still have the Injun girl," Jim broke in. It was like him to speak up, trying to prize out information. In his mind's eye Boone saw the Indian child, a little splinter of a girl who was all eyes in a thin face. His gaze went to the stern of the *Mandan*, where Jourdonnais had rigged a buffalo-robe shelter for her against the cargo box. He heard again what Jourdonnais had said the first night out. "You men, you leave the Indian *enfant* alone. No talk. No play. No hands on her. Summers will shoot, by God, dead anyone who monkey. Leave alone! You understand?"

Answering Jim, Jourdonnais' voice was soft. "The little squaw. Ah! With an eye like the bluewing teal."

"We'll raise hell in the Blackfoot nation," said Summers. "Alcohol and guns and powder and ball."

"Good business. They want it."

"The other side of Leavenworth," the hunter went on, "all we have to bother ourselves with is the Company. And afterwards, if we slide by that new fort, Union, there's the Blackfeet and maybe the British."

"Business is danger. We lose, maybe. Maybe we make money."

"It ain't worth it, for the money."

"You go," said Jourdonnais. "You are my partner."

"Not for the money so much."

Jourdonnais' shoulders came up to his ears and fell back. "All hunters are crazy. You like the lonely fire, the danger, what you call the freedom and, sometime, the squaw. We like silver in the pocket, people, wine, song, women. We ascend the river only for the return."

"This child don't feel easy in his mind about them sick ones in the boat."

"We do what we can. Now it is up to God." Jourdonnais went back to his subject. "But you are not all mountain man, Summers. Half of you is grayback farmer."

"So?"

"Oh, not that you are not brave, my frien'. *Oui*, you are brave for a certainty. But you are not hard and rough and cruel, like some. You do not go off, like the hermit, to stay forever."

"Maybe so." Summers was silent for a minute. "You ascend the river only for the return. You ought to shine when the steamers run."

"Never!"

"They're on the Missouri a'ready."

"The *Duncan*! And to Leavenworth only!"

"They aim to try the whole distance."

Jourdonnais' dark head shook. "It is foolishness. The Missouri never know where she run, here today, over there tomorrow. Sandbanks, sawyers, towheads, *embarras*. The steamer be smash' before she start."

"You'll see," promised Summers and sucked on his pipe. The breeze died and the walnuts quit whispering. From the boat there came the sound of coughing and a long moan.

"If only we get there," said Jourdonnais.

"This child'll see about those poor bastards," the hunter said, rising.

The patron put out an arm to hold him back. His gaze was on the ruffled shimmer of the river. From it there came a shout.

"Ahoy!" shouted Jourdonnais. "Who is it?"

Boone turned to Summers. "It's a raft, ain't it?"

"Pirogue."

"Bercier, Carpenter and La Farge."

"*Mandan,* Jourdonnais." The patron had started for the bank. The others followed him. The pirogue was a black patch on the water. The paddles caught the moonlight as the men brought her in under the stern of the *Mandan.*

The steersman said, "We thought to be in St. Louis before now."

Jourdonnais caught the mooring rope. "The food is warm. Coffee we have. *Beaucoup,*" he said, as if coffee was a rare thing on the Missouri.

The paddlers rested their oars. "The good God help me," said one, "but my ass aches!"

Boone's eye caught the barest movement on the *Mandan* and made out, by squinting, that it was a small head poking up, the head of the little squaw looking down on the pirogue.

Summers asked, "What's the cargo?"

"Bear oil. Lard for St. Louis."

"Bear oil, in March?"

"Cached it last season. It's sweet enough still."

"Climb ashore," Summers invited.

Stiffly the men started to rise. Half-risen, they stopped and listened. Their faces turned up to Jourdonnais. "Bellyache," he explained. "Two got the bellyache." The men at the paddles looked at each other and aft at the steersman. After a long silence the steersman said, "We are behind already."

"The moon she's up for long time," said one of the paddlers, and let himself sink back.

"*Merci beaucoup,*" acknowledged the other. "We move along. The oil maybe spoil."

Jourdonnais tossed the painter back to them and with his foot started the pirogue into the current. The paddles glistened, the patch of black receded, until Boone could not tell what was boat and what was wave.

The patron's gaze was out on the water. "You watch camp," said Summers. "I'll see about the sick."

Boone and Deakins followed Summers to the fire, where he cut and lighted a spill. They went back to the keelboat with it, climbed the side and let themselves down in the bow. There was a smell there, a hot, sour smell that made Boone wrinkle his nose. The moaning had stopped. They heard, instead, a strangling, snoring breath. Summers handed the spill to Boone. "It's fever of some cut," he said.

Two men lay side by side on buffalo robes, half-covered by blankets. "Can't keep covers on 'em, but still I got an idee sweatin' is the ticket." One of the men had turned on his side and lay there without moving. The other was on his back. His eyes glistened in the light of the flame. "Water?" asked Summers. The man's hard breath caught at his cheeks, puffing and pulling them as he breathed in and out, changing his face from thin to fat. Boone heard the rattle of phlegm in his chest. He felt a movement on his leg and started from it. It was Painter, the black cat, rubbing against him. He put his free hand down and felt the cat's spine against it. The cat meowed once and began to purr, like a small imitation of the sick man. From the cargo box six pairs of green eyes looked out, the bodies behind them lost in the cage and the dark. Boone felt a little shiver along the back of his legs and up his spine, thinking they were wanting to get out to feed on man flesh. Painter arched ahead, purring.

Summers stood up. "François has gone under," he said, and stooped again and brought the blanket over the face. "Zephyr's nigh gone." He stood thoughtful and unafraid. "Come on. We'll tell Jourdonnais." First, though, he took the rag that had slipped from the sick man's forehead and wet it again in the river and smoothed it back. "All right. The poor bastards."

Jourdonnais met them at the bank.

"François's dead, and Zephyr won't last till sunup, I'm thinking."

The patron thrust up his hands. "Quiet!" he whispered. "Quiet! Not one will be left. It is time enough in the morning."

His warning given, the patron crossed himself.

10

From the cargo box Jourdonnais shouted, *"A bas les perches!"* The wind took the words from his mouth and blew them away. It flattened his clothes against his ribs and caught hold of the left bar of his mustache and swept it to the other side, so that he looked almost as if the hair grew only on the right.

Jim Deakins lowered his ash pole and felt it catch on the river bed. He brought the ball of it into the hollow of his shoulder and set his legs to driving, feeling the boat give under his feet. Ahead of him on the walkway that the Creoles called the *passe avant* the men were bent low with strain. One of them clawed ahead with his hand and caught a cleat and with arm and legs drove against his pole. *"Fort!"* Jourdonnais cried. *"Fort!"* The keelboat slid under Jim's feet. *"Levez les perches!"* The boatmen straightened, swung about and hurried forward. *"A bas—."* They caught her before the current stopped her, and it was push again, step by step, while the ball ground into a man's shoulder and his lungs wheezed.

Damn the wind! It hit at Jim, throwing him off balance when he went forward, trapping the breath in his lungs as he angled against his pole. It was a cold bully of a wind, full of devilment and power, letting up for a moment and coming on again, stronger than ever, just to plague a man. At that, it was better to be on the wind side where, if a man faltered, he was pushed against the cargo box. On the other side, where Boone was, a body could go overboard as easy as not. He could see Boone when the crew straightened, just the head and the straight neck and the strong shoulders of him over the box, moving forward to get a fresh hold with his pole. Boone didn't look much to right or left. He kept his eyes ahead of him and tended to business, unsmiling and silent. Jim reckoned Boone wasn't himself yet, from having his gun stole and being jailed and whipped. Once Boone had showed him the marks of the whip, which still lay long and dark on his back like old scars.

"A bas . . . levez . . . fort." The words were a chorus in Jim's head. He heard them at night and awoke to find his legs moving under his blanket. Or if it wasn't poling it was pulling, straining from the bank on a thousand-foot line that ran to the mast of the keelboat. It was like pulling in a fish, like pulling in a whale, except

that a man never got her in until nightfall and had to scramble over the rocks and through the willows and in the mud from sunup to dark.

They had had just one easy day, when the wind was right, and Jourdonnais had the square sail put up, and the boat moved along so well that the rowers he had sent to the oars sang songs and only played at rowing.

That was the day Jim had tried to talk to Teal Eye, while Romaine was at the rudder and Jourdonnais up front in the bow. Remembering that day, Jim tried to get a look at her when he came to the end of his push and straightened up, but all he could see was a little of the top of the shelter Jourdonnais had made out of a couple of sticks and a buffalo robe. She was sitting down probably, with Painter near her and the caged cats close by, out of the wind. Mostly she sat by her makeshift tepee, quiet as a rabbit. She might be asleep, except that her eyes were never still. They looked big and fluid in the thin, dark face—too big for her, too big for the small shoulders over which she kept drawn a tatter of blanket, too big for the legs that came from under the white man's calico and ended in a small pair of worn moccasins. For all that Jourdonnais had said, the men rolled their eyes at her when they got a chance and showed their teeth in smiles, but she just looked at them and looked away, her face as straight and set as some little carving of wood. If any had a notion to go further, Jim reckoned the thought of Jourdonnais and his promise and of Summers with his cool gray eye was enough to hold them back. At night a guard was posted, to see the men didn't desert, to watch the boat, and, Jim imagined, to see no one tried to get with Teal Eye. She was mighty young and small, but still you couldn't tell what a man might try—a French boatman, anyway. Jim felt sorry for her, truly sorry, thinking of her as little and lonesomer than a man might believe. Later now, two or three years ahead, he might think of her as the boatmen did, but not now, not while she was so young and helpless and alone.

"Howdy," he had said on that day he tried to talk to her. He smiled. Her eyes flicked to his face and went on, as if they were seeing nothing and still had seen all. "Heap good day," he tried. He pointed toward the sun. "Heap good." The small face didn't change. He had a sudden notion that there was some old wisdom in her that found him not important enough to take notice of. Her eyes were liquid, as if dark water ran in them. Following her gaze, he saw Boone Caudill standing on the *passe avant*, standing still, looking west beyond the river. A man might have thought the country was saying something to him. It occurred to Jim, studying Boone's sharp, dark profile, that Boone might have been an Indian himself. Two men in the stern started singing a song, looking at Jim and laughing and singing in French. He'd ought to had better sense than to speak to her with the damn Creoles around. For a bluff he got out his knife and tried the blade with his thumb and looked at them again, and they stopped laughing.

Summers could get Teal Eye to talk, though, and even Jourdonnais a little. One or the other always took her plate to her, and sometimes on shore Jim heard murmurs from the stern where they were. He reckoned they set a high value on her, the way they fed her and watched her and scared everybody else away. Labadie said she was a Blackfoot—a daughter of a chief—that a boat had picked up half dead the year before and carried to St. Louis.

It would be good, Jim thought, as one foot felt for a cleat and his aching shoulder fought the pole, to be Jourdonnais, up there on the cargo box managing the rudder, or to be Romaine, the bosseman, who stood in the bow with his pole to fend off snags and help steer. Sometimes, lying awake under the stars, he wondered whether François and Zephyr, back on the bank with dirt and rocks piled over them, didn't like it better, just resting and letting others do the work.

Against the wind Jourdonnais put the *Mandan* into shore beneath a cut-bank. Romaine went over the side with the painter and waded to the bank and tied her up.

"We rest," said the patron, "until dark and the moon." The sun was still up, slicing through the trees to the brown water that wrinkled to the wind. Here the wind only came by accident, in puffs that slid down the bluff or found a way around it. It made a noise, though—a hollow whining like hounds tied up.

The cook struck steel to flint. After a little a feather of smoke arose, fell back, and arose again, shifting in the eddy of the wind. "Plenty food, Pambrun," Jourdonnais ordered, "and coffee again. The night will be long."

Jim sat down and rubbed his aching shoulder. Boone came over and let himself down beside him. Jim chewed on a stick. Out of the side of it he said, "My shoulder'll be wore to a nub, come morning. By littles the damn pole is pushing it clean away."

Three of the Frenchmen, sitting cross-legged, were singing. Jim guessed it was a dirty song. They made mouths over it and their eyes rolled. Two others wrestled on the bank, tumbling over and over and laughing as they tumbled.

"Mules," Jim said. "Just mules. Git 'em out of harness and they roll and heehaw." He looked at Boone. "You got a misery, Boone?"

Boone's gaze went to his face and then to the ground, and it was a little while before he answered. "Just a bellyache, I reckon," he said, but Jim knew it wasn't. Boone got up and went toward the fire, walking stooped at the middle.

Jourdonnais was going from man to man, his forefinger hooked through the handle of a jug. He held it up for Jim. "A drink?" The liquor was like a flame in the mouth, like a fire in the windpipe, like a hot coal in the belly.

"Much obliged."

"Good," said Jourdonnais, of his alcohol and water. "Good whisky."

Pambrun beat a pan with a long-handled spoon. The songs broke off, the wrestling ceased, the men came to their feet and all pushed forward. It was beans again, and lyed corn, and pork strong with salt. In Kentucky people would be looking ahead to wild greens cooked with hog jowl and corn bread and maybe young onions and buttermilk cool from the spring. Jim heaped his plate and sat down against a tree, smiling to himself at Labadie, who was squatted at the water's edge washing his face and hands. For God's sake, who cared about a dirty face?

Summers was talking out of a full mouth. A couple of little pieces of food fell out with his words. "I be dogged! I will, now. Just one deer so fur and a taste of turkey." He shook his head. "Settlers are doin' for 'em." Way early every morning, while darkness still lay on the river and woods, Summers slipped out of his bed and went ahead to hunt, meeting them later on the bank or hanging his game on a limb where they couldn't miss it and going ahead to hunt some more.

As the men finished their meal they took their plates over to

Pambrun and went back and lay down, or sat, leaning forward, and pulled deep at their pipes. Jourdonnais had piled a plate to the brim. He slid a spoon in at the side and started to the keelboat.

As the sun sank the wind died. It was just a whisper overhead now, a fretwork on the water, a breath on the fire, and after a while it was nothing at all. Leaning against his tree, Jim wondered what had happened to it. Was it still tearing on east of them, rolling the dead grass of last year, bending the trees and whining? Did it leave an emptiness where it came from? He let his back slide from the tree and put his elbow under his head.

It was dark when he woke up. He lay motionless and chilled, feeling the stiff ache of his shoulder, seeing the moon ride low and red in the east. Jourdonnais and Summers were seated near him, smoking.

"Pole or line?" asked Jourdonnais. "What you think?"

"You know the river."

"*Non.* Not the east bank."

"I reckon not. Everyone puts in at Leavenworth."

"*Oui.*"

"Look open, from the west side?"

Jourdonnais shrugged. "Some trees, brush, sand. You know."

"We ought to warp 'er, maybe. It would be quieter."

Jourdonnais thought it over. "Good," he said, blowing out a mouth of smoke.

"We could go across, maybe under sail." Summers put his head up, feeling for the wind. "Little breeze is beginning to stir, and it's right. Then we pole her along, close as we dast, and tie up, and send the men up with the cordelle."

"Good!" said Jourdonnais again. His head moved. "The moon, she's right. They never see us in the shadow."

"They better not."

Jim caught the faint shine of Jourdonnais' teeth. "Goodbye the alcohol. Goodbye the permit."

"Goodbye us. It'll take Teal Eye and strong water and a heap of luck to set us right with the *Pied Noir.*"

Jourdonnais put his palm to the ground and lifted himself up. "It is time." He went from man to man, waking each quietly, as if already the need for silence was on them.

The breeze along the river was soft, hardly filling the sail. Jourdonnais sent the men to the oars. The boat went into the current gently. The water slid under her, shining dimly. The west shore pulled away, standing sharp in the moonlight. Over there a man could almost see to sight a rifle. The east bank climbed above them, climbed to the moon and beyond it, taking them into its shadow. Jourdonnais had the sail hauled down. "Quiet," he said. "Quiet now, all. No song, no curse. Quiet." He moved among them. "To the *passe avant. A bas les perches.*" He was on the cargo box, with the rudder making his boat keep to the shore, his face thrust forward.

The boat swam ahead, noiseless except for the careful scuff of leather on the walkway. The crew acted without directions, putting shoulders to poles, feeling for the cleats with their feet, straining at knee and thigh until the first of them, arrived at the end of the *passe avant,* stood straight, and, seeing him, the others all swung about and trooped back and turned again and reset their poles, slipping them into the water. The dark bank moved by them, its trees and undergrowth, its ledges and sand coming out of the darkness and showing themselves and falling into the darkness astern. The water murmured against the boat. Farther out, beyond the line of shadow, it was a wrinkled glimmer under the moon.

Ahead of them and high on the far shore the moon picked out a huddle of buildings. When he lifted his pole and turned and walked back toward the bow, Jim could make out doorways and windows like eye sockets and the dark strokes of sidewalls. From one window a light gleamed like a caught star.

Jourdonnais and Romaine were bringing her in again. Romaine was a shapeless movement in the dark as he went over the side. The men leaned against the cargo box, breathing deep. "The cordelle," said Jourdonnais, low-voiced, as he let himself down among them. "Come." He went forward. "Summers?"

The hunter's buckskins set him off from the rest. "Git the cordelle," he muttered, "and follow close after me." They strained at the heavy coil of line and lifted it to the gunwale. "Watch now." He gave a hand in getting it ashore.

Summers had cat eyes. He never stumbled, never seemed at a loss for a way, never lunged as branches caught him. The others struggled after him, drawing the heavy line along, cursing in whispers as switches slapped them. He kept them close to the bank, avoiding the trees that arose on their right. "Careful," he warned, turning. "We got to wade." His feet went into the water like an animal's, sure and quiet.

They were upstream from the huddled buildings, as far above as the boat was below. "All right." Summers took the end of the line and tied it around the heavy trunk of a tree, testing the knot after he had made it. "Back, now, and quiet." He led the way and stood aside when they came to the boat and then followed the others aboard.

"Take the line," said Jourdonnais. He carried the slack loop of it past the bow, along the walkway next to the shore. The men took it in until it went taut. "All right." Romaine untied her and came aboard and, straining mightily with his pole, worked her nose out from the bank. The men set themselves and began to pull, the line passing from one pair of hands to another.

This way was quieter. Only the smothered grunts of the crew sounded, and the whisper of the waves along the boat and the sound of the line working in the brush up the shore. Jim heaved on the line, relieved to have the pole's knob out of his shoulder. This, he thought, was like the whale swallowing the line, and keeping on swallowing it until it had brought itself to the bank.

Romaine grunted at his pole, forcing the boat out into the river, testing the depth after each push. Once they heard sand running along the keel, and the pullers halted at Jourdonnais' hiss, while Romaine felt for the bar. He waved them on and they pulled again and the boat moved, still working out of the shallows until the *Mandan* was on the very edge of the shadow of the hills.

The high cluster of buildings floated downstream, floated by slow inches until it stood over them. Jim felt a breeze along his cheek. It had veered around and was coming from the east. From the quiet huddle of the buildings a dog began to bark, furiously, as if set on waking folks to things their own senses didn't tell them. "Steady," said Jourdonnais. The dog must be running up and down along the bank, the way his barking sounded. Jim strained his eyes to see. A door opened in the building in which the light shone, and the light ran out in a yellow mist. Jourdonnais whispered "Wait!" and the men stopped heaving and the boat lay dead in the outer shadow of the bank. Jim made his breath come easy. He felt, rather than saw, the man standing outside the door, looking down across the river, standing there quiet and watchful, prying at the night with his eyes while the dog tried to tell him what he knew.

Summers squatted in the bow. He cupped his two hands over his mouth. Jim's hackles raised as he heard the howl, starting low and rising—the wild, lonely cry of a wolf, challenging the dog and the night. It might have come from upstream or downstream, from near or far, from anywhere or everywhere. The dog went into a regular fit. His barking ran up and down the shore, carrying clear and sharp across the quiet water in the air that had gone still again. They heard a man's voice. The barking ended in a sudden, surprised yelp. A door slammed, putting out the yellow mist. Jim breathed. Jourdonnais murmured "Pull!" The boat began to move again.

When they came to the end of the line Summers got out and untied it, and the crew went to the poles again, still working quietly. The patch of buildings on the other shore moved downstream and lost itself.

The moon was nearly overhead when they pulled the *Mandan* in on the eastern bank. "*Mon Dieu*, what a wolf!" chuckled Jourdonnais. "What a howl! Summers, you are crossed with the bitch wolf." His hands were busy with the lashings on the cargo box.

Summers went ashore and came back to report. "Nigh perfect. There's a good bunch of willows. Here, you."

The alcohol gurgled in its short flag kegs as Jourdonnais lifted it from the cargo box. He brought the kegs over the side, to the men who stood in the water and waded ashore with their loads to the willows where Summers waited. When they were done Jourdonnais brushed his hands together. Jim came back aboard with Summers. "Shipshape," Summers said. "You left some?"

Jourdonnais began lashing down the canvas. "*Oui.* Enough. What the permit allow."

"Enough," supplied Summers, "to keep the damn agent from gettin' suspicious?"

"*Oui.* A little more than what the permit allow, so the *Mandan* do not appear too pure, like the lily." He chuckled.

"It leaves a hole in the cargo."

"I fix it in the morning so no one would know."

Summers said, "You, Deakins, and you, Caudill, you stay with me. Get a rifle. We're the guard." He put some blankets under his arm. "Pambrun, give us a pot. We'll have empty paunches afore you get back, I'm thinking."

Jourdonnais had the canvas tied down. "We get back about sundown," he said. "Ready."

Jim went over the side of the *Mandan* after Summers and Boone. They stood on the shore, watching the keelboat swing around, seeing the shadows creep over it as it moved with the current.

Jim said, "What—?" and let his voice trail off.

"Jourdonnais'll drop downstream fur as a day's journey up. Tomorrow he'll put in at the fort, show his trader's permit and git his cargo inspected, aimin' to git here just afore dark. We'll load up, come night, and be all set to go next morning. Slick."

They moved off toward the willows. "How much whisky you allowed?" Boone asked.

"Gill a day for each boatman, but for four months only. The big outfits do a sight better. This nigger's knowed land brigades to git a gill a day for a whole year for each man, makin' out they was boatmen, and of course not a boatman in the lot, as everybody knowed." He walked on. " 'Course, the crew does git some of it."

They dropped their blankets near the willows, and set down the pot and can Pambrun had given them. "Might as well sleep," Summers said. "It's a long pull to the Blackfoot Nation. First, though, we'll make a little fire and dry out."

11

The *Mandan* was making time. The wind stayed at her stern, a gusty, notionable wind, but good enough to keep her moving. With all twenty oars working, the boat slid along. The voyageurs sang to the stroke, sang sounds that Boone had come to know by heart though he did not know their meaning.

> *Dans mon chemin j'ai recontré*
> *Trois cavalières bien montées.*

Sometimes Jourdonnais, at the steersman's post on the cargo box, joined them, singing in a big, hoarse voice. Romaine stood in the bow, watching the river, his long pole held level in his hands. Now and then he turned and grinned, looking back towards Jourdonnais.

> *L'on, ton, laridon danée*
> *L'on, ton, laridon, dai.*

The sky was blue, bluer than in Kentucky, and patched here and there with slow white clouds. The sun looked down from it, bright as could be. Painter lay on deck in the sunshine, his green eyes half open, flexing his claws once in a while as if to keep in practice. The trees along the banks of the river were bright green with leaves still curled from the bud.

> *Trois cavalières bien montées,*
> *L'une à cheval, l'autre à pied.*

Boone pulled to the time, laying the long blade far back and pulling it through, trying for the easy skill of the Creoles. The Missouri wasn't made for a white man, not the way it was for the French. They were like ducks, or like beavers, sure and happy on the water and clumsy and half-scared off it. Jourdonnais wouldn't have taken him and Jim on, Boone reckoned, except he couldn't find a full crew of Creoles.

Jourdonnais was singing now, singing along while the crew waited.

> *Derrière chez nous, il y a un étang,*
> *ye, ye ment.*

The voices of the oarsmen blended with his.

> *Trois canards s'en vont baignans,*
> *Tout le long de la rivière.*

Singing this way, rowing to the time, Boone almost forgot about himself, except when he pulled too hard and felt a quick little stab in his pants. When that happened, he remembered the smarting and the wet spot that touched his leg when he leaned back at the end of his stroke, and a cloud came into his mind. He wished he could take his jeans down and have a look, away from everybody. A man didn't have a chance to take stock of himself, working all day with the boat. And come night, he couldn't see. He had a pretty good notion what it was all right. He hadn't lived to be growing on eighteen without finding out a few things. It wasn't anything, or not anything much, and he wouldn't pay it any mind except that it worsened day by day and kept his thoughts down in his pants. Maybe he would ask Jim about it, or maybe Summers, just to ease himself. They were older; likely they could put a certain name to it and tell what to do. There were some things, though, that rightly were none of other people's knowing, like the scars he carried from the whip and finally let Jim see, he asked so much. It wasn't he was ashamed of it. A sight of men must have miseries like it, maybe some of the crew; maybe that was what they said their French jokes about at night, making funny faces to go along with their talk. But he hated to seem like a green 'un; and, more, he hated people to be sizing him up and maybe laughing, knowing there was something wrong. Already Summers looked at him sometimes, and Jim, too, and Jim asked questions when he walked stooped to favor himself as he had to when he first got up, now that it had grown so bad.

The Creoles' song floated out on the water, out to the shore and maybe farther, out to where maybe buffalo heard it, or elk or deer, standing quiet and out of sight, wondering, or maybe to where an Indian heard it and hid himself by the bank and watched while the boat pulled by. They were getting close to real game country, Summers had said. So far, the hunter had shot three deer and some turkeys and one evening a whole passel of pigeons that they had all had to help Pambrun ready for the pot. "Deer run sceerce from here on," Summers had said as they passed the Nadowa. "The brush thins out, that's why. But we'll find elk up a piece and then buffler, a galore of fat cow, more'n you could ever count."

The sun was farther down than Boone had thought, halfway from overhead already and aiming around to the west. It slanted at him, warming his neck and the peak of his right shoulder, darkening hands already as dark as a nigger's.

Thunder rumbled up the river and rolled down on them, and some of the crew looked over their shoulders to the dark cloud that was rearing in the sky. While they looked the wind changed, veering round to the side and then clear around. The big sail snapped to it, and the keelboat sat back, giving to the violent gust. The Creoles looked up, their eyes uneasy, while their arms weakened at the oars.

"*Halez fort! Halez fort!*" Jourdonnais was shouting, and they steadied to his order, looking toward him out of wide eyes while they grunted at their work.

The bank was slipping ahead. Boone could mark it, sighting past the corner of the cargo box. Jourdonnais had the sail hauled down, but still they lost ground, inch by inch, as the wind strengthened.

Summers stepped over Painter and peered up river, studying the cloud. He turned around, toward Jourdonnais, and gestured toward the bank. The *Mandan* angled for the shore and the Frenchmen began to sing again, but softly, relieved that the boat had quit her heeling, happy to be through with work.

When they got to the bank, though, Jourdonnais ordered them out with the cordelle, and they looked at him, disappointed and reproachful, like a dog scolded home, and went over the side with the line while the wind tugged at their clothes.

The dark cloud hung like a blanket in the sky. A bolt forked down from it, and, after a little, thunder rattled in the valley. The trees bowed before the wind, thrashing branches knobbed with bud.

The crew went upstream with the line, and came to the end of it and pulled. It was like pulling a balky horse. The *Mandan* settled back and then lunged to their heave and settled back again. After a while the towers came to a thick patch of woods growing down to the water, and Jourdonnais motioned them in, moving his arm with a jerk like a man disgusted.

Jourdonnais and Romaine were snugging her in when the crew got back, and Pambrun was readying a fire. A few drops of rain fell, blown to spray by the wind. A rainbow curved from the edge of the cloud, which was moving east as if it would miss them, but the wind kept racing down the valley.

Boone walked out from the water's edge, past Pambrun and his kettles, and pushed through the willows and came into larger growth—cottonwood and cedars, mostly, and here and there a small oak or ash. It was easier walking here than down river where the rushes that they called scrub grass grew so tall and thick a man could hardly pass. Through the trees he could see the greening hills that came down and leveled off for the river.

Boone looked around and then opened his jeans and let them drop. Goddam that woman at St. Louis! He saw her again, and felt her and smelt her, an old woman with a whiny voice who complained that he was rough. Rough! If he could get hold of her now she'd know what rough was.

"How."

It was Summers, the hunter, walking quiet as a cat. Jim lagged along behind him. Their eyes looked at him and flicked away. He buttoned his pants. The hunter's gaze was poking into the woods and scanning the hills. He had his rifle in his hand.

"It beats all," he said, while Jim sat down on a fallen log, "how game pulls back one year after another." He sat down alongside Jim and motioned Boone to a seat. There was a silence, as if no one knew what to say, and then Summers hitched around and looked straight at Boone while the beginning of a smile worked at the corners of his mouth. "It's the clap you've catched, I'm thinking."

He waited, his gaze still on Boone and the little smile still drawing at his lips.

Jim leaned over, to see past Summers. "Nee'n to think you're the only man ever catched it, Boone."

"I reckon it's a man's own business what he's got."

Jim said, "Don't get on the peck, Boone. We'll leave it your business if you say so."

The hunter looked at the ground and then up at the hills. His voice was old with things remembered. "Fifteen year, anyhow, since I put out for Platte first. This child was no older'n you be, and a greenhorn like you, too. We drank some, we did, the week afore we put out. I be dogged, I had a head! Come time to go I didn't know whether my rifle had hindsights or not. I was that close to the horrors I like to gave up the trip. Missed the boat, I did, and had to catch 'er at St. Charles." He leaned his rifle on the log and took the knife from his belt and began shaving a twig with it, as if it were important to pare off a shaving no thicker than a leaf.

A few drops of rain sifted through on them. Summers scanned the sky. "Rain'll blow over. We won't move ag'in this day, though, with that wind."

"How fur'd you go?" Jim asked.

"To Platte and up it, tradin' with the Wolfs. This nigger was learnin' to clerk. That's a smart way to get dollars in your possibles, if a man can hold hisself to it. I didn't shine, clerkin', makin' figures and givin' out beads and vermilion and powder and takin' in plews and robes and packin' 'em while all the time a man could be outside, free as air, trappin' beaver and eatin' fleece fat and makin' camp when you wanted to and goin' on when you were a mind to, with none to hinder."

"No," Boone said.

The hunter smiled. His gray eyes were far away, seeing the Wolf Indians, Boone reckoned, and the trading, and then the beaver country and the buffalo, and himself, a greenhorn then like Boone, finding what it was like to be on his own, out where a man had elbow room.

"It was the first time," Summers said as if to himself, "that this child ever had a runnin' anywhere save his nose."

Jim asked, "What you mean?"

"A purty little whore at St. Louis, at a fofaraw house called a place of entertainment, she give it to me, a regular case."

Boone didn't say anything.

"Well, now, I figgered I was gone beaver, knowin' no better. I did, sure enough. I looked at it and cussed that little whore, wonderin' if I would end up no man at all and maybe broke down in the back to boot."

"How long before you got all right?" Boone asked.

"A man gets over it, like a cold. It ain't much, even if it drags on, some."

"I kin say amen to that," Jim put in.

"It's natural, like ager. This nigger's had it four or five times since, and like as not will have it again. Can't miss it and still shine as a man."

Summers went silent, whittling on his stick. His eyes would lift from the stick and look around and come to Jim and Boone and go to the stick again.

"A nigger wench p'izened me," Jim said, "but I don't recollect I worried my mind with it. I thought I was pretty slick, catchin' it so young. I made some brags about it."

"I mind the Rees afore their lodges burned, in eighteen twenty-three or four that was," Summers said after a while. "They're some punkins, them Ree squaws, best outside of a Taos woman, I'm thinkin'. Light-colored and tall and long-legged and purty as a young filly, and nigh every one of 'em willin', for beads and vermilion or a lookin' glass not as big as your hand. A man got calluses, handing the price to the bucks the squaws belong to. Leastwise, I did them days. I could shine then. And nigh every squaw with the clap and every man catchin' it, and not payin' it no more mind than a sniffle."

Boone asked, "Sure enough?"

"It didn't amount to nothin', not if you didn't have whisky and salt. Not up there. Ain't anything corrupts on the upper river."

"They just let 'er go?"

"Mostly. Tied a piece of beaver h'ar on it and let her go. Some with bad cases, like maybe you'd catch from a white woman, they dug niggerhead roots and made tea. It lets up after a while, regardless."

The hunter straightened himself, as if the subject was closed. "Wisht we could raise some meat."

"Did the tea do good, for bad cases?"

"Maybe. Some said it did, but a man can't tell. When I first catched it, there on the Platte, the bourgeois had this child thinking it was mighty big medicine to bed with a squaw, like gettin' shet of a wart by givin' it to someone else. It ain't so, though."

"Sure enough?"

"Oh, it don't hurt any. I give it a good trial, nigh every night."

Summers flicked his nubbin of stick aside and put his knife back in his belt. His hand reached for his rifle. "I'll put some beaver out, for them as needs it," he said. "There's an old plew aboard. Beaver's mighty fine medicine, whatever's wrong. And maybe the niggerheads are coming up, and a man could find a root."

The hunter arose, as if to leave. Boone got up, too, saying, "I ain't told nobody."

"We ain't heerd nothin' to tell, have we, Deakins?"

Jim said, "Nary word. On'y, Boone, it don't do any good to shy away. A man keeps hisself shut up, and by and by a p'izen gets into his head, like. I figger the mind needs air or she goes sour on you, and gits ideas that ain't natural."

"I reckon my mind's all right."

Summers said, "Rowin' hurt ye, boy, or strainin' on the line?"

"A mite."

"Make water all right?"

"Stings."

"It's clumb some, I'm thinking." Summers was silent for a minute. "Wrastlin' a boat's poor doin's, anyways, for an American. He don't shine there."

"We done our part, didn't we?"

"Sure. This child ain't belittlin'. Only we need more hunters, and it'll do ye good."

"You mean we can hunt?"

"You'll have to row and pole and pull some, too, short as we are, but the both of you can help me. One hunter ain't enough. Zephyr was going to hunt, too, only he went under. I'll take one of you out, then t'other, till ye l'arn."

"Sure enough?" asked Boone. Jim's blue eyes were twinkling.

"It's the French ought to handle the boat. They're right for it, long as we feed 'em and watch 'em and keep the brown skin away. Me and Jourdonnais didn't figger on you two as boatmen so much. We took you on to help us in a fix. Come a fix, the Frenchies shout for God. Most of 'em, that is. I've knowed some, like Romaine, that don't scare much, and some, like that Jourdonnais, that don't scare any. Canadians are worst that way."

Boone said, "I can shoot pretty good."

Summers had his rifle in the crook of his arm. "Time I moved along. This child's froze for meat. Even poor bull is rich doin's besides beans."

He started off. "I'll get the h'ar out." Farther on he called over his shoulder, "Cryin' over spilt milk just makes the nose run." Boone thought he heard him chuckling.

The storm cloud was a ridge on the far horizon, but the wind continued, hard and steady. The sun was down almost to the hills.

"It'll be pie to hunt," Jim said. His hand was on Boone's arm. Boone watched Summers move away, watched him moving, quiet and quick and alert, like a man who knew what he was about. Already the trouble in Boone's breeches seemed gone, or anyhow just about.

12

The Missouri was boiling. It overran its bed, clucking among the willow and the cottonwood. It gouged at the bluffs, undercutting the shore. Great sections of bank had slid into it or toppled over, making slow splashes which the current caught up and carried on and lost in its own hurry. Trees came down when the banks gave, falling slow at first and then faster, to the sound of torn air, and lying out in the water, anchored to the broken shore, making dams against which the drift piled. The water moved up against the dams, climbing as it felt for weaknesses, and turned and raced around, breaking white as it found its course again. Out in the channel the current rose, like the back of a snake.

The Missouri was a devil of a river; it was a rolling wall that reared against the *Mandan* and broke around her and reared against her again; it was no river at all but a great loose water that leaped from the mountains and tore through the plains, wild to get to the sea.

As far as a man could see, rain was falling—falling small-dropped and steady, so that the air itself was watery and came into the lungs wet and weak. Looking up river, feeling the breeze square on his face, Jourdonnais lost the river in the mist. The far shore was a shadow. He could see the towline, running from the mast through the bridle, bellying of its own weight, and going on to nothing, toward the crew that was a slow-moving blur upshore.

It was no time for boating, no time for sail or oars or poles or line. A man could lose his boat before he knew it. A shelving bank would wreck her, or a planter, or a sawyer. Most of all, Jourdonnais feared sawyers. A half a dozen times this day he had seen the moving water break and the great limbs spring out like thrashing legs, standing for a moment against the current, naked and huge, and then yielding again and sinking from sight. One leg under the *Mandan* would be enough. Jourdonnais watched the dark water as if he might see beneath it. Romaine stood ahead of him in the bow, a watchful giant of a man who handled his long pole as if it were no heavier than a cane.

It was no time to be moving, but the *Mandan* had to move—ten miles a day, five miles, one, whatever they could strain out. And so they had rowed and poled and towed and put up sail and had to haul it down and put it up again, hoping for long reaches and favorable winds. They had worked from dawn to dark, snatching breakfast and dinner aboard and making camp only when the light was done. Where the shore water was deep they had moved into the bank and the men had stood on the *passe avant* and on the decks, grasping for the brush, pulling the *Mandan* ahead hand over hand.

There was complaint among the crew. They looked at Jourdonnais—not directly, but out of the corners of their eyes—and he had heard them grumbling over their food at night and in their blankets of a morning, waking to the dawn sore and resentful. Every morning now and every night he passed the whisky jug. He led them in songs and made jokes and swore at them and praised them, as if they were children. He and Summers talked at night when they were camped, telling about the Pawnees, who were bad when they found a white man alone. It was just last year, Summers said, that two deserters had gone under on the Platte.

The rain fell in a tiny lisp against the cargo box and ran down the sides. The deck was filmed with water. Pretty soon they would have to bail. Jourdonnais felt uneasy about Teal Eye, though she had a robe to sit on and an extra blanket, and he himself had rearranged the buffalo hide that made her little lodge. It would not do for her to get sick. He must save her from sickness and the men. *Mon Dieu*, the men! He would tell them again and have Summers stare at each with that so-hard eye of his. The cats in the cage on the box looked small with their hair wet. They moved around, mewing, not liking the rain. There were only four of them left now. Two had been taken by Francis Chouteau, the trader on the Kansas, for the price of a good plew each, for the price of an Ashley beaver. Painter was in the stern with Teal Eye, protected by the robe.

Jourdonnais squeezed the water from his mustache with the knuckle of his forefinger. April nearly at the half, and the Platte still ahead! He shook his head, thinking about it. How far was it to the Blackfoot Nation, past the Roche Jaune, past the Milk and the Musselshell, maybe clear to the Great Fall? Twenty-three hundred miles? Twenty-five? It was a long summer's work, that was sure. The *Mandan* wouldn't make it unless they used every minute, or maybe would make it late, maybe in time to be frozen in, in country so cold the air cracked like ice and the sun froze and even the *Pieds Noirs* kept to their lodges, dreaming ahead to summer and war parties while they sharpened their scalping knives.

Les Pieds Noirs! A little cold lump came into a man's bowels when he thought about them. Even Lisa had had to give up, and the bones of Immel and Jones and how many others rotted in the Trois Fourches or along the Roche Jaune? Jourdonnais shook himself, pushing uneasiness from his mind. It could all be accounted for. The Blackfeet knew Lisa as the friend of their enemies, the Crows. Immel and Jones had set their traps in country forbidden. And neither Lisa nor the others had had Teal Eye, the little squaw who was daughter of a chief. The white trader was bringing her home because the white trader was kind and wanted to be a brother to the Blackfeet. He had journeyed many sleeps and encountered many dangers just to get her back, and he brought with him a red uniform with gold facings and silver buttons that would mark the chief as the great man he was in the nation. Also, he had for his brothers beads and vermilion and guns and powder and some of the drink called firewater. He had brought them past the Sioux, past the Rees, past the Assiniboines, so that his friends, the Blackfeet, might have what other nations had.

All would be well, Jourdonnais told himself again, if only the *Mandan* got there, and got there in time. He would manage. Starting from nothing, as a common voyageur, he had worked himself up, by labor, by saving, by being bolder than other men. And now, along with Summers, he was a bourgeois, for all that he served as his own patron, a trader with all his savings and borrowed money, too, invested in an old boat and in traders' goods. He had a chance, a gambler's chance, to make very many dollars, and he would manage. He would push ahead as he had always pushed ahead, and by and by perhaps he and his Jeannette could build themselves a big house far away from Carondelet, and who could call him a *Vide Poche* then?

Out of the bushes along the shore the hunter appeared. He waded out and came aboard as Jourdonnais brought the boat in. His wet buckskins hugged his body. He said, "Jesus!"

"Bad," Jourdonnais agreed.

Summers said "Jesus!" again. "This bank ain't made for the cordelle."

"Or the bed for poling, or the current for rowing, or the wind for the sail. We move, a little, anyway."

"The damn trees, right down to the water."

Jourdonnais looked at the sky. "The river she's straight now, above the Nishnabotna, and the wind wrong, like always."

"*Embarras* ahead," Summers announced.

"Another?"

"Worst yet."

Jourdonnais swore. He looked toward the far shore, across the brown flood and its traffic of drift. "We waste the time going back and forth like a damn ferry. All the time, point to point, we cross and cross again."

Summers' eyes were inquiring.

"Maybe we try, anyhow."

The hunter moved his head dubiously. "The mast might go, or the line, I'm thinking."

"It is not safe, even to cross," Jourdonnais answered, pointing across the water.

"Risky, all right."

"I look, anyhow."

For a hundred feet from shore the fallen tree dammed the current. Drift was piled deep against it, soggy cottonwoods and cedar and dwarf pine from far up river and willow still swollen with buds, making a litter that pulsed with the current and drove tight against the bar of the tree, so that a man might walk on it. Around the end the water swept, smooth-muscled at first and then broken, flying in foam and spray, filling the ears with a steady gushing. The air stank a little with decay, from the bloated bodies of buffaloes that had drowned up river and now were caught in the jam and made little hills of brown in the drift and sometimes pushed around it and ran bobbing in the waves.

Jourdonnais signaled for a halt below the *embarras*. He studied it, his lids half-drawn over his eyes. "We have to drop back, to cross," he said to Summers, and waited for the reply.

The hunter only nodded.

"Even so, we run the risk." He motioned again toward the channel. "We could be wreck' there, also."

Summers grinned, but his eyes were sober. "I'm thinking we would tie up if we had a fool hen's sense."

Jourdonnais said, "*Non!* Mother of God! Do we spend the summer on the bank?"

"Let's try 'er, then," the hunter said. "You need three men anyhow in the boat, but we need as many hands as we can git on the line."

"Go on. Romaine and I, we will handle her."

Romaine poled the boat toward the bank, and Summers splashed ashore. "We'll take a hitch around a tree and then r'ar at her," he called to Jourdonnais. Romaine was working the *Mandan* out again. Jourdonnais came down from the cargo box and gave him a hand, ignoring Romaine's heavy frown. He saw Summers stride along the bank, walking as a man of purpose walks, his figure blurring with rain as he drew away.

Summers waved his hat. "Ready," Jourdonnais said to Romaine, and climbed back to the helm.

The *Mandan* inched ahead while the water boiled against her nose. The cordelle straightened from its sag, running almost in a line. The rain was thinner now, and Jourdonnais could see the crew, bent and scrambling on the rough and cluttered shore.

The boat came close to the dam, came even with it, out from it by a dozen feet but still in the tow of the current that raced around it. The *Mandan* began to swing like a kite, running out and suddenly turning back toward shore, getting her nose to one side as if to swing around and then overanswering to the towing line and the bridle and the steering oar in Jourdonnais' hand. Romaine jumped from side to side, swinging his pole around with him.

Jourdonnais heard himself saying *"Fort! Fort!"* His body strained to urge her ahead, but she lay at the crest of the sweep, running before it but not pushing into it, like a scared horse before a fence. *"Fort! Fort!"* The men could pull her well enough but for the lack of footing. He saw water squeezing out from the cordelle and standing in beads like sweat. The mast arched with the strain on it. The rain was thick again, making a blur of the crew. He should have told them to take a shorter hold on the line, for the power it would give them.

"Fort!" he grunted again, between his teeth, and fell ahead, seeing the brown current streaking under him while his hands clawed for a lashing. Romaine made a splash in the water, and came up and began pawing for shore, bending his streaming face around to see the *Mandan*.

She had reared and spun around as the bridle broke and now she lay tilted while the water beat against her side, held by the line and the mast bending to it. Sprawled on the cargo box, clutching a rope, Jourdonnais said, *"O mon Dieu! Mon Dieu!"* The boat ran in and out, like the weight at the end of a pendulum. He saw the mast arching over him, the mast that he had insisted be made of hickory, and felt the slant of the cargo box under his belly. "Line! Give line! Easy!" he shouted, knowing he couldn't be heard above the water. He saw Romaine pull himself from the river and stand dripping for a minute, staring at the *Mandan*, and then begin lunging up shore through the mud.

He worked himself off the cargo box and crawled to the spare pole and got it over the side while he braced himself on the slope by one foot and a knee. He forced the pole through the water and felt for the bottom, hoping to bring the *Mandan* part way round. The *Mandan* and all that he might be and all his years of work and purpose tilted on the brink of nothing, held by a hickory stick and a string, tilted for a minute, for an hour, for a lifetime that seemed as long as forever and no longer than yesterday. He heard himself shouting, crying for the crew to ease up.

His voice seemed prisoned, kept within the *Mandan* herself by the rush of water on her side, or lost beyond her in the little, busy rain, but at last he felt the line give, felt the boat rock and come to balance against the cordelle again, and saw the *embarras* easing upstream.

He poled her in after a while, and Romaine came up, puffing, and made her fast to a tree. After him came Summers and the crew.

Jourdonnais turned and looked the boat over. "The cats," he said, "I did not see them go." And suddenly he thought, "Teal Eye!" and jumped to the *passe avant* and ran along it to the stern. He saw Painter, standing stiff-legged on a blanket. He yelled, "Gone! Look, everybody! Along the bank. She is gone. Teal Eye!"

He jumped from the boat and plunged ashore, motioning. "All! All! Look!" He started running. "You, Summers, you have eyes like the Indian."

They scattered into the brush and came out of it farther down and looked out at the water and along the banks. "Go on! Go on! Farther down! She could be farther."

It was the young Kentuckian, Caudill, who found her. They heard him shout and ran to meet him and found him carrying her through the brush. "She was holdin' to a loose log," he said. "Near done in, too. I had to swim for her." He looked down at his dripping jeans.

Jourdonnais took charge of her. "We get some dry clothes, little one," he said, "and then the fire and food." She looked at him, saying nothing, her eyes melting in the thin face that seemed all the thinner now. Her clothes hung to her small limbs. "She look like the wet cat but chic, still," Jourdonnais thought. Aloud he said, "Tell her to get dry and change clothes, Summers. She understand you better. She get the fever, maybe."

The girl seemed to understand. She barely nodded. Jourdonnais lifted her into the stern.

He walked away then and stopped when he came even with the nose of the *Mandan* and looked across the rolling water and up it, feeling tired but glad with a fierce gladness. "Four cats," he said. "You great big damn tough river, you only get four cats." He turned back. "Come on. We all have a drink."

13

My old man allus said, if trouble's sartain, try and enjoy it."

Jim Deakins sat on a slope of grass, slapping now and then at a mosquito. The *Mandan* was tied up again, on the southwest shore, behind the protection of a tree that slanted into the water. Boone was lying on his back, only half listening, looking at the sky across which the low sun sent a streamer. Summers had said they would go out, looking for buffalo, pretty near any day now. Boone rubbed his cheek. "Don't reckon your old man could enjoy these gnats." He was wondering whether he and Summers would get any buffalo their first try.

"He could kind of put 'em out of his mind, like. He had a way."

"They say this ain't nothin'. They get bigger and thicker all the way up, till they got a stinger like a pipe stem."

Boone rolled over on his side. Jourdonnais was making a fire. He pulled up a handful of dead grass, screwed it into a nest and put a piece of tinder in it. He struck fire into the tinder, brought the straggling ends of the nest into a handhold and swung it in a circle with a motion of his wrist. The grass broke into a blaze, and he pushed it under his little pile of shavings and bark.

"Why you reckon we tied up?" Boone heard himself asking, while in his mind he saw a fat buffalo cow and himself leveling on her, sighting just behind the shoulder. "We could be movin'."

"You can't work even a mule day and night. Don't you know that? They git mean and wore out." Jim pointed beyond Jourdonnais to the men who sprawled on the ground, or just dragged around, too tired to sing or even to rest, their voices no more than a mutter. "Time Jourdonnais gives 'em a drink and fills their stomach, they'll go again. We ain't done for the day."

"River's falling, or anyways not going up." Boone had just pulled the trigger on the cow and heard the punkiny sound of the ball as it went home.

"I was sayin' about my old man. When God got to him, he was mean to live with."

"Sure enough?"

"Oh, he'd git over it, until they was another meeting. But while

God had him, He had him good. I was thinking, them days, that God rode a cloud and had lightning in both hands to throw at people just for being theirself." Jim paused and went on, "Sometimes I do yit."

"I reckon my pap was too mean even for God." The cow had lunged once and fallen forward and was kicking in the grass.

"You can't beat God for bein' picky. No, sir. If He catches you playin' cards or sayin' one swear word, or with your hand on a woman, even a nigger, it's to hell with you forever and ever, amen. Even thinkin' is mighty dangerous. As a man thinketh, that's how he is, and to hell with him ag'in. Why you reckon He gave us a thinker, then? It's a sight better to be a dumb critter and enjoy yourself, not thinkin', than to think and burn for it."

"I reckon."

"God is some busybody. You'd think He had enough to do, just mindin' the world and the stars and such and keepin' an eye on the devil, so's not to be tricked. But no. He pokes his nose into every piddlin' thing. Even go to the backhouse, and there's God, lookin' spang through the roof or peekin' through the moonhole, bein' almighty curious about what you're doin'."

Summers said you skinned a buffalo belly side down, planting his feet out to hold him right.

"My old man, now, I reckon he thought some mighty low thoughts to git tied up with God that way, every so often, and worryin' about hell and hereafter. We had to pray and read the Bible and repent the livin' day and some of the night, too, unless you could go to sleep and forgit God was watchin' you. I didn't know what repent was, but I done it. Yes, sir. I done my share of repentin'. Mostly, now, I just figger what the hell, and let 'er rip. So far, ain't no lightnin' struck." Jim looked at the sky. "You can't tell, though." He slapped at the mosquitoes and reached out and pulled a stem of grass and stuck it between his teeth. The tassel at the end of it danced when he spoke. "Mostly, my old man was all right. When he went on his own hook, without lookin' yonder—" Jim's thumb waggled at the sky—"he was a right clever body. He was right about trouble."

"Why you keep talkin' about trouble?"

"Nothin', Boone. Nothin' much, anyways. Only we git to the Platte tomorrow or next day, Summers says."

"Uh-huh."

Jim's eyes slid over to Boone, as if they were studying him on the sly. "Let's leave 'em have their fun. Shavin' and such."

"I ain't aimin' to kick," Boone answered, and saw the slow grin that came over Jim's face.

"Good for you. You're a sudden man sometimes, Boone."

"I'm feelin' better, a sight better. Reckon it's the beaver, or what?" He let himself smile, looking into Jim's mild blue eyes. A short growth of red beard was sprouting from Jim's cheeks, glinting like wire.

"Might be. Or not drinkin', or maybe she's wore herself out, natural-like."

Jourdonnais left the fire and started around with his jug. Pambrun began warming the pot. "Take a beeg wan," Jourdonnais was saying.

When the jug came to him Boone shook his head. "I kin drink for two, I reckon," Jim said and gulped deep. He wiped a splash of liquor from his chin.

Jourdonnais called back to them. "Over the line, greenhorns, into the upper river. We shave the head on you two, *parce que* you keep the whiskers close. Maybe tomorrow, eh?" His teeth were like corn under the sweep of his mustache.

They ate—wild goose meat and eggs that Pambrun had gathered on an island and mush made rich with tallow—and went on afterwards, using oars and poles and part of the time the sail, which bellied and went limp and bellied again with the breeze. The river was wide and still high, but quieter now along an open shore and almost free of drift there. The boatmen's songs went out again, while the sun fell behind the hills and a paring of moon came up, pale as the sail against the light. Snipe tilted along the banks, some dove gray, like Bedwell's coat, and others showing red underneath. Nighthawks made a whimper in the sky, like a thrown chip, and from the hills that were a flowing ridge to the west Boone heard the cry of some animal, thin and quavering and lonesome. A little shudder shook him, traveling up his back and tingling the hair on his neck. This made living worth a man's time. This, and buffalo ahead, ready to be shot. He felt the beaver hair in his jeans and he had to smile to himself while he put his shoulder to the pole, thinking how worried he had been. It wasn't nothin'. A man got over it, like a cold. "*L'on, ton, laridon, dai.*" Would it be a bull or a cow him and Summers would see first?

They struck the Platte when the sun was high and a good breeze blowing. The *Mandan* kept to the far side of the Missouri, but Boone could mark the Platte coming in, around both sides of an island that was almost covered with water now. Only the center of it stood dry. At the sides the river washed the branches of the trees. The Platte curved out of round green hills that were bare as an egg except for a little tree here and there, standing stunted and alone. Boone imagined if a man got to the top of those hills he could look on and on forever, without anything to stop the eye, unless it was a herd of buffalo, or maybe a war party, all painted and feathered, raising the dust as they galloped.

The men who had been up river before had been busy all morning, busy whispering, busy going around, smiling at one another and looking at Boone and Jim and Labadie and Roi and the others who were crossing the Platte for the first time. And now that they were abreast of it Pambrun began yelling in his high, cracked voice and waving a razor, and Jourdonnais and Summers, Romaine and Fournier and Chouquette and Lassereau and the rest were grinning and rubbing their hands as if there was fun ahead. Jourdonnais turned the helm over to Menard and came down and sent little Teal Eye to the bow along with all the greenhorns. The wind pushed the boat along easy with only half the sail up. Teal Eye stood apart from the men, far up in the bow, looking at them out of her small, sober face and looking away. Boone met her gaze and let himself smile a little, while the men laughed and jabbered behind him and pushed one another around. Her eyes went away from his and came back for a long minute, but she didn't smile. Didn't she ever smile? Didn't she know what a smile was?

"Mister Deakins!" Summers stood on the *passe avant.* "Are you willing, or do we come and git you?"

"Onwillin', but comin'." Boone watched Jim walk alongside the cargo box, toward the arms that reached for him. There was a scramble, and Jim went down and out of sight. Boone could hear him yelling, letting out regular war whoops, while the others yelled, too, and laughed fit to kill, setting up a racket that scared a wild duck off the water. Boone studied Teal Eye again. Would she be purty, older, like she was now? Purty as a Ree woman? And willing? Willing if a man was a sure-enough buffalo hunter?

Summers yelled, "Mister Caudill." His face was screwed up, fierce, but underneath his eyebrows his eyes had a twinkle. Boone jumped to the *passe avant* and walked along it. From behind, Summers gave him a push, and he lunged into the crowd, trying to keep his feet, while hands grabbed at him and an arm clenched around his neck and someone got him from behind in a bear hug. They surged around the little deck. Once he broke loose and caught a glimpse of Jim with his head shaved slick at the sides and the center of it hogged like the mane of a mule, and then they were on him again. He felt the weight and pressure of them all around him, felt the breaths panting on his neck and the hands reaching and grabbing. For a minute a crazy fright came up in him, and something else, something rising from deep down in him, a mad spell or a laughing spell, one, while voices shouted in his ears. He jerked and squirmed with a sudden, wild strength. Summers puffed, "This hoss be as strong as a young bull." He heard himself laughing then, hollering and laughing, while they pinned his arms and got him by the feet and bent him down on his butt on the deck. Jourdonnais said, "We initiate *l'enfant*," and Summers answered, "This nigger feels like raisin' h'ar." Hands came from behind him and clamped over his eyes. "We made a Pawnee out of Deakins. We'll make a Maha papoose out of this hoss." It was Summers again. Boone felt the razor on his scalp, moving and catching and moving again while the blade sang. "There, by beaver!" He ran his loosened hand over his head. It was as bare as a stone, except for a tuft in front and one behind. They were circled around him, laughing. He looked up at the eyes on him and the mouths wide and tried to keep on laughing himself, but he felt the blood coming into his face and a notion came into his head to hit out at somebody or get up and clear out of sight. Then he saw Jim again, looking as funny as a body ever could with just the ridge of hair running down the middle. Jim was a mule himself, with a cut red mane, a mule with tears running down his face he was laughing so hard, and laughing all the harder, Boone realized, because now he was laughing, too.

Jourdonnais tugged at him, offering a tin cup, not alcohol and water this time, but good French brandy. Boone tasted it, feeling his tongue tingle.

Labadie was on the *passe avant,* looking worried. "For this," he cried, "I get across. Yes? No?" He held up a bottle.

"Good! *Oui!*" They snatched the bottle from him, sucking at the mouth of it like men half-dead for a drink.

"For that," said Romaine, "we not shave you. We give you bath only." His great arm flashed out and caught Labadie and yanked him down. Labadie squealed. "Easy now," Romaine said. "Easy." He dropped a loop of rope over Labadie and lifted him and lowered him over the side, dunking him like a piece of corn bread on a string. Labadie screamed in French and came back cursing and strangling, and Romaine beat him on the back until he flung free and fled to the bow.

"Next wan," said Jourdonnais.

When it was over, the Platte lay behind them, lost beyond its hills. Though the breeze kept up, Jourdonnais put in early and treated them to more brandy, looking relieved and almost happy now, while the boatmen drank and sang and wrestled on the bank. At dawn they went on, using the cordelle along the open banks, for the river turned and turned again, like a running snake.

"Buffler country yit?"

"Soon, now. Soon. I'll tell ye." Summers' eyes were always on the banks or the bluffs above them, seeing things maybe another man wouldn't see. The trees grew smaller and scarcer here, stringing along the bottoms as if they had given up the hills for good. They were cottonwoods mostly, with here and there an ash or a wild plum just beginning to break white with bloom.

Banks sliding by, sunup and noon and sundown, and the river leading on, flanked by the pale green of new leaves. Pelicans flapping over at twilight, a passel of them, flying wedge-shaped to the north. Wild geese along the shore in the cool mornings, with tiny goslings strung along behind, making quiet V's in the water. Whippoorwills calling. An eagle's nest high in an old tree, and Indian hunting wigwams, empty and falling down. And always the line or poles or oars and sometimes the sail, on and on, on a river without an end, on a river that flowed under them and led ahead, to Council

Bluffs, to the Yellowstone, to the Blackfeet, to buffler, catching the sky at evening and winding on like a silver sheet.

"We put in at Cabanné's," Jourdonnais said at night, and Summers' eyes raised and asked a question, and Jourdonnais went on, "I know him for long time. He is all right. A friend."

"Works for the company, allasame."

Jourdonnais nodded. "We stop for a minute only, to say hello. Also, to find out what goes on above. We maybe get some jerked meat, from the Mahas."

"Meat aplenty soon. Just a jump or two to buffler. Caudill, here, aims to shine at makin' meat, eh?"

Boone said, "I aim to try."

"Meat ahead," said Jourdonnais. "Also Sioux and Rees. Better to have a little meat on board."

They went ahead under sail at dawn. On the left bank the poplars stood naked, dead from fire, their limbs reaching out at the sky like the bones of a hand. Beyond them, past a creek, a chain of green and wooded hills rolled up. There were huts on the bank along the river, and bigger buildings above them on the bluff. A half-dozen Indians stood on the bank watching. The boatmen yelled at them and waved, and they lifted their hands and let them come down slow, as if they were tired or disappointed because the boat didn't come in. A squaw in a blue dress that hung around her like a sack kept watching, her broad face turning with them, until she was only a patch of blue on the shore.

Cabanné's post stood white against the green, stores and cabins and a two-story house with a balcony overlooking the river.

"Mahas, Otos, and maybe a few Ioways," said Summers, sizing up the crowd on shore while Depuy blew on a trumpet to give notice that the *Mandan* was coming in. A few rifle shots sounded as a welcome from the post, and four guns from the *Mandan* answered. Some of the Indians were dressed in buffalo skins, hairy side out, and some had blankets striped with paint. Children stood among them, potbellied and chill-looking without a stitch of clothes on them. The Indians moved aside a little as the *Mandan* came in, to let through a man who walked importantly and put out his hand as Jourdonnais jumped ashore. They stood talking as Frenchmen did, with their eyes and hands as much as their mouths. Boone reck-

oned the man must be Cabanné. The Indians had their faces painted, some of them with red stripes that ran down their cheeks and
others with raw blotches of red, still showing wet from the spit, on
their foreheads and chins.

Jourdonnais called back. "Do not leave the boat! *Non!* We go
on quick. Let no one on, Summers."

A squaw with eyes as small as beans and hair hanging loose
down her back pressed to the front, her hands out, putting one
forefinger on top of the other and then the other on top of the first,
making a sign. She pointed between her legs and looked up while
she made the sign again, her little eyes asking a question. From the
boat Romaine called "Hah!" and held up a coin, and then added another to it, but she shook her head, still making the sign with her
fingers. The men were jeering at Romaine, looking at the squaw
and then at Romaine and jeering, their eyes sharp and hungry.
Romaine pocketed the coins and pointed down at himself and then
held his two hands out, a foot apart, like a man giving the size of a
fish. His eyebrows lifted in a question. The men shouted, making
little of his brag, but the squaw just looked at him, unsmiling, her
fingers still fiddling. Underneath the old skin dress that was pulled
in at the middle Boone could see the fat of her breasts jiggle. He
turned his head toward the boat and saw Teal Eye gazing out, her
face for once lively and off guard.

An old Indian, with one eye and a face so pitted a man would
think hawks had pecked at it, came up to Boone and Jim, who had
jumped from the boat and stood at the edge of the water. His empty
socket was sunken and red-lidded and weeping a thick yellow drop
that he tried to brush away with the knuckle of one hand. In the
other he held a long black pipe, ringed with circles of lead. Grunting, he put his finger in the bowl to show that it was empty. His
hand reached out to them, begging.

Jourdonnais and Cabanné came from inside the post followed
by four Indians. Jourdonnais said something to Lassereau, who
went up the bank and returned carrying a skin bag and went back
and got another. It was jerked buffalo or pemmican, Boone imagined. "Tobacco," Jourdonnais said to Summers, who undid a lashing on the cargo box. The Indians all crowded around Jourdonnais
as he took the dark twists. They talked in their throats, as if it were

the throat that shaped the sound, and held out their hands. Jourdonnais paid the four and looked around at the empty hands and dropped a twist into the palm of the old man with one eye.

Cabanné shrugged when the deal was done. "Better the Mahas and the Otos than the Blackfeet. No?" he said to Jourdonnais. "You get the beaver, maybe. More likely they take your scalp."

Jourdonnais ran his fingers through his thick head of hair. "I do not need so much."

Cabanné's face was troubled. "Take care, my friend, of Indians, and other things, too."

For an instant Jourdonnais' eyes searched his. "Yes?"

Cabanné looked away, shrugging again, saying nothing, as if what he had said was enough, and maybe too much.

"*Allons!*" cried Jourdonnais and shook hands with Cabanné.

The banks sliding again and the river winding on, past an old fort at Council Bluffs, where Summers said three hundred soldiers died from scurvy once; through a stretch of river thick with snags, through country low for a while and then hilly again, bare of trees but green with grass; past Wood's Hills where a million swallows had nested in the yellow rock.

"Buffler country yit?"

"Quick now. Purty quick."

To Blackbird Hill, where a chief was buried; to Floyd's Bluff, the river slackening and the banks lying low and the Big Sioux coming in; to Vermilion creek, where Summers pointed out the silver berry bush that the Creoles called the *graisse de boeuf;* on toward the Riviere à Jacques and the Running Water, on by stroke and pull and push and sail, day on day, while the sun came up and circled the sky and hid behind the hills.

It was still dark when Summers prodded Boone. "Time to shine." Boone lay for an instant, blinking, seeing one star like a hole in the sky. "Buffler!" he said to himself and scrambled up.

14

Boone picked his way among the sleeping men. Jourdonnais' face, faintly horned with the spikes of his mustache, was a dark circle against his darker robe. He was snoring the long deep snore of a man worn out.

"I got you a Hawken," Summers said from the keelboat, keeping his voice low. He handed a gun and horn and pouch over the side to Boone. "It's the real beaver, for buffler or anything."

Boone hefted the rifle and tried it at his shoulder. It was heavier than Old Sure Shot, and it was a flintlock, not a cap and ball, but it felt good to him—well-balanced and stout, like a piece a man could depend on.

A kind of flush was coming into the sky, not light yet but not dark, either. The men lying in their blankets looked big, like horses or buffalo lying down. The mast of the keelboat, dripping with dew, glistened a little. Boone could hear the water lapping against the sides of the *Mandan*. Farther out, the river made a quiet, busy murmur, as if it were talking to itself of things seen upcountry. Once in a while one of the men groaned and moved, easing his muscles on the earth.

"It's winter ground mostly," said Summers, coming down from the boat, "but might be we can get our sights on one."

They started up the river, moving out from the fringe of trees to the open country at the base of the hills, hearing a sudden snort and the sound of flight from a thicket. "Elk," said Summers. "Poor doin's, to my way of thinking, if there's aught else about. We'll git one, if need be. They're plenty now."

"Poor? I was thinkin' they're tasty, the ones we shot so far."

"Nigh anything's better. Dog, for a case. Ever set your teeth in fat pup?" Summers made a noise with his lips. "Or horse? A man gets a taste for it. And beaver tail! I'm half-froze for beaver tail. And buffler, of course, fat fleece and hump rib and marrow bones too good to think of."

"That's best, I reckon."

"You reckon wrong. Painter meat, now, that's some. Painter meat, that's top, now." Summers' moccasined feet seemed to make no noise at all. "But meat's meat, snake meat or man meat or what."

Boone turned to study the hunter's lined and weathered face, wondering if he had eaten man meat, seeing an arm or leg browning and dripping over the fire.

"Injuns like dead meat. You'll see 'em, towin' drowned buffler to shore, buffler that would stink a man out of a skunk's nest. This nigger's et skunk, too. It ain't so bad, if he ain't squirted. The Canadians, now, they set a heap of store by it. It's painter meat to them."

The stars had gone out, and the sky was turning a dull white, like scraped horn. A low cloud was on fire to the east, where the sun would come up. Boone could make out the trees, separate from each other now and standing against the dark hills—short, squatty trees, big at the base, which could hold against the wind. They walked slow, just dragging along, while Summers' eyes kept poking ahead and the light came on and Boone could follow the Missouri with his eye, on and on until it got lost in a far tumble of hills. The ground was spotted in front of them with disks of old buffalo manure under which the grass and weeds grew white, as in a root house. When he turned one over with his toe, little black beetles scurried out into the grass.

"Ain't any fresh," he said. His eyes searched the hills and the gullies that wormed up through them from the river bottom. "Reckon we won't find any?"

Summers didn't answer right away. He would look east, up on the slope of the hills and west to the woods and river and beyond them to where other hills rose up, making a cradle for the Missouri, and sometimes his eyes would stop and fix on something, as if it might be game or Indians, and go on after a while and stop again. Boone tried to see what he was seeing, but there was only the river winding ahead and the slopes of the hills and the gullies cutting into them and here and there a low tree, flattened at the top, where birds were chirping.

Half the sun was showing, shining in the grass where the dew was beaded. There wasn't a cloud in all the sky, not even a piece of one now that the one to the east had burned out, and the air was still and waiting-like, as if it were worn out and resting up for a blow.

"Sight easier to kill game along the river, where a man don't have to tote it," Summers said, following the valley with his eyes. "Let's point our stick up, anyway." He turned and started uphill.

From the top Boone could see forever and ever, nearly any way he looked. It was open country, bald and open, without an end. It spread away, flat now and then rolling, going on clear to the sky. A man wouldn't think the whole world was so much. It made the heart come up. It made a man little and still big, like a king looking out. It occurred to Boone that this was the way a bird must feel, free and loose, with the world to choose from. Nothing moved from sky line to sky line. Only down on the river he could see the keel-boat showing between the trees, nosing up river like a slow fish. He marked how she poked ahead. He looked on to the tumble of hills that closed in on the river and wondered if she could ever get that far.

Summers had halted, his nose stuck out, like a hound feeling for a scent. "Air's movin' west, if it's movin' at all, I'm thinkin'. All right." He stepped out again, walking with a loose, swift ease.

The sun got up, hot and bright as steel. Off a distance the air began to shimmer in it. Summers kept along the crest of the hills, going slow when they came in sight of a gully or a swale.

It was in one of them that they saw the buffalo, standing quiet with its head down, as if its thoughts were away off. Summers' hand touched Boone's arm. "Old bull," he said, "but meat's meat." The bull lifted his great head and turned it toward them, looking, his beard hanging low.

"He seen us," Boone whispered. "He'll make off."

"Shoo!" said Summers, putting his hand on the lifted barrel of Boone's rifle. "They can't see for nothin', and hearin' don't mean a thing to 'em. It's all right, long as he don't get wind of us." He started forward, walking slow. "You kin shoot him."

"Now?"

"Wait a spell."

The bull didn't move. He stood with his head turned and down, as if for all his blindness he knew they were there. Boone's mind went back to his blind Aunt Minnie who could always tell when someone was around. Her head would pivot and her face would wait, while she looked out of eyes that didn't see.

"Take your wipin' stick. Make a rest. Like this." Summers put the stick out at arm's length and had Boone hold it with his left hand and let the rifle lie across his wrist. "Let 'im have it."

The rifle bucked against Boone's shoulder, cracking the silence. The ball made a gut-shot sound, and a little puff of dust came from the buffalo, as if he had been hit with a pebble. For an instant he stood there looking dull and sad, as if nothing had happened, and then he broke into a clumsy gallop, heading out of the gully. Boone watched him, and heard another crack by his side and saw the bull break down at the knees and fall ahead on his nose. He lay on his side, his legs waving, his breath making a snore in his nose.

Summers was reloading, grinning as he did so. "Too high." Boone felt naked in the bright blue gaze of his eyes, as if what he felt in his mind was standing out for the hunter to see. Summers' face changed. "Don't think nothin' of it. Nigh everybody shoots high, first time. Just a hand and a half above the brisket, that's the spot. It's a lesson for you. Best to load up again, afore anything."

Quicker than Boone could believe, Summers charged his gun. He hitched his pouch and powder horn around, drew the stopper from the horn with his teeth, put the mouth of it in his left hand, and with his right turned the horn up. He was ramming down his load before Boone got his powder measured out.

The buffalo's eyes were fading. They looked soft now, deep and soft with the light going out of them. His legs still waved a little. Summers put his knife in his throat. "We'll roll him over, and this child'll show you how to get at good feedin'." He planted the four legs out at the sides, so that the buffalo seemed to have been squashed down from above. The hunter's knife flashed in the sun. It made a cut crosswise on the neck, and Summers grabbed the hair of the boss with his other hand and separated the skin from the shoulder. He laid the skin open to the tail and peeled it down the sides, spreading it out. "Can't take much," he said, chopping with his hatchet. "Tongue and liver and fleece fat and such. Or maybe one of us best go and git some help from the boat. Wisht we had a pack mule."

"There's a wolf."

Summers looked around at the grinning face that watched them from behind a little rise. "Buffler wolf. White wolf." He spoke in jerks while his knife worked. "I seen fifteen-twenty of 'em circled round sometimes."

"Don't you never shoot 'em?"

"Have to be nigh gone for meat. Ain't enough powder and ball on the Missouri to shoot 'em all."

Boone found a rock and pitched it at the wolf. The head disappeared behind the rise and came into sight again a jump or two away.

Summers kept looking up from his butchering, turning to study every direction, and then going back to the bull again. "See them cayutes?" Boone watched them slink up, their feet moving as if they ran a twisting line, their eyes yellow and hungry. They came closer than the wolf and sat down. Their tongues came out and dripped on the grass. "Watch!" Summers threw a handful of gut toward them. The bigger one darted in, seized the gut, and made off, but he hadn't got far before the wolf jumped on him and took it away. The coyote came back and sat down again. "Happens every time," said Summers. He had the liver out, and the gall bladder. He cut a slice of liver and dipped it in the bladder and poked it in his mouth, chewing and gulping while he worked. "For poor bull, it ain't so bad. Want some?"

Boone took a slice. While he was making himself chew on it, he saw the cloud of dust. It came from behind a little pitch of land maybe two miles to the north, and it wasn't a cloud so much as a vapor, a wisp that he expected to disappear like a fleck in the eye. He wondered whether to point it out to Summers. The wisp came on to the top of the pitch. There was a movement under it. He said then, "Reckon you catched sight of that?"

Summers looked long, the knife idle in his hand. "I be dogged! Hold still now! It's brown skin, sure as I be, but maybe just Puncas." After what seemed to Boone a long time, he added, "Let's back up toward cover. We can cache, maybe. Here's a hoss as don't like it."

He peeled off his shirt and spread it on the ground and put on it the parts of the carcass he had cut out to save, folding the shirt over afterward. Boone narrowed his eyes against the glare. Those were horses under the dust cloud, with riders on them.

"Might be we can git back with this here," said Summers.

"They seen us all right." He lifted his parcel. "Poor doin's, anyhow, to let Injuns think you're runnin'. Even the squaws get braved up then, and full of hell. Ease away, now." His voice was sure and quiet.

Boone scanned the river, looking for the *Mandan*. "Ain't hardly had time to pull this fur," said Summers, "with no breeze to help."

They dropped down behind the crest of the hills, out of sight of the Indians. "Hump it! Hump it some!" They broke for the thin timber two hundred yards and more away, with Summers holding his bundle out from him so as not to hinder his leg.

"I'll take 'er," Boone panted, but Summers only shook his head.

"All right." Summers slowed to an unhurried walk. The Indians came to the top of the hill and halted, outlined against the sky.

"We'll make peace sign." Summers put his parcel down and fired his rifle at the sky. Afterwards, he took his pipe out and held it high for the Indians to see.

The Indians looked and talked among themselves, until one of them yelled and all joined in, a kind of high, quavering yell. They sent their horses down the bluff, the hoofs making a clatter in a patch of stones.

"Gimme your Hawken and load this 'un." They were still a throw away from the fringe of woods along the river. Summers took the wiping stick from its slot while he watched. "Sioux, by beaver, or this nigger don't know Injun. They can't circle us here, anyways. Git ready, old hoss, but hold fire till I give the sign." He planted his wiping stick out before him and laid the rifle on its rest. "That's it, hoss, and line your sights on the belly, not the head."

A hundred and fifty yards away the Indians pulled up. Boone counted them. Twelve men. They were naked from the waist up, unless a man counted the feathers stuck in their hair. Their skin looked smooth and soft, like good used leather. It would make a better strop than the one he'd left in Louisville. Three or four had guns in their hands, and the others bows. Their horses minced around as they waited.

"It ain't a war party, anyhow," Summers said, as if he was making talk at night around the fire.

"How can a body tell?"

"No paint. No shields. They're huntin', I'm thinkin'."

Summers stood up. His voice went out, rough and steady and strong, in language Boone didn't understand, and his hands made movements in front of him.

The Indians listened, sitting their horses as if they were grown on them. Sometimes as the horses moved Boone could see the Indians' hair, hanging far down in plaits. The foremost of them, though, the one who seemed to be the leader, had chopped it off short.

Summers' voice came to a halt. To Boone he said, "A man never knows about Sioux."

The Indians sat their milling horses. Their heads moved, and their hands, as they talked to one another. The Indian with the short hair rode out. The tail of some animal hung from his moccasin. His voice was stronger than Summers' and came more from his chest.

"Asks if we're squaws, to run," Summers translated. "And what have we got for presents? His tongue is short but his arm is long, and he feels blood in his eye."

The Indian halted, waiting for Summers' reply. "I'm thinkin' they just met up with an enemy and got the worst of the tussle. That makes 'em mean as all hell. I'll tell 'em our tongues ain't so long either, but our guns is a heap longer'n them crazy fusees." His voice went out again.

Suddenly, while the rest watched, the Indian with the short hair let out a yell and put his horse to a gallop, coming straight at them. He was low on his horse, just the top of him showing and the legs at the sides.

Summers dropped to one knee again and leveled his gun, and nothing seemed to move about him except the end of the barrel bearing on the rider. Boone was down, too, with his rifle up, seeing the outflung hoofs of the horse and the flaring nostrils. He would be on them in a shake. The horse bore out a little, and the cropped head moved, and the black of a barrel came over the horse's neck. Summers' rifle spoke, and in a wink the horse was running free, shying out in a circle and going back. The Indian lay on his belly. He didn't move. "That's one for the wolves," Summers said. His hand came over and gave Boone the empty rifle and took the loaded one and drew away with it. "Load up!"

The Indians had sat, watching the one and yelling for him. They hushed when he fell and then all began to yell again, the voices rising shrill and falling. They set their horses to a run streaking to one side and then the other, not coming directly at Boone and Summers, but working closer as the line went back and forth. Sometimes one, bolder than the rest, would charge out of the line and come nearer, waving his gun or bow while he shouted, and then go back to the line again. "Hold your sights on one," said Summers, "the one on the speckled pony. Hold fire till I tell you. Then plumb center with it." He had taken his pistols from his belt and had them out before him, ready to his hand.

The Indians made themselves small on the horses, swinging to the off side as they turned. "Shoo!" Summers said. "They can't ride for nothin'. Can't shine with Comanches, or even Crows."

"Why'n't they charge, all of 'em?"

Summers' eye ran along the barrel of his gun. "They got no stummick for that kind of doin's, save once in a while one likes to shine alone, like that nigger out there."

A rifle cracked, and in front of them the ground exploded in a little blast of dust. "Steady. Time to go ag'in." Out of the corner of his eye Boone saw smoke puff from the gun. A running horse stumbled and fell. The Indians shouted, higher and wilder. The fallen horse lay on its rider. Boone saw the rider, just the head and jerking hands of him beyond the horse, trying to pull his leg free. Summers handed over the empty rifle. Two Indians flew to the one who was down, slipped from the off sides of their horses, and, stooping behind the downed horse, rolled the withers up. The fallen rider tried to arise and went off crawling, dragging one leg.

The others, driven back a little by the shot, began to come in again, working to and fro. One of them bobbed up and swung his rifle over. The ball sang past Boone. He had the rifle primed again, and the Indian on the speckled pony on his sights. "Kin I shoot one?" He didn't wait. The sights seemed to steady of themselves and fix just above the pony's neck. His fingers bore on the trigger, like it had a mind of its own. The rifle jumped.

"I be dogged."

The speckled pony shied off. Behind him a man squirmed on the ground, squirmed and got up and went back, bent at the middle.

"Slicker'n ice, Caudill."

The Indians bunched up, talking and gesturing. "They had nigh enough, I'm thinkin'," said Summers, raising his cheek from his rifle. He added, "For now."

"That's the boat."

The trumpet had sounded, cutting through the still air, rolling up river and out to the hills and coming back on itself. Boone saw the *Mandan*. The oars made little even flashes as the men laid them back. Someone was busy in the bow. It looked like Jourdonnais. It was him, working at the swivel gun, which was a bar of light in the bow. The Indians looked, holding their horses tight, easing them backward away from the river. The swivel belched smoke, and the sound of it came to them, a rolling boom like thunder. Jourdonnais got busy with it again.

"First shot was just to skeer 'em. Second'll be business."

But the Sioux drew off, turning back and shouting and shaking their arms as they went. Boone watched them long enough to see that they picked up the two crippled warriors.

Summers put his pistols back in his belt and fitted his wiping stick to his rifle. He and Boone walked ahead, to the Indian who lay still in the grass. Summers stooped over. His knife cut into the scalp and made a rough circle, from which the blood beaded. He got hold of the Indian's short hair and tore the circle loose, leaving the piece of skull naked and raw. "Take his gun. This Injun's had a grief lately. Some of his kin's gone under—a brother, maybe. That's why he chopped his tails off. Looks recent, don't it? Like as not it just happened. That's why they was so froze for our scalps, so's they wouldn't have to go home beaten and with nary thing to shine with." He went back and picked up his bundle of meat, carrying scalp and bundle in one hand.

The *Mandan* pulled in, so close they could hop aboard. Jourdonnais' bold, dark face questioned Summers. The Creoles looked at him, too, their eyes big and watchful like the eyes of a frog ready to jump if a man took another step.

Summers said, "We put one under and winged two." The barrel of his rifle swung toward Boone. "There's a hoss as'll shoot plumb center." In tones that Boone barely overheard he went on, "We ain't seen the last of 'em, I'm thinkin'."

15

Summers was right; but for a day and part of another, while they went by the Rivière à Jacques and headed on toward the L'Eau Qui Court, Jourdonnais told himself that he wasn't. There wasn't one sign of Indian, not even to Summers, who watched the shores, hour after hour, searching with his trained gray eye. Summers' face was sober but not worried. Jourdonnais wondered if he ever worried, this big, loose-built man who was like a wise old dog. Watching him, gazing down from his place at the steering oar, Jourdonnais wondered that Summers had gone in with him. Summers didn't care for money or a nice house or pretties for a wife, if he had one. He lived like a wild thing, to eat and frolic and keep his scalp, not thinking from one day to another, not putting by against the future. If Jourdonnais hadn't found him fresh back from a good hunt in the country of the Arapahoes, Summers wouldn't have had money to put into cargo, the way he was spending it. As it was, Jourdonnais in his desperate need for funds had had to beg, holding out the possibilities of rich profits in the Trois Fourches. Looking at Summers, seeing the alert face that was untroubled by regrets or ambition, Jourdonnais thought that Summers had joined him for the fun rather than the profit. He was glad that Summers was an easy man, without the dark strain of violence that ran so often in mountain men.

He was thankful, too, for the favor of the wind, grudging and unreliable as it was. It would take a gun, almost, to drive the Creoles to the bank now. He wouldn't order them to tow unless he had to. A hundred Indians could hide in one small thicket and kill the crew to the last man as they pulled up to it. It was good that the river was down. The time was coming on to June, and the Missouri would flood again when the snow in the mountains ran off.

As much as he could, Jourdonnais kept the *Mandan* to the left bank, away from the side on which Summers and Caudill had come up against the Indians. Sometimes he put the crew out with the cordelle on the long sand bars that divided the current, lying in the water like the backs of hogs cooling off in the muck. The men rowed, each with a rifle by his side, and for all of Summers' looking, they looked, too, putting only half their attention on the oars and the other half on the bank, as if every bush hid an Indian. Sometimes Jourdonnais felt ashamed for his people, who had neither bravery nor pride like Americans.

"The Sioux go away, eh, Summers?"

Summers came over and leaned against the cargo box and gave a half-shake of his head. "They're like to pop up on a bank any time and rain arrers down on us. Now's when we need two boats, one on each side, the other lookin' out for us and us lookin' out for them. We can see the far shore a heap better'n this one. I'm thinkin' they're comin' along, maybe lookin' for a way acrost."

The hunter looked down from his six feet and said something in Indian to little Teal Eye, who was standing by her lodge with one hand on the box letting the breeze blow her. She answered and let her gaze slide back to the shore.

"You sure about Sioux?" Jourdonnais asked. "They make no trouble for long time."

Summers' tone had a faint edge. "This child ought to know a Sioux."

Jourdonnais agreed, smiling to soften the other's irritation. "You have sleep with them enough? Maybe *beaucoup* Sioux babies by Summers?"

The hunter didn't answer at once, and when he did speak it was to explain. "Sioux or what, two white men alone make Injuns itchy."

"So?"

"They had blood in their eye to boot, I'm thinkin'." He pointed to the scalp that had been tucked under a lashing, raw side up, to dry. A big blue-green fly, shining with bloat, was working on it. "Hair's cut short. Means that hoss was grievin'."

"Yes."

"Injuns ain't never so mean as when they've took a beatin'. They're half-froze to make up for it, don't matter on who."

They pulled up to a sand bar for the night. The river ran on both sides of it, making an island—a flat little island on which the willows had commenced to poke up. It might wash away with the next high water. The wind played among the willows and picked up the sand and threw it at them, so that there was sand in the eye and in the meat and in the beds. Pambrun had set up his stove on top of the cargo, in a box filled with sand. Here in the middle of the river the Creoles felt safe. Some of them took off their clothes and sported in the water. That was one thing about his people, Jourdonnais thought; they had the light heart. He let himself have one of the Spanish segars that he reserved for special occasions, though he hardly felt right in smoking it. A man could keep himself poor, letting small money get away from him. "By damn," he said to Romaine while he wiped an eye, "the wind blow the gnat off and the sand on. One damn thing or another." As the night began to close down Pambrun set out his fishlines, baited with bird gut.

They stood watches that night and went on before the sun was up, their bellies working on catfish and roast liver and tenderloin that was half-raw and tough but full of strength. Great yellow-breasted larks sang as the sun came up, and with his fowling piece Summers shot half a dozen prairie hens that had watched them from an island, their heads up and turning until the bird shot knocked them over.

There was no wind at all in the early morning, and the river seemed to have a new strength, as if it had just awakened to find how far they had invaded her. The absence of a breeze, the renewed force of the current, the Indians maybe somewhere along the bank, all seemed to Jourdonnais, squirming at the helm, the proof of conspiracy against him. *Enfant de garce*, wasn't the river easier above the Jacques, always! He thought of distance as the enemy, as a slow and crawling thing that stood between him and a new house and money in pocket and the big men of St. Louis saying "Monsieur Jourdonnais." The left bank lay open, inviting him to tow. He motioned Summers to him.

"The cordelle?" He was asking for advice. He motioned toward the bare bank.

Summers' chin closed, so that his mouth was the thin mouth of thought. "Put in," he said at last. "This child'll scout. See me wave, send the crew out." He lifted his gun that seemed always in his hand now and refreshed the priming. "Better send a hunter with 'em, to boot." Before he started for the shore he studied it. "All right." Jourdonnais saw that they had scared up a heron, which flopped away with its legs out, using them for a rudder.

It seemed a long time before he saw Summers again, standing

half a mile up on a little tongue of land, motioning them on. Jourdonnais said, "The cordelle. We tow," loud enough for the oarsmen in the bow to hear him. The men's eyes went to the bank and then to him. They got themselves up, as if they had weights in their pants. "*Non!* Not the guns. *Mon Dieu,* you think to pull with rifles in the hands?" They stood shifting from foot to foot, muttering to themselves. "Summers, he's looking ahead. I send Caudill with you, to lead. Here, all have a drink. It is all right."

The woods were still, but not too still. Things moved in them and made noises, a brown thrush flitting in a thicket of buffalo berry, a coyote trotting at the edge of the meadow that flowed out from the trees and led on up to the hills, a bunch of magpies cawing in a tangled cottonwood. Summers' eye caught the movement of the thrasher. It was no more than a shadow passing in shadows, but he saw it and identified the bird, and his eye climbed the bushes until it found the nest. The magpies were a brood. The young ones made an unsure clamor, like boys with their voices changing.

Summers went on, letting a part of his mind roam and keeping a part of it open for the messages of the woods. A man had to learn how to divide his mind that way, to think and remember in some far-off part of it and yet to note and feel what was going on about him, and to be ready to act without thinking. The far-off part of his mind saw Caudill aiming at the Indian, his face set and maybe a little pale but not scared. Caudill, for all he was an odd and silent boy, would make a mountain man. Maybe so would Deakins, though he didn't seem cut out so clear for it. Trading would suit him; he got along with people. It was something, what traders would do to make money—like Jourdonnais stewing over his nickels. Christ, even when you had a heap of beaver what did you have?

He went to the water line and motioned an "All right," waiting for Jourdonnais' answering wave, and then let the woods swallow him again and that far piece of his mind go on with its thinking. He knew he wasn't a mountain man as some men were. He liked to get to St. Louis once in a while and sleep in a sure-enough bed, with a white woman that smelled of perfume instead of grease and diamond-willow smoke. He didn't mind farming, too much. It was still getting outside. And he hadn't lost his taste for bread and salt and pies and such. They were a heap better than squaw meat, which men had been known to butcher and eat, probably after bedding with the squaws first.

Above him, out at the edge of the brush, a curlew was calling. Its sharp two-toned cry seemed to hang in the air. He caught a glimpse of it, with its wings outspread and just the tips of them fluttering as it glided. He waited for it to land, waited for the muted little trill that would tell him it was aground again and satisfied. The bird's shadow sped along the leaves over his head. It hadn't lighted. It wasn't going to light. The two-toned cry kept sounding, as if something had stumbled on the nest.

Summers waited and watched and after a while moved ahead again, going as softly as a man could. Except for the curlew and the magpies that were half a mile behind him now, the woods had no voice at all, and no movement. He came to a small open space and stood at the edge of it, unmoving except for his eyes. Through a screen of brush he could see a patch of the river shaded by the trees above him. The water seemed still as pond water, gathered in a small elbow in the bank. While he watched, a mallard hen came into the patch, swimming steadily downstream, watching for the string of ducklings that trailed behind her. They didn't make a sound.

Summers thought, "Injuns about, sure as God," but still he didn't move. A man couldn't run off yelling Injun without knowing where they were and who and how many. After a while he slipped ahead again, and stopped, and went on. A willow branch made a little whisking noise along his buckskin. He halted and put it back of him and waited again. The curlew was still circling, still crying about her nest.

The boats were stowed carefully in the brush, so as not to be seen from the river. There were seven of them in sight, the round bullboats of the upper Missouri, each made from the hide of a single bull stretched over a willow frame. They appeared old and were wet yet, but not dripping, as if they had been used the night before and hadn't had time to dry out there in the shade. Summers looked at them through a clump of low willow. He made out a moccasined track pointed upstream.

After what seemed a long time, he crouched down and sidled over toward the bank of the river. He thrust his head from the brush slowly, like a squirrel peeking from behind a limb, knowing it was movement and not shape that caught the eye. Up the current, less than an arrow shot away, the river made a slow turn. The willows grew lush there, probably where a tree had gone over and caught the sand and made a bank. The boat towers would have clear going until they got there.

Summers couldn't see anything among the willows, not so much as a branch bent out of shape or the grass trampled where a man might have gone through, but he knew the Sioux were there.

He brought his head back, still slowly, and turned about, to see an Indian screened in the brush only an arm's length away. Two black stripes ran down the Indian's cheeks. They pulled downward as the Indian caught his movement. There was one still instant—a flash of seeing, in which nothing moved or sounded—and then the Indian jerked up his battle-ax. Summers leaped to one side, hearing the empty whistle of the club before it thrashed the brush. There wasn't room or time for the rifle. Summers dropped it and leaped ahead, straight through the thin willows at the Indian, trying to beat the second swing of the club. The Sioux grunted and went down over a root, chopping with the bladed club as he fell. Summers felt the point of it stabbing his left shoulder. He got hold of the hand. His right hand went down for his knife. The Indian gave a sudden heave, snapping himself at the crotch. They rolled over, Summers underneath now, hugging the Indian to cramp his swing. He knew he ought to call out, to warn the crew oncoming with the cordelle. He felt the Indian's legs on either side of his knee and jerked the knee up. The force of it pounded the Indian ahead. The Indian let out a grunt that settled into a thin whine. Summers got his knife then, got it out and around and brought it down, feeling it hit and skid and go on. The Indian flopped from him and lay straining and got himself on his butt and sat, unable to do more. Summers was on his feet. He had his right hand back, with the knife in it.

The Sioux's fingers lay loose around the handle of his tomahawk. Summers thought his eyes were like a dog's, like a pitiful goddam dog's. He had to let him have it. The eyes followed Summers' arm up to the knife, waiting for it to come down. The far-off part of Summers' mind told him again he wasn't a real mountain man. Eyes like a goddam hound's. The knife went in easy this time.

Summers wrenched himself around and lurched through the brush to the shore. He could feel his shirt sticking to his back. The boatmen strung along the cordelle pulled up, their mouths dropping open, as he burst out almost on top of them. He made himself be deliberate. "Back!" he said. "Quick, but be careful!" He heard the Indians begin to shout behind him, from the clustered willow. Their arrows made a small fluttering noise, and their fusils boomed. He thought, "Injuns always use a heap too much powder," while he shouted at the Creoles, trying to put order in their flight. They had turned like sheep and started to run and fallen down and run again and fallen, as the fleeter overran the others. He was shouting, more to himself than to them, "Easy! You French sons of bitches." An arrow was sticking from Labadie's arm, but it didn't stop his running. It just made him yell. Christ, a man would think it had him in the heart!

The Indians shouted louder, but not from the willow any more and not like men standing still. Summers could hear them breaking through the brush, their cries broken by the jolt of their feet. The Creoles were a frantic tangle down the bank. Closer, Caudill stood, his dark eye fixed along the rifle barrel, and behind him was Deakins, unarmed but waiting. "Hump it!" cried Summers, humping it himself. The *Mandan* lay like a dead duck at the edge of the stream, her sail down and useless as a broken wing. Free from the towline, she was settling back with the current and pulling out, drawing away from them. While Summers watched, he saw Romaine splash into the water and run up on the bank and take a snub on a tree, and then splash back to the *Mandan* as if the devil was on his tail.

"Go on!" shouted Summers. "Hump it, you goddam fools!"

Caudill's rifle went off almost in his face, and then they were running at his sides, Caudill and Deakins were, running and looking back. An arrow whizzed over their heads and buried its head in a tree before them. A rifle spoke again, sounding as if it had been fired right behind their heads. "Goddam it, run, you boys!" Summers felt his legs playing out on him. His head was dauncy, as if it wasn't fixed rightly to his neck. All of a sudden he realized he was old. It was as if all his life he had run among the sleeping dogs of the years and now at last they had wakened all at once and seized on him. He knew he couldn't make it. "Git on, you two," he panted. Back of him he could see the Indians, running in the open now and yelling their heads off, sure that they would get him.

And then the swivel spoke. The black smoke belched out of it, cored at first with fire, and hung in a black cloud, tattering at the edges as the air played with it. The shot silenced the yells of the Indians and the footsteps. When Summers looked back he couldn't see a Sioux, except for two that lay there for the wolves. After a while, above the slowed sound of his own moccasins, he heard them again, but thin this time and lost in the brush. He called to Jourdonnais. "Let's move on up and get them scalps. They'll help a heap with the Rees and Blackfeet."

16

Boone lay on his back and looked at a night sky shot with stars. They were sharp and bright as fresh-struck flames, like campfires that a traveler might sight on a far shore. Starlight was nearly as good as moonlight here on the upper river where blue days faded off into nights deeper than a man could believe. By day Boone could get himself on a hill and see forever, until the sky came down and shut off his eye. There was the sky above, blue as paint, and the brown earth rolling underneath, and himself between them with a free, wild feeling in his chest, as if they were the ceiling and floor of a home that was all his own.

Boone had his shirt close around his neck and a handkerchief half over his face to shut off the mosquitoes. They made a steady buzzing around his head, for all that he and Jim had built a smudge and bedded down close to it. He could hear Jim slapping his face and rubbing the itch afterwards.

"Worse'n chiggers," Jim said, "these damn gnats. Listen to 'em. It's their war whoop they're singing." Boone set his mind to listening. The whole night seemed filled with the small whining of their wings. "What's the good of a gnat, anyways?" Jim asked.

"They'll quiet down some, if it cools off."

"They don't serve no purpose, unless to remind a man he ain't such a somebody."

"I dunno," said Boone, knowing Jim was turning the question in his mind as he did with everything. When it came to an idea Jim was like Boone with a rock or a buffalo chip, tipping it over to see what was underneath. Boone figured it was better to take what came and not trouble the mind with questions there was no answer to. Under a rock or a chip, now, a man could spot bugs and sometimes a snake.

"Maybe the pesky little bastards is asking themselves what God wanted to put hands on a man for," Jim said after a while. "Maybe they're thinkin' everything would be slick, except their dinner can slap 'em. Maybe," he went on after another pause, "maybe they got as much business here as we have. You reckon?"

"I wouldn't say as much."

"They're here, ain't they?" Jim's hand made a whack against his cheek. "And we're here, ready for 'em to feed on. I bet they figure we're made special just for them. I bet they're sayin' thank you, God, for everything, only why did You have to put hands on a man, or a tail on a cow?"

Boone could look down along the shadows of his cheeks and see the *Mandan's* mast, standing sharp and black.

"Or maybe they're sayin', like my old man would, we know it's a punishment for our bein' so sinful and no-account. Forgive us our trespasses, an' God's will be done."

The boat got to be part of a man, like his pants or his shoes. Only Boone didn't have shoes any more, but moccasins bought from the squaws. Everybody was dressed like an Injun now, or half like one, with long hair and moccasins and hunting shirts and some of them leather leggings. Even his hair and Jim's, shaved off away down on the Platte, was beginning to come around the ears. He could make tails, almost, from the tufts they had left. He had got himself a slick outfit, trading glass beads that Jourdonnais had put up against his pay and a turkey tail that Summers had given him. It was something, the store the upper Injuns set by turkey tails to make headpieces with. Summers said it was because you didn't see turkeys, leastwise not very often, above Little Cedar

Island. His outfit had been made by the Crows, the Mandans said, and had quills on it and some beads. A man could cut a figure in it.

Sometimes, lying out this way at night listening to Jim, he thought about home and Bedwell and the sheriff and the horse he had stolen and sold at St. Louis. Mostly, though, when he thought about things like that, he thought about home. Not that he wanted to go back. God's sake, no! Still, a man wondered about his ma and brother. And if he had it to do over again, he wouldn't be scared of Pap. He could handle Pap now, all right, even if he was still just seventeen. He had got on to a lot in a mighty little while. He brought his left hand over and felt the muscle of his arm. He could pick Pap up and shake his teeth loose without so much as taking a long breath. When he thought about leaving home and the tears coming into his eyes and the lump aching in his throat, he wondered if he was still the same body. It would take something to make him cry now. It would take something to make him worry, even, the way he had worried when he found he'd caught a case of clap. Summers was right; a thing like that kind of wore out after a while, and a man got so he didn't give it any heed.

It seemed like a year he'd been with the boat. Like his whole life. A body lost track of time. One day melted into another, passing into full summer and beyond, and no one took note or cared except Jourdonnais and maybe Summers a little, and even Jourdonnais was smiling, for it was as if the wind that had deviled them for so long suddenly had got ashamed of itself. Past the Ponca country it had switched around. Day after day it had kept behind them, pushing them along, turning when they turned as if it was trained to it, getting ornery only once in a while and pretty soon giving up and working with them again. Jourdonnais shook his head, saying one time after another, "I never know it like this," while his mustache pointed up with his smile. They had passed a sight of country. It ran through Boone's eyes as he eased off toward sleep, as if he were seeing it for the first time again: the hills changing, some of them as flat as a table and others undercut and weathered off, looking like old forts or fancy places that kings had lived in long before; the wild currants and cherries and gooseberries above the White, where Carolina pigeons whooed and blackbirds rasped; islands run around with cedar or cottonwood, with little, secret meadows in-side; the black veins striping the river bluffs, which Summers said was coal and sometimes caught fire, making the pumice stone that the river carried and that the squaws used to finish hides; dead In-dians lying on scaffolds and some of them falling to pieces and lit-tering the ground, making a stink, and the buzzards sitting in the trees around; Summers lying above the Big Bend with a handker-chief flying from a stick and an antelope dancing and circling and coming closer, out of curiousness, until Summers' bullet knocked it over; sandbanks and sandbanks and prairies and prairies and al-ways the strange hills and the big sky.

Jourdonnais stood at the wheel, steering right by Fort Te-cumseh, which belonged to the Company and hung to a bank the river was undercutting. He let the men answer the welcoming shots on the shore with a volley from half a dozen muskets, but steered on by just the same, the sail full and the flag whipping from the mast, while he looked dead ahead as if his mind was on trouble.

The hills were easy and wooded at the mouth of the Cheyenne, and farther on cottonwood and a few elms and small ashes and buffalo berry and currant bushes made a lane for them. They saw elk—thirty of them in one bunch—and white wolves chasing along the bluffs, and once Boone and Summers and Jim came on a little place fenced in with poles, which had a post in the center painted with fading red and a buffalo head raised on a small mound of earth. Summers said it was medicine, to make the buffalo plenty. They saw trees scarred high by the ice that had gone out in the spring, and beaver cuttings and beaver tracks galore. Summers looked hungrily at the sign, and explained that hunters let this country be because the Rees claimed it for their own.

The Ree villages sat round-topped on the west bank, the two divided by a stream and each closed in by a fence of stakes that had commenced to rot and fall down. The houses were made of reddish-white clay and each had a square hole in it for a door. And beyond the villages were the Cannonball and the Heart, and buffalo, pound-ing over the high ground, making knee-deep paths along the bluffs, swimming in the river. Summers killed a cow with a knife, jumping in the river and swimming to her and running the blade around her throat as she hit shore. How much fresh meat could a man eat?

It went into the stomach and spread right out into blood and strength, leaving the belly ready for more.

Summers shot a deer, not a whitetail but what they called a mule deer, larger than the other and darker, with ears almost like a jackass. It was young and juicy, and the head that had been buried in the coals made Boone's mouth water, just thinking.

The river went on, to the Mandans, to the Minitari, to the Knife River, to the Little Missouri, the brown never-ending river, idling and tearing and twisting and gouging, the river that ran full of silt and drift and rotting buffalo, leading up from the deep woods and the closed hills and the scrub grass of the down country to country that kept getting freer and bigger until sometimes, looking out over it from a rise, Boone felt he was everywhere on it, like the air or the light.

"Goddam, Jim!" he said.

"What?"

"It's slick, ain't it?"

"What?"

"This here. Everything."

"These pesky gnats—"

Jim's words got mixed with Boone's remembering. He thought back to the night that was closing down over the Ree camp. It wasn't dark yet, not so dark a man couldn't see, but the boatmen and the squaws didn't care. In the open grass behind the clay huts they made moving heaps, the men writhing over the squaws, rising and pushing and writhing and sometimes groaning like a stud horse as the stuff of them pumped out. Once in a while you heard a giggle from a squaw or a Frenchie, before they settled down to business. The dusk was thick and soft, like smoke you couldn't smell. Boone could hear the old squaws quarreling in their houses and the barking of the wolf-dogs that showed their teeth to white men, but they seemed far away, like echoes running across a stillness. Here there was just the single voice in a laugh or the throat in a groan and the grass rustling. By and by other boatmen would be coming along with their squaws. It was early yet.

Boone's squaw lifted her gown and sat down and lay back. There was no get-ready, no kissing or hugging or hunting with the hand. It wasn't that a man needed any, not with what was going on

126

around him, and the heart big and urgent in the throat. The squaw
lay waiting, thinking likely about the scarlet cloth her man had
bargained for and taken only after he had gone back to her to ask if
it was enough. She wasn't bad—straight and young and so light-
colored a man might take her for white in the dusk. The smell of
her came into his nostrils as he got down, the smell of lodge
smoke and warmth and meat grease and woman and the smell of
bruised grass.

Afterwards he got up without a thank-you or a how-de-do,
walking with the loose, easy fag of a man who had spent himself.
There were a passel of dogs in the village and more blind people
than a body would think for. He met Summers. The hunter's eyes
studied him. "This child wasn't lyin', was he, about the Ree wom-
en? They ain't so many as before, but still good. The Rees are
movin'."

"Why?"

"Sioux, mostly. The Sioux keep pressin' them. Likely they'll
join up with the Pawnees. They're kin."

"They been oncommon friendly for folk you didn't trust."

"On account of the Sioux scalps, and on account of this nigger
hisself. They remember me all right. Some calls me brother, from
away back." Summers gave tobacco to two who came begging.
"They're tricky, though, remember, and mean fighters. Meanest
next to the Blackfeet, I do believe. Watch careful, or might be they'll
take our hair."

"I'm bein' careful."

"I'm makin' talk with Two Elks. Want to come? Best to have a
little 'baccy."

"I got a lookin' glass, too."

Buffalo robes were already spread around a small fire in the
lodge they entered. An Indian put out his hand, saying nothing.
They shook it and sat down while he filled a pipe. A squaw began
to busy herself with a kettle, waddling to the fire like an old duck.
Two Elks lighted his pipe and blew smoke to the sky and earth and
the four directions. Holding the bowl, he passed the long stem to
Summers and then to Boone. By the light of the fire the squaw had
poked, Boone could see the white and welted line of the scar that
ran along each of his arms and came together on his naked stomach.

The vermilion on his cheeks was like streaks of old blood. His hair was heavy and longer than a man could believe. It came down from the sides of his head in plaits and lay in coils at his thighs like snakes.

In the pot that the squaw had fixed was a mixture of dried corn mixed with beans and cooked with buffalo marrow. It tasted good to Boone, putting him in mind of Ma and the garden in Kentucky.

Two Elks said, "How," and waited for a minute and went on carefully, like a man making a speech, talking deep in his throat. His eyes were small and deep-set. The little fire shone in them, behind the close banks of the lids. The squaw came to Summers and studied his buckskins piece by piece. She took an awl and a piece of split sinew from a bag and went to work on a rip in his moccasin. Two Elks kept talking.

"The heart of Two Elks is full," Summers translated as the Indian paused. "His brothers, the Long Knives, have brought the scalps of the Sioux who are as many as the blades of grass, whose tongues are crooked and whose hearts are bad. While the pale brother makes war on the Sioux, the Rees will walk with him."

The fire made a ball of light in the darkness, a red bubble closing in Two Elks and his squaw and Summers and Boone. Outside there was only darkness, and sounds that came muted—the growl of a dog, a snatch of talk, the laugh of a squaw or the deeper laugh of a boatman out in the grass.

The chief spoke again, and Summers translated. "Two Elks is a poor man. He has given his goods to others, for it is below a brave man to want riches. He is very poor and needs what the white brother can give him. What he has, his brothers may have, too."

Summers reached for the powder horn at the Indian's side and held it to the fire to see how full it was. It took most of Summers' horn to fill it. Boone handed over a twist of tobacco and the looking glass he had brought along in case he needed it with a squaw. Then, because they looked so little, he took some balls from his pouch.

Summers talked with his hands and mouth. The Indian sat back listening, his eyes steady on the hunter's face, sometimes nodding and sometimes just looking through his narrowed lids. To Boone Summers said, "I told him I heerd the Rees had blacked their faces towards us, but I knew it was not true, that I had lived with the Rees and slept in their lodges and hunted with their hunters, and we were brothers. I said we brought the scalps of the Sioux and some presents, too, to show our hearts were good."

The squaw's hands picked at Boone, looking for a loose thread or a tear. Her fingers lingered on the boughten shirt he wore, which was red-checked cotton and faded with the sun, and pretty soon began to tug at it while her eyes looked into his. After a while he took the shirt off and gave it to her. She made a pleased sound. Afterwards she barely brushed his head and jaw with her fingers as if to make out what he was. He sat still, trying not to notice her, as he reckoned a man was supposed to do.

The chief pointed to the robes they sat on, to show they were gifts. The squaw left the circle of firelight, clucking over the old shirt which she held in front of her. Boone heard again the sounds that came from the rutting back of the village. One voice rose high, a Frenchman's, speaking through a bubbling of laughter.

Two Elks heard and leaned forward, his elbows outspread on the knees that slanted up from his crossed legs. His eyes were direct and asking, and his old face in the firelight seemed as open as a child's. His voice came out in a question, which Summers seemed not to understand, for he said something short and Two Elks asked again.

Summers looked puzzled but nodded his head and spoke. Two Elks' gaze went down to the fire and thought made a cloud on his face. He was silent, as if trying to figure something out.

A dog was barking at the edge of the village. He set off the others until there was nothing but the sound of dogs out in the night. When they quieted the other sounds took up. By listening close Boone could hear voices in other lodges, where Jourdonnais and maybe Jim and Romaine were visiting. Above them he could still hear the sounds out in the grass behind, coming through the clay of the lodge.

"Two Elks don't understand," said Summers. "He wants to know, ain't there any squaws in the land of the Long Knives?"

As long as he lived, thought Boone as he squirmed for comfort on the ground, he would remember that question and Two Elks' open face asking it. "No squaws in the land of the Long Knives?" In a way it was so simple it made a man want to laugh.

Jim snored lightly, fallen away from his thoughts. Jim always seemed to go to sleep quick, and to wake up feeling good, with a glint in his eye. The campfire was a dying glow in the night. Across it Boone could see other figures, lying loose and all spraddled out as if the touch of the ground rested them. Most of them made noises in their sleep, sucking in their breath and blowing it out. Only Romaine was up, taking the first watch. It would be Boone's turn next, and then Jim's. Jourdonnais and Summers always took the early-morning watches, figuring they were the dangerous ones. Romaine went over by a tree and stood there a minute and then let himself down, his back against the trunk. It was a mighty poor way to stand guard. After a while he began to tip over, a little at a time, like a bag not set quite right. Boone knew he was asleep.

Except for the men's breathing and the river forever talking to itself along the shores, there was hardly a sound tonight, bar the coyotes that sang at the sky. A man couldn't tell where a coyote was from his singing. His voice came from the hills somewhere, sharp-pitched and sorrowful, and threaded through the night like a needle. Closer, he heard the sound of a wing as a bird settled itself better for the night.

Boone lay on his side with his eyes half-open, looking down toward the *Mandan* and the water that caught the lights of the stars, looking and thinking and trying to drop into sleep. He saw himself shooting the white bear, and the bear turning as if to bite the ball out and falling and loosening away into death and Summers looking at him and smiling.

Sometimes bears sneaked into camps, looking for a piece of meat or a lick of sweetening. For a moment, through his widened eyes, Boone thought it was a bear he saw, waddling slow and quiet toward the boat. His hand went over to waken Jim, but Jim had rolled out of reach. Romaine was lying as flat as anyone now and as sound asleep. Boone felt for his rifle. He sat up, holding the weapon in his hands. The figure lengthened from its crouch as he looked and framed its upper part in the star shine of the river, and he saw it was a man, working down easy toward the keelboat. Boone brought his gun up and ran his eye along it, and then he thought about Teal Eye in her little lodge in the stern, and brought the weapon down. He rolled from his bed and started ahead on all fours, hearing his heart thump in his chest. It was an Indian—a Ree, maybe, or a Sioux, or a Blackfoot. There'd be others with him, though. He halted and hunted with his eyes, but saw no one except the man creeping to the boat. He was of a mind to let out a shout or to crawl to Summers and wake him up. For all he knew, though, the man was just one of the Frenchies. That was it—a Frenchie sneaking up on Teal Eye, going against the orders that Jourdonnais had given out many's the time. Goddam, a man would think they'd had enough for a spell! He'd learn him. He crawled faster, less careful now of making noise. The man inched along like sneaking on a goat and only one bullet to his name. Boone put his rifle aside, stood up and jumped.

His weight brought a whoof of air from the man. Boone got his forearm under the neck and up on the other shoulder and levered the man's chin up, straining the neck bones while he held him flat on his stomach with his weight. The man was hitting behind himself with his right hand. The knife in it ran hot along Boone's thigh. He grabbed for the hand, and they rolled over, making a crackle among the dead twigs. The camp came to life all at once as Summers let out a whoop. Boone heard shouts and moving feet, and the crack of a gun stock against bone. "That'll tame him." Boone had the wrist in his hand. The two hands, his and the man's, made a wide circle. The man quit wrenching of a sudden and got his butt up and bucked like a horse, trying to free himself. Boone hung to a handhold on his hair as he would have hung to a mane. Another pair of hands worked on the arm. "You can let him up for air, I'm thinking," said Summers.

Pambrun had kicked the fire into life. The crew was milling around it. Summers had Boone's man by the seat of his pants and the scruff of his neck. He pushed him into the firelight like a man pushing a boy. "Now, by Jesus, we'll make out what kind of a varmint you are! Bring t'other'n, Jourdonnais."

The man said, "Son of a bitch," and Summers cuffed him on the back of the neck with his fist.

Jourdonnais and Romaine came dragging another man, Jourdonnais saying sharply, "You 'ave the nice sleep, I hope, Romaine," and Romaine answering, "For a minute only. *Mon Dieu*, a man gives out."

They let the second man fall on his face in the dirt. Summers was tying the other up with a length of hide. He was a small man, dressed in skins and with his hair in three plaits, but a white man for all that. His face was as sharp as a mole's. It turned about, first one way and then another, as if to find something to bite. His eyes were small and wicked.

The man lying on his face was coming to. He got his elbows under him and pushed up and rolled over on his butt. His eyes looked around, at the bound man by his side, at Jourdonnais and Summers and the crew gathered about. A slow understanding came into them. He rubbed his head where the gun stock had clubbed it. He looked at the hunter, and a little smile worked at his mouth. "Dick Summers. Heap time no see."

"You want a kiss?"

"We had a awful dry. We was tryin' to scout up a drink."

Summers said, "Snake shit!" He had another length of hide in his hands.

"All back to bed!" Jourdonnais yelled. "The party she's done for now. In the morning she goes on again. We see about it then." He turned. "Come, Caudill, we mend the scratch, with balsam and beaver."

True to his word, Jourdonnais waited for dawn. Then, as the light came up in one big streamer he walked over to the two visitors. Summers had untied them, and they sat rubbing their wrists and ankles. Boone squirmed up, feeling the shallow cut on his leg pull with his movement, and went over and sat down by Jourdonnais. He saw Deakins open his blue eyes and flop over on his belly to watch. The men were stirring, getting up and stretching and chafing their beards with the heels of their hands. They lounged over within earshot. Pambrun was striking another fire, away from the dead ashes in front of the two men, nearer the shore. Already the mosquitoes were making little clouds around each man.

Jourdonnais said, "Now, by the good God, you tell us."

He had a pistol in his hand. Summers sat at his side, his rifle across his knees. Boone wondered if he had sat that way all night.

The bigger man spoke. "I told you, Frenchy. We was lookin' for a drink. We was tryin' to wet our dry." He had a head that bulged above the temples and came in and went out again, like the body of an ant. There was a bruise at the hairline where Summers had hit him. The little inquiring smile still curved the corners of his mouth.

"Tell the sons of bitches nothin'," said the smaller man out of the sharp face that seemed made for smelling. When Boone looked at him closer he was put in mind of a rattlesnake. The man had the same poisonous set of eye. When he talked it was like a snake striking.

"I've told 'em all."

"For a little," said Jourdonnais, wagging the pistol, "for a very little, I pull the trigger."

"No, you won't, Frenchy," the bigger man said. His gaze went around. "It would get back to St. Louis, sure as hell's afire. They'd raise your license and maybe stretch your neck." He put his head to one side, as if the hangman's rope were pulling it. "You're too smart for that, Frenchy. Think you could close all these mouths? The boys don't love you that much, Frenchy."

The smaller man snapped, "The *Vide Poche* bastard! Let's up and go."

"Not until we're ready and damn good and ready." It was Summers, talking soft.

Jourdonnais said, "You come from the new fort, Union—yes?"

Boone could see the smiling man was thinking fast. "Yes, from there, but not for them."

"Zeb Calloway's there, Summers; he's a hunter for the fort." Summers' glance flicked to Boone.

"McKenzie, he sent you, *n'est-ce-pas?*"

"No, we came on our own hook, I told you, nazpaw?"

"Who's McKenzie?" the little man asked.

"McKenzie," Summers said, "is the nigger that sent you here, to cut the boat loose or fire it, one, while we was asleep."

"You're an all-knowin' son of a bitch. Why'd you ask?"

Summers got up, took a step forward, seized the little man by his long hair and pulled him up. The man fought like a cat. Summers held him, waiting, and then hit him with his right fist, so hard a man would think it broke his neck. The little man thumped full length on his back and lay still, the teeth in his sharp snoot showing like a dead squirrel's.

"Your friend didn't have no mother, I'm thinkin', to teach him else but cuss words."

The other man shrugged, appearing hardly to notice.

Summers said, "This child can give you some of the same, Long Face, if it'll make you shine."

Long Face still smiled. "When a nigger's froze for a drink he's like to do anything."

"Like cuttin' a boat loose or settin' it afire?"

"Like raisin' a keg, or even a jug."

Jourdonnais fanned at the mosquitoes. "We can make them tell," he half-whispered. "So many ways to make the talk come, if a man know how. Fire, or water, or rope, or maybe the live snake."

Jourdonnais and Summers waited, watching the man's face. The smile was still on it. The little man closed his mouth. By and by he moved and got himself up to a sitting position again. The side of his mouth was swollen, and a little trickle of blood worked down from it.

"Ain't no call for it, Jourdonnais," Summers said.

"What?"

"We know, by God. This is Company doin's. They ain't wantin' us to horn in." Suddenly Boone thought of Cabanné down at the post at Council Bluffs and the trouble in his face and his careful words, "Take care, my friend, of Indians, and other things, too."

"You would let them go?" Jourdonnais asked.

"You're comin' close. Let 'em go, but without the horses they came on and without guns or knives or flint."

"Yes?" asked Jourdonnais, for Summers' tone showed he wasn't through.

"And with nary stitch of clothes. Rich doin's for the sting flies and such."

"Yes," said Jourdonnais with no question in his voice. "How far to Union?"

"Hundred miles and more."

"Far enough for *beaucoup* bellyful to the gnat."

Summers looked at the two men as he might have looked at dumb brutes. "They'll git ganted up some, too, carryin' empty paunches, and like as not have to dodge some Injuns or git their h'ar raised."

"Good. Good. And nex' we make a call on Monsieur McKenzie."

Out of his broken mouth the little man spit, "You're some, you are, now. Goin' to fight Union, like a rabbit after a b'ar. We'll see your scalps, we will, hangin' in the wind."

"If you get there, little snake," Jourdonnais said softly.

The bigger man studied their faces, and there was only the leavings of a smile on his face now. "We just aimed to raise a drink," he said.

17

When Boone thought back to the sneak-up on the camp he shook himself to set his senses right, remembering the heat that had come up in him when he thought one of the boatmen was stealing on Teal Eye. She was just a kitten, ten or twelve years at the outside, not truly old enough to interest a man that way. He pushed the thought of her away but still saw her, the face grave, the eyes big and noticing in a face too thin for an Indian, the front of her beginning to look like a woman sure enough when she didn't have her blanket folded across her. She put him in mind of some small, soft animal in a cage, watching, always watching, as if she had been taken out of a burrow or a woods into where everything was strange. She was more at home now than she had been, though, and moved around the deck and sometimes came on shore while Jourdonnais watched the men out of his stern black eye. Often Boone felt her eyes on him and turned and looked at her, and sometimes there was a shadow of a smile on a mouth that was as straight and neat as a good seam, but not thin like a seam. There was some fullness to it that made a man wonder if she knew how to kiss. He had seen Jim Deakins watching her many a time, his blue eyes sharp and his mouth laughing and saying little things, but she hardly seemed to notice.

Now that the *Mandan* had got to the upcountry her eyes were always on the banks, as if she thought to see a known face. One hour after another she looked to right and left, searching the bald hills, until a man almost expected to see her pappy, the chief, come galloping down the slopes with his feathers flying. Or, seeing the eyes watching and the face still and waiting, Boone figured maybe there was a hunger in her that the eyes filled, a hunger for the big bare hills and the streams running through the cottonwood and, far off and fair, the blue of a mountain like something a body might see through closed lids when he first laid himself down at night. Even when the smoke from the prairie fires was rolling and the eye couldn't see to the tops of the ridges, she still looked. Once, late at night when the moon lay bright on the river, Boone had awakened and made out her head above the side of the keelboat, pointed out where the far flames licked as if the edge of the world was on fire.

Summers gestured, saying, "Lookee!"

"What?"

"On the top of the hill there. On the rimrock."

A wild creature stood there, gazing down at them from under an arch of horn that seemed too much to carry.

"Rocky Mountain sheep," said Summers. "Bighorn. What the French call a *grossecorne*. You'll see a heap of 'em farther up."

Boone and Summers stood on the *passe avant*. Jim was rowing with the crew, not rowing very hard because a fair wind was pushing them along.

"There's a galore of 'em beyond the Yellowstone," Summers went on. "What you ain't like to see, now, is a white buffler."

"White buffler?"

"It ain't a buffler, proper, nor a white antelope, neither, though you hear that name put to it and a sight of others. They keep to the high peaks, they do, the tiptop of the mountains, in the clouds and snow. This nigger seen one once—just a skin, though, not a live one. Not many's seen a live one. A man has to climb some for that. He does, now. Come a fix in the mountains, I do believe I'd set out for one."

The sheep turned and made off, walking with little, dainty steps. "He's got a weight of horn," Boone said.

"There's them as'll say he lights on 'em, jumpin' from the cliffs, but I got doubts. Don't stand to reason. Likely he chips his horns fightin'. Sheep meat is good doin's."

Summers made a fire in his pipe. The boat slid by a thicket in which a catbird was making a racket. It occurred to Boone that they didn't hear the whippoorwill any more at evening. A swan whiter than milk paddled ahead of the boat, straining to outdistance it, swimming with its front out and neck up as if it was proud of itself. It breasted to the bank as the *Mandan* came on, and in a sudden awkward hurry flopped ashore. After the boat had passed, it eased back into the water and got hold of its pride again. The river was low and lazy now, flowing shallow between gray rock ridges that were grained slantwise and gave way here and there to hills that might have been leveled off with a saw. Romaine kept sounding with his stick. At the foot of the slopes buffalo-berry bushes shone like silver and juniper climbed in the rocks. Tongues of land ran out where the river turned, groved with cottonwood that grew from a tangle of undergrowth.

"Sooner in the season," said Summers between puffs on his pipe, "the wild roses are right purty. They pink up nigh the whole shore hereabouts."

The sun was just starting down from overhead when the *Mandan* reached the Yellowstone, which came in wide and easy, like a man slowing down after his race was won. It looked to be as big as the Missouri. Around its mouth tall cottonwoods grew, their leaves turning, making a rustling sound in the wind above the willow thickets that buffalo had crowded paths through. It made the Missouri look naked, for here the river flowed through a prairie that rolled on and on, one hill leveling off and climbing to another, as far as the eye could reach.

Jourdonnais put to on the point of land between the rivers. He was singing a song under his breath, and when his glance caught Boone's he smiled, sending the points of his mustache up. "We make 'er, the Roche Jaune."

They stepped to shore and climbed to an easy plain that ran back for two miles or more. "Gin'ral Ashley had his fort on this here tongue between the rivers," said Summers. "Don't reckon there's aught of it left." Jourdonnais gave everyone a drink.

They ate buffalo tongue and marrowbone while a flock of crows quarreled in the woods, and after a while pushed on again, taking it easy, since Jourdonnais for once seemed to have lost his hurry. Boone wished he would hump it. Just ahead was Uncle Zeb, who had led him out here, even if unknowing—Uncle Zeb, who didn't like Pap and talked of Injun country like a man under a spell. He could see him in his mind's eye: the eyes looking out from under their heavy brows and the mouth working under the long nose and the face smiling now and then at him and Dan as they begged him to tell some more. It was a long time since he had seen Uncle Zeb. Still, a growed man didn't change much. He hoped Uncle Zeb would be glad to see him.

Against Fort Union the other posts that Boone had seen along the river seemed like hunters' wigwams. Big square pickets, evened off at the top and shining bright and new, marched around it, fencing in a piece of land a man could set a cornfield in. At the southwest and northwest corners blockhouses stood, broad as a barn, rising high to pointed four-way roofs. Low down on them Boone could see loopholes for cannon. A flagstaff rose from inside the pickets, its tip moving to a flag that rolled and snapped with the wind.

The fort was on the north side of the river, maybe fifty feet from the bank, on a prairie that looked to go back for a mile before it came to a ridge of hills. There were a dozen or so Indian lodges pitched back of the fort and beyond them a little bunch of horses grazed. Standing in the stern, Boone heard a noise behind him, and turned to see Teal Eye, her head barely raised over the cargo box, the mouth a little open and the eyes looking. Jourdonnais had moved some boxes around her so's to shut her from sight while the *Mandan* was tied up at the fort. Another keelboat lay at the landing place—a bigger, fancier one than the *Mandan,* with a cabin in her and long sweep oars that men would work by walking. While Boone watched, the big gate in the front of the post began to fold open, smoke puffed from the loopholes and swept up in the wind, and the boom of the cannons sounded.

The swivel answered, and the crew shipped oars and got up and took the rifles Jourdonnais had let them have, and fired a ragged volley. Rifle shots were sounding from the fort, and people were coming from the gate.

Jourdonnais was shouting, "All right. Back to the oars. *Mon Dieu*, you think the *Mandan* get there by herself!" He crooked a finger at Boone. "You watch the little one," he said. "See she stay among the boxes, with the robe thrown over. No one must see. Summers try to tell her, these Rocks, they maybe kill her. And McKenzie, no. He must not find out. You see?"

Boone stepped back and put his hand on the head that peeped above the cargo box. She went down willingly, her gaze lingering on him, and he fixed the robe so's to leave her some air. Afterward, seeing Painter lying stretched in the sun, he put him in with her and heard him go to purring as her hand stroked him.

Indians and whites lined the shore—what they called Assiniboine, or Rock, Indians, mostly naked from the belly up except for their buffalo robes, and workmen in jeans and cotton shirts and moccasins, and here and there a man in a city suit such as a body would see in St. Louis. Boone's gaze ran among them, looking for Uncle Zeb. There weren't more than two or three Indians had leggings on; the rest were barelegged, and most of them barefooted, too. Red and white, they were laughing and talking, ready to give a hand as the *Mandan* pulled in. Some of the Indians waded out in the water.

Boone wondered if he ought to holler if he saw Uncle Zeb, or wait quiet and make himself known when the time came. Uncle Zeb was bound to be about; Long Face had said he worked for the fort. The Indians looked like Sioux, though a good many of them had their hair cropped shorter so it just hit the shoulders. One buck had it fixed over his forehead and ears like a mane. His eyes looked through it like a rabbit through a bush. He wore a little white leather cap. Their faces were red with vermilion and looked greasy in the bright sun, except for one that was painted as black as any nigger's. Uncle Zeb would know what the black was for. With their straggly hair and bare feet and such, they looked like a poor bunch. Boone saw two bear-claw necklaces but no beads or shells like the Indians down river decorated their heads with. A few of them had guns and every last one of them carried a bow. The guns had bright yellow nails driven into the stocks and small pieces of red cloth tied on the fixings that held the ramrods. Most of the men carried bird-wing fans and some of them had little decorated sticks in their hair. As Boone's eyes hunted among them, one buck pulled out the stick and began worrying at his pipe with it. The Frenchmen on the *Mandan* were eying the squaws, who stood back a little, smiling. They had on store-bought clothes, and Boone imagined they were the women that belonged to the white men at the fort. Uncle Zeb wasn't in the crowd; Boone had looked at every face.

The Indians who had waded out in the water were trying to climb aboard, and Jourdonnais was shouting, *"Non! Non!* Push off them! Push!"

As the *Mandan* eased in, a man came out of the gate and walked through the crowd, stepping like God. He wore a dark suit, fresh-ironed, that must have cost a sight of money, and a shirt with ruffles down the front that gleamed white in the sun.

"So," he said, "the *Mandan* made it." He had a broad forehead and broad cheeks and a broad chin, Boone saw between spells of shoving Indians from the side, and the hair that showed under his city hat looked soft and black as a crow's wing.

"We aim to talk to you, McKenzie," Summers said, grunting, "if we can keep the Rocks off."

The broad-faced man turned about and shouted, "Pierre! Baptiste!" as if he was used to having people jump when he spoke. McKenzie's head jerked toward the *Mandan.* "Keep everybody off." The two dark-faced men who had come forward trotted up the river bank to a willow clump and came back with long switches in their hands.

Jourdonnais said, "Your two men, who 'ave welcome us on the Little Missouri, they be along. Maybe here now. So?"

The men with the switches were laying about with them, driving the Indians back up the shore.

The cold eye of McKenzie rested on Jourdonnais without a flicker. "I don't know what you mean. Come on to the house."

"We thought you wouldn't be expectin' us," Summers put in.

Boone stood still in the stern, watching them and watching the robe that covered Teal Eye and sending his gaze among the people on shore on the chance that he might have missed Uncle Zeb after all.

Jourdonnais turned back. "No one leave the boat. We be a minute only, and then go on. You hear? Romaine?"

McKenzie said, "Come on," and he and Summers and Jourdonnais walked to the gate and disappeared inside.

Jourdonnais' eyes were busy as they walked through the grounds to the back where the house of the bourgeois stood. The flagstaff rose from the middle of the quadrangle, and near it was a cannon, trained on the gate. A half-dozen tepees were pitched near-by, which Jourdonnais supposed belonged to the half-breeds employed by the fort. Along the wall of pickets were houses for clerks and interpreters and *engagés,* and storerooms and workshops and other buildings whose uses he could only guess. Some of them weren't yet completed. Carpenters moved about them, pounding and sawing. Above the beat of the hammers and the clang of a blacksmith's sledge he heard the cackle of hens and the lowing of a cow.

Everything was new, from the high cottonwood fence and the cottonwood rifle walk that ran near its top to the cottonwood home of the bourgeois which looked at them from four real-glass windows. And everything was big and built with care, indicating money and organization and fine plans.

For a moment, as he entered the door of the large house, Jourdonnais' spirits sank. How could he, a *Vide Pôche,* succeed against so much, against gentlemen like Monsieur McKenzie, who wore a ruffled shirt and had an air that made men stand back? His whole venture seemed suddenly mad and hopeless, the picture of himself in St. Louis smoking good cigars and wearing expensive clothes, saying, *"Bonjour, Monsieur Chouteau,"* and hearing *"Bonjour, Monsieur Jourdonnais. Comment allez-vous?"* Jourdonnais shook himself as he went through the door, making himself think again of the rich trade of the Blackfeet and the *Mandan* loaded with liquor.

There was a movement in the room as they entered and then the slow closing of a door, shutting from sight the face of a young Indian woman. McKenzie motioned them to chairs that were stuffed to rest the butt and back. Summers sat forward, as if he were laying an egg. He had been on the ground too much, sitting cross-legged, to be comfortable in a chair. McKenzie got a bottle and glasses out of a cabinet. It was fine French brandy, so high in spirit that it seemed to evaporate in the mouth.

"Now, what was it?" McKenzie asked. There was a faint clipped quality in his speech, such as Jourdonnais had noted in other Scotsmen.

Jourdonnais looked at Summers, wanting him to do the talking.

"You know," answered Summers, his gray eyes unyielding before McKenzie's stare. "We catched 'em, the freeman—leastwise, he was free once—that the Indians call Long Face, and a hoss with a snoot like a weasel. I never seen him afore."

McKenzie passed Spanish segars while his eyes studied Summers and his strong face kept as blank as a rock. He refilled their glasses.

"They'll show up, maybe, if the gnats don't bleed 'em to death, or the Injuns raise their h'ar. We turned 'em loose like they was borned."

McKenzie said, "I know them. Damned nuisances. Traded in a pack and stayed around." He turned to Jourdonnais. "You understand, being a bourgeois, what a problem men like that are, hanging around after their business is done. Nuisances, and a danger, too."

"Yes, monsieur."

Summers said, "Bein' on your payroll maybe had somethin' to do with their stayin' around."

"They weren't on the payroll."

"Like hell!"

McKenzie studied Summers for a long moment. When he spoke, though, it was just to ask them to have another drink.

Jourdonnais felt the brandy strengthening him. Feeling it, and seeing Summers sitting there, hard and unimpressed, he straightened, while there edged up in him the stubborn ambition that had brought him this far.

"They thought to cut the boat loose, or fire it," he said, making himself look straight into McKenzie's face.

"How do you know?"

Summers answered, "Plain as paint."

McKenzie drank and set down his glass and leaned over toward Jourdonnais. "Look. We know what you plan to do. Naturally, no opposition can come up the Missouri without the American Fur Company knowing about it. We know the Blackfoot country better than you do. It's our country. We have plans for it. But the time isn't ripe, even for us. And if it isn't ripe for an outfit like ours, how close to ripe do you think it is for you?"

Jourdonnais said, "We pick it green, then."

"You'll get rubbed out, every one of you—killed and scalped and left to rot. You don't know the Blackfeet."

"We know some things," Jourdonnais said, thinking of Teal

Eye, the chief's daughter, hidden now between the boxes, under the buffalo robe. "We go on."

"Go on, and you'll go under."

Jourdonnais spread his hands.

McKenzie let his voice drop. "You are reasonable men. You know the odds are against you. As reasonable men you're going to be interested in our proposition."

"What?" asked Summers.

"We'll buy your cargo, lock, stock, and barrel, and pay you double first cost for it."

"So?"

"And that's not all. We'll pay you to take a cargo down, a full cargo—packs and buffalo tongues—and pay whatever you ask—within reason, of course."

Summers glanced at Jourdonnais, as if waiting for him to speak.

"I think we go on," Jourdonnais said slowly.

"Goddam it, man, you can't do better."

"I think we go on."

"What more do you want?"

"It ain't for sale, McKenzie," Summers said. "You might as well understand."

"For two to one, and a load back? What do you expect?"

Jourdonnais spoke slowly. "Four or five to one, maybe more, like the American Fur Company."

"We won't average two to one. Four or five to one on one deal, a total loss on another." He poured brandy into their glasses again.

"Still, we go on."

McKenzie drank and sat back while his lips savored the brandy. His gaze went from Jourdonnais to Summers and back to Jourdonnais, but it was as if, instead of them, he looked at thoughts. Jourdonnais was reminded, somehow, of a hunter putting a fresh load in his gun.

"You won't be fighting the Blackfeet alone," he said, measuring his words. "The British at Edmonton House will see that they have plenty of guns, and powder and ball to match. They'll egg the Indians on and maybe offer a secret bounty for your scalps."

Jourdonnais said, "We go on."

McKenzie's calm gave way suddenly. "You goddam fools!" The blood climbed his neck and flushed his broad face.

Summers got up—almost lazily, it seemed to Jourdonnais. "You're a little Jesus here, seems like, but not to us, by beaver! This nigger's got a notion to see if you'll bleed."

McKenzie looked at him, bold and calculating, while the anger died in his face, leaving it again as blank as a rock. "I'm sorry," he said, as if he really wasn't. "Sit down. No insult intended." Summers perched on his chair again, and McKenzie poured brandy.

"All right," McKenzie went on after a pause. "You won't sell at any price. You don't want to talk reason. I have just one more thing to say. We can send a keelboat up, too, and fort up right next to you and offer more goods and undersell you clear down the line." He was studying them again. "Sometimes we do that, taking a loss just to discourage opposition."

"You could," agreed Jourdonnais, thinking of little Teal Eye, wondering if the fort, big as it was, had such a store of whisky as was on the *Mandan*.

"You could if you have the men for it," Summers said. "Come one, come all, we'll go on."

"Very well," said McKenzie. His tone was short, and it seemed as an afterthought, as something demanded by common politeness, that he added, "You'll stay the night at the post?"

"*Non.* We pull up a little an' keep the crew together. They like whisky too well, and squaws."

"Suit yourself then."

"Zeb Calloway about?" Summers inquired.

"Drunken scoundrel. He's out for meat. May be back about sundown."

"So's we understand each other," Summers said, standing in the doorway. "We let those two niggers go. Next ones we'll make wolf meat of."

A polite smile was on McKenzie's lips. "Next ones will be the Blackfeet, unless you come to your senses. You'll have your fill of meat making." He held his hand out to them.

As they passed through the grounds and went out the gate Summers said, "Reckon we're fools not to take his offer."

"Maybe."

"Still, this child 'ud rather be scalped by a Blackfoot than skun by a nabob."

18

The long western sun lay flat on the river and plain. Down the hills to the northeast a string of pack animals filed, looking black against the summer tan of the bluffs.

"Could be that's Zeb," Summers said, squinting. "McKenzie said likely he'd get in afore dark." He and Jim Deakins and Boone stood behind the fort. The *Mandan* was moored two miles up river, where Jourdonnais was watching cargo and crew. Summers had suggested that the three of them come back to the fort to talk to Calloway. "That hoss knows a heap," he had said to Jourdonnais, "besides bein' kin to Caudill. I figger I better see him."

A little piece from where they stood a dozen lodges of the Assiniboines, set in a half-circle, pointed at the sky. Once in a while smoke came from one of them, rising from the smoke hole at the top in a thin wisp, as if a man with a pipe was blowing through it. The voices of the Indians, of the men talking and the squaws laughing and squabbling and a baby squalling came clear in the evening air. Dogs nosed around the lodges and sometimes faced around in the direction of the three white men and barked as if they had suddenly remembered to do something forgotten.

"Let's set," said Summers, letting himself down to the ground.

The pack string snaked down from the hills and headed toward them across the plain. A mounted man was at the head of it, and another one at its tail.

Summers smoked and watched and said presently, "I do believe it's your Uncle Zeb, Caudill."

It was Uncle Zeb, all right, looking older, and gray as a coon. A man couldn't go wrong on that long nose and the eyes that peered out from under brows as bushy as a bird's nest.

Boone wanted to get up and shout hello and go out and give his hand, but something held him in.

Summers got to his feet easy, so's not to affright the mules that were packed high and wide with meat. "H'ar ye, Zeb?"

Uncle Zeb stared out of his tangle of brow like a man sighting a rifle. "How," he answered, his voice stiff .and cracked as a man's is after a long silence. Then, "This child'll be a Digger if it ain't Dick Summers."

Summers motioned. "This here's someone you seen afore."

Uncle Zeb fixed his gaze on Boone. He spit a brown stream over the shoulder of his horse. "So?"

Summers waited, and Uncle Zeb looked at Boone again and said, "Ain't my pup, I'm thinkin'."

"Close," answered Summers. "Don't you know your own nephy, old hoss?"

Boone asked, "How you, Uncle Zeb?"

"For Christ sake!"

"I reckon you don't know me, I've changed that much."

Uncle Zeb spit again and put his mind to remembering. "One of Serenee's young'ns, ain't ye?"

"Boone Caudill."

"For Christ sake!"

Uncle Zeb didn't smile. He sat on his horse, his shoulders slumped and his mouth over at one side, making his face look crooked. A calf was bawling inside the fort as if he had lost his ma. "Stay thar," Uncle Zeb said at last. "I'll get shet of these here mules. Ho, Deschamps." The string got into slow motion, the heads of the mules jerking as the slack went out of the tie ropes. The rider at the tail was an Indian, or a half-breed anyway. For a bridle he had a long hair rope tied about the lower jaw of his horse. The stirrups of his saddle were made of skin and shaped like shoes. He stared as he went by, lounging on his horse, with his rifle carried crosswise before him.

Jim and Summers glanced at Boone. He picked up a blade of grass and tied a knot in it. "It's a spell since he seed me."

The Assiniboine squaws were playing a game, laughing and squealing as they played. Three bucks passed by, making toward the fort. They stopped on the way to ask for some tobacco. A little sand rat that Summers called a gopher came out of a hole and sat up, straight as a peg. He whistled a thin pipe of a whistle that struck the ears like the point of an awl. Boone tossed a pebble at him, and he dived into his hole and then nosed back up, just his head showing, and the black unwinking eye. The sun had got behind a bank of clouds and painted them blood red. It was like an Indian had spit into a hand of vermilion and rubbed the western sky with it. Boone got out the pipe he had traded for down river.

In a little while Uncle Zeb came back, walking stiff and uneven from the saddle. His leggings were black and worn, with no more than a half-dozen pieces of fringe left. He wore an old Indian shirt smeared with blood, which had a colored circle on the chest made of porcupine quills. Instead of a hat he had a red handkerchief tied around his head. He took a bottle out of his shirt and sat down and got the cork out, not saying anything. Summers brought out another bottle. Uncle Zeb passed the first one round, watching it go from hand to hand as if he could hardly wait. The first thing he said was, "Can't buy a drink on'y at night, goddam McKenzie!"

It was getting cold, with the sun low and hid, too cold even for the gnats that like to ate a man alive. A little breeze ran along the ground, making Boone draw into himself. Off a piece he could see some whitened bones, and beyond them some more, and beyond them still more where buffalo had been butchered. Three Indian dogs that looked like wolves except for one that was blotched black and white were smelling around them. The dogs were just bones themselves, with spines that humped up and ran crooked so that the feet didn't set square underneath them. The calf inside the fort was still bawling.

As if it didn't make much difference Uncle Zeb asked, "How's Serenee makin' out?"

"All right, last I seen her."

Uncle Zeb grunted and lifted the bottle and took a powerful drink. He slumped back, in a mood, as if waiting for the whisky to put life into him. He said, "Christ sake!" and took another drink.

Summers said, "This here's Jim Deakins, crew of the *Mandan*."

"Pleased to meetcha," Jim said.

Uncle Zeb got out tobacco and stuffed it in his cheek and let it soak. "Why're you here?"

"I fit with Pap."

"Measly son of a bitch. By God! If'n you're any part like him—?" He spit and sucked in his lower lip afterward to get the drop off.

"He's some now," Summers said. "He's true beaver. Catched the clap and fit Indians and killed a white b'ar a'ready."

Uncle Zeb looked at Summers. "Never could figger why my sister teamed up with that skunk, less'n she had to." He turned. "How old be ye?"

"Comin' eighteen."

Uncle Zeb thought for a while, then said, "You got no cause to be set up, account of your pap."

"Be goddammed to you! You take after Pap your own self."

"Sic 'im, Boone!" It was Jim, looking across at him with a gleam in his blue eye.

Uncle Zeb only grunted. He started the bottle around again, taking a swig of it first himself and ending the round with another. "This nigger's got a turrible dry."

Summers was smiling at the ground as if he was pleased. "Caudill and Deakins, here, aim to be mountain men."

"Huh! They better be borned ag'in."

"How so?"

"Ten year too late anyhow." Uncle Zeb's jaw worked on the tobacco. "She's gone, goddam it! Gone!"

"What's gone?" asked Summers.

Boone could see the whisky in Uncle Zeb's face. It was a face that had known a sight of whisky, likely, red as it was and swollen-looking.

"The whole shitaree. Gone, by God, and naught to care savin' some of us who seen 'er new." He took the knife from his belt and started jabbing at the ground with it, as if it eased his feelings. He was silent for a while.

"This was man's country onc't. Every water full of beaver and a galore of buffler any ways a man looked, and no crampin' and crowdin'. Christ sake!"

To the east, where the hill and sky met, Boone saw a surge of movement and guessed that it was buffalo until it streamed down the slope, making for them, and came to be a horse herd.

Summers' gray eye slipped from Boone to Uncle Zeb. "She ain't sp'iled, Zeb," he said quietly. "Depends on who's lookin'."

"Not sp'iled! Forts all up and down the river, and folk everywhere a man might think to lay a trap. And greenhorns comin' up, a heap of 'em—greenhorns on every boat, hornin' in and sp'ilin' the fun. Christ sake! Why'n't they stay to home? Why'n't they leave it to us as found it? By God, she's ours by rights." His mouth lifted for the bottle. "God, she was purty onc't. Purty and new, and not a man track, savin' Injuns', on the whole scoop of her."

The horses were coming in fast, running and kicking like colts with the coolness that had come on the land. The gopher was out of his hole again, moving in little flirts and looking up and piping. It was beginning to get dark. The fire in the west was about out; low in the east one star burned. Boone wished someone would quiet that calf.

Summers said, "'Pears you swallered a prickly pear, hoss."

"Huh!" Uncle Zeb reached in and fingered the cud from his mouth and put a fresh one in.

"Beaver's a fair price, a mighty fair price. It is, now."

"Price don't figger without a man's got the beaver," Uncle Zeb said while his mouth moved to set the chew right.

The horses trotted by, kicking up a dust, shying and snorting as they passed the seated men. Behind them came four riders, dressed in the white blanket coats that the workmen at the fort wore.

"I mind the time beaver was everywhere," Uncle Zeb said. His voice had turned milder and had a faraway tone in it, as if the whisky had started to work deep and easy in him. Or was it that he was just old and couldn't hold to a feeling? "I do now. Everywhere. It was poor doin's, them days, not to trap a good pack every hunt. And now?" He fell silent as if there was nothing fitting a man could lay tongue to.

"Look," he said, straightening a little, "another five year and there'll be naught but coarse fur, and it goin' fast. You, Boone, and you, Deakins, stay here and you'll be out on the prairie, hide huntin', chasin' buffler and skinnin' 'em, and seein' the end come to that, too."

"Not five year," said Summers. "More like fifty."

"Ahh! The beaver's nigh gone now. Buffler's next. Won't be even a goddam poor bull fifty years ahead. You'll see plows comin' across the plains, and people settin' out to farm." He leaned forward, bringing his hands up. "They laugh at this nigger, but it's truth all the same. Can't be t'otherwise. The Company alone's sendin' twenty-five thousand beaver skins out in a year, and forty thousand or more hides. Besides, a heap of buffler's killed by hunters and never skinned, and a heap of skins is used by the Injuns, and a passel of 'em drownds every spring. Ahh!"

"There's beaver aplenty yit," replied Summers. "A man's got to go after them. He don't catch 'em inside a fort, or while makin' meat."

"Amen and go to hell, Dick! On'y, whisky's hard to come by off on a hunt. Gimme a pull on your bottle. I got a turrible dry."

Boone heard his own voice, sounding tight and toneless. "She still looks new to me, new and purty." In the growing darkness he could feel Uncle Zeb's eyes on him, looking at him from under their thickets—tired old eyes that whisky had run red rivers in.

"We're pushin' on," said Summers, "beyant the Milk, to Blackfoot country."

"This child heerd tell."

"Well, now?"

"This nigger don't know, Dick. It's risky—powerful risky, like you know. Like as not you'll go under."

"We got a heap of whisky, and powder and ball and guns, and beads and vermilion and such."

"You seen Blackfeet drunk, Dick?"

"A few."

"They're mean. Oh, by God, they're mean! An' tricky and onreliable. But you know that as good as me. Got a interpreter?"

"Just this hoss. I know it a little, and sign talk, of course. We ain't got beaver for a passel of interpreters."

"You dodged Blackfeet enough to learn a little, I'm thinkin'."

"Plenty plews there."

"They don't do a dead nigger no good. Pass the bottle."

"How are you and McKenzie?"

"The bourgeway bastard, with his fancy getup and his tablecloth and his nose in the air like a man stinks! Y'know the clerks can't set to his table without a coat on? And the chinchin' company, squeezin' hell out of a man and chargin' him Christ knows what for belly rot! McKenzie pays this child, and this child kills his meat, but that's as fur as she goes. I'm just tradin' meat for whisky."

"Zeb," Summers said, "this here's secret as the grave. Wouldn't do for it to get out. It wouldn't now."

"My mouth don't run to them cayutes, drunk or sober."

"We got a little squaw, daughter of a Blackfoot chief, she says, that was stole by the Crows and made a getaway. A boat picked her up, nigh dead, and took her on to St. Louis last fall. We're takin' her back."

"Umm. Injuns don't set much store by squaws."

"Blackfeet like their young'ns more'n most."

"A squaw?"

"I know, but still?"

"Might be." Uncle Zeb was silent for what seemed a long time. "This nigger heerd something from the Rocks about that Crow party. Heavy Otter—ain't that the chief?"

"That's the name she gave. We're countin' on her a heap, Zeb."

"Umm."

"We make talk purty slick, what with her l'arnin' a little white man's talk and me knowin' some Blackfoot. Me and her together, we don't need no interpreter."

"This nigger don't like it."

"Your stick wouldn't float that way? We'll cut you in, and handsome. Better'n bein' a fort hunter."

In the darkness Boone could see Uncle Zeb's head shake. "It ain't a go, Dick. It ain't now."

"I recollect when it would be."

It seemed to Boone that all of time was in Uncle Zeb's voice. "Not now, hoss. Not any more. This child ain't scared, like you know, but it ain't worth it. It's tolerable here, and whisky's plenty even if it costs a heap."

"What you hear about the Blackfeet?"

"The Rocks say they're away from the river, gone north and east to buffler. Me, now, I'd say go to Maria's River, or along there, and fort up, quicker'n scat."

"Too fur. Take a month, even with Jourdonnais blisterin' the crew. Buffler an' Blackfeet would be back afore we could set ourselves."

"Uh-huh. There's mostly some Injuns around Maria's River all the time. Anyways, get your fort up fast."

"That's how this child figgered. A little fort, quick, ready for 'em when they come back to the river."

"It's risky doin's, anyways you lay your sights."

"You figger the Company's like to take a hand in this game?"

"McKenzie's got plans for the Blackfeet. He's makin' medicine. He is, now. Come fall or winter, he'll p'int that way, or try to. But he'll let ye be, likely, thinkin' the Blackfeet and the British'll handle things. He's slick. He ain't wantin' a finger p'inted at him, now you're so fur up."

"He said he might send a boat up, to buck us."

"No sech. He ain't got the hands right now. If this nigger smells a stink afore you pass the Milk, he'll get word to you one way or t'other."

"Heap obliged, hoss."

Uncle Zeb got up unsteadily, his knees cracking as he straightened them out. "If it gits to talk, ask for Big Leg of the Piegans, and give a present, sayin' it's from me. We're brothers, he said onc't."

"That's some, now. Obliged again."

Uncle Zeb walked away, swaying some and not saying goodbye. The three others made off in the direction of the *Mandan*, waking the Indian dogs, which started barking all at once. They could hear loud voices and laughs and sometimes a whoop from inside the fort. "Liquorin' up," said Summers. The calf had stopped bawling.

Boone's head swam with the whisky. It was the first he had let himself drink much of in a long time. "I reckon old age just come on Uncle Zeb," he said. After a silence he added, "It's fair country yit." Summers was keeping them in the open, away from the river.

"It's fair, sure enough," Deakins agreed.

Summers said, "Watch out for them pesky prickly pear. They go right through a moccasin."

19

Already autumn was coming to the upper Missouri, the short northern autumn that was here and gone like a bird flying. Flecked in the green of the cottonwood trees, telltale leaves hung yellow, giving limply to the breeze. The blood-red berries of the *graisse de boeuf* sparkled along the silver limbs. It was often chill in the morning, warming as the sun got up and lay on the land in a golden glow, and cooling again as it finished its shortened arch and fell in flames among the hills.

The men were lean and hard, and brown as the Blackfeet who populated Jourdonnais' mind. Day on day he drove them, routing them out before the sun was up, keeping them at the line until the hills darkened and the light lay pale along the water like something remembered from the day. It was nearly always the line now, the line which was the last resort and main reliance, for the wind was seldom good. The men went half-naked along the soft shores, sinking to the knee, to the crotch, sometimes to the belly. They floundered in the mud, or waded out into the water or jumped from point to point among the drift, falling sometimes and coming up wet and sputtering but going on. Where the river permitted they splashed into it and pushed the *Mandan* with their hands; when they had to, they climbed along the bluffs like the *grossecorne*.

They were a crew now, such a crew as not even the Company could boast, wise in the ways of the Missouri and the keelboat, strong and long-enduring and not so timid as before, though the rattlesnake frightened them, and the great bear. Always with them he had Summers or Caudill or Deakins to kill the snake and shoot the bear, and to watch for the *Pieds Noirs*. Not an Indian had they seen all the way from Union to the Milk and beyond—not an Assiniboine, not a Blackfoot, not a man of any kind. It was as if the land was deserted, except for the elk and the deer and the buffalo and the bear. Everywhere one saw them, at every bend, on every island, on every bar—not the great herds of buffalo that made the earth tremble, but wanderers, three or four or a dozen, browsing on the bottom grass, drinking in the stream. The hunters killed enough meat for half a dozen crews, taking only the choice parts, spiking them to a great pair of elk antlers that had been placed in the prow. At night and in the early morning the wolves howled over what was left. Along the wild meadows bones were clustered, one skeleton and then another, where Indians and maybe the bold mountain men had butchered in their turn. *Mon Dieu*, what a place for game! The Kentucky hunters could not be restrained. They awakened eager every morning, to shoot more bear, more buffalo, more elk and deer and bighorn, coming in later with the red meat slung all around them and maybe with the head and claws of a bear or the rough roll of a rattlesnake with the head smashed flat.

The *Mandan* went on, the river lessening and the land rising into shapes that no one could believe, like castles and ruins that old folk remembered from France, like forts and battlements, like shapes a man would see only when he had the fever or a craziness in the head. Yellow, red, and white along the shores, and flashings like the mirrored sun and, above and beyond, the prairie, the so-big plains rolling on, yellow and dry now so that even the single wolf left a slow trail of dust. A raw, vast, lonesome land, too big, too empty. It made the mind small and the heart tight and the belly drawn, lying wild and lost under such a reach of sky as put a man in fear of heaven. It was the little things that made one at home in the world, that made him happy and forgetful; neighbors to hail and supper on a table and a good woman to love, and the tavern and fire and small talk, and walls and roofs to shut out the terrors of God, except for glimpse enough to keep the sinner Christian.

Often discouragement rode Jourdonnais, making his voice harsh and his way hard. It seemed to him then that not even the good God could help him. For success, all must turn right and in its time: the Indians must stay away until the fort was built; they must come when it was ready, and come with fine furs—beaver and otter and mink; he must do his business quickly and be gone, before ice closed the river. How could he know that the Blackfeet had furs? Maybe already they had been to Fort de Prairie and traded with the British. How long to build a fort? Two weeks? Three? More? How keep the Indians friendly? How keep them off the boat? How prevent them from overrunning the fort, if the fort really ever was built? How manage them drunk? How get word to them when all was ready? How make them hold back the shot or the arrow until they could hear about Teal Eye?

When his thoughts were dark he made himself think about Teal Eye, who was like a cricket now, happy and active, looking out, saying things as if to herself, with an expression on the little face of one coming home and seeing maybe the remembered gate, or the old fence, or the house in the trees after a long time away. The daughter of Heavy Otter coming to her father's lodge. The daughter being brought home by the white brother. Yes, if the nation wished, he, Jourdonnais, the white brother, would keep a post among them and send not one boat but two and maybe three every season, and perhaps build more posts so that the Blackfeet had not to travel far. Let them bring their beaver to him, and he would bring them strouding and paints and sky-blue beads and powder and ball and alcohol and all that made a nation happy and great.

Little Teal Eye, like a bird, like a fledgling hopping! It could be that this journey was not a single gamble for a few thousand dollars only, for one cargo of fine furs and then the end, but the beginning of a big trading house, like American or Hudson's Bay, dealing in fine furs and in coarse, in robes and buffalo tongues. Maybe he would wear a ruffled shirt and a fine suit, and people would stand back waiting on his words. *Peut-être. Peut-être.*

The little squaw, with an eye like the bluewing teal! How the young Caudill had fought when Chouquette had tried to slip into the bushes after her! There was a flame in his eye and a look like thunder in his face, for all that he hardly spoke. Chouquette was a thick and powerful man, wise at fighting with fists and knees and thumbs and, need be, the knife, but he was no match against the other's fury. Even his knife failed him, kicked away as he got it out and tried to arise. And at the end, before those flames in the eye and the storm in the face, he had cried out for mercy. It was good, Jourdonnais thought, to have another to protect Teal Eye, but it puzzled him still that one should have fought for her who seldom looked at her and then only with an unmoving face. He shrugged inwardly, telling himself the way of Americans was often strange.

For all the want of Indians, he and Summers were more careful than before. Two men stood each watch now, and at night the *Mandan* tied up on the south shore, away from the side the Blackfeet were thought to roam in. The swivel always was trained on the bank. The crew slept on board, lying crowded fore and aft except for a little space around Teal Eye's lodge, where he or Summers lay.

The men looked like corpses, with their blankets drawn over their faces as a protection against the mosquitoes that made a cloud about every man, day and night, unless the wind blew or the cold came. The mosquitoes flushed out of the willows in the daytime, out of the sedgy grass that the feet of the boatmen disturbed, in streams that ran like wisps of smoke and grew into wheeling circles around each head. Let a man stop to light his pipe or load his rifle and before he was done they covered his hands and face. They plagued the men at the cordelle, who rubbed mud thick on themselves and learned to fight with one hand and pull with the other without losing more than a little of their pace. Only the grasshoppers, a crawling carpet in the faded grass above the bluffs, were so many, and grasshoppers were no bother except when a stiff wind caught them and drove them hard against the face. They only crawled or flew away clacking, showing red or yellow wings spotted with black.

This place, Summers? *Non?* It is clear and behind it the wood is plenty for the fort. *Non?* You think the hill too close, so Indians could fire inside the palisades. Time passes, Summers. South bank or north? No matter? This place? It is beautiful. *Non?* This one then? *Mon Dieu,* we do not have eternity! It take time to build a fort and do the trading. Another day, you think? Two? How many? *Enfant de garce!* Here? Here? Ah, now, at last!

They were eighteen days out from Fort Union, above a stream that Summers thought was Teapot Creek. The hunter's hand had gestured toward a little flatland that ran back treeless for two hundred yards and more. "Good as we'll do. She's clear enough at the sides, and the trees at the back ain't too close but still close enough to give us timber. No hills near enough to bother."

"Good! Good!" Jourdonnais blew the breath from his lungs, letting himself relax for a moment, but only for a moment. He looked at the sun. "We 'ave time for a start."

Summers nodded. "Time to fort up some." He went forward and adjusted the swivel.

They pulled to and put the crew ashore, distributing powder and ball first. Afterwards Summers studied the hills with the glass. "I'll get 'em going. Caudill! Deakins! Take a look yonder." To the crew he said, "We'll stack the rifles where they're handy." He set the boatmen to dragging in fallen logs and piling them close to shore so as to make a low three-sided enclosure which opened on the river. "Injuns l'arned me this. It's a help, come a fight."

It was growing dark when they finished. Pambrun was warming food in the fire he had set above the cargo box. "Best put her acrost," said Summers, scanning the hills. "Don't hurt to play safe." He whistled for Caudill and Deakins, giving the high two-toned cry of the curlew. "Tomorrow we can get to work on a sure-enough fort."

"*Oui.*" Jourdonnais' heart was lighter than it had been in days. He felt assurance rising in him, as if he had had a big drink of good brandy. In two weeks, of a certainty, they could build the fort and be ready. He let himself see the Indians streaming down from the hills, shaking the hands of the white men who had brought one of the nation home. He saw quick and peaceful trading, much fine furs, money. As the *Mandan* moved into the south bank he looked down at Teal Eye and smiled. She was like one of them now. If not quite easy in their company, she had a kind of shy and watching confidence, like a wild thing nearly tamed. She would speak for the white man, that was sure, for the trader who had brought her all the long miles, who had seen that no harm came to her. She was a good child and a pretty one, with her black hair and oval face and fine eyes. Almost, he hated to give her up, even for beaver.

He went to sleep thinking about her and about plews and wealth and the new house and, on the rim of things that could be, a great trading company that alone enjoyed the trade of the Blackfeet.

When he awakened in the morning, Teal Eye was gone.

Every day before he let them put across from the south shore Summers went off with the ship's glass while Jourdonnais fretted, striding back and forth on the bank or pacing the boat, looking over the river to the growing pile of cottonwood pickets, looking upstream, looking down, looking for Summers to come back, and swearing in French because he had to wait.

Boone scouted while the men worked, he and Deakins and Summers did—Boone up the river and Deakins down it and Summers straight away up the gulch that flowed out into the little prairie they were building the fort on. Often when the plains seemed peaceful and a man couldn't see anywhere the rising dust that might mean buffalo and might mean Indians, one of them would come in and give a hand. They shot meat when they needed it, but mostly in the late evening when the men were easing up and the chance of bringing Indians on was least.

Half the men and more worked in the trees that spread down from the gulch, cutting down cottonwoods, lopping off the bigger branches and the tops and toting the trunks to the others near the bank for shaping up as pickets, to be set later in the trench they had dug. One in every five men took a gun with him. Rifles for the others were stowed behind the three-sided breastwork they had built. The men kept busy early and late, working like niggers while they swore and dripped sweat in the autumn sun, driven by Jourdonnais' rough voice and led on by him, too, for he did the work of three men, helping chop, helping trim, helping shape. Since Teal Eye ran away he was like a man with a fever in him. His hard square face never smiled now. When the teeth shone under his black mustache it was because he was swearing at the men or calling on God to see what he had to put up with. The men growled and often sassed him, their anger showing black in their eyes, but they did as he said, maybe afraid to balk or run away, maybe knowing they had best stay with him for all he was so cranky. "Come Indians," Summers had told them while their eyes flicked from one to another, "make for these here logs and grab a rifle. Shoot plumb, too. Noise don't kill Injuns. We can hold off a heap of Blackfeet if you do right."

Lying on the deck or standing guard at night or looking for Indian sign by day, Boone thought often about Teal Eye. Things didn't seem the same without her though she wasn't much more than a papoose. Why did she run away? Did she get back home to her pappy? Summers had tried to track her down that first morning but had come back at noon shaking his head. "She just lit out. She did now. Ain't nobody can trace her, I'm thinkin'."

Jourdonnais' jaw muscles ridged his face. "Someone pay for this," he promised. "Someone asleep on guard let her go. I find out."

"We didn't look for her to run," Summers reminded him. "Ain't anybody's fault more'n our own."

From a rise up the river Boone could see the men working and the felled trees lying naked near the bank. Jourdonnais' voice carried to him, small with distance but still full of fury. "You, Chouquette! You, Lassereau! You think we have the year to build! Goddam!" Boone could look up to the crest of the bare hills on the north shore and southward across the river to the top of the slope and beyond, where the yellow prairie lay. Jourdonnais and the men and the axes biting into wood were the only noises in the world, except for a bird sometimes and late in the evening the nighthawks whimpering in the deep sky. He wondered whether Teal Eye heard them, too. He wondered if ever he would see her again. All the time his eyes kept busy, looking for movement, looking for color, looking for something out of place. After a while he would go on, down to the river, maybe, watching for moccasin tracks, or up on the plain where he spent a good part of his time, his eye out for moving streamers of dust. When the sun sank he would start for the boat, seeing from the rise the lazy plume that Pambrun's fire sent up from the cargo box.

When Summers returned with the glass on the third morning of their stay, he drew Jourdonnais aside and then motioned to

Boone and Deakins. "Something this nigger don't know about, south."

"So?"

"Heap of dust, makin' this way. Maybe just buffler, maybe Injuns. I best see."

"We go across without you," Jourdonnais suggested. "We never get the fort up, waiting."

Summers nodded. "Keep your eye peeled. Do it, now."

Jourdonnais got out a segar and chewed on it, forgetting to light it.

"I'm thinkin' you better let Caudill and Deakins scout afore you put the men out." Summers turned and walked away and was lost to view in the brush.

They rowed across, losing ground against the current and afterwards bringing her upstream with the line. Boone and Jim leaped ashore. The sun had just got itself clear of the hills and shone round as a plate. The chill was lifting off the river in little lines of vapor. "We'll git back, quick as we see," Boone said.

"Go! Go on!" Jourdonnais' voice was harsh. "We be all right."

Boone made for the woods at the back of the clearing, from the side of his eye seeing Jim going on downstream. The grass was wet as rain with the dew. Things looked as they always had. There was the big cottonwood, with the broken limb flying its yellow leaves, the buffalo-berry bush showing silver and red, the game path going into the woods, marked with fresh tracks from the night. A striped squirrel played along ahead of him.

The first notion he had that things weren't right came with a small shifting in a thicket a hundred yards or more away, a patch of brown that faded out before the eye and might have been nothing. He saw a puff of black smoke and felt a tug high on his shoulder, close against the neck, and heard the crack of a rifle. Then all the quiet woods came alive. From behind trees and clumps and thickets Indians leaped, whooping. He saw them in one confused instant, the feathered headdresses, the medicine bags bobbing, the faces daubed with red and black, the mouths open, the guns puffing smoke, and the taut wood of the bows leaping against the strings. He heard bullets whistle and the flutter of arrows. Then he did what he had been told to do. He gave one sharp cry of warning and turned and ran for the breastwork. Before him the crew broke into a scurry like half-grown birds that a hunter had stumbled on. One of them ran ahead, making for the boat.

Boone fell behind the logs and slewed around and rested his rifle and pressed the trigger and saw a heavy-set buck falter and go over. The Indians weren't more than fifty yards away, the closest of them. The shot slowed them but they came on. Jourdonnais lay beside him, and Romaine, sighting along his rifle. Jourdonnais' voice sounded above the cries of the Indians, calling on the crew to come and help. His rifle spit out a cloud of smoke. Boone reached for a loaded weapon. Romaine's gun exploded in his ear. Boone shot again. The wave of Indians faltered, and suddenly there was no wave at all, but only the top of a headdress showing over the grass or the black of a scalp above a hump and the noses of the muskets poking out and the arrows being fitted to the bows.

"*Non! Non!*" It was Jourdonnais, screaming as if a pain was in him, Jourdonnais, turned half-about and screaming at the crew. Boone caught one glimpse of them splashing in the water, climbing wildly aboard the *Mandan*. Someone had cut the boat loose. It was edging out and down with the current.

"*Non! Non!* Mother of God!" It was as if nothing but the boat counted with Jourdonnais. It was as if the boat pulled him to his knees, to his feet, to his full height. He began to run for it. He shouted over his shoulder, "Romaine!"

Someone on board touched off the swivel. Its boom beat against the hills, wiping out all other sounds, halting the crawling Indians in the grass. Boone looked behind him. Jourdonnais had staggered round, a great hole showing in his chest. He fell sprawled out. There was no one in the breastworks now but Boone. He fired once more and dropped the gun and scuttled for the shore, seeing behind him the Indians rising and coming on. Their shouts pounded on his ears. Romaine was on his hands and knees with half the shaft of an arrow sticking from his back. He motioned Boone on with a weak and helpless gesture of the hand that left him face down in the grass.

Something told Boone to keep away from the boat. He ran, hearing the bangs of muskets and the feathered whisper of the arrows, and dived into the river, turning upstream after he hit the water so as to keep close in to the shore, swimming under water until his lungs were like to burst. He turned over and let his lips up for air and went under again, stroking with arms and legs while the trapped breath in his lungs went to nothing. Branches scratched his arms and chest and he let himself up easy, his head poking into the brush of a fallen tree. He saw bodies lying humped and sprawled on deck. The air was full of a wild shouting which the water cut off as he went under again. He heard instead only the river murmuring by his ears. He came up and sank and swam, came up and sank and swam. After a while the cries of the Indians began to seem distant. He pulled himself into the bank, into a thick cluster of red willow, and sat there for a long time, watching through his screen. It was all over now, except for the yelling and the prancing and the sound of muskets shooting into dead men. When the Indians passed Jourdonnais' body or the big lump that had been Romaine, they pointed and fired, or fell on their knees and beat the heads with rocks. Boone reckoned it was scalps they waved around their heads. Squaws and naked children had flocked out of the woods like chicks at the call of a hen. They started beating at the bodies, too, aiming mostly at the crotch. A squaw with a knife went to work on Romaine, holding up her cut afterwards for everyone to see.

The *Mandan* had been brought to again. Boone couldn't see the bodies for the Indians on her. The men were all dead, though, dead and being shot up and cut to pieces with the tomahawks he saw raised. High on the mast clung Painter, his dark coat fuzzed out. Some of the Indians had painted their faces coal black.

Boone fingered the hole by his neck that the ball had made. It had no feeling in it. The blood had seeped down and made a watery stain on his chest. He crawled away with a coldness on him, inside and out, thinking of people who beat a man's brains out or cut off his pizzle after he was dead. His heart made a slow, heavy thump in his chest. His wet buckskins chafed him. He wished he had his rifle.

The river made a slow turn to the left, leaving the Indians in sight whenever a man wanted to stick his head out of the shore bushes. They were still yelling, still shooting, still prancing around. He saw one of them carrying a keg. He was safe for a spell. They wouldn't leave there until they had drunk up the whisky. He looked across the river, thinking he might see Summers. Did Jim get away? He was down river, out of the charge. Jim seemed far off, like someone he had known a long time before. He couldn't put his face together in his mind. He could see the blue eyes and the red hair and the mouth smiling, but he couldn't fit one to the other and make Jim's face.

He kept going, traveling soft as he could. He didn't seem to feel the mosquitoes that found a man no matter what. The sun swung up and started down. The point of land that the curve looped shut off his view of the Indians, but he could hear them yet. After a while they were only a lost echo. Would it be Teal Eye that set the Indians on them? It didn't matter, he reckoned. The sun went behind the hills and the air was still as glass and the sky deep. When he stopped, the silence seemed to sing above the little whine of the mosquitoes and the sound of water. He pulled himself into some thick bushes and lay flat with his head on his arm, feeling empty and loose like a sack. A bird hopped on a limb and for a long time looked at him out of its round eye and then went on with its business as if he wasn't there. He heard the silence and the mosquitoes and the river. By and by he remembered he was hearing something else, something far off across the water, something he had heard before in another time of his life. It was a sharp, rising whistle such as the curlew made.

PART III

1837

20

The wind was warm, coming over the mountains, and notionable. Sometimes it cried shrill and wintry in the branches
of the trees and then it would ease up and be no more than
a whisper that the ear wouldn't catch unless it listened. When it
quieted Boone could hear water dripping in the dark, dripping from
the iced tree limbs and the shoulder of rock that rose just behind
the camp. The wind blew most of the time in this country, squeezing out of the canyons and sweeping on to the high plains, until a
man got so used to it he hardly paid it any mind, except sometimes
at night when he'd wake up and hear the wild, sad sound of it and
hunch down farther in his blanket and buffalo robe, feeling safe,
somehow, and good. By and by sleep would come on him again,
and the wind would be like a river flowing, running along with his
dreams.

Out from the circle of the camp with its center of fire the snowy
land seemed to float off into darkness, rising or falling or stretching
out, depending on which way a man looked. In the west the mountains made a high broken line against the night sky.

Summers reached out and got a branch from the fire and lighted his pipe with it, his weathered face coming out red as he drew
on the stem. He had taken his cap off, and the fire played along his
hair, bringing out the white in it. Jim was chewing at a bone. Out
of the side of his mouth he said, "Comin' time to git busy."

Summers squirmed his tail farther down on the sheep's skull
he sat on and rested his elbows on the horns that arched up at his
sides like the arms of a chair. It was like his hair got whiter every

day, or maybe it was just that the white showed more with the hair reaching down to his shoulders. "Ain't spring yet, I'm thinkin'. Winter'll get in another lick or so." He puffed slowly on his pipe, looking into the fire.

"Grass can't shine too soon for me," said Boone. He brought his knife along the length of cottonwood he held between his knees. The bark peeled off in a long, limber shaving. He cut the shaving crosswise into small pieces and tossed the pieces onto a little pile to feed his horses in the morning. "Horses eat enough bark to keep one of them there steamboats going."

"We got to git somewheres ahead of the rest," Jim said.

"We'll git somewheres," Summers answered. "If it ain't the Wind or the Grey Bull or the Popo Agie, it'll be another."

"Might be they're trapped out."

"We'll find beaver. Always have."

If a man took his eyes away from the fire and kept them on the sky the stars seemed to come close, burning brighter all the while. The Big Dipper stood out plain, the sides of it pointing to the North Star, which was small but steadier than most, not winking like the others did. Boone brought his eyes back to his work. He picked up another stick and began shaving it. A man had to keep his horses fit. He had seen horses that had gnawed each other's tails down to a nub, they got that hungry. Right now when he listened he could hear their own horses stamping the snow out in the darkness, trying to get down to grass.

"I reckon beaver won't be no higher," said Jim, "and no thicker, neither."

Summers roused himself to say, "We won't be seein' any twelve-dollar plews, I'm thinkin', like they paid onc't at Fort Clark. Fat meat like that couldn't shine long."

"The damn Company's got us by the tail now, since Fitzpatrick and Bridger throwed in with 'em. Ain't none to bid ag'in 'em. That's what ails beaver."

"That," Summers said, nodding, "and them Londoners makin' hats out of silk, if what we hear tell is right."

"It'll come back," Boone put in. He had heard that kind of talk for two winters or more. "It ain't done. You'll see."

"I got a piece of land around Independence, Missouri State,

if it's still there," Summers said as if he wasn't talking to them but just thinking to himself.

"It don't matter so much about the beaver. Not to me," said Boone. "Just so a man ketches enough for tobacco and powder and ball and sometimes some whisky."

To Summers Jim said, "All Boone hankers for is fat meat and a fire and to be away from folks."

It was good enough, Boone thought to himself. What did a man want as long as he had marrowbones and hump ribs and a fire to keep him warm and a free country to move around in? It took something to beat a place where you could kill a buffalo every day and not half try and take just the best of it and leave the rest to the wolves. What more could anyone want, unless maybe it was a good squaw to keep camp and to lie with him at night?

"A man gets a feeling when the years pile up on him," Summers went on, still as if he was talking to himself. "He ain't so spry sometimes in the mornin', and at night he has to keep rollin' out to let off water, and his bones hurt, and he figures he's certain sure to lose his scalp if he keeps on."

"You been talkin' thataway, Dick, since God knows when," Boone said.

Summers didn't answer.

"Git back there, and they couldn't tie you to stay. You're still sassy as a setter pup, pointin' anything that shakes its tail."

The mention of God set Jim off, like it always did. He locked his hands behind his head and leaned back against a stump. "I reckon God don't like a man to set his sights too high. Time he overaims, God sics something on him. Reckon He thinks nobody's got a right to feel big savin' Himself. Ain't room in the puddle but for one big frog. Maybe that's why we're still kickin'; we ain't aimin' at nothin' except keepin' our hair on and our bellies full, and havin' a time at rendezvous or maybe Taos. Ain't nothin' in that to git God's dander up."

Summers didn't seem to be listening. He was just looking into the fire with his eyes slitted as he did many a time now. Boone started on another length of cottonwood.

"Like Jourdonnais now," Jim argued. "He thought to be a mighty big nabob. He did, now, till God cut him down."

"McKenzie didn't do so bad."

"Only for a spell, Boone. Then the government found he was makin' whisky there at Union, and you ain't heerd of McKenzie since. I reckon that was God workin' through the government."

"It was tolerable liquor, too," Summers said, stirring. "A sight better than some. Seems onlikely God had anything to do with it, though; He ain't in the liquor business. This nigger wishes he had a can of it now."

"It ain't so long till rendezvous." Jim ran his tongue around his mouth. "That's what I'm living for, is rendezvous. Whisky and playin' hand, and the Injun girls all purtied up, yours for a cut of cloth or a hawk's bell or a Green River knife for her man. Jesus!"

"Things don't figure to shine so much," answered Summers. "Not with Bonneville back in the army and Wyeth in Boston. Be a plenty of Indians, but not so many packs and not so much money. Not so many mountain men, either, the way they been pullin' out."

" 'Member how the Snakes looked at Bonneville's bald head, wonderin' if the hair had been left off apurpose so's he couldn't be scalped?" Jim chuckled.

Boone answered Summers. "We get beaver enough."

"By travelin' by ourself. By taking chances. Trappin' small and quiet, a man can ketch beaver yet, if he don't lose his scalp."

"And lose out on some fun, too," Jim said, his gaze fixed on Boone. "It wouldn't have hurt our ketch, nohow, to've rendevoused for winter with Bridger's men on the Yellowstone."

"This here suits me," Boone answered.

It had suited him for a long time now, this life along the streams and in the hills—so long it seemed like forever. Jim was always letting fret get into him and wanting to put out for St. Louis or Taos or anywhere that people were. Taos was all right when it came to that; he had followed along after Jim and Summers a time or two. And maybe St. Louis would be all right if a man took just long enough to wet his whistle and didn't let himself get tangled with the law; but once, when he had thought to go with Jim and Summers, he had turned back at the settlements, feeling strange and uneasy and caged in.

This life had suited him a long time, saving the weeks they had spent on foot dodging Blackfeet after Jourdonnais and the crew went under. Once in a while those days would come back to him yet, as real as if just happening, and he would hear the curlew's cry coming from across the river and would fear to answer it and would make his legs carry him upstream along the bank until he found a log and pushed off with it for the other side. Summers and Jim had watched him coming, and they fished him out of the river and half-carried him away, stopping after a while in a thicket where Summers had a look at the wound by his neck.

Summers' voice would come to him, low and friendly and with the edge of a joke in it. "One little musket ball won't put you under, hoss. This place ain't nothin'. I seen holes as bad made by a sticker bush." Summers' eyes were smiling. Boone looked up into the gray of them and over Summers' bent head saw the sky dulling off to night. He reckoned he ought to smile back but he didn't have the will for it.

The days ran together when he thought back to them, so that what he remembered wasn't time set off and divided, with this and that happening on such and such a day. What he remembered was the fear on him like a weight, the long hiding, the pushing ahead when his legs were limber and his breath dry and fast in his throat, the wound hurting steady, and Jim helping him, and Summers, and Jim looking anxious when he thought Boone didn't see. They walked one day after another, keeping when they could to the brush or the cuts the water had made, but always walking, step and step—always walking, each time putting a teensy bit of ground under them while they looked ahead on plains land that flowed on and on forever. Some places it was so bare that even a rabbit couldn't find a good place to hide, and a man got the feeling then that the Blackfeet were perched all around, watching from where the plains rimmed up to the sky. Their moccasins wore out, and the rawhide from the buffalo Summers had dared to shoot clung stiff and clumsy to the foot; and step and step they went on, the spines of cactus angry in the flesh, and their bellies drawn up in their ribs and the taste of wild-rose berries and raw prairie turnips in their mouths, for not often would Summers take the chance of striking a fire or shooting meat. The sun swam across the sky and went down early, and a keen chill flowed on the land, so that they shivered in their buckskins and slept close for warmth and roused early when the night was coldest and went on, heading east and south for the Yellow-stone and the friendlier country beyond, heading across the endless tumble of plain, and lying one time in the grass when a party of Indians came into sight and passed by and grew into nothing. They kept on, joked and cheered and pushed along by Summers, and then—in the early morning, it was—they met up with six hunters from the Rocky Mountain Fur Company and went with them to winter rendezvous on the Powder.

It wasn't so far, that rendezvous, from where they were camped now—not so far by miles, anyhow. By time it seemed a long way off.

Summers nosed the logs farther into the fire, which had been built Indian fashion, with the ends of the wood rather than the middle in the blaze. A little shower of sparks arose, until the wind woke up and sent them streaming. Flames licked at the logs and then came up in one tongue, lighting the camping place. Through the wide mouths of the skin lodges, set close against the shoulder of rock, Boone could make out robes and blankets and their small bags of fixings. The graining block stood behind him, a half-worked deerskin on it. Close by ran a pole, set in crotches, that they hung their meat on. There wasn't but a chunk or two of fresh meat on it now, and the meat they had dried for winter was all eaten up; tomorrow he'd kill a cow, and he and Summers and Jim would feast on the young one she carried in her. Farther out, he could see the white trunks of quaking asp glimmering as the fire flickered. A horse sneezed, unseen in the darkness, and out still farther, rumped on some hill, a wolf howled. Boone shivered inside his hunting shirt, feeling lonely and good with the darkness crowding around him and the spot of fire holding it back and the wind sad in the trees.

His gaze went to Summers and saw him tighten a little and grow still, as if all the strength of his eyes and ears was brought to one point. That was the way it was with Dick. He would seem to be drowsing, and then there would be a sound somewhere or a movement, and you would see that he was alive and quick all the time, quicker and more alive than anybody, as if his senses told him things even in his sleep. His hand went over and curled around his rifle and brought it, slanting out, across his knees.

Jim started to say something but fell silent as Summers let out a low hissing noise.

Boone heard it now, too, the sound of feet coming toward the fire, coming careless and loud, crunching in the snow, as if the man swinging them hadn't a fright in the world. He had his own rifle in his hands. The nose of Summers' weapon moved to the right and steadied.

Into the circle of firelight a top-heavy figure moved and grew to be an Indian carrying an antelope across his back. He dumped the carcass by the fire and straightened and looked around, first at Summers, then at Jim, and then at Boone. His ugly, bony face creased into a sudden smile that showed he had two teeth missing in front. He had a crooked nose that came down almost to his lip and seemed about to poke into the hole that the teeth had left. "How," he said, and began to laugh, a laugh that started deep in him and bubbled out, until a man hearing him had to laugh, too, it was so true and silly.

"How," said Summers.

The Indian brushed a tangle of hair out of his eyes and took the bow and quiver from his shoulder and let them drop. For a hunting shirt he had on an old deerskin that had been doubled over and a hole cut for his head. He had it tied with whangs under his arms. "Talk English, me," he announced. "Heap good. Plenty good."

"So?"

The Indian slapped himself on the chest. "Good."

"Talk it then, hoss."

"Eat. Drink. Piss. Goddam."

Jim got a surprised look in his face and then began to howl.

A little smile worked at Summers' mouth. "Dogged if that hoss don't run the circle," he said to Boone and Jim.

The Indian said "Son a bitch" as if it was a word he'd just thought of.

"You shore shine at trapper's talk. You do now. Who be ye, Injun?"

The Indian squatted down by the fire, where Boone could see his leggings were old and thin with hardly a fringe left. The cloth shirt he wore under the deerskin was probably red once.

"Blackfoot, me." His words ran into Indian talk. Summers listened close, nodding that he understood.

When he was through Summers said, "Here's a nigger without a nation. Says he's a Blood, but had a set-to with them for some reason, and so he run off. Lived with the Kootenai for a spell, and the Flatheads and Shoshones. Looks more like a Poordevil Injun —no gun and nigh bare-assed—but he don't act that way."

The Indian smiled again. The fire showed his tongue working behind the gap in his teeth. "Love Long Knives, me. Love whisky. Love whisky heap." He looked around, smiling a kind of baby smile under the long, hooked nose, as if he expected one of them to offer him a can. "Drink heap whisky, me."

"I'm thinkin' he's a true-blue Blackfoot." To the Indian Summers said, "No got whisky. No medicine water. All gone. Eat?" He invited, and pointed to a piece of meat still skewered on a stick that slanted over the fire. The Indian jerked the meat from the stick and set his jaws into it and took the knife from his waist and ran it in front of his nose, cutting a bite from the chunk. He gulped and laughed his strong, bubbling laugh again for no reason at all unless because he felt good.

"Ask him does he know Heavy Otter," Boone said to Summers.

Summers' voice went out, hoarse and choppy. The Indian stopped chewing and made a face and combed his greasy hand through his hair. Then he said "Goddam" and went on chewing.

Jim was watching him, his face screwed into a questioning grin as if he had never seen his like before. "Kin we keep him, Pap?" he asked as a young one would have asked it.

When the Indian had finished the meat he combed his hair again, looking pleased and friendly. He yawned then and suddenly let himself down, squirming onto his back on the pine boughs that Summers had spread over the last snow. "Sleep," he announced and closed his eyes.

Summers looked at Boone and Jim. "We got a partner, if'n we want him."

The wind had strengthened again, wailing through the trees. Through the wailing Boone could catch the sound of the creek, beginning to run with thaw.

"You can't kick a man out brings meat to camp," Jim said, motioning toward the antelope. "Besides, he does me a sight of good."

"Acts like he's asleep a'ready," Boone said, "like a baby or a pup or something. For all he's so damn ugly, he tickles a man."

Summers didn't say any more, but got up and went inside his shelter and came back with an old robe. "This is like feedin' a lost dog," he warned. "I'm thinkin' we can't get shet of him." When Jim and Boone didn't answer he dropped the robe over the Indian. He looked out into the dark then, looked out and listened while he thought. "Wind feels like spring, sure enough. This nigger thinks if need be we could go acrost to the Bear or along Lewis Fork and down the Snake a ways."

Boone lifted himself from the ground and stood straight and looked at the dipper again and at the North Star it pointed to, the North Star shining steady, lying over the Blackfoot country, lying over Jourdonnais' bones, which were likely rotted and gone now, lying over the lodges of the Piegans, and Teal Eye maybe in one of them. It was a time since the *Mandan's* crew went under. He counted back. Seven seasons. Seven seasons since he had seen the Indian girl with an eye like the bluewing teal. She would be growed now, and most likely have a man. He wondered what had set him to thinking so keen about her. It couldn't be just a foolish runaway Blackfoot with a long nose and a gap in his teeth—not him alone, anyhow. From high overhead he caught the faint honk of geese driving north to nesting grounds.

21

There was still snow above the Wind River plains, a deep snow with an old crust that skinned the front legs of the lead horse after he had broken through. Boone and Jim and Summers took turns breaking trail, so as to even the hurt among the horses. Loaded with furs and traps and bedding, the two pack animals followed along, one behind Boone and one behind Jim, and at the rear came Poordevil, riding the horse they had spared him and singing out "Hi-yi" every once in a while. Whenever Boone looked back Poordevil gave a big grin, showing the slot in his teeth. Sometimes he would pull out of the trail and lunge up alongside of Boone and grin again and say some fool thing just to hear his own voice. "Heap beaver heap quick betcha goddam." Down from the hills the plains looked almost dusty, and warm and quiet, as if below the reach of the winds that on the ridges were like a hand pushing into a man's face. Boone could see

buffalo below, like a fluid stain on the tanned grass, and bunches
of trees, and antelopes moving light and easy as birds. The sun-
light lay yellow and soft on them all, seeming to have a warmth
down there that it lost on the high places. Across the plains to the
west the Wind River mountains climbed into snow banks.

Boone told himself they would find fur, traveling few and quiet
this way. Big parties, like Jim Bridger's, put such a fright into
beaver they wouldn't stir from their lodges or wouldn't come to
medicine if they did. Even when the parties thought it was safe
enough to split up, they left more beaver than they caught, what
with one man holding a rifle and the other setting traps and both
of them splashing along and maybe talking. A man took chances,
hunting small; Indians might happen on him any day. If he kept
his scalp, though, he got plews. And the risk wasn't so great with
Summers along—not with a man along who could tell from the eye
and ear of a horse or the set of a buffalo whether there was aught
about. Boone figured he and Jim had got good themselves at smelling Indians; they wouldn't have their hair if they hadn't. He had
seen men at rendezvous wouldn't know a war whoop if they heard
one. Some of them were dead now, and others were bound to be, in
time, if they didn't learn better, or if they didn't quit the mountains, as some of them were doing, and some true trappers, too.
They had hurt the hunting, though, pushing up every trickle of water until there was hardly a place a man could feel was fresh any
more.

It gave him a little pinch when he thought about them, about
pork eaters from Canada and Missouri graybacks and Yankee traders and men from Kentucky and Tennessee moving in, traveling
along streams and through passes that a man liked to think were
his own, just as it gave him a pinch when he thought back to
last year and remembered the white women that a couple of crazy
preachers had brought to rendezvous on Horse Creek, bound on
across to the Columbia. Damned if they weren't on wheels, those
preachers and their women! He heard later they got a cart as far
as the British post on the Boise. White women! And wheels! They
figured to spoil a country, except that the women would leave or
die. Ask any hunter who had fought Indians and gone empty-
stomached and like to froze, and he'd say it was no place for wom-

en, or for preachers, either, or farmers. And no place for wagons or carts, except maybe to bring trade goods as far as rendezvous. The rocks would knock them to pieces, and the rivers wash them down, and the sun shrivel the wheels apart. All the same, he got a pinch of misery, thinking, just as he had sometimes in Kentucky when he'd be out in the woods, feeling good that he was alone, with everything to himself, and then he would spy someone and it would all be spoiled, as if the country wasn't his any more, or the woods or the quiet.

Ahead of him, Jim's hair streamed from under his hat like a lick of fire. Jim let his hair hang long and loose, like Summers. For himself, Boone liked it better in a couple of plaits, like the Indians wore it, tied at the end with red cloth. He would get himself some new ribbons, come the rendezvous, and a new hunting shirt and leggings, with some hawks' bells and colored strings for the fringes. Buckskin got old and greasy in a year and lost its fringes, one by one, as a man needed laces for his moccasins. He would buy himself a new rifle, too, a percussion Hawken, about thirty-two balls to the pound; people were coming to see that a cap and ball was better than a flintlock, just as he had always said. And he would play some hand and drink some whisky and have himself a squaw, and then he would be ready to go on. There wasn't any sense in staying when a man's beaver was spent.

Summers pulled up and swung his leg from across his horse and stood looking down at the plains, which seemed close but would take a spell to get to with the going like it was. Though spring was coming on, Summers still wore his old capote with the hood that came up from it and went over his head. He reached inside and got out a piece of roasted liver and began to munch while his eye traveled north and south and back again. Jim dismounted, too, and then Boone, and from the back Poordevil came galloping up and threw himself from his horse, showing off, and fell in the snow. Summers handed him a piece of liver when he got up. Poordevil grinned and bit into it and cleaned the slot with his tongue and took another bite.

Summers said, "This nigger's had enough of sagebrush fires and cold camps. That there timber looks good."

"It's like someone forgot to put a tree between the Powder and the Popo Agie," Jim said. "I aim to put my feet to a sure-enough fire and cook meat over quaking ash and set and set and eat and eat. It wears a body down, pullin' stems to keep a blaze."

Over nothing, Poordevil said, "Oh, goddam!" and laughed.

"You can't tell from what that nigger says what's bitin' him." Summers' gray eye was studying the Indian.

"He just talks to hear hisself, like a boy shootin' a new rifle at nothin'."

"All the same," Boone said, "he's comical. I wouldn't care no more for a bear cub."

Poordevil saw they were talking about him and felt big for it. He hit himself on the chest. "Hi-yi. Love whisky, me."

"Git on your medicine dog, you crazy bastard," Summers said. "We're goin' to kill us a bull and build a fire." Before he mounted he added, "We'll poke along the Popo Agie and the Wind and maybe up the Horn, dependin'. We'll catch beaver enough with the plews we got from fall, I'm thinkin'."

Jim faced half around to the north. "Reckon we'd fare better up a ways?"

"With Bridger's men thicker'n wolves around a hurt cow!"

Boone said, "Rendezvous is comin' soon enough, Jim. You'll see all them as is on Clark's Fork."

Summers said to Boone, "Ol' Red Head is a sociable nigger."

The horses stood slack in the snow, their eyes sad and lifeless, their ribs showing through the long winter hair.

"I'll break the way for a spell," Boone said, and stooped and examined the knees of his horse. "Come to Tar Springs, I'll doctor ye, Blackie," he promised. Blackie was a good horse, for all that he was ganted up now. Let the Indians have their white and spotted buffalo ponies; he would take a solid dark.

The bull Boone killed was young and fat enough, fatter than a cow would be now with a calf pulling on her and the grass scant yet. A couple of wolves loped up out of nowhere at the sound of the shot, and from a sky that didn't have a bird in it three crows came flapping. They lighted a little piece off and stepped back and forth, all the while keeping their sharp eyes on the butchering. The wolves rumped down to wait, their tongues hanging out and dripping, their gaze following the tenderloin and tongue and liver and marrowbone that Boone and Summers packed on the horses. The horses had come alive, now they were out of the snow, and kept cropping at the grass, eating it clear down into the dirt.

There was a good camping spot, with a small meadow almost shut in by the trees, near where the Wind and the Popo Agie joined to make the Horn. The four men pulled the saddles off and hobbled the horses with rawhide and turned them loose to graze. Summers took a long look around first, saying as he nearly always did, "It's a sight better to count ribs than tracks," and meaning it was better to keep a horse tied up and hungry than to turn him loose and let him get stolen by Indians.

Poordevil gathered wood, and Summers laid it and struck fire. In a little while all of them had sticks slanted over the blaze with chunks of liver on the ends. Jim had put a pot on the fire, too, into which he had cut pieces of bull meat.

Summers said, "Wisht we had some coffee," and Jim put in, "I hanker for salt," but straight meat and river water were good enough. They kept up a man's strength and never made him sick, no matter how much he ate, and made his blood good, too. A mountain man never got a running sore or a toothache or shook with a fever—or almost never, anyway. After a while he lost his taste for salt and bread and greens and such.

It was warmer down in the valley and clear of snow except where the trees grew thick and kept the wind and sun away. The sun was shining now, far off, giving only a touch of warmth when it lay on the back of a man's hand. It was making downward for the Wind River mountains that reared up, white where the snow lay and blue on the bare rock. From the west the wind was puffing.

After he had a bellyful Boone stretched out with his feet to the fire and his head on the saddle and slept. When he awakened the sun was near to the mountains, fixing soon to sink from sight.

"Jim went downstream, him and Poordevil," Summers informed him. Summers was spreading skins over some saplings to make a lodge.

"I'll point up, soon's I get my outfit on." He peeled off his leggings and got into a pair that had been cut off at the knees and pieced out with a blanket. There was nothing gave a trapper misery like hide drying tight on the legs, unless it was moccasins that hadn't been smoked enough and pinched a man so, drying out, that he had to cripple out of his bed at night and dip them in the water again. Boone's own moccasins were made from an old lodge skin that was half smoke itself.

There were beaver left all right. Boone saw cuttings along the stream and after a little came to a dam and peeked over. The pond lay smooth at first, and then a wedge of ripples started close to the bank and the point of it came toward him and sharpened into a head and turned and went the other way and sank into the water without a sound, leaving just the ripples running out and whispering along the banks.

Boone slipped along the shore, walking soft in the snow that lay old and coarse underneath the trees, keeping back from the ice that edged the pond where the water was shallow. When he found a likely place, he walked around it and went beyond and laid his traps down. He leaned his rifle against a bush, cut and sharpened a long, dry stick and cocked a trap, and then, carrying rifle and stick and trap, went to the spot he had chosen. He rested his rifle on the bank there, felt for footing on the fringe of ice, stepped on it once and then beyond it, into the water.

The water was cold—so cold it knotted the flesh, so cold it made a man wish for a larger stream where he could use a dugout and poke quietly along the banks, dry as could be. He lifted a foot out of the water, grunting a little with the cramp in it, and put it back and brought the other one up. After that, they didn't hurt him any more, feeling only dead and wooden in his moccasins. He felt the mud stiff and thick under his soles and saw bubbles rising around his ankles and smelled the sulphur smell they brought up.

He stooped and put the cocked trap in the water, so that the surface came a hand above the trigger, and led the chain out into deeper water until he came to the end of it. Then he slipped the stick through the ring in the chain and pushed the stick in the mud, putting all his weight to it. He tapped it next with his ax to make sure it was secure enough. Back at the bank he cut a willow twig and peeled it, and from his belt took the point of antelope horn he kept his medicine in. The medicine came to his nose, strong and gamy, as he took the stopper out. He dipped the twig in the medicine, restoppered his bottle and put it back, and stooped again and thrust the dry end of the twig into the mud between the jaws of the trap, so that the baited end stuck about four inches above the surface of the water. It wouldn't be long, he reckoned, until a beaver came to medicine. Backing up, he toed out the footprints his moccasins had left. With his hands he splashed water on the bank so as to drown out his scent. He reached out and got his rifle then and waded along the edge of the pond. When he came opposite his traps he stepped ashore.

By the time Boone had set four traps it had grown too dark to place the other two. He went back to camp with them, to find Summers and Jim and Poordevil eating boiled bull off pieces of bark, as the Snake Indians did. He found a chunk of bark himself and spooned meat on it and took the knife from his belt and ate. The spoon and kettle and one can, and the knives they wore, were all they had for cooking and eating since the Crows had paid them a visit in the fall.

"Beaver about," Jim said, and Boone nodded and went on chewing.

Summers was looking out into the closing darkness. He got up after a while, stiffly, and took his rifle. "Travel weather. I'm thinkin' we'll see Injuns any time. Best to bring in the horses and peg 'em close."

Poordevil said, "Medicine dogs all gone."

"Don't git to it afore it happens," Boone answered. "You mean medicine dogs'll be all gone."

"All gone. Goddam." He trailed along after Summers to bring the horses up.

Afterwards they all sat around the fire for a time, smoking and looking into it and not saying anything much. When his feet were dry Boone went into the lodge and laid himself down. He heard the others getting up and yawning and making a splatter on the ground before they came to bed, and then he didn't hear them any more, for the wind was flowing along with his dreams, flowing in the north country, rippling the grass, singing around lodges he had never seen till now.

The days were gone when a man could sleep as long as he wanted and get up lazy and eat some meat and lie down again, glad for warmth and a full stomach and even the ice that put the beaver out of reach. It wasn't quite sunup when Boone awakened, hearing the sharp chirp of a winter bird that spring was giving a voice to.

The others were sleeping, except for Summers who was sitting up and shivering a little. Poordevil was snoring a kind of whistling snore, as if the gap in his teeth gave a special sound to it. Every time the bird cheeped, he would stop and then start in again, maybe getting the cheep mixed up in his dreams. Jim's head was covered by his blanket. You would think he was a dead one, back in the settlements, lying there quiet with the cover over him from toe to scalp lock.

There was still some fire left, and some meat in the pot. Shaking in his buckskins, Boone threw some grass on the coals and nosed sticks over them. The flame came up, making him feel warmer just from the sight of it. The sun bulged up from the eastern hills, catching the Wind River mountains first and turning the snowbanks whiter than any cloud. Not a thing moved as far as Boone could tell, and not a noise sounded, except for Poordevil's whistling snore and the fire busy among the sticks. Even the bird had fallen silent. The wind itself was still now, blown over east and gone, and a man listening heard only his ears straining.

Boone set the pot by the fire and went to the horses, standing dull and patient, hobbled and tied to their picket lines. Blackie nickered and nosed Boone's shoulder as Boone bent over the knot.

When the horses were watered he tied them up again. They would have time to graze later after the morning hunt was over.

"Fair morning," Summers said when he came back. "Good thaw, though, or a rain, and the streams'll be too high for huntin'." He was looking west, to the snowbanks that looked clean-washed on the mountains.

They set out after they had eaten, Jim and Poordevil downstream and Boone up, and Summers across to the Wind.

The pond lay quiet as a sheet of ice. There was no sound in it or in all the woods, except for the quiet gurgle of water finding a small way around the dam. A fish nosed the surface while Boone watched, and the water riffled and lay flat again. From the dam he could see that his stick was gone, the stick he had forced into the mud to hold the trap. Sometimes a man worked so quiet he didn't do right. Like as not the beaver lay drowned in deep water now, and he would have to wade out and maybe swim for the plew and the twelve-dollar trap that held it. Only it wasn't once in a coon's age a beaver pulled loose on him, he sank his sticks that deep. He walked to the setting place, searching with his eyes for the stick floating and the ring of the chain around it. After a while he made out the float, lying free along the edge of ice, with the ring gone from it. A man couldn't tell where the beaver was, without he drowned quick, close to where the trap grabbed him. Boone waded out and looked into the water, following it while it got deeper and darker until the bottom was lost to his eye.

He straightened and shifted his rifle to the other hand, and stepped back toward shore to ease the ache in his legs, and then he heard a small noise in a clump of willows behind him, a bare whisper in the limbs. He looked around and saw the end of the chain, not knowing it for what it was, at first. He stooped and seized it and pulled her from the bushes, a young she in the prime. She crouched down when he had yanked her into the clear, not trying to run, but just crouching, looking at him while her nose trembled and a little shivering went over her.

"Got ye," he said, and cast about with his hand and picked up a dead stick big enough to kill her with.

He saw now that she had been at work on her leg. A little bit more and she would have chewed herself free. There were just the tendons holding, and a ragged flap of skin. The broken bone stuck out of the jaws of the trap, white and clean as a peeled root. Around her mouth he could see blood.

She looked at him, still not moving, still only with that little shaking, out of eyes that were dark and fluid and fearful, out of big eyes that liquid seemed to run in, out of eyes like a wounded bird's. They made him a little uneasy, stirring something that lay just beyond the edge of his mind and wouldn't come out where he could see it.

She let out a soft whimper as he raised the stick, and then the stick fell, and the eye that had been looking at him bulged out crazily, not looking at anything, not something alive and liquid any more, not something that spoke, but only a bloody eyeball knocked from its socket. It was only a beaver's eye all the time.

He skinned her, and cut off the tail and knifed out and tied the castor glands so they wouldn't leak and rolled them in the plew and reset his trap and went on. He got two more beaver. The fourth set was untouched. It was a good-enough morning.

Walking back to camp, he thought about rendezvous—and after. Jim wanted to hunt the Bear or the Sick River and head on south for the winter, to Taos, which people sometimes called Fernandez. A man couldn't tell what Summers would do, maybe not even Summers himself. Boone wondered whether Poordevil would want to go back to the Blackfeet. Thinking about the north country, of a sudden he knew what the beaver's eyes had put him in mind of.

22

Trapping or traveling, Jim Deakins watched the country for dust and the buffalo for movement, as any mountain man would. Winter and summer, the Blackfeet were pushing south from the Three Forks to war on the Crows, and going on, a many a long camp from home, to rub out white men as they trapped the streams and made over the passes. It wasn't Indian sign he wanted to see, though; Bridger's men ought to come out of the north any time now, pointed for rendezvous. Allen would be with them, maybe, and Lanter and Hornsbeck and others that he had had himself a time with before.

Hunting was all right, and wintering the way he and Boone and Summers had, but a man got lonesome finally and hankered for people and for frolics. It was good to tell stories sometimes and to hear stories told and to brag and to laugh over nothing and play horse while the whisky worked in you, and to have the good feeling in the back of your head all the time that when you were through talking and betting and drinking and wrestling there would be an Indian girl waiting for you; and, afterwards, you would lie quiet with her and hear the coyotes singing and the stream washing and see the stars down close and feel the warmth of her, and the lonesomeness would all be gone, as if the world itself had come to set a spell with you.

Take Boone, now. He never seemed to get lonesome or to want to see folks, except once in a while for a squaw that he was through with almost as quick as he got her. He was like an animal, like a young bull that traveled alone, satisfied just by earth and water and trees and the sky over him. It was as if he talked to the country for company, and the country talked to him, and as if that was enough. He found his fill of people quick; he took his fill of whisky quicker, drinking it down like an Indian and getting himself good and drunk while another man was just warming up. Then one morning before rendezvous was more than half over he would wake up and want to make off, to places where you wouldn't see a white man in a coon's age.

Summers was the same in a way, but different, too, for Summers seemed to live in his head a good part of the time, as if it was the years kept him company. He would sit at the campfire and smoke or go about the horses or tend to the skins, and a man would know that he was away back in his mind, seeing old things, things that had happened long ago, before the *Mandan* ever put out from St. Louis, seeing himself as a boy maybe in Missouri or a young man down on the Platte. Summers liked company, all right, and liked drinking and frolics as well as anybody, but in a quiet way, as if nothing that happened now was as important as what had gone before. It was age getting him, likely; a man was lucky if he didn't grow too old and have to think that the best of what was going to happen to him had already happened. God was mighty mean in some ways, letting a body get on to the point where he always hungered to turn back, making him know he wasn't the man he had been, making his bed cold but keeping in his mind the time when it wasn't. It was like a man was pushed backwards down hill, seeing the top getting farther from him every day, but always seeing it, always wishing he could go back. Sometimes God seemed pretty small.

Summers was in one of his spells now, just sitting and smoking and thinking, and saying only a word or two, and then only if spoken to first. Boone had dug a hole where the fire was and put a deer's head in it and raked the coals over. In the kettle there was meat cut small, cooking with wild onions that Jim had pulled, remembering food back in Kentucky.

"We might as well be gettin' on, with the water so high," Jim said. "Be rendezvous time before it goes down."

Summers asked "Reckon?" as if he wasn't listening.

Boone and Poordevil sat away from them a little. As Jim watched, Boone put his finger on his eye and Poordevil sounded the Indian word for it. Boone tried the word then, practicing with it until Poordevil smiled and bobbed his head that he had got it right.

Jim bent over the moccasin he was making, pulling a whang through the holes his awl had bored. Boone had got so's he spent a deal of time talking with Poordevil that way, learning the Blackfoot words for things.

The sun was coming down from overhead. They would eat and maybe sleep a little, and then it would be time to look at the traps again. Even with the water as high as it was, they caught a few beaver. It might be he would go out first and kill some meat. The cows were thin yet. Bull was better, or mountain sheep. There was a mess of mountain sheep on the shoulders of the Wind mountains—rams and ewes and lambs full of play. They leaped along slopes that would affright a bird, never falling, never hurting themselves.

Jim looked up from his work and let his eye go all around, and then he took to his feet and looked harder, at the buffalo running north of them.

Summers saw him and got up and looked, too, and reached over for the rifle he had leaned against a tree. He jerked his head as Boone lifted his glance. They stood watching, seeing the buffalo stream to the east, leaving a slow rising cloud behind them.

Without speaking Summers moved off toward the horses and so started them all that way. The horses snorted as they trotted to them, and tried to shy off, rearing and plunging with the hobbles but making a poor out at getting away. Back at camp, the men threw saddles on them and led them into a patch of brush.

Summers squinted through the branches. The cloud that the buffalo had left was sinking, and at the tail end of it Jim could see horsemen coming through. "Can't tell," Summers said. "Injuns or hunters. They ain't like to sight our fire at this time of day without they ride close."

"Long Knives," Poordevil announced. "No Injuns."

"We'll see. Looks to be six or ten."

Except for Poordevil, who stood at the side of his horse without even his bow in his hand, they brought their saddle horses in front of them as the horsemen approached, looking over the backs of them and on through the branches with their rifles rested across their saddles. Summers' eye slid to Poordevil. "Can't figger how that nigger's lived so long."

If it was Long Knives it would be Bridger's men, Jim thought— Bridger's men making for rendezvous on the Seeds-kee-dee which some folks were calling the Green River now.

Summers relaxed. "Injuns don't carry rifles that way, I'm thinkin'." He stepped from the brush.

The horses pulled up short, and the riders swung their rifles on him until he shouted at them and fired his own weapon in the air. Jim fired his gun then, and heard Boone's go off next to him, and then there was a quick scattering of shots and voices shouting and hoofbeats thudding on the ground as the horsemen swept up.

"Dogged if it ain't Allen and Shutts and Reeson. How, Elbridge? How, Robinson?"

The men slid from their horses and shook hands around, yelling "Hi-yi," some of them, and strutting like Indians, making a show for all that their buckskins were worn and black with grease and the fringes down to nothing. One of the eight kept to his horse, though, a big, loose man whose slouched shoulders made a wide arch over his saddle horn. His eyes went around and fixed on Poordevil, as if Poordevil had done something against him. Still looking, he pulled off the handkerchief he had about his head, and Jim saw that a plume of hair grew solid white from a scar at the hair line in front.

"Ain't you gonna light, Streak?" Lanter asked. "Or are you gonna let your tail grow to that there mare?"

They all moved around, talking, telling about the winter, filling the quiet air with sound, all except the big man who still sat his horse with no smile on his face and no word in his mouth.

"Where's Bridger and the rest?" Summers asked.

"Comin' along. We took out ahead."

"How's beaver?"

"We catched a few. The damn Blackfeet give us trouble again, a heap of it."

"Damn the goddam Injuns!" It was Streak speaking, speaking as he looked at Poordevil. "What's that one?"

Summers looked up but didn't answer right away, and Boone put in "Blackfoot" and looked afterward as if he knew he shouldn't have said it.

"What!"

"More like a Poordevil," Summers said. "Let's smoke."

Streak got down off the horse and stood holding his gun. It was a smart rifle, decorated with brass tacks and a pattern of vermilion, as if he had just done fancying it up.

"We got ourselves a few plews," Summers was saying, talking to the rest but keeping the tail of his eye on Streak. "Not so many, though. It's poor doin's, account of floodwater."

Boone stood a little apart, listening.

"A goddam Blackfoot, is he?"

Lanter said, "No need actin' like a sore-tailed bear, Streak."

"This child'll rub that bastard out."

"You'll get kilt yourself." Boone had stepped in front of Streak, between him and Poordevil. Poordevil just stood there, not quite understanding, his eyes going around and his mouth open showing his broken jaw, and his crazy deerskin shirt hanging comical on him.

"By God!" Streak turned his head around to look at the others, who fell silent one by one and shifted a little, expecting trouble. "You hear what I did? Leave 'im alone, he says, leave 'im alone, us as've been fighting Blackfeet all winter. Leave 'im alone, like as if the Blackfeet didn't send Bodah under, like as if the Blackfeet ain't dogged us all along and put lead in some of us."

He turned on Boone, and his finger pointed to the scar on his hairline. "Whar you think I got this? From old age? Blackfeet, by God, four years ago. Knicked my mare and knocked her over, the devils did, and took me for dead, lyin' there, but we raised runnin', me and my mare, afore they lifted my scalp."

"It wasn't Poordevil done it."

"One's like t'other, much as two peas."

Jim saw two of Bridger's men nodding as they agreed with Streak. The rest just stood there, waiting for what would happen next, their faces sober and their eyes sharp. Come a fight, he and Boone and Summers and Poordevil figured to get the worst of it, with eight on the other side.

Boone was looking Streak in the eye, giving him a sort of dark, wild look, the kind of look Jim had seen him give just before his temper broke. Boone was a sudden man, acting first and thinking after. Jim wondered that he held in so good now.

"This nigger can outrun, outdrink, outstud, and outfight any son of a bitch that sides with a Blackfoot. Stand out of my way! This hoss aims to raise h'ar."

Jim saw the look on Boone's face that meant he wouldn't stand any more. He saw the look and saw Summers slide between them, moving quick and easy like a young man. "Hold in, now. We aim to get along nice and sociable. I reckon we're plumb glad to see you. But we don't aim to have Poordevil kilt, not by anyone. Not by you, Streak, and not by any of the rest—you, Shutts, or you, Reeson, or Allen, or any of the rest if you're a mind to stand with Streak. If it's blood you want you'll have it, but some of it'll be yours, I'm thinkin'." His gaze fixed on Streak and then went to the others, and there wasn't anything in his face except quiet. Jim stepped over by him, his unloaded rifle in his hand, and there were the four of them together looking at the eight and waiting, four of them counting Poordevil, who had lost his foolish smile, Jim noticed as he moved, and stood quiet but sharp and alive, like an animal waiting for a man to make a move.

For a moment things seemed to hang, like a rock teetering on a slope, not knowing whether to roll or settle, and then Russell said easily, "I wouldn't fight Dick Summers for the whole damn Blackfoot Nation and the Rapahoes to boot." It was like the rock settling.

Lanter grunted. "Me neither. These here are friends. Y'hear, Streak?"

After a silence Streak gave in. "I wasn't fixin' to fight any but that Blackfoot. I'd like his scalp for my old leggin's. I would, now."

He let himself be turned around to the fire and sat down and by and by smoked with the rest, not like a man with a fright in him, but like one just waiting his time.

"We ain't fixed good for company," Summers said while he moved around the fire pushing wood into it.

"We got meat," Lanter said, "a sight of good bull meat—a little blue, maybe, but not as blue as some I've et." He got up, and Robinson with him, and went to one of the pack horses and came back carrying cuts of it.

The others got out their knives and carved themselves pieces and speared them on roasting sticks. Lanter, who looked as old as time and as weather-beaten as any rock, yelled as one of them bent over the meat. "Don't be cuttin' that meat ag'in the grain! Other way saves the blood and juice. Y'hear?"

The dark little man he spoke to looked up, his great eyes seeming to swim in his head, and nodded and went to work with his knife again.

"No more sense'n a fool hen, that greenhorn Spaniard," Lanter muttered. "He'd sp'ile young cow, he would." He watched his own cut beginning to sizzle over the fire. "Treat it right, nigh any meat is good."

"Savin' snake meat," Hornsbeck put in. "This nigger's throat plumb shuts up at snake meat. I et it onc't, after wreckin' a bull boat and losin' everything 'cept my hair, an' I do declare it were a long fight 'twixt my pore paunch and that there snake."

Lanter turned his stick. "Meat's meat, I say, bull or cow or snake or whatever. But man meat ain't proper meat to this child's way of thinkin'." He took his knife and cut a slice from his roast and spoke while his jaws worked on it. "I put tooth to man meat onc't, down with the Diggers, who made out it was jerked goat when they traded. Stringy, it was, and kind of white, and it grew in the mouth while a man chewed on it." He swallowed his mouthful. "It ain't proper doin's. It ain't, now. This child's et skunk and goose cooked Injun style with the guts in and a roastin' stick pushed through from honker to hole, and raw fish and old moccasins when there was nothin' better, but my stomach is real delicate on man meat."

Poordevil had squatted by Boone, like a dog by its owner. His mouth was open, and through the hole in his teeth Jim could see his tongue lying pink and wet. As the meat browned, the men would carve off the outside, leaving the inside red and dripping to cook some more.

When the meat was gone Russell got up and stood waiting for the rest. "We best be getting on," he announced.

"How you pointin'?" Summers asked.

"To the Sweetwater and over. Come along."

Jim wanted to say "Sure," but Summers' gaze came to him and flicked on to Boone and Streak and Poordevil, and he said, "Reckon not, Russell. We can find us a few beaver yet, now the water's goin' down. Reckon we'll go up the Wind and over to Jackson's Hole and to rendezvous that way. We got time enough."

"We'll go on, then."

Streak turned in his saddle as they rode off and stared at Boone and then at Poordevil and hitched himself and went on. Jim figured he might as well have said he wasn't done yet.

Jim knew that Boone saw him, too, but Boone didn't say anything. He just watched the men ride away and by and by turned to Poordevil and put his finger to his eye and said, "Nō-waps-spa," and Poordevil bobbed his head.

23

Dick Summers pulled the hood over his head and brought his capote closer about him. There was no place in God's world where the wind blew as it did on the pass going over to Jackson's Hole. It came keen off the great high snow fields, wave on wave of it, tearing at a man, knocking him around, driving at his mouth and nose so that he couldn't breathe in or out and had to turn his head and gasp to ease the ache in his lungs. A bitter, stubborn wind that stung the face and watered the eye and bent the horses' heads and whipped their tails straight out behind them. A fierce, sad wind, crying in a crazy tumble of mountains that the Indians told many a tale about, tales of queer doings and spirit people and medicines strong and strange. The feel of it got into a man sometimes as he pushed deep into these dark hills, making him wonder, putting him on guard against things he couldn't lay his tongue to, making him anxious, in a way, for all that he didn't believe the Indians' stories. It flung itself on the traveler where the going was risky. It hit him in the face when he rounded a shoulder. It pushed against him like a wall on the reaches. Sometimes on a rise it seemed to come from everywhere at once, slamming at back and front and sides, so there wasn't a way a man could turn his head to shelter his face. But a body kept climbing, driving higher and farther into the wild heights of rock, until finally on the other side he would see the Grand Teton, rising slim and straight like a lodge-pole pine, standing purple against the blue sky, standing higher than he could believe; and he would feel better for seeing it, know-ing Jackson's Hole was there and Jackson's Lake and the dams he had trapped and the headwaters of the Seeds-kee-dee not so far away.

Summers bent his head into the wind, letting his horse make its own pace. Behind him plodded his pack horse, led by the lariat in his hand, and behind the pack horse came Boone and Jim and Poordevil and their animals.

It was known country to Summers, the Wind range was, and the everlasting snow fields and the Grand Teton that could come into sight soon, known country and old country to him now. He could remember when it was new, and a man setting foot on it could believe he was the first one, and a man seeing it could give names to it. That was back in the days of General Ashley and Provot and Jed Smith, the cool half-parson whom the Comanches had killed down on the Cimarron. It was as if everything was just made then, laid out fresh and good and waiting for a man to come along and find it.

It was all in the way a man thought, though, the way a young man thought. When the blood was strong and the heat high a body felt the earth was newborn like himself; but when he got some years on him he knew different; down deep in his bones he understood that everything was old, old as time, maybe—so old he wondered what folks had been on it before the Indians themselves, following up the waters and pitching their lodges on spots that he had thought were his alone and not shared by people who had gone before. It made a man feel old himself to know that younger ones coming along would believe the world was new, just as he had done, just as Boone and Jim were doing, though not so strong any more.

There rose the Grand Teton at last, so thin, seen from here, it didn't seem real. Summers pulled up to let the horses blow and felt the wind driving through to his skin and clear to his secret guts, with the keen touch of the snow fields in it. Boone yelled something to him, and Summers shook his head, and Boone cupped his hands around his mouth and yelled again, but sound wouldn't come against the wind; it blew backward down the pass, and Summers found himself wondering how far it would blow until it died out and was just one with the rush of air. He shook his head again, and Boone grinned and made a signal with his hand to show it didn't matter, and afterward tucked his chin around to the side to catch his breath. High to his left Summers could see a mountain sheep standing braced and looking, its head held high under the great load of horn. The trees grew twisted from cracks in the rock, grew leaning away from the wind, bowed and old-looking from the weight of it.

He let his gaze go to the back trail, to Boone and Jim and the horses standing hunched and sorry, their hair making patterns under the push of the wind. They were good boys, both, though different, brave and willing and wise to mountain ways. They were hivernans—winterers—who could smell an Indian as far as anybody and keep calm and shoot plumb center when the time came. Summers wondered, feeling a little foolish inside, that he still wanted to protect them, like an uncle or a pappy or somebody. It was Boone he felt most like protecting, because Boone thought simple and acted straight and quick. He didn't know how to get around a thing, how to talk his way out or to laugh trouble off, the way Jim did. Not that Jim was scared; he just had a slick way with him. Come finally to a fight, he didn't shy off. Boone, now, was dead certain to get himself into a battle at rendezvous with the man called Streak, and not in a play battle, either. It would be one or t'other, Summers was sure, and shook his head to get shut of the small black cloud at the back of it.

When they were going again his thoughts went back. As a man got older he felt different about things in other ways. He liked rendezvous still and to see the hills and travel the streams and all, but half the pleasure was in the remembering mind. A place didn't stand alone after a man had been there once. It stood along with the times he had had, with the thoughts he had thought, with the men he had played and fought and drunk with, so when he got there again he was always asking whatever became of so-and-so, asking if the others minded a certain time. It stood with the young him and the former feelings. A river wasn't the same once a man had camped by it. The tree he saw again wasn't the same tree if he had only so much as pissed against it. There was the first time and the place alone, and afterwards there was the place and the time and the man he used to be, all mixed up, one with the other.

Summers could go back in his mind and see the gentler country in Missouri State, and it was rich, too, if different—rich in remembered nests and squirrels and redbirds in the bush and fish caught and fowl shot, rich in soil turned and the corn rising higher than a boy's head, making a hidey-hole for him. He could go back there and live and be happy, he reckoned, as happy as a hoss could be with the fire going out of him and remembered things coming stronger and stronger into the mind.

Anyhow, he had seen the best of the mountains when the time was best. Beaver was poor doings now, and rendezvous was pinching out, and there was talk about farms over on the Columbia. Had a mountain man best close out, too? Had he best go back to his patch of land and get himself a mule and eat bread and hog meat and, when he felt like it, just send his mind back to the mountains?

Would he say goodbye to it all, except in his head? To rendezvous and hunting and set-tos with Indians and lonesome streams and high mountains and the great empty places that made a man feel like he was alone and cozy in the unspoiled beginnings of things? Could he fit himself back among people where he dassn't break wind without looking about first?

A man looking at things for the last time wanted to fix them in his head. He wanted to look separately at every tree and rock and run of water and to say goodbye to each and to tuck the pictures of them away so's they wouldn't ever be quite lost to him.

Jackson Lake and the wind down to a breath, the Three Tetons rising, the Hoary-Headed Fathers of the Snakes, and night and sleep and roundabout to rendezvous, trapping a little as they went, adding to their packs, going on over the divide from the Snake to the headwaters of the Seeds-kee-dee, and then seeing from a distance the slow smoke of campfires rising, the men and motion, the lodges pitched around, the color that the blankets made and the horses grazing, and hearing Boone and Jim yelling and shooting off their rifles while they galloped ahead, drumming at the bellies of their horses. They made a sight, with feathers flying on them and ribbons and the horses' manes and tails woven and stuck with eagle plumes. A greenhorn would take them for sure-enough Indians.

Rendezvous again, 1837 rendezvous, but rendezvous of other times, too, rendezvous of 'thirty-two and 'twenty-six and before, rendezvous of all times, of men dead now, of squaws bedded with and left and forgotten, of whisky drunk and enjoyed and drained away, of plews that had become hats and the hats worn out.

Summers' horse began to lope, wanting to keep up with the others, but Summers held his rifle in front of him undischarged. A man got so he didn't care so much about putting on a show.

24

oone felt Summers' gaze on him and, when he looked, saw it sink and fasten on the ground, as if Summers didn't want the thoughts he was thinking to be found in his eyes.

Summers said, "This nigger couldn't hit a bull's hind end with a lodgepole after five-six drinks."

"I ain't had too much," Boone answered after a silence. "I can walk a line or spit through a knothole." He drank from the can of whisky by his side. "It ain't true, anyways. You was some, now, yesterday, firin' offhand. You come off best."

"Didn't have more'n a swallow."

Summers and Jim were rumped down on either side of Boone. Poordevil lay on the ground in front of them, snoring, the whites of his eyes glimmering through the parted lids and the spit running from one corner of his mouth and making a dark spot in the dirt.

"Reckon Poordevil thought he could drink the bar'l dry," Summers said.

"I ain't fixin' to drink no bar'l dry."

It was getting along in the afternoon, and over a ways from them a game of hand was starting up, now that the horse racing was about over for the day, and the shooting at a mark. The players sat in a line on either side of the fire. While Boone watched they began to sing out and to beat with sticks on the dry poles they had put in front of them. Every man had his stake close to him. It was skins they were betting, mostly, and credit with the company, and some trade goods and Indian makings and powder and ball, and sometimes maybe a rifle. They weren't worked up to the game yet. Come night, and they would be yelling and sweating and betting high, they and others sided across from other fires. A man could make out Streak easy, with his head bare and the sun catching at the white tuft of hair.

Up and down river Boone could catch sight of Indian lodges, moved in closer than usual to the white camp, maybe because the rendezvous was smaller. Nearer, horses were grazing, and still nearer the mountain men moved, talking and laughing and drinking and crowding up with some Indians at the log counter that Fitzpatrick had set the company goods behind, under cover of skins. The tents of the company men clustered around the store. In back of them, pack saddles and ropes and such were piled. The lodges of the free trappers, from where Boone looked on, were west of the others, away from the river. Behind the counter two clerks kept busy with their account books. In front of it a couple of white hunters showed they had a bellyful. They were dancing, Indian style, and by and by began to sing, patting their bellies with their open hands to make their voices shake, and ending with a big whoop.

> *Hi—hi—hi—hi,*
> *Hi-i—hi-i—hi-i—hi-i,*
> *Hi-ya—hi-ya—hi-ya—hi-ya,*
> *Hi-ya—hi-ya—hi-ya—hi-ya,*
> *Hi-ya—hi-ya—hi-hi.*

The white men were Americans and French from Canada, mostly, but some were Spanish and some Dutch and Scotch and Irish and British. Everybody had arrived by now—the free trappers and the company men and Indians from all over, coming by the Sweetwater and the Wind and over from the Snake and from Cache Valley to the south near the Great Lake, from Brown's Hole and New and Old Parks and the Bayou Salade, coming to wait for Tom Fitzpatrick and trade goods from the States. Just yesterday Fitzpatrick had pulled in, with only forty-five men and twenty carts drawn by mules, but bringing alcohol and tobacco and sugar and coffee and blankets and shirts and such, all the same. At the side of the counter two half-breeds were working a wedge press, already packing the furs for the trip back to St. Louis, making steady knocking noises as they drove the wedges in.

It wasn't any great shakes of a rendezvous—not like they used to have, with companies trying to outdo each other and maybe giving three pints for a good plew. Now there were just the American Fur Company and Bridger and the rest of his old outfit working for it, and whisky cost four dollars and beaver went for four to five a pound, for all there wasn't much of it.

The Crows hadn't brought in more than a mite. They and the other tribes were restless and cranky; they talked about the white man hunting their grounds and about the Blackfeet warring on them and the traders putting low prices on fur and high ones on vermilion and blankets and strouding. They were crying—that's what they said—because the white brother took much and left little. The mountain men grumbled, too, trading pelts for half what they used to bring and hearing talk that maybe this was the last rendezvous.

It wasn't any great shakes of a rendezvous, but still it was all right; a man couldn't growl, not with whisky to be had and beaver still to be caught if he went careful, and the sky over him and the country clear to him any way he might want to travel.

Over his can of whisky Boone saw a little bunch of Crow girls coming on parade, dressed in bighorn skin white as milk and fancy with porcupine quills. Some of them would catch themselves a white man, and their pappies would get gifts of blankets or whisky or maybe a light fusee and powder and ball, and they would be glad to have a white brother in the family, and the white man would ride away from rendezvous with his squaw and keep her while she pleased him, and then he would up and leave her, and she would be plumb crazy for a while, taking on like kin had died, but after a while, like as not, she would find another mountaineer, or anyway an Indian, and so get all right again. Sometimes squaws got sure-enough dangerous when their men left them, especially if they left one to take up with another.

Boone saw that Jim's sharp eye had picked up the girls. "Them Crows are slick sometimes. They are, now," Jim said. He added, "And mighty obligin'."

"You ought to know," Summers said and smiled, looking at Jim as if he could see through him, looking at him with a little cloud in his eyes as if he wished he could go back to Jim's age. "Reckon maybe you should take one away with you, and not buzz yourself around like a bee in clover. They ain't after one-night rumpuses so much. Steady is what tickles 'em."

"Jim hankers for the whole damn tribe."

"You ain't so bad yourself, Boone, or didn't used to be. Can't figure you out. Bet you ain't had two women this spree. A body'd think you was still feared of catchin' a cold in your pants."

Some of the Crow girls were smart-looking, all right, and some of the Bannocks and Snakes and Flatheads, too, as far as that went. A man didn't get to see so many Blackfoot girls, but there was one of them, if she kept coming along and grew up to her eyes, would make these other squaws look measly.

Boone said, "Must be there's a right smart more goat in you. I had enough colds so's not to be afraid."

The three of them sat for a while without speaking, watching Russell come lazing over from the store, smoking a pipe.

"How, Russell."

"Hello," said Russell, and stopped and drew on his pipe while his eyes went over Poordevil. Poordevil didn't have anything on but a crotch cloth that came up under his belt and folded over and ended in red tassels. The sun lay on his brown body, catching flecks of old skin and making them shine. Russell put out his toe and poked Poordevil with it as if to see if he could rouse him. To Boone Russell said, "He isn't worth fighting about, he or any of the rest."

"I reckon I'll make up my own mind."

"As you please."

Russell was a proper man, and educated, but a good hunter, so they said, and cool in a fix. "Too bad you arrived late," he said to Summers. "We had some excitement."

"I been hearin'."

"Such impudence! Those Bannock rascals coming in to trade but still refusing to give up the horses they had stolen!"

"Injuns think different from whites."

"You mean they don't think."

"Stealin's their way of fun," Summers explained.

"They'll have to learn better, even if the learning comes hard. We gave the Bannocks a lesson. Killed thirteen of them right here and chased after the rest and destroyed their village and shot some more during the three days we fought them. In the end they promised to be good Indians. Bloody business, but necessary."

"Maybe so."

"The only way to settle disputes with hostile Indians is with a rifle. It writes a treaty they won't forget."

"Maybe," Summers answered again.

"They'll sing small in a few years. A wave of settlers will wash over them. The country won't be held back by a handful of savages."

Boone said, "What 'ud settlers do out here?"

Russell gave him a look but didn't answer.

"Where you aim to fall-hunt?" Summers asked.

"Upper Yellowstone again, I guess. Fontanelle and Bridger are taking a hundred and ten men to Blackfoot country."

Boone asked, "Far as the Three Forks, or north of there?"

"I wouldn't think so. They're enough Blackfeet on the Gallatin and Madison and Jefferson without going farther."

Russell strolled off, still sucking on his pipe.

Boone drank again and then let himself back on his elbows, looking west, yonder to where the sun was about to roll behind the mountains. A current of air whispered by his ear, making a little singing sound. When it died down, the other noises came to him again—the hand players calling out and beating with their sticks, the Indian dogs growling over bones, the horses sneezing while they cropped the grass, and sometimes the Indian children yelling. The sun shed a kind of gentle shine, so that everything seemed soft and warm-colored—the river flowing, the butte hazy in the distance, the squaws with their bright blankets, the red and black and spotted horses stepping with their noses to the grass, the hills sharp against the sky and the sky blue, the lodges painted and pointed neat and the fire smoke rising slow, and high overhead a big hawk gliding.

It was funny, the way Jim and Summers had their eye out for him, not wanting him to frolic until he and Streak had had it out. Boone knew how much he could hold and still move quick and straight. He knew how much he could hold and it was a considerable—as much, maybe, as any man at rendezvous. He wasn't going to cut down on his fun—not much, anyway—just so's to be on guard. Besides, Streak hadn't acted up, not to him, or picked on Poordevil, though he had made his brags around, saying he didn't walk small for any man and would get himself a Blackfoot yet, saying he could whip the likes of Caudill day or night, rain or shine, hot or cold or however. Summers allowed that Streak had held in because there wasn't any whisky in camp until yesterday.

Boone rested back on his elbows, feeling large and good, feeling the whisky warming his belly and spreading out, so that his arms and legs and neck all felt strong and pleasured, as if each had a happy little life of its own. This was the way to live, free and easy, with time all a man's own and none to say no to him. A body got so's he felt everything was kin to him, the earth and sky and buffalo and beaver and the yellow moon at night. It was better than being walled in by a house, better than breathing in spoiled air and feeling caged like a varmint, better than running after the law or having the law running after you and looking to rules all the time until you wondered could you even take down your pants without somebody's say-so. Here a man lived natural. Some day, maybe, it would all end, as Summers said it would, but not any ways soon —not so soon a body had to look ahead and figure what to do with the beaver gone and churches and courthouses and such standing where he used to stand all alone. The country was too wild and cold for settlers. Things went up and down and up again. Everything did. Beaver would come back, and fat prices, and the good times that old men said were going forever.

Poordevil groaned and opened one red eye and closed it quick, as if he wasn't up, yet, to facing things.

"How, Blackfoot."

Poordevil licked his lips. "Sick. God sick damn." He put his hand out, toward the can at Boone's side, and his eyes begged for a drink.

"First time I ever heerd goddam split," Jim said. "Seems onreligious."

"Not yet, you don't," Boone said to Poordevil. "Medicine first. Good medicine." He heaved himself up and went toward the fire and picked up the can he had set by it. It had water in it and a good splash of gall from the cow Summers had shot that morning. "Bitters. That's medicine now." He lifted the can and let his nose sample the rank smell of it. Before he handed it to the Indian he took a drink himself. "Here, Injun. Swaller away."

Poordevil sniffed of the bitters, like a dog at a heap of fresh dung, and brought up his upper lip in a curl that showed the gap between his teeth. He tilted the can and drank fast, his throat bobbing as he gulped. He threw the can from him and belched, and held out his hand for the whisky. He had a dull, silly, friendly look on his face like a man might expect to find on a no-account dog's if it so happened a dog could smile. Between the red lids his eyes looked misty, as if they didn't bring things to him clear.

Of a sudden Boone felt like doing something. That was the way it was with whisky. It lay in the stomach comfortable and peaceful for a time, and then it made a body get up and do. All around, the fires were beginning to show red, now that dark was starting to close in. Boone could see men moving around them, or sitting, and sometimes a camp kicker jerking a buffalo ham high from the fire to get off the ashes. There were talk and shouts and laughter and the chant and rattle of the hand players. It was a time when men let go of themselves, feeling full and big in the chest. It was a time to talk high, to make jokes and laugh and drink and fight, a time to see who had the fastest horse and the truest eye and the plumb-center rifle, a time to see who was the best man.

"I aim to move around," Boone said, and picked up his empty can.

"Last night you wasn't up to so much, Boone." It was Jim talking. "Me and Dick, we kep' our nose out of the strong water, just in case."

"Goddam it! You going to be dry all rendezvous? I ain't skeered."

Jim didn't answer, but Summers looked up with his little smile and said, "Not the whole livin' time, Boone. Just long enough, is all."

"Best get it over with right now, then."

Summers lifted himself and felt of the knife in his belt and took his rifle in his hand. "This nigger wouldn't say so, son. It's poor doin's, makin' up to trouble. Put out; we'll foller."

"Git up, Poordevil." Boone toed the Indian's ribs. "Whisky. Heap whisky."

Poordevil hoisted his tail in the air, like a cow getting up, and came to his feet staggering a little. "Love whisky, me. Love white brother."

"White brother love Poordevil," Jim said with his eyes on Boone.

"Love Poordevil heap. He's bound to, ain't he, Dick, with whisky four dollars a pint? Nigh a plew a pint."

Poordevil put on a ragged cotton shirt that Boone had given him earlier.

"What's beaver for?" Boone asked, leading off toward the counter. "Just to spend, ain't it? For drinks and rifles and fixin's? You thinkin' to line your grave with it?"

All Jim answered was, "That Injun can drink a sight of whisky."

From the store they went to a fire that a dozen free trappers were sitting around, telling stories and drinking and cutting slices of meat from sides of ribs banked around the flames.

"Make way for an honest-to-God man," Summers ordered.

Boone put in, "Make way for three of 'em."

From the far side of the fire a voice said, "Summers' talk is just foolin', but that Caudill, now, he sounds like he sure enough believes it."

Boone squinted across and saw that the speaker was Foley, a long, strong, bony man with a lip that stuck out as if for a fight.

A little silence came on everybody. Boone stood motionless. "I ain't one to take low and go down, Foley. Make what you want out'n it."

There was the little silence again, and then Foley saying, "Plank your ass down, Caudill. You git r'iled too easy."

Summers lowered himself and put his can of whisky between his knees. "How," the others said now. "Move in and set."

Foley started the talk again. "Allen was sayin' as how he had a tool once would shoot around a corner."

"I did that. Right or left or up or down it would, and sharp or gentle, just accordin'. Hang me, I would have it yet, only one time I got 'er set wrong, and the ball made a plumb circle and came back to the bar'l like a chicken to roost. Knocked things all to hell."

"This child shot a kind of corner onc't," said Summers, "and I swear it saved my hair."

"So?"

Summers fired his pipe. "It was ten years ago, or nigh to it, and the Pawnees was bad. They ketched me out alone, on the Platte, and there was a passel of 'em whoopin' and comin' at me. First arrow made wolf's meat of my horse, and there this nigger was, facin' up to a party as could take a fort."

Allen said, "I heerd you was kilt away back then, Dick. Sometimes be damned if you ain't like a dead one."

"Ain't near so dead as some, I'm thinkin'. It was lucky I had Patsy Plumb here with me." Summers patted the butt of his old rifle. "This here piece now, it don't know itself how far it can shoot. It scares me, sometimes, dogged if it don't, thinkin' how the ball goes on and on and maybe hits a friend in Californy, or maybe the governor of Indiana State. It took me a spell to get on to it, but after while I l'arn't I could kill a goat far as I could see him, only if he was humpin' I might have to face half-around to lead him enough. Yes, ma'am, I've fired at critters an' had time to load up ag'in afore ball and critter come together."

"Keeps you wore out, I'm thinkin', travelin' for your meat."

"That's a smart guess now. Well, here this child was, and the Pawnees comin', and just then I see a buffler about to make over a hill. He was that far away he didn't look no bigger'n a bug. I made the peace sign, quick and positive, and then I p'inted away yonder at the buffler, and the Injuns stopped and looked while I up with Patsy. I knowed 'er inside out then, and I waited until the critter's tail switched out of sight over the hill, and then, allowin' for a breeze and a mite of dust in the air, I pulled trigger."

Summers had them all listening. It was as if his voice was a spell, as if his lined face with its topping of gray hair held their eyes and stilled their tongues. He puffed on his pipe, letting them wait, and took the pipe from his mouth and drank just a sip from his can of whisky.

"The Pawnees begun to holler again and prance around, but I helt 'em back with the peace sign and led 'em on, plumb over the hill. Took most of the day to git there. But just like this nigger knowed, there was Mr. Buffler, lyin' where the ball had dropped down on him. I tell you niggers, the Pawnees got a heap respectful. One after the other, they asked could they have meat and horns and hair, figgerin' it was big medicine for 'em, till there wasn't anything left of that bull except a spot on the ground, and dogged if some of the Pawnees didn't eat that!" Summers let a little silence come in before he spoke again. "I ain't never tried any long shots since."

"No?"

"I figger I ain't up to it. I swear I aimed to get that old bull through the heart, and there he was, plain gut-shot. Made me feel ashamed."

They laughed, and some clapped others on the back, and they dipped their noses into whisky, and their voices rang in the night while the dark gathered close around, making the fire like a little sun. In the light of it the men looked flat, as if they had only one side to them. The faces were like Indian faces, dark and weathered and red-lit now, and clean-shaved so as to look free of hair. Boone drank from his can and pushed closer to the fire, feeling the warmth of it wave out at him. Poordevil squatted behind him, seeming comfortable enough in his crotch cloth and cotton shirt. Around them were the keen night and the campfires blazing and the cries of men, good-sounding and cozy, but lost, too, in the great dark like a wolf howl rising and dying out to nothing.

"I reckon you two ain't the only ones ever shot a corner," Jim said.

"Sharp or curve?"

"Sharp as could be. A plumb turnabout."

"It's Company firewater makes a man think things," Allen said. "He gets so he don't know goin' from comin'."

"In Bayou Salade it was, and we was forted up for the winter." Jim was getting to be a smart liar—as good as Summers, almost. "I took a look out one morning, and there not an arrer shot away was the biggest by-God painter a man ever see. 'Painter meat!' I says and grabbed up my rifle and leveled. The painter had got itself all stretched out, and lyin' so's only his head made a target. I aimed for the mouth, I did, and let 'er go, only I didn't take into account how quick that painter was."

Jim looked around the circle of faces. "He was almighty quick. The ball went in his mouth fair, and then that critter swapped ends, faster'n scat. I ain't hankered to look a painter in the tail since." Jim fingered his cheek gently. "That bullet grazed my face, comin' back."

The laughing and the lying went on, but of a sudden Boone found himself tired of it, tired of sitting and chewing and doing nothing. He felt a squirming inside himself, felt the whisky pushing him on. It was as if he had to shoot or run or fight, or else boil over like a pot. He saw Summers lift his can again and take the barest sip. Jim's whisky was untouched beside him. Goddam them, did they think they had to mammy him! Now was a good time, as good as any. The idea rose up in him, hard and sharp, like something a man had set his mind to before everything else. He downed his whisky and stood up. Summers looked around at him, his face asking a question.

"I'm movin' on."

Poordevil had straightened up behind him. Summers poked Jim and made a little motion with his head, and they both came to their feet.

Away from the fire Boone turned on them. "Christ Almighty! You nee'n to trail me. I aim to fix it so's you two dast take a few drams. Come on, Poordevil."

He turned on his heel and went on, knowing that Poordevil was at his back and Jim and Summers coming farther behind, talking so low he couldn't hear. He looked ahead, trying to make out Streak, and pretty soon he saw him, saw the white hair glinting in the firelight. The players chanted and beat on their poles, trying to mix up the other side, and the side in hand passed the cache back and forth, their hands moving this way and that and opening and closing until a man could only guess where the cache was.

The singing and the beating stopped after the guess was made, and winnings were pulled in and new bets laid while the plum-stone cache changed sides.

Boone spoke above the whooping and the swearing. "This here's a Blackfoot Injun, name of Poordevil, and he's a friend of mine."

Some of the players looked up, holding up the bet making. Streak dragged his winnings in.

An older man, with a mouth like a bullet hole and an eye that seemed to have grown up squinting along a barrel, said, "Set, Caudill. Who gives a damn? Me, I had a pet skunk onc't, and it wasn't hardly ever he'd piss on a friend of mine, and when he did the friend like as not didn't stink no worse, but only fresher."

Lanter said, "Let's get on with the game."

"What happened to your skunk friend?" Jim asked.

"It was goin' on the second winter that I had him, and I was holed up with two old hunters, like o' Lanter here, and one night old No-Pee just up and left without givin' no reason at all."

"Likely his pride finally got the best of him," Lanter said.

"'Twer'n't that. I figgered it out all right. Livin' close up with two hard cases like you, Lanter, his pore nose got so it just couldn't stand it no more."

Boone waited until the voices had quieted down. "I ain't aimin' to let no one pester Poordevil. Anyone's got such an idee, sing out!"

In front of him a man said, "Jesus Christ! My beaver's nigh drunk up already."

Streak's eyes lifted. His face was dark and his mouth tight and straight. A man couldn't tell whether he was going to fight or not. Boone met his gaze and held it, and a silence closed around them with eyes in it and faces waiting.

Streak got up, making out to move lazily. "The damn Blackfoot don't look so purty," he said to the man at his side. His glance rose to Boone. "How'll you have it?"

"Any way."

Streak left his rifle resting against a bush and moved out and came around the players. Boone handed his gun to Jim. Summers had stepped back, his rifle in the crook of his arm. Over at the side Poordevil grunted something in Blackfoot that Boone didn't understand.

Streak was a big man, bigger than he looked at first, and he moved soft and quick like a prime animal, his face closed up and set as if nothing less than a killing would be enough for him.

Boone waited, feeling the blood rise in him hot and ready, feeling something fierce and glad swell in his chest.

Streak bent over and came in fast and swung and missed and caught his balance and swung again before Boone could close with him. His fist struck like a club head, high on Boone's cheek. Boone grabbed for him, and the heavy fist struck again and again, and he kept driving into it, feeling the hurt of it like something good and satisfying, while his hands reached out and a dark light went to flashing in his head. He caught an arm and slipped and went down with Streak on top of him. A hand clamped on his throat and another clinched behind, and the two squeezed as if to pinch his head off. The fire circled around him, the fire and the players and Summers standing back with his rifle and Jim with his mouth open and his eyes squinched like he was hurting and Poordevil crouching as if about to dive in. They swung around him, mixed and cloudy, like something only half in the mind, while he threshed against the weight on him. He heard Streak's breath in his ear and his own wind squeaking in and out. He caught Streak's head in his hands and brought it down and ripped an ear with his teeth. Streak jerked the ear free, but in that instant Boone got a gulp of air, and the dizzy world steadied.

He had hold of Streak's wrists. He felt his own muscles swelling along his forearms as he called on his strength. It was as if his hands were something to order the power into. It came a little at a time, but steady and sure—a little and then a wait and then a little more, the hold on his throat barely slipping each time and then loosening more until he held Streak's straining hands away. He called on all his strength and forced Streak's left arm straight, and then he dropped his grip on the other and whipped his free arm across and clamped it above Streak's elbow, straining the forearm back while he bore on the joint.

The arm cracked, going out of place, and Streak cried out and wrenched himself away and lunged to his feet, his face black and twisted and his left arm hanging crooked. As he came in again, his good arm raised, Boone caught the dark flicker of a knife and heard Jim's quick cry of warning.

He hadn't time to get out his own blade. As he twisted away, the knife came down and cut through his shirt, and the bite of it along his arm was like the bite of fire. He snatched at the wrist and caught it. Above the whistle of their lungs Summers' voice came: "By God, he asked for it!"

His hands fought the wrist, the knuckles, the clutched fingers, and caught a thumb and bent it back. He jerked the hand around under his chest and saw it weakening, one finger and another letting up like something dying and the handle coming into sight. The knife slipped out and fell in the grass. Boone snatched it up, holding to Streak with his other hand. A word stuttered on the man's lips, and the campfire showed a sudden look of fear in his face, a look of such fear that a man felt dirtied seeing it. The eyes flicked wide, flicked and fluttered and came wide again and closed slow as Boone wrenched the knife free and drove it in again.

Boone pushed with his hand. Streak fell over backwards, making a soft thump as he hit, and lay on his back, twitching, with the knife upthrust from his chest.

Poordevil let out a whoop and began to caper around, and Jim joined in, dancing with his knees high and yelling, "Hi-ya!"

Summers' rifle still was in the crook of his arm. "I'm thinking the trouble's over," he said, and nobody answered until Lanter spoke up with "Let's git on with the game. The parade's done passed. Any of you niggers want to take Streak's place?" Boone heard him add under his breath, "That damn Caudill's strong as any bull."

Boone turned to Summers. "Maybe you're ready to wet your dry now?"

"'Pears like a time for it, after we doctor you."

"It ain't no more'n a scratch. To hell with it! Let's have some fun."

Summers looked at the long cut on Boone's arm. "Reckon it won't kill ye, at that."

The men went back to playing hand, leaving Streak's body lying. Closed out from the firelight by the rank of players, it was a dark lump on the ground, like a sleeper. A man had to look sharp to see the knife sticking from it.

Boone passed it again, near daylight, after he had drunk he didn't recollect how much whisky and had had himself a woman and won some beaver. There was the taste of alcohol in his mouth, and the gummy taste of Snake tobacco. He held his arm still at his side, now that the wound had started to stiffen. He felt fagged out and peaceful, with every hunger fed except that one hankering to point north. With day coming on the land, the world was like a pond clearing. From far off on a butte came the yipping of coyotes. Suddenly a squaw began to cry out, keening for a dead Bannock probably, her voice rising lonely and thin in the half-night. A man could just see the nearest lodges, standing dark and dead. There was dew on the grass, and a kind of dark mist around Streak's carcass, which lay just as it had before, except that some Indian had lifted the hair, thinking that that plume of white would make a fancy prize.

25

Summers took one last look from the little rise on which he and Boone and Jim stood.

The camp had begun to stir now that morning was flooding over the sky. Squaws were laying fires and fixing meat to cook, and so were the white hunters and company *engagés* who didn't have a woman to do the squaw's work. He and Boone and Jim hadn't taken up with the squaws so much as the others, except for a time or two. As far as Summers knew, they hadn't fathered a child either, not anywhere, though like as not they had. Already one Indian was at the counter, probably asking for whisky. Summers saw a squaw come poking out of a lodge and after her two half-breed children, whom the French called *brulés* on account of their burned look. He wondered whether even the squaw knew who their pappy was. Farther off, horses were running, bucking and kicking up and nipping at one another in the early chill. The sun touched the tops of the hills, but lower down the dark lay yet. Against the morning sky the mountains were still dead, waiting for day to get farther along before they came to life.

"Me," said Jim, "I'd wait and go east with the furs."

Summers didn't answer, but it went through his mind again that he didn't want to go back with anybody. He wanted to be by himself, to go along alone with the emptiness that was in him, to look and listen and see and smell, to say goodbye a thousand times and, saying it, maybe to find that the hurt was gone. He wanted to hear water at night and the wind in the trees, to take the mountains and the brown plains sharp and lasting into his mind, to kill a buffalo and cook the *boudins* by his own small fire, feeling the night press in around him, seeing the stars wink and the dipper steady, and everything saying goodbye, goodbye.

Goodbye, Dick Summers. Goodbye, you old nigger, you. We mind the time you came to us, young and green and full of sap. We watched you grow into a proper mountain man. We saw you learning, trapping and fighting and finding trails, and going around then proud-breasted like a young rooster, ready for a frolic or a fracas, your arm strong and your wind sound and the squaws proud to have you under a robe. But new times are a-coming now, and new people, a heap of them, and wheels rolling over the passes, carrying green-horns and women and maybe children, too, and plows. The old days are gone and beaver's through. We'll see a sight of change, but not you, Dick Summers. The years have fixed you. Time to go now. Time to give up. Time to sit back and remember. Time for a chair and a bed. Time to wait to die. Goodbye, Dick. Goodbye, Old Man Summers.

"We didn't do so bad," Boone said, "what with beaver so trapped out and the price what it was."

Summers wondered whether he had done bad or good. He had saved his hair, where better men had lost theirs. He had seen things a body never would forget and done things that would stay in the mind as long as time. He had lived a man's life, and now it was at an end, and what had he to show for it? Two horses and a few fixin's and a letter of credit for three hundred and forty-three dollars. That was all, unless you counted the way he had felt about living and the fun he had had while time ran along unnoticed. It had been rich doings, except that he wondered at the last, seeing every-thing behind him and nothing ahead. It was strange about time; it slipped under a man like quiet water, soft and unheeded but taking a part of him with every drop—a little quickness of the muscles, a little sharpness of the eye, a little of his youngness, until by and by he found it had taken the best of him almost unbeknownst. He wanted to fight it then, to hold it back, to catch what had been borne away. It wasn't that he minded going under, it wasn't he was afraid to die and rot and forget and be forgotten; it was that things were lost to him more and more—the happy feeling, the strong doing, the fresh taste for things like drink and women and danger, the friends he had fought and funned with, the notion that each new day would be better than the last, good as the last one was. A man's later life was all a long losing, of friends and fun and hope, until at last time took the mite that was left of him and so closed the score.

"Wisht you'd change your mind," Boone said. "It'll be fat doin's up north, Dick."

Fat doings! Jim and Boone wouldn't understand until they got old. They wouldn't know that a man didn't give up the life but that it was the other way about. What if the doings were fat? What if beaver grew plenty again and the price high? He had seen times right here on the Seeds-kee-dee when beaver were so thick a hunter shot them from the bank, and so dear that a good pack fetched nigh a thousand dollars. Such doings wouldn't put spring in a man's legs or take the stiffness from his joints. They wouldn't make him a proper mountain man again.

The sun was coming up over Sweetwater way. The first red half of it lay lazy on the skyline, making the dew sparkle on the grass. To the west the mountains stood out clean, the last of the night gone from the slopes.

Summers looked east and west and north and south, hating to say goodbye.

"Fair weather for you," Jim said.

"Purty."

Boone's eyes came to his and drifted off.

These were Summers' friends, the best he had in the world, now that the bones of older ones lay scattered from Spanish territory north to British holdings. There was Dave Jackson, who started for California and never was heard from again, and old Hugh Glass, put under by the Rees on the Yellowstone, and Jed Smith, who prayed to God and trusted to his rifle but died young for all of that, and Henry Vanderburgh, a sure-enough man if green, who lost his hair to the Blackfeet, and Andrew Henry, the stout old-timer, who had died in his bed back in Washington County; there were these and more, and they were all gone now, dead or vanished from sight, and sometimes Summers felt that, along with some like old Etienne Provot, he belonged to another time.

And yet it had all been so short that looking back he would say it was only yesterday he had put out for the new land and the new life. A man felt cheated and done in, as if he had just got a taste of things before they were taken away. He no more than got some sense in his head, no more than hit upon the trick of enjoying himself slow and easy, savoring pleasures in his mind as well as his body, than his body began to fail him. The pleasures drew off, farther and farther, like a point on a fair shore, until he could only look back and remember and wish.

These were his best friends, he thought again, while for no good reason he took another look at the pack and saddle and cinches on his two horses. They were his best friends—this Boone Caudill, who acted first and thought afterwards, but acted stout and honest just the same; this Jim Deakins, who saw fun in things and made fun and had God and women on his mind.

"This nigger oughtn't to be takin' your Blackie horse," he said to Boone.

"Might be you'll need him, goin' alone."

"I ain't forgettin'."

"It ain't nothin'."

"Not many gives away their buffler horse."

"Ain't nothin'."

"Wisht I had him to give," Jim said.

Summers turned away from them. It was sure enough time for a mountain man to give up when his guts wrenched and water came to his eyes.

"Whar'll you camp tonight?"

What did it matter? It was all known country to him, the Seeds-kee-dee Agie and the Sandy and the Sweetwater. There was hardly a hill he didn't know, from whatever direction, or a stream he hadn't camped along. He could say goodbye to one as well as another. Leaving, a man didn't set himself a spot to make by night. There wasn't anything waiting for him at the end, except a patch of ground and a mule and a plow. He would take it slow, looking and hearing and remembering, while one by one the old places faded away from him and by and by he came on the settlements, where men let time run their lives—a time to get up, a time to eat, a time to work, a time to be abed so's to meet time again in the morning, a time to plow and sow and harvest. A man didn't live off the land there. He worked it like he would work a nigger, making it put out corn and pigs and garden trash. He didn't go out when he got hungry and kill himself a fat cow. He didn't see his living all around him, free for the shooting of it. He had to nurse things along, to wait and figure and save.

Things pressed him all around. He had to have money in his pocket, had to dicker for this and that and pay out every turn. Without money he wasn't anything. Without it he couldn't live or hold his head up. Men in the settlements gave a heap of time just to trading money back and forth, each one hoping he had got the best of it and counting his coins and feeling good at having them, as if they were beaver or rifles.

"You bound to go north?" he asked, knowing they were.

"Boone is," Jim said.

"We'll get us aplenty of beaver on the Teton and Marias and along there," Boone explained.

"If the Blackfeet'll let you. If the Piegans ain't trapped it out for Fort McKenzie."

"We'll get it."

"Teal Eye would be how old now?"

Jim said, "Old enough to have a man, and young'uns, too. Eh, Dick?"

"We'll get us beaver," Boone said.

The campfires sent up a thin blue smoke, so many campfires that a man wouldn't want to count them. The smoke rose straight, growing thinner while it climbed, until you couldn't see it at all, but only the clear empty sky it had lost itself in.

"Reckon Poordevil will stick by you?"

"Sure."

"Boone's l'arn't a right smart of Blackfoot talk."

"I taken notice."

"It'll come in handy. You'll see."

He wouldn't hear these sounds again, Summers told himself, or see these sights, or smell the smoke smell of quaking asp. He could hear the sharp voices of the squaws and the throaty talk of their men and the cries of children. The tones of the hunters came to him, too, and the knock of axes. He looked at the lodges standing in the glistening grass, standing clean against the blue distance. He looked at the dogs and children trotting about the lodges, at the horses done with their playing now and moving purposefully out to good pasture, at the river flowing steady between its fringe of trees, winding forever to the south to strange land he had never seen. It all was a regular town, of a kind, and it all made a smell and a sound and a picture. Could he get it again in his ear and eye and nose, once he was back in Missouri with time nudging him and his hand always feeling for money?

His eyes went to Jim and Boone. More than ever, the feeling of being father to them rose in him now that he had to leave. It was as if he was casting his young'uns loose to shift for themselves and feeling uneasy at what might happen to them.

"Well," he said, "time to put out. It is, now." He held out his hand. "This nigger can't make talk all day."

He got on his horse and reined it around, toward the rising sun, toward the east from which young Dick Summers had come a long, long time ago.

26

oordevil hung back, his face screwed up and anxious, and his eyes searching around like the eyes of an animal that had got a whiff of danger.

Jim was slewed half-around in his saddle, watching him. "Come on, Poordevil," he called. "If'n elk can pass along here, I reckon horses can."

Poordevil called back, "Heap, heap bad," and went off into Indian talk that Jim couldn't understand.

Jim turned around, so that his voice would carry to Boone at the head of the file. "What's he sayin', Boone?"

"Didn't hear," Boone answered over his shoulder.

"Say it again, Poordevil. Make loud talk."

The Indian raised his voice above the creaking of the leather, the clunk of the packs and the hollow thump of the horses' feet.

"Says it's the doin's of bad spirits," Boone translated.

"They put a proper name to it, all right, callin' it Colter's Hell."

Hell might lie underneath, sure enough, in the great unseen hole that echoed to the horses' feet, in the fire that burned under all the land and sent water boiling out of the ground and jets of steam that hissed up and trailed off in clouds on either side of the elk trail they were following. A low stink hung over everything. North and south and east and west the ground was crusted white, like a salt desert. Unless he looked beyond, to the line of hills or the trees sitting dark and hazy on the slopes, a man wouldn't think he was in the mountains. The sun blazed on the white crust, and the crust blazed back into the eyes, so that a rider went along with his face pinched and his lids narrowed.

Poordevil's voice came to Jim in a sudden throaty cry, and then the sucking of a hoof and the scramble of a startled horse, and, looking back, Jim saw the hole that the hoof had made in the crust and the blue steam coming from it.

"Devil nigh catched you that time, Poordevil," he said. "It's skeery, sure enough, Boone," he went on, knowing Boone couldn't hear him but talking all the same. "Almighty skeery."

Boone's hunched shoulders bobbed ahead of him, looking strong and bony under the slack cotton shirt. Beneath the red handkerchief he had tied on his head, his plaited black hair swung to the gait of his horse. His eye was always looking, to right and left and ahead, and his rifle was held crosswise and ready, but Jim knew it wasn't the devil Boone was watching for. Boone didn't worry about hell, or heaven either, but about Blackfeet and the thieving Crows and meat and beaver. He was a direct man, Boone was, and God didn't figure with him. What he could see and hear and feel and eat, and kill or be killed by, that was what counted. That, and sometimes a crazy idea, like this notion of going on beyond the Three Forks where the Blackfeet were thicker than gnats and always hungry for the Long Knives' scalps. Beaver, Boone said he was after, but Jim knew better. It was little Teal Eye, held secret in Boone's head all this time, and all the time growing and taking hold of him, until finally his mind was made up and God himself couldn't change him.

It was a crazy idea, all right, crazy as could be. Even Bridger, bound just for the upper Yellowstone and the Madison and the Gallatin and the Jefferson, was taking a parcel of men with him so's to be safe. Jim and Boone and Poordevil made only three. And what if Poordevil was a Blackfoot himself, as Boone argued? That didn't mean the Blackfeet would hold off. Jourdonnais had figured the same way, having Teal Eye with him, but he was dead just the same.

Sometimes Jim wondered why he hung along with Boone. There wasn't much fun in Boone. He was a sober man, and tight-mouthed, without any give in him unless it was with Summers. Go with Boone and you went his way. A man would think Boone would be satisfied now, having his own say-so about going north, but still he fretted because they took it slow and easy according to the promise Jim had finally pinched out of him. There was no sense in hurry, not with boiling springs to be seen and the great canyon of the Yellowstone and other doings that a body couldn't believe. It was only high summer, going on to fall, and the service berries were fat and purple on the lower slopes, and higher up the wild raspberries shone red along the ground. There was meat on hill and hollow, and the sun shone round and warm, and the wind had slackened, saving up for fall. It was a time to loaf, being as beaver wasn't good now anyhow.

Boone was a true man, regardless, cool and ready when there was danger about. He didn't know what it was to be affrighted. And you could depend on him, no matter what. There weren't many would stand as steady with a friend, or go with him as far, or stick through thick and thin. For all that he gave in to Boone, Jim felt older and a heap wiser and he knew that Boone depended on him. Some ways, Boone was like a boy still, needing just a careful word to be dropped to see things right and wise. Shooting buffalo or catching beaver or fighting bear, Boone was as good as the best, but with people it was different. He didn't know how to joke and give and take and see things from different sides and to find fun instead of trouble. All he knew was to drive ahead. Sometimes when he was about to get himself in a fix, on account of not taking time to think, a little piece of talk, said so as to seem offhand, would set him right and steady him or maybe hold him back. Jim reckoned Boone was grateful, as a boy would be grateful without having words to say so.

Jim squirmed in his saddle to watch Poordevil. The grin was gone from the broad and foolish face. You wouldn't know he was a merry one to see him now. His mouth was tight shut, closing the hole in his upper jaw, and his black eyes kept moving, seeing a spirit underneath every squirt of water and every puff of steam. Jim bet if a man nudged his hind end unbeknownst, he would jump clear off his horse.

"I reckon God is just putting on," Jim said to his horse, watching one long ear slant back to listen. "Could be, don't you reckon? God must like to get off by Himself sometimes and caper. Must get mighty tiresome, keepin' tally on folks and gettin' the sun up and tuckin' it in bed and bringin' the rain on and all, and all the time actin' stiff and proper." That surely was it. God must like to throw

Himself around some and be silly if He felt like it. So He came here, to the top of the world where the rivers met, and cavorted about and blew steam out of holes and squirted water just to show Himself what He could do, like a boy playing and no one to see him.

Thinking that way made a man feel friendlier toward God. Most folks made God out to be a mean somebody, putting notions in people's heads and sending them to hell if they acted according. God must have aimed for a man to enjoy himself, so He gave him a hankering for women and put women around him, and when a man pleasured himself, he was doing what God expected all along. Where was the sense in it otherwise? Why were squaws so many and so easy, if not for a purpose?

You couldn't tell, though, the different ideas there were. Maybe the folks were right who thought God just tempted men to be sinful, meaning to roast them forever and ever for doing what He had given them a weakness for. Maybe He aimed to trip them up. Or maybe it was the devil kept a man sinning. You couldn't tell where one left off and the other took up. Do what God gave you a taste for and the devil got you; don't do it and God took you to heaven. It all sounded against nature, but men believed it and a man couldn't tell.

After a while the white crust and the boiling water gave way to tangled pines, and the pines later to a plain with clumps of trees on it. To the south and west of them lay Yellowstone Lake, quiet in the late sun, with little circles running from the rising trout.

Boone checked his horse and raised his rifle and shot an elk that had just poked out of a clump of trees. The elk jumped once and fell and lay thrashing. "Likely place to camp," Boone said as he set about reloading his rifle.

"Heap bad," said Poordevil, his eyes fixed on another hot spring that sent up a feather of steam.

"Heap good, you goddam Injun," Boone said. "Love hell, me. Love hell heap. We got meat, and hot water to cook with, and we ain't like to be bothered with Blackfeet here, bein's they don't like it no better than you."

He got off his horse and went over to bleed the elk and came back and began to take off his saddle, looking around at Poordevil and grinning while his hands worked at the leather.

They tethered the horses and cooked elk meat and boiled a can of coffee, and afterward Jim sat back smoking and looking at the hills and the sky. The sun was gone, and dark was beginning to creep on the wooded slopes beyond the lake, but the sky was clear and light yet and the lake lay bright against its edging of earth and timber, like a piece fallen from above. To the east the sun lingered on the very tops of the mountains. Up there a man could see the ball of it yet and get some heat from its shine, but from where they sat Jim could see only a little cloud that it had set afire as it passed. He hunched his shoulders inside his shirt as he felt the evening chill coming on. Overhead, from somewhere or everywhere, there was a high, fine singing. Only when a man was quiet did he hear it, but there it was then, thin and coming on and fading and coming on again, and it might have been the high pines talking, or the mountains, or time humming, far off and old, so that a body felt little and short-lived, so that he felt lonesome and hungry for people so's to forget how big the world was, so's not to be thinking how long a mountain lived. The air was so quiet that the fire smoke climbed straight as a stem. Jim could hear the fire murmuring at the wood and once in a while the sound of a grazing horse, but that was all, except for the thin singing.

He wished for Summers, with his gray eye and slow smile and his easy, knowing way. A body never was so sad and lonesome like this with Summers around. Summers understood how a man felt, and he understood animals and nature, too, and they all seemed to fit together with him and make him at home wherever. Jim could tell that Boone missed him, too, being even silenter than usual and straight-mouthed, with no ear or tongue for small talk. It was as if something was lost to them when Summers left, something that helped to make a trapper's life good and satisfying. Jim asked himself why he should keep on hunting the rivers and being alone and half-starved for folks and sometimes at night having the deep, secret fear of death with him like something that shared his bed and pricked him away from sleep; but he knew he would keep on for a while anyway, no matter why. A hunter's life was a good-enough life if you weren't cut out especial for something else. After a spell you grew into it and just kept going, not knowing anything better. Probably people on farms or in stores or on the river levees got almighty sick of one another and wanted to get off by themselves. For all that he liked company, there wasn't anything could be more tiresome than people.

He sat half-dozing, letting his ears listen. And then he heard Boone say, "Sheepeaters, likely," and he sat up and saw four figures at the edge of the woods behind him. When Boone got up, his rifle in his hand, they melted back into the trees. Boone put his rifle down and stood silent, and after a while they came out again and stood in a line, all of them looking and all waiting.

"I'll see," Jim said. He arose and started toward them without his rifle, wondering if they knew the peace sign, wondering if they could understand his Shoshone talk. He kept a smile on his face and moved slow, and by and by motioned them to come to him. They were a man and a squaw, he saw now, and two young ones, and they stood uncertain and curious, wanting to dart back into the trees but wanting to see more, too. A little flutter of uneasiness went over them as he drew closer, and he stopped, waiting for them to get used to him, as a hunter would have waited to calm down his game.

"The white brother's heart is good," he said in Snake. "The white brother has but one mouth and one tongue."

They listened, understanding but still wary, standing pale in their bighorn skins against the dark of the woods. The man's bow dangled in his hand. Four dogs carrying packs slipped from behind them and saw Jim and growled and then sat down. After a while, as he stood silent, the dogs began to grin.

It all might have been a picture except for the little movement, the Indian's eyes going over him and the squaw watching and putting out her hands to stay the little ones, and the little ones, forgetting fright, making small, jerky motions like sandpipers.

"The white brother has meat. Will his brothers eat?"

Jim could see the thought working in their heads. Their eyes were still now, and fastened on him as a man might fasten a glass on a distant thing, but fastened inward, too, on the food that he offered.

"The red powder and tobacco and beads and a medicine glass to look in." Jim motioned behind him, toward the fire.

The squaw said something low-voiced to her man, and they took a forward step, still watchful and uneasy, but venturesome, too.

Jim turned and made for the fire, and sat down there with

Boone and Poordevil, and all of them looked away toward the lake in which a slow cloud floated. No one spoke or peeked until the Indian gave a little grunt, and they turned about to see them standing, open-faced and simple, the man on one side and the squaw on the other, with the two children in between.

Jim took a brand from the fire and touched it to his pipe and pointed the stem up and down and around and held it for the Indian. After he had puffed on it, the Indian held out an old and battered fusil, with the pan open and rusted, pointing to it to show he lacked powder and ball. A three-foot sheep's-horn bow ornamented with quills hung from his arm. Jim took lead from his pouch and poured powder from his horn into the Indian's chipped one. The man smiled then and began to make Snake talk. Pretty soon the squaw was talking, too, and the young ones chirping.

"That old musket wouldn't shoot, no matter what," Boone said. "And take a look at the arrer. These is Poordevils, sure enough. Got a stone head, it has." He dug into his possibles and brought out a small looking glass backed with paper, and handed it to the squaw. She looked into it and made a sudden little noise and smiled to see herself. The children crowded into her and gazed at themselves. Their eyes went to hers, asking questions; for no reason at all they broke out laughing, high and clear like bells. They darted around to the other side of the fire and smelled the meat and pointed to it, wanting some.

Not until then did the man seem to notice Poordevil, but when he did his eyes widened suddenly and narrowed, and he made a motion as if to push his family back.

"Don't be skeered," Jim said, and switched to Shoshone. "The Blackfoot has traveled far with us. He is a brother. He wants peace." Jim studied Poordevil as he spoke. Poordevil let up on his anxious look long enough to give a smile.

The Sheepeater studied Poordevil a while longer and then, as if his fright was over, began talking again. Did the white brother have tobacco? Did he have a knife or an awl? Would he trade ball and powder? Did he want the skins of the beaver or the otter? Beaver were few in the streams now because the Indians had had to make meat of them. They had saved a few skins.

The four dogs were haunched around the fire, smelling the elk meat while their tongues hung out dripping. The Indian went to one of them and from the travois to which it was hitched took a small bundle of furs. He dropped it at Jim's feet.

"Beaver and otter," Jim said to Boone.

The Indian said, "They belong to the white man. Give us what you like."

When they had traded and eaten they moved off, happy at having a butcher knife and an awl and a few rounds for the fusil. Their talk and the laugh of the little ones came to Jim after they were lost from sight, and by littles thinned to an echo and then were gone.

Afterward, when night had closed in, Jim lay on his back facing a sky prickled with stars. It was like the beginning of the world here, high and lonesome and far off from men's doings, and the Sheepeaters might have been the first people, shy and simple and full of trust when their fright was gone. The beginning of the world, with the fine singing filling the sky and the boiling water sounding low, and a man wondering how things got started, and was God sitting on one of the stars, looking down and maybe grinning or maybe frowning? A man felt lost if he let his mind run, lost under the sky, lost in the high hills, lost and as good as dead already while time flowed on and on forever.

"Boone," Jim asked, "you taken notice that Poordevil's got Streak's scalp?" But Boone already was asleep.

Jim wished he had a woman. It kept a man's mind close to himself.

27

Boone lay on his belly, screened by the quaking asp that grew on the nub of a hill. Before him rolled the great Yellowstone plain, dipping and rising and stretching on until the sky curved down and closed it off. Far away, so that it seemed like the ragged shadow of a cloud moving across the sun, he could see a herd of buffalo headed out from water to the rich brown grass of the slopes, now that the afternoon was cooling off. Closer, half a dozen antelopes played, moving quick and delicate like flutters in the wind. The sun bore down on the back of his neck and spread on out over the plain, making a warm tan of it like the summer coat of the weasel. Earlier, for all that the time was early fall and the wild plums were ripening, the heat waves had danced out of the dust, and animals kept to the shade and water, but the sun had gentled now and a cool breath came off the mountains. Mosquitoes buzzed around him, and one big blue fly that acted as if it expected him to die any minute. He wondered whether, if he lay still enough, the fly would blow him. How did a fly know when a critter was dead? Maybe the fly was like Jim, figuring there was more than a chance he would go under, but not scolding over it the way Jim had done.

"It's risky, Boone," Jim had said, "and onnecessary to boot."

"I'll be all right, I said."

"Sure. Sure. You'll be all right, except maybe dead. Or maybe the Crows hot on our tail, and us only three and strange to these here parts besides. Crows ain't squaws, you know, or dogs. They kin fight."

"Won't let 'em sight me. They can't fight what they don't see."

Jim shook his head. "I'll tag you then. It ain't safe to let you out alone."

"Don't want you along. This is one man's work."

Poordevil sat before the early-morning fire. His big nose squatted down at the tip as his mouth spread into a grin. "Me big thief," he said. "Damn fine thief. Catch 'im horse quick."

"Me catch 'im horse," Boone answered. "I'll be back, come dark," he said to Jim, and then he had left them camped snug where the Yellowstone began to come out of the mountains. He had known Jim's uneasy gaze followed him as he rode away.

Behind Boone, where the asp was thicker, his horse moved, cracking the twigs, and he looked around to make sure it was all right. The horse looked back at him, sleepy-eyed and dull, while its tail waved at the mosquitoes. It was Summers' old horse, Poky, a slow animal but a stayer and gentle as a pet dog. It was just the thing for what he aimed to do.

He sent his eye back to the plains, seeing the buffalo again and the antelopes and the sunshine lying long on the grass, but mostly he kept his gaze on the Crow village that lay not a half-mile away. It was a fair-sized camp, being forty lodges, he figured, and it was coming to life now with the heat cooling. He saw squaws scraping skins and carrying wood, or chasing the no-good dogs that would pull the wood in if only you could catch one of them. Sometimes when the wind stilled he could hear the squaws screeching at the dogs like magpies. The smoke of fires was rising here and there and bending and going off with the breeze. Men moved from one lodge to another, making plans for a hunt, maybe, or for a war party, or bragging on themselves or maybe just talking. Greenhorns thought Indians always talked high and solemn, but that was just when they were holding palaver; around camp, with no nabob about, they talked small and sometimes so dirty that even a trapper noticed it. The men's hands moved as they talked. A bunch of horses was drifting out to grass, cropping on the way. Boone studied them, one by one, trying to search out the best. There were some smart horses in the herd, the smart ones mostly hobbled and having to walk short or to lift up and lunge to get anywheres.

After a while he settled on the horse he wanted. It was a red horse with a narrow blaze and a deep chest and legs quick and slender, and it carried itself proud. An Indian wouldn't trade off a horse like that, not for anything, even if the horse wasn't white or speckled. About the only way to get a war horse was to steal it.

Boone lay still, waiting on time. A man got so he could lie patient and quiet as a hunting cat, not pushing against time but letting it run while the sun shone on him and the breeze hummed by his ear. He was like a tree or a chunk of earth, except that his mind looked back and forward and made pictures inside his head. Old Chief Heavy Otter would prize that red horse, he reckoned. He saw himself offering it, with the painter skin he had got from the Utahs falling rich across its back. There was nobody knew how to dress skins like the Utahs. And he had vermilion, too, and tobacco aplenty, and powder and ball. He was a good hunter and a brave warrior, and his heart was good toward the Blackfeet. He would help the chief when he grew old and be a son to him and keep meat in his lodge when the chief's arm was weak with the arrow and his legs too stiff for the hunt. While he watched, the red horse took a sudden fright and shied out and ran lunging with the hobbles, but moving fast and easy just the same, and then stopping with his head high and turned, and the sun shining white on the blaze. He was a proud horse; Heavy Otter was bound to like him.

He could see Teal Eye, not like she was but grown and rounded now, but still with the big eyes and the slender face, and eagerness in her like in a bird. It was strange how a hankering got into a man and stayed with him and finally pointed him in a certain direction. Maybe it was that he wouldn't want Teal Eye now. Maybe it was only a notion that would go away when he saw her. Maybe Teal Eye had a man already, and a lodge full of young ones. Anyhow, he and Jim and Poordevil would find beaver, a many of them, in country that other trappers feared to hunt. The white hunter had brought the good red horse as a gift, and he had brought the painter skin and powder and lead to Heavy Otter to show he loved the Blackfeet.

The blue fly lit on his hand and flexed itself up and down while its fat tail looked for a place to lay. Boone brushed it away, and it arose with a little drone of wings and circled his head, not giving up. Could a fly know when a man was going to be meat and to lie for the wolves and worms and the quick gray bugs that worked deep in the stink?

That was something that Jim would think about and have an idea for. Jim thought a heap—too much for a good mountain man —going along sometimes and not seeing anything except what was in his head. Jim was a smart one, all right, only Boone didn't see any sense in pestering himself with things he couldn't do anything about. The mind dug into a thing and got itself tired and cranky and then had to back out the same hole it had gone in.

The slow afternoon wore on. The sun inched down, no longer shining on his neck but just peeking through the trees, making a speckle of light and dark. A striped squirrel, no bigger than a mouse, flirted along a log close to him, its eye big and moist and darkly shining. When he moved, it let out a surprised squeak and dived from sight and by and by came back to look at him again, as if to make sure he was real. Patches of shade appeared on the plain. Out from each lodge a pointed shadow lay. Nowhere in all the sky was there a cloud. The breeze had stopped. Even the nervous leaves of the quaking asp hung sleeping. A man having work to do tonight would want to get it done before the moon came out, if he could. He would want to get it done and be away, so's to meet up with Jim and Poordevil, waiting westward and ready for an early start in the morning. Likely Jim was thinking now about hot springs and mud boiling up and the great canyon of the Yellowstone and the yellow rock that gave the river its name; likely he was thinking about them and other queer doings and trying to find where God figured in it all.

The red horse had hobbled out a piece from the rest. While Boone watched he raised his head high and looked around. A good horse, he was, with strong, clean lines and a sure, high manner. A man came riding out from the camp and cast his eye around and saw nothing and after a while turned and went back, thinking all was well. Boone reckoned the Crows would bunch the horse herd closer before night, but it didn't seem likely they would stake them or post a guard, not while they felt so safe.

The sun fell behind a mountain, and the sky turned a deeper blue, and the mosquitoes began to swarm sure enough, but the big blue fly was gone, maybe hunting a likelier place or maybe chilled and discouraged and squatted down somewhere. Behind Boone the tail of old Poky kept up a steady swishing.

Boone put his head on his hands and slept a little, slept lightly as an animal, with his ear cocked for sound and his mind on the edge of wakefulness. He stirred at the time he had set and studied the camp and plain again. The dark was drifting down, so that all the horses looked of one color and the campfires winked red. He could make out the one horse, though, still off a ways from the rest and still nibbling at the grass. Three or four men, now, could make off with the whole herd, he reckoned, but he didn't want a war party on his tail. He wanted just one horse, and then to be away, across the Yellowstone and on towards the Missouri.

Three riders came out and rounded up the horses and headed them toward camp, yelling to make them move. Boone kept his eye on the red horse. He would know him now in the dark, as long as he could see the lines of him. With the riders gone, the bunch loosened while he watched, still nosing out for grass. The red horse pointed towards Boone, grazing independent of the rest. If he stayed where he was, or close by, Boone figured he could go to him in the deep dark, smelling him out like a hound, hunting for him like an owl. There was hardly a rock or a hump or a rabbit track he didn't know after lying there looking all afternoon.

The horses grew into a darker blackness in the black of night and by and by were lost to sight. Overhead the stars began to shine, not bright and alive but sleepy, opening dim on the darkness.

Boone got up and stretched his muscles and went back to Poky. He stroked the bare back before he untied him. A saddle could give a man away. He led Poky down the slope, his moccasined feet feeling under him the trail he had marked while the sun was up.

At the bottom he halted, smelling for the wind. A breeze from the east, now, would be the thing, or no breeze at all. A west wind or a south one would take the smell of him to the horses and to the Indian dogs. The air played about him, coming first one way and then another, but then steadying, flowing from the north and east as he had wished. It was a good sign. The wind blowing as a man wanted it was a good sign. He held his old horse short and moved on, aiming toward where he had last been able to make out the red horse.

The night crowded thick all around; he hadn't a tree or a rock to go by, or the top of a hill against the sky, but only what he had put in his head while he had lain watching, only what his feet and his hands felt. Still, by a clump that raised out of the blackness when he was nearly on it, or a slope that dropped away under his moccasins, he knew that he was right. He pulled up his horse now and got to the off side of it, so's to be shielded from the herd, or from Crows if there were any about. The old horse stepped ahead, slow and easy like a free animal, answering to the hand under his neck as if he knew what to do without being told. The breeze blew steady, flowing out of the northeast and over the camp to Boone. The sounds of a dogfight came to him, and then a man's voice and the thump of a club and the keen yelp of hurt. Maybe he would have done better to wait until the camp slept, but maybe not; the Crows wouldn't be expecting company so soon after sundown.

It was here that the red horse should be, he told himself, but there was no horse about—only the grass whispering to his steps, only the dark and the emptiness. The herd had drifted after night settled down. He would have a time finding the red horse, with the bunch shuffled and the night so black a man couldn't see his hand.

He held up, thinking, trying to sharpen his eyes to the darkness, and then, eastward, he saw a pale bulge of light that told the moon was coming up, the moon that would show him the horses and that might show him to the Crows. He squatted down, holding the lead rope while old Poky stood quiet, waiting on him as if waiting was a proper part of life, too. A wolf was howling from the west, and closer by the coyotes yipped, and all at once the Indian dogs began to answer, barking deep and high-pitched and hoarse and shrill, and quieting all at once, too, while the wolf and the coyotes kept on.

The moon got its edge over world, and by and by the fat bulge of it, and then lay red and swollen, as if resting up before starting its journey across the sky. Even so, it cast a light, making big, deep patches on the land. Boone could see the red fires in it, could see it turning lazy like a ball turning. It climbed an inch or two, no longer resting on the line of earth but sailing, the flames going from red to yellow like a campfire getting hot. Things began to grow out of the darkness, a clump of bushes close at hand, the swell of a little hill, and the weaving black line the trees made yonder toward the river. After a while he saw the horse herd, moved in now toward camp.

He started the old horse then, letting it plod along like a stray coming back to the bunch while he hid himself at the side. He mustn't hurry; slow was the caper. Easy, hoss, easy. Goddam the cactus!

He knew without looking that he had come up to the horses. It was as if he could hear them staring at him, as if he could hear them standing with their ears pointed and their nostrils wide, though all he heard were the little sounds of the village and all he saw were the slow legs of Poky and the earth passing under his feet.

He looked under Poky's neck and saw a horse reared before him as if it had sprung out of the ground. The breath rattled in its nose. He stopped Poky and waited, not wanting to pass the horse and so give him his scent. The horse snorted again, shorter and lighter this time, and then turned and made off slowly.

Some of the horses lay flat. They rolled up as he neared, resting on their bellies with their heads high and watchful. He slowed his own horse to a bare creep, letting the herd look and listen and smell for him.

To the side of the others he spotted the red horse, spotted the fine line of his back and the high head, and he eased toward him, keeping behind Poky, peeking under the old neck. The red horse's nostrils fluttered in a little sound, and his feet moved nervously, but he didn't turn to run.

Poky knew the horse Boone wanted. Once pointed that way, he kept on, moving one heavy foot and then another, narrowing the distance as the red horse watched. They touched noses, the breath of the red horse drawing in in a long tremble. Boone slipped under Poky's neck, trying to move fast without seeming fast. His hand flipped the end of the rope over the arch of the neck. The red horse snorted loud and reared and tried to spin as Boone's other hand caught the end of the rope beneath the throat. Boone held on while the horse lunged. His breath said, "Whoa, now! Whoa! Ain't nothing going to hurt you, boy." His arms started from their sockets as his body jerked ahead. His legs leaped to keep up and then fell behind and dragged in the dirt. "Whoa, you snorty bastard!" The words came out in grunts. "Whoa, now!" He caught his feet and held still while the horse stood stiff and scared. "Whoa, boy!" His hand went out and stroked the neck, feeling the muscles quiver. After a minute the red horse let himself be pulled over to Poky.

The other horses had run and faced about. He could see the fronts of them, rising tall and stiff. He could hear their forefeet stamp a challenge and the breath snorting into their lungs. Even against the wind the village might have heard them. Maybe it could hear them now if it listened.

He stood quiet, letting his eyes pry into the darkness, letting his ears feel for sound. After a while, at the very end of his sight, he caught movement. It could be a wolf. It could be a Crow who had heard the noise of the horses and had come out alone, hoping maybe to get a scalp and so be able to brag on himself. It could be one of a parcel of Crows. Anyhow, he'd have to wait. There wasn't time for a getaway. With the moon higher now and the light touching things up, even a poor shot could knock him from his horse. Boone stepped the red horse around, so as to be in his shadow. He stooped and ran the free end of the lariat under the hobbles and, pulling strong and slow, brought the head down and tied a knot to hold it there. He carried a pistol in his belt, but if there was work to be done it was work for the knife. He brought the knife out, feeling the keen steel while he crouched in the shadow of the horse and squinted under its belly. He put his hand up and stroked the horse's shoulder, wanting to keep him from fighting the rope. The horse strained against it, not wild, though, but easy, as if trying the knot. The head came around then and took a long quivering smell of Boone.

The movement had stopped, and whatever had made it was melted into the darkness. When it came to Boone's eye again it was like the darkness dividing, like a piece breaking off and going on by itself. It was just one Indian walking, a bold Indian walking by himself, going slow and watchful. It could be he would pass by if Boone held still and the red horse behaved himself. The Crow stepped careful, his face showing vague against the shine of the moon, his heart hoping, likely, to find a Blackfoot and to kill him and take the hair.

A Crow scalp would be a pretty thing, now, to carry to the Blackfeet. It would help with them. The white hunter was a friend of the Blackfeet. He had fought their enemies and put them under. Here was a scalp to show that he spoke true.

Boone's hand felt in the grass and found a rock. He pitched it over the Crow's head and heard it thump and saw the Indian switch about. He ducked under the horse and heard it kick at him and felt the hoof grazing his hip. And then he was up, running soft and fast. He leaped as the Indian turned. His left arm went around the neck under the chin and clamped off the cry that struggled in the throat. His right arm drove the knife deep.

It was over almost before a man could say Godamighty. An Indian wasn't a match for a white man, not for a real man with two good arms. The Crow stiffened and went limp, and his knees folded under him. Boone let him sink. Before he ran the circle with his knife and ripped the scalp away, he studied the land again. The red horse had thrown himself, trying to run, and lay thrashing on his side. Poky hadn't stirred a step. The herd had galloped off. Boone seemed to remember that they had made quite a ruckus doing it. The wind blew steady, though, and the sounds from camp were the small sounds of calm. He stuffed the scalp under his belt. The hair on it was long, as Crows' hair was, reaching down, maybe, to the back of the knees.

He went to the red horse and untied the lariat and cut the hobbles. The horse struggled to his feet. "Steady, boy." He climbed on old Poky and headed west, leading the other horse, keeping to the shadows and the swales while his ears listened. The noises still were little noises. Even the dogs went silent after a while except for a halfhearted bark now and then. When a patch of timber closed him off from the village, Boone put Poky to a trot. It had all been dead easy, thanks to wind and luck and a pair of arms a man could take a rightful pride in. It wasn't safe to let him out alone, wasn't it? The Crows would get him, or come chasing after? Risky, Jim had said it was, and unneccesary; but his scalp was still on and no one trailed him, and at the end of the lead rope trotted such a piece of horseflesh as anyone would itch for.

The white hunter would be a son to Heavy Otter and would keep meat in his lodge and fight his enemies. The white hunter was a great warrior. Here was a scalp fresh-taken from the Crows. And here was a buffalo horse as fast as the wind and stout and long-enduring as the moose deer. The buffalo horse was Heavy Otter's, it and the painter skin and the tobacco and the red earth for the face and the powder and ball. The white hunter wanted the daughter of Heavy Otter for his squaw.

28

It was stern country they traveled, pushing north along the Gallatin, a country high and chill at night, swept by western winds. Sometimes in the mornings the frost lay white-grained on the grass. The wild plums that hung rich and ready on the Yellowstone had petered out, along with the salt weed that kept the horses stout in wintertime. Already the chokecherries dripped black, soft and sweetened by the frost, and a man going along would strip himself a handful and chew the flesh loose and blow the seeds out, making a tube of his tongue, aiming at a leaf or a chip along the way.

Boone pulled up on a hill. "Whar's your brothers, Poordevil?"

Poordevil grinned. "All gone."

"Beats me," Jim put in. "Here we are, long acrost the Yellowstone and nigh to the Tree Forks, and nary a Injun about."

"Ain't saw an Injun since I stoled the red horse." Boone looked back at the horse. With his mane roached and his tail combed he made a pretty sight. And he had got gentle, too, and trail-wise, and a man taking note of his quick ears and delicate nose and watching eyes would know when to go careful. "If it's Piegans hunt the Three Forks, where in hell are they, Poordevil?" Poordevil was a Blood, himself, but he ought to know where the Piegans hunted. They were all Blackfeet together.

"A man gets chilly quick," Jim said, "with that wind blowin'. Cools out the horses in a shake." His hand felt the neck of his horse, which was stiff where the sweat had dried.

"Be winter soon," Boone answered. He let an edge come into his voice. "We're behind time, what with all our foolin' around."

"It didn't help any, turnin' east to steal the red horse," Jim said quickly. "We could have hit straight up the Madison."

When Boone spoke again it was to say, "Blackfeet's bound to be around somewheres."

"Maybe north, gone to buffler. Or east."

"Time's past. They ought to be back on the river."

Boone clucked to his horse. Poky stepped slow, always taking his time while he kept his head down watching the footing. The red horse came along light and easy, hardly needing the line on his neck.

The country stayed empty, except for dumb brutes and varmints. There were deer and elk about and wolves and coyotes and, on the little prairies, rabbits big as jackasses that bounced away half-flying. Already they were changing from gray-brown to white, so's to be hard to see against the snow. The long-billed curlew had flocked and gone, leaving in Boone's head the echo of its rising cry. He would hear it in his mind and see the Indians running at him again, and Jourdonnais falling with the hole in his chest, and Painter clinging high and fuzzed up on the mast of the *Mandan*. He would see Teal Eye, too, not with the Indians but on the keelboat, her eyes warming on the bare hills of home. The great meadowlarks had ceased their autumn singing, though they flushed out from underfoot sometimes, big-bodied as the bobwhite he remembered from long ago. The young ducks swam four and five and six along the streams, waiting for the storm that would send them south. In the beaver ponds the winter's store of cottonwood and quaking asp stood ready, poked in the mud against the time ice held the beavers under. For all that beaver sign was plenty, they hadn't trapped much. Sometimes when they camped on the edge of dark Jim put traps out, and made his lift early in the morning, but mostly they passed by the ponds, Boone being set and pointed now and keeping the others on the go.

Not hide nor hair of an Indian anywhere, but they still traveled careful, wanting to choose their own time and way of meeting. Often they made cold camps after cooking when the sun was high and smoke and flame were harder to see. If they built a fire when dark was coming on, they pushed ahead afterward for a mile or so before making camp. Many a man had gone under because he wasn't careful that way.

The country climbed and fell and rolled away in such great sweeps that a man sometimes felt small as any ant. It was a country of stone and timber and quick, clear creeks and the Gallatin rushing through it, turning and twisting, and the noise of it beating steady against the ears. Lower down, the river slid into the mixed waters of the Madison and Jefferson, making the Missouri sure enough. Here was the heart of Blackfoot land, the Three Forks, where many a hunter had died, where even big parties didn't like to go, knowing war parties would be after them thick and fierce as hornets; but there were no Indians about them now, only signs of them, only cold campfires and gnawed bones where villages had stood and old clumps of sod the squaws had dug to hold the lodge skins down. Upstream to where the Madison and Jefferson came together and farther up along both streams it was the same.

"Might as well turn about and foller the Missouri north," Boone said. "Injuns are bound to be somewheres." Lying awake at night, hearing the sound of water and the wind in the trees, seeing the dipper sitting close and steady, he told himself the Piegans were sure to be about. A nation didn't just up and leave a country. He would find the Piegans and Heavy Otter's band. He would find Teal Eye, or learn what had happened to her. There wasn't anything hard about it or out of reason. The first Piegan they met would know where Heavy Otter was. A mountain man could find his way anywhere, to anybody. He could set out looking for a friend he hadn't seen in a coon's age, and he could point his way to him, over the mountains and across the rivers and through the timbers, as Boone had done himself more than once before. It was only time that made the hunt seem hard, only the seasons that had come between that made Teal Eye seem like someone he had built up in his head.

It was the red horse that took notice first, just a jump beyond the Three Forks. He pricked his ears and snorted softly. Slower to catch on, the others plodded along until by and by they lifted their heads, too, and looked and whiffed the air, and all of them slowed and came to a halt. Ahead of him Boone heard the cackling of magpies.

Jim said, "Probably no more'n a bear."

Poordevil's blunt nose was pointed up and his face was squeezed together as if all his senses were bent ahead. "Sick," he said. "Smell sick. Smell goddam dead."

Except for the magpies, though, there wasn't a sound. There wasn't a wisp of smoke. Boone's nose found nothing except the smell of horse and pine. "Easy!" he said, and started on.

Around a belt of trees the village came in sight, a village of fifty or so lodges and all seeming dead. Not so much as a dog moved among them, and no horses grazed about.

A puff of wind blew from the lodges and carried to Boone. "Holy Christ!" The stink on the wind was like a blow in the face.

Jim's hand went up and closed his nose. "Whew!" he said, and spit over the shoulder of his horse as if the smell was in his mouth.

The magpies, which had quieted at the first sight of them, took up their racket again when they saw the horses didn't come on.

"Piegan camp, Poordevil?" Boone asked.

"All goddam gone."

"Been a fight, maybe, and all went under."

"Sick. Smell sick."

"Best not go closer, Boone. Hear?"

"I aim to see."

"The stink's enough to sicken a man. I'm fixin' to puke a'ready."

"Bad," said Poordevil. "Injun sick, dead, heap go under."

Boone dropped from his horse and started ahead, carrying his rifle.

The magpies quieted again, and one by one flapped off, scolding as they went.

Two coyotes slid from among the lodges and slunk away, looking full-bellied and heavy, as Boone approached. The stink made a man's hair rise. He breathed short and quick, not wanting to get the air deep in him.

He pulled the flap of a lodge wider and closed it quick, snorting the smell from his nose. He made himself pull it open again and look in while the rotten air from inside poured over him. There were three bodies there, chewed some by coyotes, looking so black and bloated a man would have taken them for extra-fat niggers. In another lodge it was the same, except there was just one Indian in it, sprawled dead and black, the flesh puffing tight against his clothes. A squaw rested on her back outside another, and a young one alongside her. The magpies had been busy on them, and the coyotes. A whole damn village dead and gone, put under by a sickness, men and squaws and young ones lying stiff and bloated, and some with their eyes pecked out by birds, leaving pockets in the dead fat faces that maggots worked in.

He heard a thin whimpering, like a pup weak and hurt, and followed the sound of it and came to another tepee in which he saw a boy lying. The boy's face was one solid scab.

"How?"

There was a dead squaw inside the lodge and a dead buck to one side, likely the boy's parents.

"How?"

The thin whimpering kept on, trembling out with the boy's breath and stopping while he drew in and then trembling out again.

Boone raised his voice. "What ails you?"

It occurred to him that he had been talking white talk. He thought out some Blackfoot, shouting so's to get it through to the boy's mind.

Only the whimpering answered him, and it growing weaker and far apart. While Boone watched, the body stiffened and the scabbed mouth fell open. The lungs let out a long shuddering breath, snatched once at the air and then gave up. Boone backed out of the entrance, feeling his nostrils shrunken and his belly crowding close in his throat. He walked beyond the tepees into the wind, letting his lungs drink. At the edge of the camp he passed the bodies of a man and a squaw, part-eaten but not black or scabbed.

Each had a knife wound in the chest. Blackened with blood, the knife lay close by the man's hand.

After a while Boone turned and walked back into the stink. He made himself look into every lodge, made himself look at every woman's face. The lodge skins were brown and thin with time, so that light came through them as it couldn't come through new ones. Some of the lodges were empty, but partly readied up all the same, with robes lying in them or a kettle or a can standing or a horn spoon resting by the fire stones, as if the owners expected to come back directly, or as if they had taken a sudden fright and run away, snatching up what they could carry. A man couldn't tell one face from another, swollen the way they were and scabbed, and sometimes eaten on. There wasn't one person alive. The boy had been the last.

He walked back to where Jim and Poordevil sat. They had got tired waiting and had unforked from their horses to sit on the ground. To the question in their eyes he answered, "All dead. Every damn livin' soul dead."

"Sick," said Poordevil, nodding. The slot showed between his grinning lips as he came out with "*Petite vérole. La petite vérole.* You betcha."

"You hear that, Boone? French talk for smallpox!"

"I heerd it."

"God Almighty! Reckon he knows what he says?"

"Could be."

"You been doctored so's not to catch it, Boone?"

"I had it onc't. A man don't take it twice."

"How about you, Poordevil? You catch 'im ever? *Petite vérole?*"

Poordevil's face was one big smile. Everything was a joke to that fool Indian, except Colter's Hell. He bobbed his head and pointed to pits that lay along his hair line.

"Best I stayed away, I reckon," Jim said.

"There was a squaw and her man stabbed," Boone told Jim. "I don't git the reason of that. And some of the lodges are empty, with fixin's left around."

"That would be people runnin' away from the smallpox, Boone."

"What about the stabbed ones?"

Jim's eyes studied the ground. The stubble on his chin was a match for the hair of the red horse. "Could be they were Injuns that knew they had to die and wanted to do it quick. Could be they kilt themselves."

"Could be."

"Don't you git it, Boone?" Jim went on. "That's why we ain't met up with Blackfeet. They're all dead, likely, and them as ain't are runnin' from the smallpox."

"A whole nation don't die."

"A whole camp did, all the same."

"Not all of them. Some run away."

"You reckon that's Heavy Otter's band, Boone?"

Boone didn't answer.

"You reckon, Boone?"

A crow coasted over them, throwing a shadow on the grass, and let itself down among the lodges.

"I say, you reckon that's Heavy Otter's band?"

"How's a man to know? Goddam it!"

"I didn't go to r'ile you."

"You don't have to be askin' all the time. Askin' this and askin' that till you git a man crazy. Goddam it!"

"I said I'm sorry, and that's enough. Git mad if you're bound to."

"God hisself wouldn't know Heavy Otter, chewed up and black and swole the way them Injuns are."

Poordevil said, "Heap beaver now. Injun all gone."

Boone mounted his horse and led the way around the lodges, hearing the magpies come crying in after they had passed. He kept nudging at Poky, wanting to get along. A man moving, giving to the twist and the rise and fall of his saddle, could ease himself away from his mind. He rode straight and stiff, feeling Jim's eyes on him, and answering goddam it with the set of his back.

When they came to a little flat Jim rode up alongside. The little smile on his mouth put Boone in mind of Summers. "I reckon I know how you feel, Boone," Jim said. "I didn't aim to fly off at you."

After a silence Boone answered, "They can't all be dead, Jim. Not the whole nation. Not the whole damn Blackfoot Nation."

Jim gave him a long look. "I'm hopin' you're right," he answered, and let his horse fall behind as they entered timber again.

The Missouri valley wound north before them, opening and tightening some and opening again, the valley that was as empty as if not a man ever had lived there. Once they saw a single lodge, half blown down, and bones lying around, picked almost clean of meat, and skin clothes scattered and torn by the teeth of wolves, and once they came on a couple of campfires, cold but not more than a day or two old. A child's body was hoisted in a tree close by, but not wrapped careful. Already the birds had pecked away into the flesh.

One day and another of travel, and the valley still empty and the Blackfeet gone from the face of the earth. At night now they camped careless, building big fires and eating elk or deer meat, or one of the buffalo that had wandered up the valley into the hills. They camped silently, except for Poordevil, who grinned and talked as before, carefree as a young one who didn't know what made his elders solemn. Jim spoke little jokes now and then, trying to get shut of the cloud that hung over them but making a poor out of it. The sun rose bright in the morning and shone white and glaring in the day and left the western sky ablaze at night. Later the sky cooled to a red like an old wound, and still later the stars popped out, seeming low and plain as candles in the dark. It was prime weather for fall hunting, prime weather and prime country, but even Jim had quit laying his traps. A quiet hung over things, except for the cawing of crows and the chatter of magpies and the wind's whining in the trees, whipping the yellowed leaves away. At night the call of wolves beat back and forth in the valley, and the whistle of bull elks hot for cows, leaving the night emptier than before. By day Boone would watch the wind riffling the short grass and worrying the trees on the eastward slope and flowing on out of sight, farther than a man could know, to places a man never had heard tell of. The grass was curled and dry, headed out in darker brown. The feet of the horses raised puffs of dust from it that fell back if the wind was quiet, or streaked away. Riding all day in the wind, a man felt the grit in him, in his clothes and down his neck and against his skin, and grating between his teeth. He rode hunched against the wind, one shoulder up shielding his chin, and his mouth tight-set and dry, tasting the dirt.

Slanting out from the west bank of the river, they came from the valley into a basin and threaded through a growth of trees, and it was then they saw their first live man. He sat a horse a quarter of a mile away, and when his eye caught them he wheeled about and cut his pony with his quirt, high-tailing for a finger of timber. Boone slid from Poky, handed his rifle to Jim, and with the lariat took a quick hitch over the red horse's nose. "Foller along." He leaped astride the red horse, took back his rifle, and kicked the red belly. He felt the horse leap into movement under him and steady into an easy, long-striding run. He saw the proud head lifted and the small ears pointed ahead and the ground streaming under them. There wasn't a horse he ever knew could match that pace. The rider before him grew bigger and plainer in the eye. The rider's arm rose and fell with the quirt, and the horse answered to it with all he had. He was a buckety runner, though, galloping stiff and short. With the red horse after him it was as if he was standing still.

A musket shot short of the timber, the man saw he couldn't make it. He pulled up and got off and stood quiet, his arms hanging at his sides and his hands empty and his bow dangling from his shoulder. Boone slowed the red horse to a walk and after a while dismounted and led him, going slow toward the Indian. The Indian didn't move. Not even a muscle in his face moved. He didn't act like a Blackfoot. It came to Boone, studying him, that there was nothing in the face to see, except that he was reminded of a beaten dog. It was as if hope was gone and all good feeling and all proud spirit. Here was a man wouldn't fight against anything, not even death, but would only run like a rabbit and hunch down and wait, humble and sad before it. While Boone watched, the Indian got down on his hands and knees and bowed his head. His hair fell in a tangle at the sides of his neck.

"Git up, for Christ sake! I ain't aimin' to kill you."

Boone squatted down and took his pipe from the ornamented case that hung around his neck and filled it with tobacco and struck fire.

"Howgh," he said in his throat, and puffed and pointed the stem toward the Indian. He hunted for the Blackfoot words.

"The white hunter's heart is good."

The Indian's sad face lifted.

"The Long Knife looks for Heavy Otter—for his brother, Heavy Otter, the Piegan."

The wind played with the worn fringes of the man's buckskins and left him and whirled in the grass, sending up a spiral of dust.

Boone put a twist of tobacco on the prairie, to show it was a gift.

The Indian's eyes fixed on the tobacco, and a little gleam of hunger showed in them.

"The Long Knife looks for Heavy Otter—for his brother, Heavy Otter."

Only the Indian's eyes seemed alive, fixed on the twist.

Boone turned around and beckoned for Poordevil and Jim to come on. They trotted up, bringing the pack string.

"Tell him the Long Knife looks for Heavy Otter," Boone said to Poordevil. "Ask him whereabouts Heavy Otter is."

Poordevil slid from his horse, took a hungry suck at Boone's pipe, and then put the question.

"He don't care to talk," Jim said, grinning from his horse. "Ask him has the cat got his tongue, Poordevil."

"Shut up, Jim! Is he a Piegan, Poordevil, or what?"

"Piegan, him."

"Ain't nothin' like whisky to ile a rusty tongue," Jim said.

"Sometimes you talk sense, Jim. Damn if you don't." Boone went to a pack horse and loosened a rope and from the pack took the bottle he had saved. He came back and took the cork out and set the bottle alongside the twist. "Good whisky. Good medicine water."

The Indian reached out suddenly, like a man snatching at a varmint, and caught the bottle and held it up. Some of the whisky spilled out over his chin.

"There's an Injun as would drink a still dry," Jim said, still sitting his horse.

The Indian brought the bottle down and spit and belched and wiped his mouth.

"Ask him whereabouts is Heavy Otter, Poordevil."

Poordevil only grunted.

"Take a drink yourself then, goddam you!"

Poordevil's mouth spread happily, then closed over the mouth of the bottle. Boone took the whisky from Poordevil's hand and set it close by his side. "No more until we make talk. By and by, whisky. Tell him that, Poordevil." The Piegan's face was turned on the bottle. It was still a sad and humble face, but with a hankering in it now that saved it from being dead. With whisky a man could get nearly anything he wanted from the Indians—from all of them, anyhow, except the Comanches, who didn't care for drink. "Ask him where at are the Piegans. Ask him about Heavy Otter."

The Indian listened while Poordevil spoke. As an answer, he brought up his hands and rubbed the palms together.

"Rubbed out?" Boone asked sharply.

The Indian spoke, spoke hoarse and deep in his chest. Boone shook his head. It was only the Blackfeet words he had practiced that he knew. "What's he sayin', Poordevil? I don't git it all."

Poordevil talked part by sign and part by tongue. "Big sickness come. Long Knife bring sickness in fire canoe."

"How's that?"

"Boat that walks on water bring sickness to big house."

"To Fort Union?"

Poordevil and the Indian talked again before Poordevil went on. "Long Knife bring sickness up river from big house. Big medicine. Big sickness. White man medicine too strong. Sickness come. Blackfoot run. Sickness run more. Blackfoot cry, know Great Spirit mad. Sickness rub out Blackfoot. All gone."

"Christ sake! He don't know they're all dead," Boone said to Jim, who sat slouched on his horse, listening. "He ain't dead hisself, is he?" To Poordevil he said, "Ask him where Heavy Otter's band ran to. Ask him was there a young squaw ran. A daughter of Heavy Otter. More whisky, by and by."

"Heavy Otter sick," Poordevil translated. "Him run."

"Run where?"

They talked again, and then Poordevil shrugged. His hands took hold of his breasts. "May be."

Boone asked, "Titty River? Breast? Teton?"

"Titty," said Poordevil.

"Same as Tansy," Jim put in. "You recollect Summers told us?"

"Heavy Otter dead now sure. Goddam dead."

"He ain't seen him dead, has he? He thinks he is, is all."

The Piegan held out his hand, wanting the pipe, not snatching for it or making high and mighty talk, but asking for it humble. With it in his hand he squatted back on his heels and puffed, drawing each mouth of smoke deep into his lungs the way the Indians did. A man couldn't tell he had had even a little drink, his face was so set and quiet. A slow glow was in his eyes, though, under the rat's nest of hair.

"Ask him to write the way to the Titty, Poordevil." Boone picked up a stick and made a mark in the dirt, to show he wanted a map made.

When Poordevil had spoken the Indian took the stick and sighted around him and at the sun as if to get his directions. Then he drew a long line that bent off to Boone's right, talking to Poordevil while he did it. "River," said Poordevil. "Missouri, him." He put his finger at one end of the line and brought it to the other, to show which way the stream flowed.

"Curves off northeast," Jim said. He had got off his horse and come to stand over the map.

North of the bend the Piegan drew another line, connecting with the first from the west.

"Dearborn," said Poordevil.

Boone nodded. Summers had mentioned the Dearborn, too.

Poordevil said, "Medicine," pointing to another line farther to the north.

"That's the same as the Sun River, Boone. 'Member?"

Poordevil was smiling a silly smile. That Indian could get himself drunk quicker than scat. "Poordevil know," he said putting his finger on the line. "Me know." He looked at a new mark the Piegan was making still farther north. He punched his finger on it. "Titty. Betcha."

"How far?"

Poordevil turned to the Piegan. When he looked at Boone again he held up two fingers, then added a third.

"Two-three camps?"

The Piegan tossed the stick aside. His gaze went to the bottle. Boone handed it over. Poordevil watched him drink and took the bottle from him and raised it to his mouth. When he put it down, the whisky was all gone.

"Ask him where the squaw is, Poordevil. Ask him about the daughter of Heavy Otter."

The Piegan handed the pipe to Boone and sat back with his arms folded and his head seeming to think. Boone had the feeling that the sadness had come over him again, as if the whisky had pushed it away for a while and then brought it on all the stronger. Poordevil talked to him, and the Piegan listened and then talked back, using just a few words and rounding them out with his hands. Boone could hear beyond his voice to the sounds the horses made cropping at the grass. Only old Poky stood quiet, wanting to rest instead of eat.

"Maybe dead," Poordevil said. "Heap die." He gestured toward the Piegan. "Don't know, him. No want talk now, him. Talk all gone."

Boone took a long look at the Piegan, then got out another twist of tobacco and put it on the prairie. "I reckon we can't dig any more out'n him. Let's git on." Riding away, he saw the Indian hunch forward and take the two twists of tobacco, his face still sad and dull, like the face of a critter that had lost its young.

29

They struck north out of the basin and camped in a chain of low mountains that night and went on, coming out of a canyon into foothills on which the pines grew dwarfed and crooked. The Missouri had swung off eastward, starting the bend, Boone reckoned, that the Piegan had traced in the dirt.

"This here must be the Dearborn," he said while they stopped and let the horses drink at a stream.

The mountains crowded high and close to the left but farther on, beyond the Dearborn valley, they veered to the west, standing blue and jagged against the sky. High along the slopes of the peaks the snow lay patched. Between the mountains and the Missouri was high, bare country, where a man on a rise saw buttes swimming in the distance and the distance itself rolling off so far that he lost himself looking into it. It was a dusty country where even the sage grew spare and short and wood was so wanting that they made their fires of buffalo chips. For all its dusty bareness there were a sight of buffalo on it, and antelope and wolves and foxes small and delicate as kittens. The big jackass rabbits started up from it, jumping short and then settling to a long, flying stride.

When the sun was high enough to loosen them up, rattlesnakes buzzed from low bushes or breaks in the sandstone, and big, stone-gray grasshoppers rose clacking, and a man couldn't always tell whether it was a snake or a hopper that he heard. The prairie squirrels that Summers had called gophers stood straight as picket pins, piping shrill, and dived into their holes as the horses neared. They were big and fat now, ready for the winter sleep.

Overhead there was more sky than a man could think, curving deep and far and empty, except maybe for a hawk or an eagle sailing. The little watercourses that had cut into the dirt ran dry or stood still in little stinking pools that snipe and duck rose from. A little willow grew along them and sometimes a thirsty cotton-wood. And nowhere was there an Indian or a lodge. The buffalo grazed peaceful, and the antelopes frisked as if they never knew a hunter. Going along one day on another, a man would think the world about had never seen the like of him.

The gophers and the sky and the rattlesnakes and the brown plains rolling put Boone in mind of the Missouri above Fort Union. It was a long time ago that he had seen it, a long time ago for a wishing to stay with a body and to drive him on. Maybe Jim was right, half-hinting he was crazy.

The plains slid down to a stream, shady with cottonwood from which the leaves were whirling. Poordevil, feeling big for what he knew, said it was the south fork of the Medicine. A wide, bare hump divided it from the north fork, which flowed clear and fast over clean stones, hardly giving the trees time to catch hold along its banks. They camped by it and feasted on fat buffalo and went on in the morning, climbing to the benchlands again. To their left the benches sloped off into a basin of red and yellow badlands, bare even of grass, that twisted and humped and finally climbed to foothills. To the north and east the land was better, growing a fuzz of grass that the buffalo fattened on. It was parched, though, and tan with the sun. A herd of buffalo making a little run raised a cloud of dust like smoke. Even the running rabbit left puffs of it behind him. It was toward evening that they came to the end of the benches and, standing close by the shoulder of a butte, looked down on a wide, green valley.

Poordevil grunted and filled his lungs and made a sweeping

motion over the land with his arm and spoke out of pride in knowing. His two hands came up and took hold of his breasts.

"It's the Titty, Boone, I reckon," Jim said while his gaze took
it in. "Seems like it's a whole world away from the Green. Seems
like we been travelin' all our lives. Seems like we're certain sure to
be in British country."

The eye could follow the river winding and see where canyons
notched the blue mountains. One peak looked like an ear turned
on its side. Trees and river and the wide valley and the brown
hills on either side floated in the fall haze, lazy and comfortable
and sleepy now with autumn. It was as pretty a place as a man
could wish, a prime place except that the world seemed dying and
a man's hankering was cold and foolish in him.

"Which way?" Jim asked.

"We'll aim upstream and come down if they ain't there." Boone
kicked his horse. The benches dropped and leveled off into the valley, where prairie hens rose drumming from under the horses' feet
and birch brush grew clumped and black. Among the silver leaves
buffalo berries sparkled red as beads. They let the horses drink
at a small stream and went on to the Teton and followed it west
and north toward a notch in the mountains, toward the ear that
lay on its side.

"Purty water," Jim said where they crossed at a game trail.
"Small, but purty as I ever see." He checked his horse.

Boone dropped off Poky and bellied down and drank, feeling
the water flowing cool and sweet on his lips, seeing down in it as
clear as air. Out from him, in the blue water of a hole, a fish
floated. He could see the gills working, could have counted every
spot if he set himself to it. On the far bank a cottontail rabbit sat
as still as stone except for the tiny spread and close of its nose.
A pretty little river. Pretty country. And the world empty and
seeming to be dying to men. Maybe that was the way of it, that
Indians and white men should die and the country go back to what
it was before, with only the dumb brutes grazing and the birds
flying under all the sky.

The sun floated behind the ragged rim of mountains, and a
stillness came on. A man speaking heard his voice like something
that didn't belong there. It came out into the quiet, sounding

hoarse and strange, and the quiet cracked to it as ice would crack to a step.

"Nigh time to camp," Jim said as they rode on, and at the same time Poordevil straightened and pointed. Ahead of them, through a screen of cottonwoods, a feather of smoke was rising.

They rode toward it and came out of the trees and, maybe a stone's throw away, saw three lodges standing and two men by them and two children and a squaw, faced about to watch them but with nothing in their faces except the slow look that a tame cow might give, seeing a man passing.

"Piegans," Poordevil announced. "Son bitch Piegans."

Boone said, "Go ahead, Poordevil. Ask 'em where at is Heavy Otter."

Jim's face turned toward Boone with a quick, queer look in it. Boone didn't explain. There wasn't any use explaining, no use telling why he hung back now, with the feeling of bad luck in him. Sometimes a man could push ahead, strong and cheerful, and then something would come into him and make his heart low and hold him where he was. It didn't stand to reason that Teal Eye was alive when so many had died.

He saw Poordevil dismount and walk ahead, and then he lighted his pipe and looked at the ground, waiting.

When Poordevil got back he said, "Heavy Otter dead. Big sickness."

"The squaw?"

"Red Horn chief," said Poordevil, motioning up river with his arm. "Talk Red Horn, you."

Jim's gaze was on Boone. He said, "That Injun finds out everything savin' what a man wants to know."

"We got time to go on a piece afore dark."

"Why'n't the Piegans camped together, you reckon? Afeard of the sickness, likely."

Half a mile farther they came on to two lodges. A man came out of one of them as they approached and stood still as a post after he spied them, with no musket in his hand and no bow.

Boone signaled for a halt and got off Poky and laid his rifle in the grass and his pistols by it. "Poordevil don't learn enough, damn him! I'll go my own self and call for him if need be," he said to Jim. With no weapon but the knife in his belt he walked toward the lodge, holding his hands together in the sign of peace. Then he closed his left hand and patted it with his right, as if loading a pipe.

When he had covered half the distance, he halted, waiting on the Indian, but the Indian didn't move. He was a young man with a look of age in his face and of the sadness Boone had seen before, and of something else, too, of high pride or anger held in. The hair on his head had been hacked short, to show he had had a grief. By the thin, curving nose and wide, hard mouth a man could see there was mettle in him.

Boone sounded the words he had learned from Poordevil, speaking loud so that they would carry. "The white hunter's heart is good."

If the Indian understood he gave no sign.

"The white hunter would make talk."

Still the Indian stood silent and unmoving, his mouth straight and strong under his beak of nose.

"Red Horn, you?"

A bare flicker of the eyes told Boone he had guessed right. He called over his shoulder. "Send Poordevil up, Jim. Get him to leave his rifle and bring that there Crow scalp."

He turned back. "The white hunter is a friend of the Piegans. He is a brave warrior. He has a Crow scalp." He took the scalp from Poordevil and held it up. "Tell him the white men come in peace, Poordevil. Tell him the Long Knife looks for a young squaw, the daughter of Heavy Otter."

Poordevil said the Blackfoot words, but still the other Indian held his tongue, seeming to study whether to answer or not. When he spoke it was in a low voice for an Indian.

"White man bring whisky," Poordevil translated. "Make Injun crazy. White man sleep with squaw. Make sick here." His hand went to his crotch. "White man heart bad."

"Tell him that's Bad Medicines. Tell him it's the French and not the Long Knives."

Before Poordevil could speak, the Indian was talking again.

Poordevil bent his head, figuring the English of it. "Piegan fight. Piegan fight heap. Keep white man away. White man bring big medicine, big sickness. Kill Piegan. Piegan heart dead." Poordevil grinned at Boone. "Goddam dead. Piegan no fight now."

Boone let his glance travel around. From the other lodge, to the right of the Indian, two faces peered, a squaw's and a child's, solemn as owls. Just the heads showed, as if they had been pinned to the side of the opening.

"Ask him about the squaw."

Through the opened flap behind the Indian Boone's eye caught movement. It was a blur inside the darkened tepee, and then a face, a young squaw's face, and two eyes big and soft as any doe's.

He made himself hold still, made his gaze go to the grass, made his hands get out his pipe, made his face stiff and straight. His mind spun and settled and began to work at the way of it while each grass stem stood sharp and separate to his eye. After a while he had the answer. A man could travel many a camp, with a hunger in him and a hope, and find at the end that he had traveled for nothing, and so his hope went dead while the hunger kept on gnawing him. He could have a feeling in him that seemed right and natural and bound to turn out, and it could be a fool feeling all along, like it had been with him. A man and a squaw in a lodge meant one thing, just one thing. He heard his voice saying, "It don't matter, Poordevil. Tell him we leave presents for him and his woman."

His legs lifted him and turned him part way round, while his ears only half brought the Indians' palaver to him.

He heard Jim yell, "How, Teal Eye! How!" He heard Jim's horse walking up.

Poordevil plucked him on the arm. "Red Horn, him."

"It don't matter."

"Chief."

"We leave presents."

Jim sat his horse, his mouth open in a big grin and his blue eye bright.

Poordevil said, "B'long Heavy Otter."

"Best get out some tobacco and beads and such," Boone said to Jim.

"No got squaw," said Poordevil. "Squaw die. Two squaw die. Whole goddam squaw die. No got squaw."

"What you mean?"

Poordevil pointed. "Squaw b'long Heavy Otter. Red Horn b'long Heavy Otter."

Boone said to Jim, "This goddam Injun don't know what he's sayin', no more'n a crazy man."

Jim's face had gone serious. He sat thoughtful, with the bristles showing red on his chin and his eyes puckered. "I do' know, Boone." Of a sudden he looked up, past Boone's half-turned shoulder. "Your man, him?" he asked. "Your brother, him?"

"Brother!" Poordevil let out the word as if he had been hunting for it. "Red Horn brother."

Jim's voice sounded again. "Hey, Teal Eye, you got yourself a man? Yes? No?"

Boone didn't look. If Teal Eye answered he didn't hear. What he heard next was Jim saying to him, "Go on, Boone! Go on! Time to ask."

He held in, so's nothing would show in his face. He saw his feet moving under him again, saw his fingers working at the pack, saw the rich painter skin, the vermilion, the tobacco. He saw in his mind, without letting himself meet it, Jim's eye sharp and curious on him. He led up the red horse. He noticed the interest rising in Red Horn's eyes as he watched, but what he noticed mostly, without fixing straight on it, was Teal Eye, with recognition in her look and what a man might take for warmth.

"Tell him the red horse is a present, Poordevil, it and the painter skin and the rest."

His tongue stumbled over the practiced words. "The white hunter wants the daughter of Heavy Otter for his squaw."

Red Horn's face went stiff and blank again, as if he had put the horse away from him and closed his head to what was said. Boone's gaze went down before that stony look and came back up and searched beyond and found the big eyes searching, too, and a softness on the mouth that might be meant for him. If only he could talk with Teal Eye, away from Red Horn and the rest!

30

If a man wanted a woman for his squaw he went to her father and asked how much the father loved her and what gifts would make his heart glad to have a son in the family. The father talked to the woman afterward and to her mother and then told the man what he wanted. If it wasn't too much, the man brought his gifts and took his squaw, and that was the way of it.

That was the way of it, except that if the woman's father wasn't alive, the man went to her oldest brother, and if she didn't have a brother, then to her nearest kin. That was the way of it, except sometimes things didn't allow for such doings and a man did the best he could, as Boone had done with Red Horn and Teal Eye.

Boone sat by himself on a gravel bank, watching the Teton flow by. It had been a full day since he had offered the red horse and the painter skin and all, and still he didn't know. Maybe Red Horn wouldn't deal with a white man, there was so much bitterness in him. Maybe he would say no while his eyes stayed hungry on the horse. Maybe Teal Eye had her head set another way, on some young Piegan who had just proved himself a brave warrior. Maybe she argued with Red Horn, telling him not to take the horse and the skin and the vermilion and the powder and ball. Boone had caught just one peek at her since the day before.

The water ran easy at his feet, talking to itself as it went. It was as clear as the evening sky over the mountains, with a brown clearness in it that came from fall and leaves the trees had dropped. Up to his right, where the Teton had cut into a bank and made a hole, a lazy trout lipped at the surface, sending out little spreading circles. A chokecherry bush hung over the hole, its green gone but with some berries hanging black and wrinkled on it. The mountains lifted blue in the west, cutting sharp into the quiet sky. High and far in them lay patches of snow. He could see the mountain like an ear and the notch by its side that the Teton ran out of, and southward he could see the canyon of the Medicine with a high reef of rock on one side and a sawtoothed mountain on the other. Between the two rivers were smaller canyons made by streams that maybe the white man hadn't put a name to yet. None of them could be as pretty as the Teton winding, busy but not hurried, with a mind and time to have a look at things as it went along. Clumps of cottonwood grew on its banks, and chokecherry and serviceberry bushes and wild rose and red willow that the Indians mixed with tobacco. No place could be prettier than this valley, with two buttes rising to the south and the tan hills ridged wide on the sides, and cottonwood and black birch and sagebrush growing, and elk and deer about and buffalo coming down from the benches to drink. It was a place a man could spend his whole life in and never wish for better.

Looking beyond the stream and over the first hills to others that rose round and pointed, Boone could guess how the Teton got its name. Some lonesome Frenchman, likely, had looked and been reminded of a woman. Some Bad Medicine, froze for squaws, had seen the hills, and it was like seeing a woman lying with her breasts arched and sharp at the nipples, and his hunger had nagged him and he had said *tetons, tetons* as if just the saying eased him.

Boone heard the water talking and the breeze barely stirring in the trees and a magpie cawing somewhere, and after a while he heard a footfall close by and leather moving and the sounds of sitting down and the sounds of breathing. He didn't start or turn or lay hold on his rifle. He had a feeling who it was. Things were turning out as he had had a secret hope they would. Things were turning out as he had wished when he walked by Red Horn's lodge and came down the game trail through the brush to the river's edge. He picked up a bright pebble and let his eye run over it and flipped it into the stream with his thumb. He saw it hit and shimmer down and lie white and liquid as the water flowed over it.

He felt her eyes on him. He saw them without looking, the melting eyes and the face young and clean-lined and the breasts swelling under the leather and the feet narrow in their moccasins.

With another woman he would have made the sign of lying down and teased her with a hand of beads or a paper of vermilion, and afterward he would have got up and gone on and forgotten her, as he had forgotten a heap of squaws in his time. With another woman he would have acted like a natural man. His eyes would have been bold and his tongue limber and his hands forward. What was it made him hold back? What was it made him sit wondering, like a boy who hadn't had a taste of women? His eye slid to the side and saw her face quiet and her gaze fixed deep on the running water, and too much thought in her ever to lay tongue to. Could it be she had been waiting for him all this time, saying no to others? Could it be, being as Red Horn had told Poordevil she never had taken herself a man?

He sat silent, feeling unsure and silly, and still it was like talking to her, like letting out how the idea of her had built up in him until he had seen her face in the sky and heard her voice in the breeze. He was that far gone that the flutter of the prairie hen put him in mind of her laugh and the bright pebbles that the stream flowed over set him thinking of her teeth and he never saw a wild goose headed north that she wasn't in his head. He wanted her to come to his lodge and be his woman and make his moccasins for him. He would raise meat aplenty; their lodge would have a galore of meat, and scalps hanging by it that he would lift from the enemies of her people.

Her breath said, "Boone. Boone," as if practicing the word, and then he turned to face her and his eyes met hers and looked into them, trying to see what lay beyond. "You fixin' to come to my lodge, Teal Eye? You aim to be my squaw? Reckon I want you bad." He pointed at her and at himself and brought the tips of his forefingers together in the sign for tepee. All the time it was like his eyes speaking to her and her eyes answering, saying things that couldn't be said with words or all understood by the mind, saying things that went back many a season to the first days on the *Mandan* and Jourdonnais talking of the little squaw with an eye like the bluewing teal. A quick, small smile came on her face.

Behind them the bushes moved and, turning, Boone saw Poordevil standing on the trail with his ugly face split into a smile and his tongue showing through the gap in his teeth. His head jerked up and down as if to tell Boone he was a smart picker.

"Goddam you, Poordevil! Git!"

Poordevil came closer. His finger motioned at Teal Eye. "Punkin," he said. "Heap punkin."

Teal Eye got up. But before she dodged around Poordevil and ran up the path she crossed her wrists quickly and put them over her heart and brought one to bear on the other. Boone saw the soft breast yield and swell out to the side. The little smile flashed, and she was gone.

Boone turned back, seeing the trout still lipping at the water and the western mountains cutting into the sky and the rounded hills that had reminded the lonely Frenchman of a woman. He heard the voice of the stream and the stirrings of the breeze and Poordevil taking a step behind him. Over the mountains the sky arched clear and deep so that a man looking let himself be lost in it like a bird floating. Crossing the wrists and hugging them over the heart was sign talk for love.

PART IV

1842-
1843

31

A man could sit and let time run on while he smoked or cut on a stick with nothing nagging him and the squaws going about their business and the young ones playing, making out that they warred on the Assiniboines. He could let time run on, Boone thought while he sat and let it run, and feel his skin drink the sunshine in and watch the breeze skipping in the grass and see the moon like a bright horn in the sky by night. One day and another it was pretty much the same, and it was all good. The sun came up big in the fall mornings and climbed warm and small and got bigger again as it dropped, and the slow clouds sailed red after it had gone from sight. There was meat to spare, and beaver still to trap if a man wanted to put himself out. In the summer the Piegans went to buffalo and later pitched camp close to Fort McKenzie and traded for whisky and tobacco and blankets and cloth and moved on to the Marias or the Teton or the Sun or the Three Forks for a little trapping and the long, lazy winter.

If the beaver were few, buffalo still were plenty, for all that the Piegans slaughtered more and more of them just so's to have hides to trade. Boone had seen regular herds of them chased over the steep bluffs that the Indians called *pishkuns* and lying at the bottom afterwards with broken necks or standing or lunging on three legs while the hunters rode among them with battleaxes and bows and arrows, and then the squaws, chattering and happy, following up with their knives and getting bloody and not caring, and everybody taking a mouth of raw meat now and then and all feeling good because they had something to set by for winter.

Boone drew slow on his pipe while his eye took in the meat drying on the racks and the squaws working with the skins and the lodges pitched around. A dog came up and got a whiff of his tobacco and made a nose and backed up and by and by went on. Off a little piece Heavy Runner lay in front of his lodge with his head in his squaw's lap. The squaw was going through his hair with her fingers, looking for lice and cracking them between her teeth when she found any. In other lodges medicine men thumped on drums and shook buffalo-bladder rattles to drive the evil spirits out of the sick. They made a noise that a man got so used to that he hardly took notice of it.

It was a good life, the Piegan's life was. There were buffalo hunts and sometimes skirmishes with the Crows and Sioux, or the Nepercy who came from across the mountains to hunt Blackfoot buffalo, being as they didn't have any of their own; the sun heated a man in the summer and the winter put a chill in his bones, so that he kept close by his fire and ate jerked meat and pemmican if need be and looked often to the western sky for the low bank of clouds that would mean a warm wind was coming. Life went along one day after another as it had for five seasons now, and the days went together and lost themselves in one another. Looking back, it was as if time ran into itself and flowed over, running forward from past times and running back from now so that yesterday and today were the same. Or maybe time didn't flow at all but just stood still while a body moved around in it. A man hunted or fought, and sat smoking and talking at night, and after a while the camp went silent except for the dogs taking a notion to answer to the wolves, and so then he went in and lay with his woman, and it was all he could ask, just to be living like this, with his belly satisfied and himself free and his mind peaceful and in his lodge a woman to suit him.

Boone didn't guess, though, that Jim ever would be shut of fret the way he was, maybe because Jim never had found a squaw that wore good with him. Jim was forever pulling up and going somewhere, to Union or Pierre or St. Louis. Boone had traveled a considerable himself, but not to places where people were; he went into the mountains or across to British country or north into Canada where the Gros Ventres lived when they weren't on the move. He liked free country, with no more than some Indians about, and his squaw.

When Jim came back from a trip he was full of talk about new forts along the river and new people moving out from the settlements and the farmers in Missouri palavering about Oregon and California, as if the mountains were a prime place for plows and pigs and corn. When Jim went on too long that way, Boone cut him off, not wanting to be bothered with fool talk that stirred a man up inside.

Jim always seemed glad to be back, even if he was always setting out again. His face would light up when he saw Boone, and his hand was warm and strong and his mouth smiling. When he looked at Teal Eye it was as if he wished her double was around somewhere. Boone would catch just a gleam in his blue eye sometimes, or a kind of long, slow look that would make a man flare up if he didn't know Teal Eye so well, that maybe would put blood in his eye if Jim wasn't his friend.

Teal Eye was the woman for Boone. He reckoned he never would take a second woman in his lodge, and never have to cut Teal Eye's nose off, either, the way a Piegan did when he found his woman had lain in secret with another man. It was a sight, the squaws you saw with no end to their noses. Cut-nose women, they were called. They went around like nigger slaves, not having a man any longer or any proper home.

Teal Eye suited him all right. There wasn't any sense in a man nosing around like a bull, or wanting to cover every new woman just from being curious. One woman was enough, if she was the right one. Teal Eye never whined or scolded or tried to make a man something else than what he was by nature, but just took him and did her work and was happy. She had got a little heavier lately but was still well-turned in her body, with sharp, full breasts and a flat stomach and legs slim and quick as a deer's. Most squaws aged early, looking pretty just when the first bloom was on them and then drying up or going all to flesh, but not Teal Eye, maybe because she never had caught herself a baby. Looking at her, Boone couldn't tell much difference from five seasons back when he had found her on the Teton with Red Horn. He couldn't tell much difference, even, from the *Mandan* time, except that she was a woman now and rounded out as a woman ought to be. Her face was still slim and delicate, and her eyes melting and her spirit quick and cheerful and her body graceful. What she cared about most was to please him. She watched while he ate the meat or tried a new pair of moccasins and showed pleasure in her face when he grunted an all right. And she was always ready for him when his body was hungry, not lying still and spraddled, either, like a shot doe, but joining in, unashamed, her legs smooth and warm and strong and her breath whispering in his ear.

Boone uncrossed one leg and stretched it out before him and studied the moccasin he wore. Teal Eye had put a decoration of colored porcupine quills on it, arranging them neat and in a nice pattern. She had tanned the leather for this foot white and for the right foot yellow, so that a person not knowing Piegan ways would think the moccasins didn't match. They were slick shoes, he thought, while his mind went to wishing that Jim would come back soon from St. Louis. He felt better with Jim around. There was more spirit in him, and he laughed oftener. There wasn't anyone could find fun like Jim, or set a man's head to working so. When he thought of it, it was as if Jim was a part of all the life he liked, as if he always had been ever since they had met up on the road between Frankfort and Louisville, and Jim uneasy with the dead body in his wagon. Take Jim away and Boone felt there was something wanting, though he still wouldn't trade his way of living for any he ever knew or heard tell of. When Jim came back, it was as if all was well again. A man went with the feeling inside him that everything was right and just about as he would order it if it was his to order. Jim ought to be back soon, Boone figured, from going down the river with a boat of furs. It could be he had made up his mind to stay the winter in the settlements and to come back in the spring when the flood water would float steamboats to Fort Union and farther. Boone reckoned not, though. Jim never stayed away for a long stretch. Likely he would come overland, maybe with a party of mountain men who had spent their beaver. For all his traipsing around, Jim was a true mountain man, with the life showing in his face and in the set of his shoulders and legs and the way of his walk.

The wind was moving out of the west, as it nearly always did, sometimes hard and sometimes easy but nearly always moving. A shadow fell on the land, and lightning flickered and thunder sounded, and a big splash of rain fell on the hand Boone held his pipe with. The Piegans spent a heap of time inside their lodges. He liked to sit outside where the sun could hit him and the breeze get at him. Sometimes he put himself in mind of the menfolk back in Kentucky, sitting around the door while the day turned by, only he didn't have a hickory chair and wouldn't sit in it if he had. A man got so he didn't feel right unless seated cross-legged. The rain wouldn't be but a drop or two. Already the cloud was sailing over him, passing on east.

Boone knocked out his pipe and sat still, letting time run by. Each part of time was good in itself, if a man knew to enjoy it and didn't press for it to pass so as to get ahead to something different.

By and by Red Horn came along and sat down by him, not speaking until he got his pipe going. Red Horn's eyes seemed to get sharper with the years, and his nose higher and more hooked. The wrinkles were like cuts at the side of his mouth though he wasn't old yet. He made Boone think of an eagle, except he didn't bite or claw any more. The hand he held the pipe with lacked the joint of one finger. He had cut it off, along with his hair, when old Heavy Otter died of the smallpox.

"We have meat enough, and hides," said Red Horn, speaking the Blackfoot tongue that Boone knew almost as well as white men's talk.

"More hides than meat."

Red Horn puffed on his pipe.

"The buffalo die fast, Red Horn."

"They are plenty."

"They die fast, with hunters killing them for hides alone."

Red Horn hunched his shoulders. "They are more now than before the big sickness. We need robes to trade."

"I hope we never want for meat."

The lines in Red Horn's face deepened. He spread his hands, as if there was no use in anything. "The buffalo will last while the Indian lasts. Then we do not care. The buffalo cannot die faster than the Indian."

"We do well enough."

"The white Piegan does not know. He did not see the Piegans when their lodges were many and their warriors strong. We are a few now, and we are weak and tired, and our men drink the strong water and will not go far from the white man's trading house. They quarrel with one another. The white man's sickness kills them. We are like Sheepeaters. We are poor and sick and afraid."

"The nation will grow strong. The white man will leave us. We shall be many and have buffalo and beaver and live as the old ones lived."

Red Horn grunted and took the pipe from his lips to speak. "Strong Arm is a paleface. He will go back to his brothers when the Piegans go to the spirit land."

"No!" Boone answered in English. "Damn if ever I go back—not for good, anyways!" He switched to Blackfoot. "Strong Arm is a Piegan though his face is white."

"Already," said Red Horn, "the white hunters make ready to trap our rivers again."

"They have no right. It is Piegan land."

"We are weak. We cannot fight the Long Knives. Red Horn will not fight. He tells his people to keep the arrow from the bow and their hands from the medicine iron."

It was no use arguing with Red Horn. The spirit was dead in him, except for a sadness and an old anger that fanned up sometimes like a coal touched by wind. He couldn't see ahead. Already the white hunter was getting scarce in the mountains, finding beaver too few and too cheap and the life too risky now that the big parties were gone and he had to travel small. It would be the same with the other white men, with the traders who crowded the river and with those who figured to settle and make crops where crops wouldn't grow. Things came and went and came again.

"Red Hair should be back soon," Boone said, watching Teal Eye come toward the lodge with water from the stream and stoop and go in while the edge of her eye looked at him and her face told him he was her man. He heard her freshening the fire. The days were getting shorter. Already the sun was dipping behind the mountain rim, well to the south of its summer setting place. The breeze began to quiet, as if it couldn't blow without the sun shining on it.

"Red Hair waits at the trading house?" Red Horn asked.

"Maybe Jim is there."

"Two suns, and we go to trade."

"Good."

Red Horn got up and looked around the village, the lines cutting into his face, as if he could see how far the Piegan lodges would stand if the big sickness hadn't come along.

Boone smoked another pipe after Red Horn had gone. From inside there came the little noises that told him Teal Eye was readying the pot for him. The smell of wood smoke was in the air and of good meat cooking. A man's stomach answered to it. The water came into his mouth. High in the sky Boone could hear the whimper of nighthawks. Looking close, he spied one of them, diving crazy and crooked and whimpering as it dived.

He knocked the ash from his pipe and got up, stretching, and ducked under his medicine bundle that hung over the entrance and went in—to his lodge, to his meat, to his woman.

32

The first snow had fallen before Jim came back. It was a wet and heavy snow that weighted the branches down and dropped from them onto a man's shoulders and down his neck as he poked through the brush along the Musselshell looking for beaver-setting. The first flight of ducks from the north came with it, their wings whistling in the gray dusk. The water in the beaver ponds stood dark and still against the whitened banks. Deep down, the trout lay slow as suckers. In a day the snow slushed off. The sun came again and the wind swung back to the west and the ground dried, but the country wasn't the same; it looked brown and tired, with no life in it, lying ready for winter, lying poor and quiet while the wind tore at it one day after another. A trapper making his lift heard the wind in the brush and the last stubborn leaves ticking dead against the limbs; he looked up and saw the sky deep and cold and a torn cloud in it, and when he sniffed he got the smell of winter in his nose—the sharp and lonesome smell of winter, of cured grass and fallen leaves and blown grit and cold a-coming on. His legs cramped in the water and his fingers stiffened with his traps, and he felt good inside that his meat was made and berries gathered against the time ahead. Now was a time to hunt, and to think forward to lodge fires and long, fat days and a full stomach and talk like Jim knew how to make.

One beaver from six settings. A poor lift, but a man couldn't expect better, not while he traveled with a parcel of other folks and trapped waters that trappers before him had worn paths along. A plew wouldn't buy much from Chardon, the new bourgeois at McKenzie. A man could put one beaver of whisky in his eye and never wink, and a beaver of red cotton for Teal Eye wouldn't much more than flag an antelope. It was good a man needed but a little of boughten things. The buffalo gave him meat and clothing and a bed and a roof over his head, and what the buffalo didn't give him the deer or sheep did, except for tobacco and powder and lead and whisky, and cloth and fixings for his squaw.

Boone picked up the beaver by a leg and went to his horse and mounted and rode back toward camp. Teal Eye would skin out the beaver and cook the tail. Her hands worked fast and sure for all they were so small. And she hardly needed to look what they were doing. She could watch him or laugh or talk, and they never missed a lick and never lagged. His lodge was kept as well as anybody's, no matter if they had half a dozen wives, and it didn't crawl with lice, either, like some did. Maybe that was because of the winter she had spent in St. Louis with the whites; more likely it was just because she was Teal Eye and neat by nature and knew how to keep a lodge right and how to fix herself pretty, using red beads in her black hair, where they looked good, and blue or white beads against her brown skin, where they looked good, too.

Near his tepee Boone saw two horses standing gaunt and hipshot and heard voices coming from inside. He checked his own horse and listened and knew that Jim had come home. Teal Eye's laugh floated out to him. He jumped off and dropped the beaver by the door and stooped and went in.

Jim yelled, "How! How, Boone!" He scrambled to his feet, holding a joint of meat in one hand. He spoke through a mouthful of it. "Gimme your paw, Boone. I reckon I'm plumb glad to be back."

Boone looked at the red hair and the face wrinkling into a smile and the white teeth showing and felt Jim's hand hard and strong in his own. "Goddam you, Jim," he said. "What kep' you? Ought to hobble you or put you on a rope. And damn if you didn't get your hair cut! Like an egg with a fuzz on it, your head looks."

Jim ran a hand through the short crop on his skull. "Done it to keep people from askin' questions back in the States. Wisht I could grow it back as quick as I cut it off."

In Blackfoot Teal Eye said, "We thought Red Hair had taken a white squaw."

"Not me," said Jim. "Too fofaraw, them bourgeways are. I got things to do besides waitin' on a woman." He changed to Blackfoot talk. "The white men in their big villages do not have squaws like you. The women are weak and lazy. They do not dress skins and cut wood and pitch and break camp. They are not like Teal Eye."

Boone could see Teal Eye was pleased. He sat down by the fire and put out his wet feet and lighted his pipe. Teal Eye came and took off his wet moccasins and brought dry ones. Jim sat down and lit up, too.

It was good, this was, this having Jim here and winter edging close and a pot of meat fretting and the fire coming out and warming a man's feet and tobacco smoke sweet in his mouth. It made Boone feel snug inside and satisfied. He wished it could be that the Piegan men wouldn't come visiting until he and Jim had had their own visit out. "You didn't beat winter but by a hair, Jim."

"I look for open weather for a while."

"Red Horn says no. Says it'll be cold as all hell."

"Some thinks one way, some another; God Hisself only knows. I look for an easy winter."

"How'd you travel—boat or horse or how?"

"Horse mostly. Steamboat to the Platte, and then traded two horses away from the Grand Pawnees and follered my nose to McKenzie. Chardon told me where you was."

"Any Indian doin's?"

"Cheyennes was all. A hunting party. I got one fair through my sights after he taken a shot at me, and give the others the slip. They pounded around a right smart, tryin' to get wind of me, but it weren't so much. Not like the old Blackfeet was. Not like them hornets."

"Cheyennes?"

"That was it, now. A man wouldn't expect it."

Sitting there in the dark of the lodge with the fire warming his feet and Jim's voice coming to his ears and reminding him of old things, Boone thought back to times he and Summers and Jim had had with the Blackfeet. They had killed more than a few, the three of them had, and come close to being killed more than once. There was no one fought like the old Blackfeet did, so fierce and unforgiving, until the smallpox came along and made good Indians of them. Put together all the Indians he and Summers and Jim had rubbed out, and it would make a fair village. "See Dick?" he asked.

"Married! Damn if he ain't! And to a white woman! He's farmin'. Corn and pigs and some tobacco."

"Pigs?"

"Pigs."

"I mind when he didn't like the notion of hog meat."

"Nor white women neither, for that part."

"How's he?"

"Good enough, I reckon. He 'lows it's better'n bein' dead, but of course he don't know about that. I allus figgured that bein' dead would save a man a sight of trouble."

"You never acted that way. Keen to keep your hair, you was."

"On account of maybe a man's got to go to hell yet. But if he don't, I mean if when he's dead he's dead and no more to it, why, then, bein' dead could be better than bein' deviled."

Teal Eye had fed the fire and seen there was plenty of meat in the pot and had sat down to work on a shirt. Boone saw her eyes go from one to the other of them as they talked, and quick understanding showing in them. She followed most things that a man might say in English, though she didn't use it much.

"The Piegan knows that he goes to the spirit land," she put in. "He does not fear dying like the white man does, because he knows."

Jim gave her a quick smile. "Some Indians think different. Some believe in the Great Medicine of the white man."

"The Flatheads," she said, "and the Pierced Noses. They have the black robes and the Book of Heaven. They are not warriors like the Piegans. They are not a great people."

Jim took a wooden bowl and filled it from the pot with a horn spoon and got his knife out and began eating again. After a while he said, "I went clean to Kentucky, Boone. Seed the place I was brung up and all."

Boone grunted.

"I left word to get to your kin, figurin' you wouldn't mind. Someone said your pap was ailin'."

"Dead now and gone to hell I hope."

"It's a poor way of doin' back there, it is."

"Looks like you wouldn't always be a-goin', then."

"A man likes to get around." Jim wiped his mouth with the back of his hand while a little frown came over his eyes as if he was studying what to say. "It's a sight, Boone, how people are pointin' west."

"Just talk, I reckon."

"A body wouldn't know the river any more, with the new forts on her and the Mandans all dead and the Rees gone. You wouldn't know her, Boone."

Boone grunted again. A grunt was a handy thing, saying much with little.

"And steamboats! Damn if ever you seed such boats, Boone, so many of 'em and so white and fancy."

"A heap get wrecked."

"That don't stop the building of 'em."

"In time it will, I'm thinkin'."

"Folks everywhere talk about Oregon and California. They aim to make up parties."

"What for?"

"To get to new land, Boone. To get where there's room to breathe, I reckon. To get away from the fever. Y'ever stop to think about the fever, Boone? How many's got ager and such? Nigh half has the shakes."

"They'll shake worse, time they hear a war whoop."

"The Piegans have sickness," Teal Eye put in, looking up from her awl. It was as if her eye didn't see them but looked into other lodges and watched the children that had caught fevers and cramps in the belly lately and had died, some of them, while the medicine men had made a racket over them trying to scare the bad spirits out. It was as if, for a little while, her ear heard only the shake of a rattle and the pound of a drum.

"It ain't nothin', the Piegans' sickness ain't," Jim answered, smiling into her still face. He got up. "I brung you a present," he said as if he had just thought of it, and went to the old trap sack he had laid inside the lodge and brought out a looking glass with a wooden back and a wooden handle. Teal Eye made a little noise in her throat as she took it.

Boone caught Teal Eye's glance and made a gesture with his head. "I left a beaver outside."

Jim had turned back to the trap sack. He brought a bottle of whisky out of it and handed it to Boone. "Just so's you can wet your dry."

Teal Eye got up and went outside to skin the beaver.

"Huntin' ain't much?" Jim asked.

"I catch a few." Boone took a drink and offered the bottle to Jim. It was sure-enough whisky, not the alcohol and water that mostly passed for whisky. He felt Jim's mind studying him, as if there was something hadn't been brought to sight yet.

"There's better ways of making money."

"Could be ways of makin' more, but not better ways."

"Easier, anyhow."

Boone drank again and passed the bottle and refired his pipe.

"Teal Eye looks slick," Jim said, as if he was just making talk while his mind worked. Before he could go on, the entrance to the lodge was darkened and Red Horn came in, and after him Heavy Runner and Big Shield. They sat down, not speaking, and seeing it was a solemn visit, Boone passed around a bowl of dried meat and berries and got out his best pipe, which had the red head of a woodpecker fastened to the long stem and a big fan of feathers above the head. He loaded it and set the bowl on a chunk of dirt and blew up to the sun and down to the earth and passed it to Red Horn on his left.

Red Horn had dressed himself up for the meeting with Jim. He wore a scarlet uniform with blue facings on it that Chardon had given him and had a company medal hanging from his neck. There was red on his eyelids and red stripes on his cheeks and beads hanging from his ears, and he carried a swan's wing in his hand. Before he smoked he spit to the north and south because that was his medicine.

Boone started the half-empty bottle around then and sat back, waiting. Heavy Runner grunted the sting of the whisky from his throat and patted his bare belly with his hand. He was one Indian wouldn't dress up for anything, but would wear his old leggings and dirty robe no matter what. He had let the robe drop around his hams, leaving the upper part of him naked and showing the two old scars he had cut crosswise on each arm. Boone guessed his squaw hadn't done such a good job on the lice; he could see one climbing out on a hair. After a while old Heavy Runner felt it moving and lifted one scarred arm and picked it off and put it in his mouth.

Big Shield let the whisky trickle slow into his mouth. His face, raised to the bottle, was red with vermilion mixed with grease. The light of the fire glistened on it and shone white on the new bighorn shirt he wore. The bottle had just a drop in it when it came back to Boone.

It was a time before they got their palavering done and even then the three stayed on looking at Jim and asking a question now and then while he took up his talk with Boone, though none of them, except for Red Horn, could follow a white man's words.

"A man runs on to some queer hosses," Jim said. "I met up with one aims to learn every pass across the mountains."

"Ain't so queer. We l'arn't a few ourselves."

"That was for beaver."

Boone used a grunt again.

"This man ain't no trapper. I can't figure what he is, exactly. Says he's goin' to be ready when people really start to move. Maybe he aims to set up trading posts along the way or hire out to take people from the settlements. I don't guess he knows, himself, yet, but he's certain sure there'll be a galore of chances for a man as knows his way in the mountains. He's an educated man, he is, educated so high and fine a man can't make out more'n half he says."

"It's fool talk all the same."

"If there's a pass as'll do, he looks for steamboats to bring a pile of settlers and traders and such to Union, from where they'll head acrost to the Columbia. He's got a flock of notions flyin' around in his head."

Boone drew on his pipe and blew the smoke out in a thin jet while he looked at Jim. "When you startin'?"

Jim's eyelids flicked. "I didn't say nothin' about startin'."

"No need to."

"He's been south and's headin' up this way. Lookin' for a couple of mountain men to show him a north pass. Dollar and a half a day he'll pay."

"It's a fool thing, a damn fool thing."

"Maybe so, maybe not. If people are bound to get to Oregon seems like a good way is from one boat to another, across the mountains. Anyhow, it's bein' a fool thing wouldn't make no difference to us."

"No," Boone said, turning the thing over in his mind.

"We get our money and he gits his l'arnin'."

"Where at you aim to take him?"

"Up the Medicine, maybe, and over. You know best."

"Best is up the Marias and yan way to the Flathead. The snow'll catch him, though, and the cold."

Heavy Runner scratched his head, and Big Shield picked at the ground with a stick. Red Horn sat quiet. Only his eyes moved. It was as if he followed the talk with his eyes.

Jim said, "It ain't such a big party, just him and a couple of pork eaters to help out, and us, if you throw in."

"And a pile of stuff to tote."

"Some."

"How far does he want us?"

"I ain't sure as to that. Boat Encampment, maybe."

"Christ! When'll he be ready?"

"Aims to get to McKenzie in about a moon."

"Late. Red Horn says it will be a mean winter."

Red Horn turned his deep eyes on Jim. "Heap cold. Heap snow."

"I ain't never knowed Boone Caudill to back away from a thing on account of weather or whatever," Jim said.

"On account it's a goddam fool thing." Boone felt the whisky giving a bite to his words. "You're bad as any greenhorn yourself, talkin' about people comin', people comin', people comin'. You seen enough to know the mountains ain't farmin' country, any of it, let alone this Piegan land. A farmer'd have frost on his whiskers before the dust settled from plowin'."

"It ain't Piegan land the man's pointin' to, except to get acrost. And I ain't sayin' it's farm country. I'm sayin' we can get us a dollar and a half a day, easy."

"I mind the time such money weren't nothin'."

"There ain't no money in rememberin'."

"A man don't need money so much."

"It don't hurt him. Look, Boone, it ain't money alone, nor any- thing alone. It's money and movin' around and havin' fun. It's a time since me and you had us some fun together—some new fun, anyhow—you been sittin' in Blackfoot country so much."

Red Horn had been waiting to speak. There was a steady, hard look under his red eyelids. He hunched forward and started slow, speaking in Blackfoot. "Our old ones fought to keep the white trader away from our enemies beyond the mountains. They watched the pass that leads along the waters the Long Knife calls Maria. They met the Flatheads there, and the Kootenai. They met the Hanging Ears and the Pierced Noses and the Snakes. They were brave. They fought many battles. They took many scalps. They drove the enemies back. The enemies no more tried to travel the pass. To go to the hunting grounds they had to turn south and travel by the River of the Road to the Buffalo and come down the Medicine Riv- er to the plains. The old ones kept the white trader away. They made him travel far to the north to get to the country of the Flat- heads and Snakes. Our old ones were wise. They did not want the palefaces to give medicine irons and powder and lead to our ene- mies."

Red Horn stopped, as if to let the words sink in. His nose point- ed at Jim like a beak, and then at Boone. Heavy Runner had quit his scratching to listen.

"The old ones were wise," Jim agreed, and added, "for their time."

"No one travels where the old ones fought," Red Horn went on. "The white man does not know the trail. The Flatheads and the Snakes have forgotten what they knew. Only the Piegan re- members—the Piegan and the people that are his brothers, the Bloods and Big Bellies."

"The old ones are dead," Jim said. "The nation comes to a new time."

"The faces of the Flatheads and the Snakes are still blacked to- ward us. It is not wise to let our enemies be armed."

Boone said, "It is not a trading party. The white men will not carry rifles and powder and ball across the mountains."

"The white trader goes to our enemies by other ways," Jim ar- gued. "He travels the Southern Pass and the trail from the Athabasca."

Red Horn smoothed his uniform over his chest, his eye not looking at what he was doing but fixed sharp as an awl on Boone. The lines were so deep in his cheeks they seemed to set the mouth off by itself. "My young men will not like it. My young men will get mad. They will feel blood in their eyes, and Red Horn will have no power over them."

"Red Horn will not fight the Long Knife. He has said so himself." Boone felt anger stirring in him. Red Horn was a man right enough, no matter if he looked silly in his red suit, but there wasn't any man going to scare him off a thing or tell him what to do.

"My young men will get mad."

Boone held the anger back. "We are Piegans, Red Horn. We are your brothers."

"The young warriors will say that a Piegan would not show the secret of the pass."

"You can keep power over your young men if you want to."

"The white brother who goes to the enemy is not a brother."

Big Shield was nodding. The shine of the fire on his red face went up and down his cheeks as his head moved.

"Goddam it! Have it that way, then! I reckon I'll do as I please."

Red Horn sat straight in his scarlet uniform, holding the swan's wing idle in both his hands, while his mind seemed working at the English Boone had used.

"No cause to git r'iled," Jim put in. "You don't even know you're goin' yet, Boone."

Teal Eye came back into the lodge, came back noiselessly and went to work again on the shirt. From the trouble in her face Boone could tell she had been listening. Christ, even a squaw cramped a man some, or anyhow wanted to!

He turned to Jim. "I been settin' on my ass quite a spell, all right."

33

Peabody was the man's name—Elisha Peabody, a name that tasted strange on the tongue and sounded strange in the ear. "I am told you know the mountains as well as any man," he said while his wide eyes pried at Boone's face. He waited for an answer, but Boone didn't make one. There wasn't any sense in answering a thing like that.

Jim broke in to ask, "How's this here trip goin' to set with the company?"

Peabody moved his plump hand around, as if the room they were in and the two wine bottles on the table were answer enough. "I have talked the matter over thoroughly with Mr. Chardon. We find no conflict of interest. None whatsoever. If one existed I hope I should be gentleman enough not to impose on the hospitality of Fort McKenzie." Peabody's round and earnest face turned itself on Jim and then on Boone and then opened in a little smile that made his mouth look small and babyish. "Sit down," he invited.

It was a clerk's room they were in, Boone thought, with a fire in it and a bed held up by cottonwood blocks and a mud-and-stone chimney and a window with a broken glass. Someone had stuffed a piece of old blanket in the hole. Through his moccasins he felt the dirt floor packed hard as a slab of rock. Over his head the sod roof had sent roots down between the timbers. He heard a mouse squeaking up there.

"Have a seat," Peabody said again while he lowered his butt to the bed.

"The company can make a man a heap of trouble, one way and another, eh, Boone?"

Boone walked to the fire and turned and stepped back. He said, "Sons of bitches!"

"What is it?" asked Peabody, and then it came to him what had been said and he ended up with "Oh."

Jim sat on a stool, looking awkward perched up that way, and began putting tobacco in his pipe. There was a lighting stick by the fire, and he picked it up and held it in the flame and got his pipe going with it.

When Boone didn't sit down, Peabody asked, "Have another drink," and got up and filled the glasses, and then returned to the bed and put his butt down again, in a neat and sort of womanish way. He was a sawed-off man, thick-set without being roly-poly, and had a spot of pink in each cheek. He was a man Boone couldn't picture in buckskins or even linsey but only in the brought-on clothes he wore and the brought-on shoes, as if he had been born in them and would look raw and butchered with them off.

Boone stopped his walking back and forth to look down at him. "There ain't any pass hereabouts like the Southern Pass, none so easy and open. It snows enough to cool off hell."

"Indeed!"

"What you lookin' for—one short and quick, or long and easier?"

"In general, of course, a short route is to be desired but not if it is a great deal more difficult. Is there one that might become a wagon road?"

"Good Christ! Marias Pass is open enough, if you don't count the dead timber, but where's the wagons as'll roll over it?"

Peabody leaned forward, and interest seemed to bring his round face to a point. "Open enough, is it? By thunder!"

"There's a heap of down timber in it."

"The Indians use it, don't they?"

"Not much. Not any more." Boone drank his wine. He couldn't figure why anyone would put out wine unless he couldn't get better. A man could swallow a river of it and never feel exactly good but only dull and lazy.

"Are there better ways?" Peabody asked.

"Southern Pass."

"I mean in this region."

"Shorter and rougher ones."

"Suitable eventually for wagons or carts?"

"Hell, no!"

Peabody lifted his rump and went over to the table. "Would you be good enough to look at the maps I have here?" He picked up a book. "Unfortunately, Mr. Irving's account of the journeys of Captain Bonneville isn't much help. The map it contains shows no detail east of the Rocky Mountains." He put the book aside. "Here, however, is the map accompanying the Rev. Samuel Parker's journal." He looked up, his eyes questioning Boone. "It is a recent work."

"Wrong as hell, just the same. It ain't but two long camps across the mountains, maybe three, startin' from the Marias canyon. This here's supposed to be Flathead Lake, ain't it? And here's the Marias. There ain't no such stretch of country between."

"By thunder!" said Peabody. His face looked pleased and eager.

"Why'n't you just go ahead and cuss?" Jim asked from the stool.

Peabody turned aside long enough to answer. "I have never found it necessary."

"Helps, though."

Peabody was opening another book and flattening out the map. "This," he said, "is the latest thing available, the *Memoir Historical and Political on the Northwest Coast of North America and the Adjacent Territories*, by Robert Greenhow, librarian to the Department of State. Notice what he calls 'the Route Across the Mountains.' " Again his face questioned Boone.

"It ain't so far wrong," Boone said slowly while he studied the map, "savin' on t'other side. The trail don't lead south of the lake to Flathead House, but north. It turns northwest here, where Bear Creek flows into the middle fork of the Flathead."

"Splendid!" said Peabody, rubbing his plump hands. "Splendid!" He added, "By thunder!" and looked over, quick, to Jim as if he expected him to say something.

Boone said, "The time is goddam late."

"I daresay we'll make it."

"If it was just gettin' across, maybe yes. But Jim here says you want to go on and down the Columbia a piece."

"That's right."

"It ain't all-summer country, yan side of the mountains. It gits cold enough to freeze the tail off of a painter."

"We'll make it, God willing."

Jim said, "A body never can tell about God."

Boone studied Peabody, starting from his feet and going up to his head, and Peabody spoke with a stiff edge in his voice. "I believe I can go where another man can."

"I think I'll have me a little drink," Jim said, getting up and pouring a big one. "Wisht old Poordevil was around. He was a man, now, for a trip. That Injun could keep warm with no more'n a rabbit skin for his pizzle. Heerd tell of him lately, Boone?"

"Last I knew he was north, with the Bloods."

Boone had seen men like Peabody before, men who were simple in a way and serious as owls and so sure of themselves that everything they said was a kind of brag without being a brag, either. When they got their comeuppance, it was something like a baby being hurt.

The room darkened as a cloud went across the sun. Through the window Boone saw a shadow running along the ground and up the pickets and over. The pound of a blacksmith's hammer came to his ears. He turned to Peabody. "Y'ever see a horse froze dead?"

Peabody's wide eyes widened more, as if he was seeing the horse now. After he had taken a good look at it, he answered, "New England weather is hardly tropical, you know."

Boone poured his glass full. "I wouldn't know as to that."

For a while nobody said anything. Then Jim spoke up, just to make talk. "Me and Boone met up with Bonneville and Wyeth more'n once."

"They didn't come out so fat," Boone said, watching Peabody's face.

"There are good reasons. Bonneville, for one, never knew what he was after. He chased one way and then another. He never decided whether he was explorer, trader, trapper, or mere adventurer. He couldn't choose between fun and furs."

"He was an all-right man, just the same," Jim answered.

"I refer to his business abilities."

"Not so different from you in looks, if only you had a bare scalp in place of that there suit of hair."

Boone asked, "What about Wyeth? There was a man knew which way his stick floated."

Peabody nodded. "I know Wyeth personally. Splendid gentleman. He was the victim of misfortune and bad faith. If the Rocky Mountain Fur Company had kept its contract with him, I dare say he would be in the mountains still, instead of cutting ice at Cambridge for the South American trade."

"Ice!" Boone said. "Kin a man sell ice?"

"All the same," Jim put in, "beaver would have petered out on him, same as on the rest."

"I'm not interested in beaver. I've told you that. It is development I'm interested in, future development. You appear to think, because the Indians haven't made use of this great western country, that nobody can."

"They live in this country. They live off of it, and enj'y themselves and all," Boone answered. "What in hell do you want. Christ Almighty!"

Peabody took a deep breath, as if to make sure he had wind enough for his argument. "When country which might support so many actually supports so few, then, by thunder, the inhabitants have not made good use of the natural possibilities." His wide eyes looked at Boone, earnest and polite but not afraid. "That failure surely is justification for invasion, peaceful if possible, forcible if necessary, by people who can and will capitalize on opportunity."

"I say it's all fool talk."

"If you live, you will realize how wrong you are. Can't you see? We are growing. The nation is pushing out. New opportunities are sure to arise, bigger opportunities than ever existed in the fur trade. Transport, merchandising, agriculture, lumbering, fisheries, land! I can't imagine them all."

"Goddam it, you talk like a man could put a plow in the land and grow corn, maybe, or sweet potatoes, or sorghum, or tobacco. The season ain't long enough to make a crop. This here's Injun country and buffler country, and allus will be."

"I doubt what you say, even as regards this Blackfoot country itself. As for Oregon and the Willamette valley—" Peabody spread his hands. "The Hudson's Bay Company has crops there, and cattle. The missions are doing well. A hundred settlers went there this past summer under the leadership of Dr. Elijah White."

Peabody's mouth was drawn straight in his round face. The pink in his cheeks had spread out so that most of his face seemed red. He took another breath deep in his belly, as if to send his big words out again, but all he said was, "I didn't come to debate but to hire guides." He sat down and rubbed his face with a white handkerchief that he pulled from the pocket of his roundabout.

Jim took the glass from his mouth long enough to say, "It's British country acrost the mountains. How you aim to fix that?"

"It isn't British country. It's joint-occupancy territory, by treaty."

"I reckon the Hudson's Bay Company ain't heard about that."

"I understand the settlers aren't being treated too badly. That question aside, do you think the United States of America will let the company, or even the British army itself, stand in the way? Nothing shall stop us. British? Spanish? Mexicans? None of them. By every reasonable standard the land is ours—by geography, contiguity, natural expansion. Why, it's destiny, that's what it is—inevitable destiny."

Jim grinned and his arm came out stiff and his finger pointed. "Hurrah for the first gov'nor!" His glance came over to Boone. "A man that can talk that high and handsome don't ever need to turn his hand."

Peabody was flushed with talking. He flushed hotter at Jim's words and got out his white handkerchief again.

"I reckon we'll have a time of it, just the same, pushin' them Britishers into the sea," Jim said.

Peabody took his cup of wine from the table and sat on the bed and took a bare nip and clamped his lips over it and held it in his mouth for a while without swallowing, as if to get all the good out of it before giving it up to his stomach.

Boone let himself down and sat cross-legged on the floor. "How far you want us?"

"To the head of navigation on the Columbia, at least."

"For big boats or small?"

"We shall have to see."

"You figure to stop at Hudson Bay forts?"

"Perhaps not." Peabody considered. "Perhaps it would be best not to. Not this trip."

"It's crazy to put out now. I say wait until summer."

Peabody shook his round head while his mouth made the tight line again above the small, square chin. "That point is settled. I am not going to lie idle because of a little unpleasant weather. If you won't take me, I shall look for someone else."

Jim had his knife out and was whittling on the stool between his spread legs. "Here's a hoss as knows his own mind."

"Mr. Chardon thinks the snow in the mountains presents no obstacles as yet."

"Could be he wants to get you froze," said Boone.

"Once it makes up its mind to snow in this country, by God she snows," Jim added. "Chardon tell you that?"

"You haven't given me your answers."

"If a man was smart now, I reckon he'd hoof it." Jim's gaze was on Boone.

"I have equipment, you know."

Boone shook his head. "Could be horses would come in handy, if we get snowed in and no game about. There's worse doin's than horse meat."

Peabody's round face got a look of surprise on it.

"And if snow kep' away," Jim said, "we'd get through that much quicker."

"Are you accepting, then?"

"Reckon I'll go, like I told you once," Jim answered. "It ain't me you need so much as Caudill, though. I never traveled this here pass. What you say, Boone?"

"I say it's a crazy idea. There won't be no sight of people travelin' this way, ever, and no sight of people fixin' to farm. It's too cold and dry and windy for folks. Them as try it will clamp their tails down and run for home, if their scalps ain't already on a coup stick. And some will starve and some will freeze. That's what I say." He watched Peabody's face. "It's plumb dangerous to go now. That's what I say, and dangerouser if we got to dodge the British forts."

"There's danger, all right," Jim agreed. "Red Horn, now, he don't want us to go."

"Goddam Red Horn!"

"I don't understand," Peabody put in. "Who is Red Horn?"

"It don't amount to anything," Boone answered. "Just Injun talk."

"He don't like it, though, Boone. Maybe we'd best give it up, account of him."

"Damn you, Jim. You just aim to get my dander up."

"Is she up enough?" There was a crooked smile on Jim's face. He went on, "I ain't just devilin' you. Come on, Boone! It won't be no fun without you. Tell the man yes."

"I don't like Red Horn to get the notion he can herd me around."

"That's he-bear talk now."

Peabody was looking from one to the other of them. A little frown sat over his eyes. "I'm not sure I follow you," he said to Boone.

"It ain't no skin off of me. Me and Jim can get us out of a fix, all right enough, not sayin' we can do the same for you. I'll p'int the way."

"Splendid!" The little man rubbed his fat hands together and reached over suddenly and got his glass from the table and took a whole swallow all at once. "I'll need help and advice getting ready. My two French Canadians won't be of much assistance there. If you want to lend a hand, I'll start your pay at once, at the agreed rate of a dollar and a half."

"Might as well," Jim said. "I'm that poor I couldn't buy a bead for my fav'rite squaw."

"Who's the French?" Boone asked.

"They're named Zenon and Beauchamp. This Beauchamp is a powerful man."

"Hope they know how to pack a horse. Me and Jim, we figger just to raise meat and lead the way."

Boone walked over and let himself out of the room. Rooms made a man feel shut in on himself; they made him uneasy, so's his mind never rightly put itself to a thing but kept thinking about a way out, like a mouse in a bucket. He walked past the cannon and the flagstaff. A sleepy gate watcher let him out of the inner gate. There were a couple of Bloods in the Indian store and one man he took to be a Cree, acting pretty well drunked up. "No whis-ky," the clerk was saying. "No got medicine water." The Cree came over to Boone, begging tobacco. He was a stout Indian, not tall, but built wide and chesty. Boone shook his head and started by him, but the Cree reached up and grabbed one of his braids of hair to hold him by, saying something in his throat while he yanked. Boone hit him in the belly and heard the wind grunt out of him and felt the hand let go the plait. The Cree bent over, his arms wrapped across his belly. Boone hit him again, striking up in the face, and the Cree slammed backwards on the dirt floor and lay still. There wasn't anything said, not by the clerk or the two Bloods. Boone felt their eyes following him as he went through the big gate to the outside.

The sun had lost itself behind some clouds to the west, and a keen chill had fallen on the land. It would be dark soon. With win-ter coming on, the sun no more than took a peek at things and then ducked behind the mountains. Smoke was coming from the tepees pitched around the fort, rising gray to the cold sky. There was the smell of wood smoke in the air, and the smell of snow. Off to his right the river ran dull as lead.

Teal Eye would be waiting for him in the lodge she had pitched. She would be waiting and wondering, but she wouldn't ask when he got there. She would see there was meat for him and that the fire was good, and all the time her eyes would be on him with the un-asked question in them, and her face with a light in it that he had noticed lately, a kind of soft gleam through the flesh. She wouldn't ask, but all her small ways would be listening ways, bringing the answer to her from his looks or his motions or the tone of his voice. A woman got a hold on a man and pushed him one way and another without so much as opening her mouth. Sensing her all around him, a man didn't feel like his own self sometimes. He wanted to shake loose and say to hell with it and strike out somewhere, with nothing hanging to him of what he had been or what he had done. He wouldn't do it, though, not forever—not if he had a woman like Teal Eye. A little time away from her was enough, four moons maybe, while he took a crazy by-thunder Yankee across to Oregon.

34

It was just as Boone had known it would be. There was jerked meat, boiled and cooked with pounded prairie turnips, and the fire warm in its circle of stones, and Teal Eye doing around while the edge of her eye kept on him and her face waited for what might come to her ear or eye. He grunted and sat down and ate out of a bowl and afterwards fired his pipe with the trader's black to-bacco mixed with the bark of the red willow. It was a soft-stone pipe he had, with a round bowl on a square base and a willow stem. He had made it himself, after the style of the Blackfeet, and while it wasn't as fancy as some that other tribes made, it was sweet and drew easy. He studied it while he smoked, letting his mind turn things over slow.

After a while, without looking at Teal Eye, he said in Black-foot, "You will go back to Red Horn and wait."

She didn't need to say anything, not with the quick look on her face.

He counted on his fingers. "After six sleeps we will start." He let his glance go to her while he pulled on his pipe. "Red Hair and I and the white man and two Bad Medicines."

She bent her head and her hands made a little flutter above her leather skirt. She said, "I will get the warm clothes ready."

It was one of the things he prized her for, that she didn't argue. For all that her eyes might say, or her face or her hands, the mouth didn't come out with it. He spoke his mind, and that was that, and he didn't have to fuss about it. It saved a man a heap of bother.

Her look questioned him again, and he answered. "In the time of the big winds I will be back, or sooner if the winter opens, in the time when the great owl nests."

She said, without looking at him, "You will come back?"

"In the time of the big winds, or sooner."

"You will come back to the Piegans?"

"I told you once I would!" he answered sharply in English. "Think I aim to stay with the Flatheads or Snakes or somebody?"

"Every day I shall look to the west." She sat quiet, looking down at her hands.

"I reckon you could get yourself another man, if it came to that."

She got up, not speaking, as if what he had said had hurt her inside.

"Jim would take you, I reckon."

The wind whistled in the tops of the lodgepoles overhead and a puff of it came down the smoke hole and chased the smoke around. Dark was settling inside the lodge, making the fire look sharper. He would sleep on his rifle tonight. A man couldn't tell what some crazy Blood might take it into his head to do after filling up on firewater.

Teal Eye was already under the robe when he went to it and put himself down with his feet to the fire. He lay there, letting things run in his head, thinking she was asleep, and then her hand came over and barely touched him and her voice said, "Strong Arm will have a son."

He said, "For Christ sake!" and thought about it some more and said, "For Christ sake!" again.

A man wondered what his young one would look like and what he would be like. It gave a man a solid feeling, knowing he had got himself a pup.

He went to sleep with his mind on it. Once he awakened, thinking he had felt Teal Eye shaking under the robe, thinking he had heard a little held-in cry, but all there was was the wind singing by the lodgepoles and the fire dying.

35

From high in the canyon one could look down on the foothills and far beyond them to the yellow plains shimmering under the early winter sun. Elisha Peabody checked his horse. It was an enormous world, a world of heights and depths and distances that numbed the imagination. One felt inclined to draw into himself, like a turtle. The mountains were loftier than any Peabody ever had seen; the streams were swifter, the wind fiercer, the air sharper, the view vaster. It occurred to him that everything had been made to giant's measure; it was as if proportion had run wild. The great sprawling magnitude of the west made the hills and parks of home seem small and artificial, like a yard with a picket fence around it.

The human soul inclined to extremes, too. Yesterday it had soared, feeling wild and free, feeling so inconsequential among these physical immensities as to be lost to the sight of God and His wrath. Last night, with the great darkness crowding in, it came back like a bird to roost, sensing the awful power and glory of God all about. Peabody knew humility then, and prayed for guidance and strength and God's favor, without which even Yankee ingenuity could be of no avail. Today there rode with him a small burden of oppression that no circumstance could account for, unless it was that the wordless vigilance of Caudill had given rise to a vague and foolish misgiving. More than once Caudill had hitched around in his saddle to study the way they had come. Under the black brows his eyes were always busy, scanning the slopes, the timber, the stream, the game trails. What his eyes told him his mouth did not utter or his expression reveal. There was the sharp awareness of a wild animal in his face, but nothing more.

A strange man, Boone Caudill, riding rawboned and slouched at the head of the column while his Indian's braids swung to the swing of his horse. A strange man, with moodiness in him, and quickness to anger and the promise of a childlike savagery. Was it the rude half-civilization of the Kentucky frontier that had made him what he was, or his years with the red Arabs of the plains? Watching him ride ahead, his strong shoulders loose and his body giving to the pace of his horse, Peabody concluded he was more Indian than white man. Outwardly he was hardly white man at all. He wore the clothes of an Indian and carried a bag of amulets —a medicine bundle, as it was called. His voice was rough and deep in his chest, even when the sounds it made were English sounds. His face was dark-eyed, weathered, and often inscrutable. He had a squaw for a wife.

Caudill could be a difficult man, even a dangerous one, Peabody imagined. One of gentler breeding sometimes felt uncertain and impotent in his presence, as if the strength and forwardness and primitive masculinity of the man dwarfed any disciplined powers. Peabody shrugged that feeling away while his eyes ranged far out on the plains. A Yankee could hold his own in any company, by wit and courage and perseverance, as Yankees had demonstrated through generations. Caudill would be a penniless white renegade among the Indians long after his own enterprise and vision had made him comfortable and important.

His eye came back up the canyon, following the winding stream, until it reached the pack string and saw Deakins sitting quiet on his horse at the tail of it, waiting for Peabody to go on. Deakins grinned, showing a flash of teeth. He and Caudill had come from different molds. Where Caudill was silent, Deakins talked; where Caudill flared out, Deakins fashioned a joke; where there was in Caudill the suggestion of quick ferocity, there was in Deakins the indication of considered action. Whimsicality was a part of Deakins' make-up, and humor, half-sly, half-innocent, so that one never quite knew the depth of his perception. The two constituted a good if godless pair, the one balancing and conditioning the other.

Peabody kicked his horse, and heard the pack animals behind him clumping into action and Zenon chattering French. He could picture the smile on Zenon's face, the mouth mobile and expressive under eyes as eloquent as any maiden's. He could see his small hands moving as he talked. Occasionally he heard Beauchamp answer Zenon's fluent words. Beauchamp was a heavy wedge of a man with the neck and shoulders of a bull and a skull inhabited by a slow brute wit. Against Zenon's quick understanding he matched his muscle, as if in the final reckoning it was force that told the measure of a man. He liked to show the knot of muscle on his biceps and to seize Zenon's arm afterward and make him wince with the power of his grip. He had liked to, that is, until Deakins interfered on their second night out from Fort McKenzie.

"If I was Zenon, now, I would shoot that damn hand of yours off, I would," Deakins had said. Peabody saw, with a little turn of astonishment, that the twinkle was gone from his blue eyes.

Beauchamp let go of Zenon. It was an instant before he answered. His gaze traveled over Deakins as if measuring his strength. Then he said, "By damn, me think you need one fusil, to stand with Beauchamp."

Before Deakins could answer, Caudill stepped around the fire. Wordless, he walked up to Beauchamp. Peabody remembered how deliberately he stepped and how suddenly he struck. Miraculously, Beauchamp kept his feet. He staggered back, almost falling, but caught his balance and stood silent as if allowing time for thought to turn in his head. He brought up his hand to feel of his jaw. His eyes dropped from Caudill's face and went to the ground and hunted around. Peabody was reminded of a mouse seeking a hole.

"There ain't no real fight in him, Zenon," Caudill said. "No need to be afeard of him. He only looks like a man."

There had been no trouble since, nor, Peabody imagined, was there likely to be any. Beauchamp was like an ox tamed by the whip, with no resentment in him and no impulse to revenge. Day by day he did his work. Altogether, thought Peabody, he had a good crew. He turned his mind away from the reasonless oppression he felt, thinking of the good crew, the open weather, the purposeful progress they were making. Oregon lay just beyond the hills. God willing, he would reach the Columbia.

As they traveled the canyon, bearing to the southwest, it seemed more and more logical to assume that God was willing, for the way lay wide and easy, except for windfall and the new growth that had sprung up along the trails that forgotten Indians had worn. On all sides the mountains lifted in great peaks and bulges of rock, thrusting so high that white clouds moved among them; the wind blew the keen breath of winter, sometimes with the spit of storm in it; but the pass rolled on, gradual and safe and bare of snow. It was more than Peabody had dared hope for, by thunder. Looking into the future, one could see pack trains climbing it, and carts and four-wheeled wagons piled with settlers' goods, bound for the fertile valleys of the Columbia. They would be free men, these, without a slave among them—free men going to free country to establish what would come to be free states of the Union, once the claims of the British had been dismissed. Afterward the lanes of commerce would open, replacing the long, slow sea route around the Horn. He could see cargoes going up and down the Missouri and the Columbia and being transshipped across the mountains over the very ground his horse trod—cargoes of processed goods and imports, of textiles, tools, rifles, coffee, tea, and sugar, flowing west in exchange for the products the settlers had wrested from the new land. How could South Pass, without the benefits of navigation, rival the course he was traveling? There would be opportunity here for men of industry and foresight. He who was early on the ground would have the better chance. He who knew the way could profit by his knowledge. There would be stores to establish and transportation lines to build and operate and land to be dealt in. Once one was familiar with the country he would know where to direct his energies. Boston men would be told of the pass, and Boston men would be acquainted with the possibilities, and Boston money, hitherto so cautious, would answer to the assurance of tidy earnings. Peabody brought his compass and notebook from his pocket. Tonight, by the light of the campfire, he would enlarge on this hasty sketching.

The column slowed and shuffled to a stop as Caudill stopped to look up and down the canyon. After a while he slipped from his horse and tied it to a limb and came back to borrow Peabody's glass. All he said when he handed it back was "Let's git on." Peabody used the glass himself while Caudill returned to the head of the string. His horse kept moving under him, nosing for spears of cured grass, with the result that his eye couldn't fix on a place. Things swam into sight and out again, the pine trees rising stiff and tall, the river winding, the mountains shouldering up to the timber line. He took the glass from his eye. The plains were shut off from sight here. One felt alone with the great hills; one felt imprisoned, and voiceless in an eternal silence; one felt buried below the ragged spires that pierced the sky. Fort McKenzie was a lifetime away, a five-day lifetime away.

Where the trail dipped down to water, Caudill brought the string to a halt for the night. The stream was little more than a trickle now, chuckling over stones slick with rusty moss. Peabody imagined he could see the divide ahead, where the sun was sinking in a fiery glory. He got off his horse and held to the saddle for a minute while his stiff legs renewed their acquaintance with earth. The sunset held him. He could lose himself in it. Melancholy ran through him, and ecstasy—a sad enchantment that made personal ambition seem almost unimportant. "Majestic!" he said under his breath. "Majestic!"

Caudill asked, "How's that?"

Peabody only motioned toward the west.

"Red as all hell. Reckon you can eat, regardless." Caudill set about unsaddling the horses while Deakins took a side of deer from a pack and began to build a fire.

"We'll keep the horses close up," Caudill said for the benefit of the Frenchmen. "Soon's we get 'em unpacked just take 'em to that little flat there, and remember to hobble 'em, every head."

"Meat's almighty scarce," Deakins observed while Peabody fumbled at his saddle. "Ain't seed elk nor deer since morning, and little sign."

Peabody pulled the saddle off and laid it for a pillow where he planned to make his bed. It gave him a certain feeling of pride to perform his share of the tasks. "At the rate we're going, we'll be in the Flathead basin before we want for more game."

"Shoo!" answered Deakins, while his gaze followed Zenon and Beauchamp as they led the horses away. "I reckon you ain't watched them pork eaters make a meal."

"Everything's working out. This pass, man! I couldn't have wished for anything better. Why, with the timber cleared away, wagons could roll across here."

Caudill was working on the venison with his knife. He said, "If anyone wanted to roll 'em."

"I'd like to have the toll rights."

"Toll! Toll! By Jesus, Jim, greenhorns no sooner see a place than they hanker to spoil it. They want to grab things for their own and close a country up. Who you think the country belongs to, anyway, Peabody?"

"I imagine the man who cleared the way would have some rights to levy on those who used it."

"It don't make no difference," said Caudill more mildly while he plied his knife. "A tollman could hold his hand out until Christ come again and never find money in it."

In his mind's eye Peabody saw the wagons rolling and the collector busy making change. His gaze went to Caudill. Something in the man was a challenge to him. It was as if self-respect demanded that he provoke him more. "It isn't too difficult to think that some day, maybe in our own time, the steam railway will be heard clanking over this pass, carrying passengers three hundred miles in twenty-four hours."

"Your head's got room for the damndest notions."

"It's ag'in nature," Deakins answered. He already had speared a chunk of meat on a stick. "Why'n't God put wheels on a man if he aimed for him to hump it so?"

"People are going against nature in four or five states already, then, and not being hurt by it. Albany and Buffalo are connected by rail now, I understand."

Caudill asked, "Where's that?"

"New York State."

"That ain't Injun country."

"I never seen a steam carriage," Deakins said.

"Me, I don't never care to see one. A horse is good enough, or these here feet, if it comes to that."

The Frenchmen trailed back from the flat and set about cutting roasting sticks. Zenon squatted down afterward with his knees up under his chin, watching his roast cook. Caudill laid the side of ribs close to the coals.

Peabody dipped a can of water from the stream and set it to heat. Straight meat was a diet that grew agreeable with use, and it so simplified the business of cooking that a mountain traveler felt disinclined to make use of the flour and meal he had packed. A civilized stomach demanded a swallow of coffee, though, with a generous addition of sugar.

Watching him, Beauchamp said, "Me think good." Beauchamp lay on his stomach, with his stick propped against a rock and his roast scorching in the fire. He was a careless Frenchman for all his muscle.

Peabody sent his gaze up toward the divide again. The sunset had burned itself out. Of it all, only one thin red streak remained above the hills, and even as he watched, it darkened and the mountains began to lose outline against the sky. Darkness seemed to squeeze around him—darkness and silence, made the darker and silenter by the little flame of the campfire and the mindless chuckle of the water. The cold crept through his woolens and lay like metal along his skin. He pushed his feet closer to the fire. Perhaps Caudill was right, saying Indian shoes kept the feet warmer than the cobbler's product.

Caudill licked his fingers and wiped them on his buckskins and drew the knife across the leather to clean it and then put it back in its case. Not until he had fired his pipe did he speak. Then he said, "We'd best set a guard."

"Set a guard?" Peabody asked. He saw the campfire mirrored minutely in Zenon's lifted eyes.

"Just playin' safe," Caudill replied.

"What is it? By thunder, you'd think I was a child."

"I ain't seen a thing to scare a man. Just got a notion, is all."

"You didn't have a notion last night, or before."

"No cause to."

Deakins put in, "His medicine's workin', Peabody. It's tellin' him."

"Telling him what?"

"It ain't medicine, but just sense," Caudill said.

"Speak so a man can understand you, will you, please?"

Zenon asked, "*Les sauvages?*"

After a silence Caudill said, "You got a right to know, only I don't want to scare the French into leavin' us. This here pass is a dog-leg. There's a shorter way across, from the hip to the foot of the dog. It's rough but quick, runnin' up Cut Bank and over to Nyack Creek." He paused for a minute and added, "That's how the old Blackfeet kep' trappin' the Flatheads and Snakes."

"Who in the world would want to trap us? You two are Black-feet yourselves."

Beauchamp was looking around into the darkness, as if the possibility of danger had just entered his dull head.

"Could be they'd foller and not cut ahead," said Deakins.

"Could be," Caudill agreed. "I didn't see nothin', though, the back way, and it ain't likely, besides. A party would've had time, now, to take the short cut and sneak back on us."

"For heaven's sake, answer! Who would want to trap us?" Peabody let his full impatience come into his voice.

Caudill shrugged. He let the words out along his pipe stem. "Red Horn, maybe, or some of his boys."

36

There was the bite of winter in the breeze the next morning and a skim of snow in the ground, stretching out white under the lingering darkness. Swift-running as the creek was, shore ice was closing it in. The Frenchmen came to the fire with their teeth chattering and rubbed their hands close over the red coals, swearing through stiffened lips.

"Get up the horses soon as you thaw out a little," Boone ordered. "We won't get across huggin' a fire." Their gaze came to his face and traveled from it out to where the night still wavered over the snow, and he added, "It's safe enough. I took a look around."

Peabody blew out his breath, watching the cloud that it made, and scuffed the palms of his hands on the skirts of his long-tailed coat. He had on a woolen cap, with flaps that came over his ears. "Cold," he said while he hunched inside the coat. "Cold for so little snow."

"You'll be seein' snow, I'm thinkin', before the day's over," Jim said. His eyes lifted, trying to make out what the sky looked like. The dark was close down, though, like a fog, and nothing showed overhead—not even a pale streak to the southeast where the sun would be climbing after a while. The breeze curled around a man, licking at him with a tongue of frost.

"Our visitors didn't appear," Peabody said. His round face, lighted up by the fire, looked fresh again after the night. The cold had brought out the red spots in his cheeks and had put another in the middle of his chin.

"Trouble with Injuns is they don't let a man know when they'll show up," Jim answered. "It ain't polite, not givin' a body time to fix for 'em."

"I see," said Peabody, smiling a little as if he didn't know quite what to make of Jim.

"Varmint scared the horses a while back," Boone said. "Painter, likely."

"Horse meat beats no meat, even to a painter. I bet he ain't had a bite since year afore yesterday, game's so scarce." Jim knifed a piece from what was left of the side of deer.

Peabody watched him fill his mouth and then went to his pack and got out a towel and walked to the creek and squatted down. Boone could see him, stooped dark against the snow, with the creek running black and small at his feet. Peabody took off his cap and loosened the collar of his coat and pulled his sleeves up. He dipped up a hand of water and rubbed his two hands together and dipped again and held his hands tight for a minute to ease the cramp the cold had put in them. Then he dipped with both hands and brought the cupped water to his face and rubbed hard and fast, like trying to get a spot out. He came back blowing.

Jim said, "Shoo, that ain't nothin', Peabody. Wait'll you have to wash that there face with a icicle. You ain't a true *hivernan* till then."

The Frenchmen, and the horses behind them, took shape across the stream. The dark was drawing off, leaving the sky gray all over —the same kind of gray, with no light spot in it even yet.

"I et," Boone said, "so's I could take out ahead. You bring my horse along."

Jim nodded, but Peabody put a quick question. "You're not going to walk!"

"Thought I would."

"Why?"

Jim answered, "Same reason a war party walks. A man ain't so plain to see. He can get where a horse can't."

"And be run down more quickly, too."

"If he lets hisself be seen, maybe. And if t'other man has the stummick for it. Ain't many would want to chase after Boone, not if they knowed him."

"Do you really expect trouble?" Peabody asked Boone.

"I wouldn't say, either way. Only, if Injuns are after us, I figure they'll cut across and come at us from the front or sides."

"I can't believe anyone has designs against us."

"Maybe not, but the wolves have et many a feast on men as thought that way. You don't take chances, not if you know Injuns." Boone lifted his rifle to the crook of his arm.

"We'll see you later, then," Peabody said. Greenhorns kept saying things that didn't need to be said, nor answered either. A fool would know he would see him again, saving only that maybe his eyes didn't see any more.

Zenon and Beauchamp came up with the horses, which were snorty and touchy with cold. "Make them Bad Medicines hump it," Boone said to Jim. "I'm thinkin' hell is fixin' to freeze over." He set out up the canyon.

Daylight had come, or as much of it as ever would come on this day. The sky lay low over the mountains, so low that their tops were lost to sight. A man felt closed in, with no distance for his eye. It was as if the sky lay on his shoulders, bearing him down. From somewhere ahead the wind came, with a growing strength in it and a sting that drew up the face. The snow squeaked under his moccasins. Red Horn's young men would be shivering in their robes if they were out today. They would be shivering but looking just the same, seeing the snow and the trees black against it and the mountains climbing and the slopes dimmed with gray. Their eyes would be poking for distance, watching for color, watching for movement.

A man got so's he could foot it fast and easy like a wild thing. He got so's he could cover ground without trying and go quiet without taking pains, so that his mind was free to think and his eye to look and his ear to listen. Jim was right, saying game was scarce. There was hardly a track in the snow, except now and then for the skittery print a mouse had left. The shoulders of the hills lay quiet and empty. A man walking alone got the notion that everything was gone except him, everything except him and the hills and the gray sky and the running wind.

The wind pinched his nose and cheeks and got a cold whisper inside his clothes sometimes. He would stay warmer than most, though, come no matter what, with wrappings of blanket under his leggings and fur-lined shoes made with long flaps that wrapped around his lower legs, too. Teal Eye had cut the blanket and made the shoes herself and seen to it that all were put into his pack. Blanket and fur and buckskins were better than boughten clothes anyway you took them, except that the Nor'West capote that he wore, with a hood that fitted over the head, was a good thing.

The stream dwindled to a swift trickle that fed off snowbanks high on the slopes and splashed down in little falls and made a bed and ran away, bound for the Marias and the Missouri. Another day like this one and the warmth that the sun had put in the earth would go out altogether and the snowbanks would close tight and the last of the water would freeze in long icicles over the faces of rocks where it fell now. Already the ice hung at the sides of the falls.

Along toward the middle of the day, beyond where even a trickle of water ran, Boone climbed the last lift to the divide. One way the land pitched down to Oregon, to the Flathead and Clark's Fork and the Columbia and the western sea; the other, it fell off to the Marias and Missouri, to Blackfoot country and Red Horn's band and Teal Eye carrying his young one in her. It was strange that a man could go off and leave a part of him living behind him and have no power over it and no say-so but only the knowledge that there was a live piece of him that wasn't with him. It was as if a man couldn't get free from what he had been and done. He couldn't be himself alone; he had to be all the other men he was, in the season before and the season before that and the season before that. He couldn't stand just by what he did now; he had to stand by what he had done in the past, too. Old Dick Summers would understand if he was around to be talked to. Still, it was all right, all right this time. A man knowing he had got himself a young one was all right. It gave him a different feeling from what he had had before, a kind of secret fullness in the chest.

Boone looked back the way he had come, squinting for Jim and Peabody and the pack string. He took off his glove and rubbed away the water that the wind had brought to his eyes and looked again. Except for the trees bending stiff to the wind there wasn't a movement below. Jim was a piece back, or behind a shoulder or a bunch of trees. One thing sure, he hadn't run into trouble with Indians, for there hadn't been hide or hair of an Indian about, all the way to the divide. If there had been a sign of one Boone was sure he would have spotted it, careful as he was to watch. He turned and walked ahead and studied the land in that direction and saw nothing. Maybe he was wrong about Red Horn. Maybe the notion that had come up in him and grown as they traveled along, maybe the notion was a crazy notion. It was just that a man couldn't tell about Indians, no matter if he lived with them. They were prideful and easy to please or to anger and quick to act in ways a man might not look for and for reasons he might not think of.

Boone stood with his legs apart, braced against the wind. Here on the high hump of the world the wind rushed at him from every which way. It was as if winds from all over came together here, winds from the east and winds from the west and winds from north and south, all chasing wild up the canyons and meeting and matching their strength and making him catch for breath no matter how he faced. They made a sound that wasn't a whine or a howl but just the sound of movement—a rushing, torn, lonely sound.

The wind got to a man when he stood still, chilling his sweat and making him shiver beneath his skins. It filled him full; it blew into him through his eyes and nose and mouth and drove through his skin; it streamed into him through his ears and rushed around inside his head. It was something he didn't feel alone or hear alone but that he knew in every part of him as a man swimming would know the water.

Far off, the wind picked up a sound and brought it up the canyon and whirled it away. Then it brought another and another, all seeming part of the wind until something back in the mind separated it and shouted it out for what it was.

Boone wheeled. It could be Jim had jumped game. It could be that three of them had taken a shot at it before they brought it down. He knew better, though. He began to run, striding long and hard down the way he had climbed. How far was it back? A man didn't think about distance until he had to cover it quick. The wind came at him from the east, pushing fierce against his face and chest. He turned his head to the side and screeched in a long breath. His notion had been right all along, except that he had misfigured on Red Horn, thinking he would take the short cut and double back on them. Red Horn had outthought him, that was what. Goddam Red Horn for a smart Indian! He screeched in a lung of air again, keeping running all the time, dodging the breaks of rock and jumping the fallen timber.

A raw branch whipped his face, stinging double because of the cold, and his foot slipped on the snow and caught under a root and he fell full length, saying, "Goddam it! Goddam it!" Back on his legs he held up to listen and to look. All he heard was the wind wailing. All he saw was the mountains and the timber and the creek again, and the snow blowing low on the wind. If there had been fighting, it was done now, and Jim and Peabody and the French were dead or else the Indians had been beaten off. They would have howled in retreat and the howling might have carried to his ears, but he hadn't heard howling.

Jim's face ran with him as he ran again, with a smile on it and the white teeth showing and the eyes blue under the short red hair. He would kill himself a chief if Jim was dead. He would stand Red Horn's scalp on a stick by his lodge no matter if Red Horn was kin to him by woman. He heard his breath wheezing in and out and felt his heart pumping and the sweat beginning to roll under his shirt.

From a rise he saw Peabody, standing stiff as a stick in his boughten coat and then bending stiff like a knife over something on the ground. Boone slowed. There wasn't an Indian around, or a horse or a Frenchman or Jim, but only Peabody in his long coat leaning over something.

Before Boone went on he studied the little open space in which Peabody stood and then sent his eye beyond it and to the sides. At the edge of the open space, half-hidden by a clump of brush, he made out a man lying sprawled in the snow. The woods to the side and the patches of timber beyond seemed clear of Indians, but a careful man would scout around before he came into the open and so made a target of himself. Boone began to run again.

The game trail he followed dipped into the trees and straightened out and led through more trees to the opening where Peabody stood. Peabody heard him coming and switched around, empty-handed, with fear and fight both showing in his face. When he saw who it was he called out, "Thank God! Thank God, it's you!" He moved toward Boone, and Boone could see now that it was Jim he had been leaning over. "Terrible! Terrible!" Peabody said with a choke in his voice and his mouth twisted. "The red devils!"

"Git away! Let me see Jim."

Peabody followed along. "They rushed us, twenty or more of them, yelling and waving things and frightening the horses."

"How you, Jim?"

Jim lay with his mouth half open and his face pale. There was a bullet hole in his coat and a spot of blood on the snow.

"Jim! For Christ sake! Hurt bad?" Boone knelt by him.

Jim's eyes came over slow and looked at Boone for a while. Then his mouth closed and one corner of it tried to turn up. His voice was drained down to nothing, almost. "Hoss," he said, as he might have whispered something to a woman, never moving his eyes from Boone's face. "Hoss."

"The equipment's gone, the horses, everything. And poor Zenon lies dead over there," Peabody put in.

"I'll fix that Red Horn!"

Jim's fingers touched Boone's sleeve. "Warn't him, Boone."

"Who, then?"

It took Jim a time to answer. "Young Piegans. Soldiers."

"Let it go. No time to talk now, Jim."

Jim's lips kept moving, letting the words out small and each by itself. "They didn't aim to raise hair. Horses, they was after, so as to make us turn back. Then Zenon fired—"

"No need to talk now. You got from now on to talk, Jim. And you, too, Peabody. Get a fire goin', there!" Boone pointed to the spot. "Easy, Jim." He opened the shirt to see the wound.

"Beauchamp, the coward, ran away," Peabody said while he cast around for wood. "I almost hope they caught him."

"Missed your lights, Jim. They did, now." Inside himself Boone was saying it was a mean wound. Inside, he felt empty and alone, knotted up by a fear he couldn't let show. He unwound a strip of blanket from his leg and tore it across and went to the stream and wet the two pieces. "Keep some blood in your carcass and you'll come sassy again, I'm thinkin'." He packed the pieces of blanket over the holes the ball had made.

Peabody trailed by, dragging a dead log. "I never got a shot," he said to Boone, as if he were cursing himself. "I never got my rifle from its case."

"Didn't figure you would, but shut up now and keep workin'. Sure Zenon's dead?"

"The ball passed through his head."

"Time we get Jim fixed up we'll lay some rocks over him to keep the wolves off. Get plenty of wood first. And get that damn fire started, hear?"

Peabody let the log drop. "I'll do anything I am able to do, except take orders as you are giving them." Boone saw that the small, square jaw was clamped tight. After he had spoken, Peabody picked up the log again.

Jim's eyes still swam on Boone's face. "Feisty," he said, letting the word trail off.

"I aim to build a lodge around you, Jim, out of sticks and such, and the fire right at the door to keep you warm. We been in worse fixes. Hold still, now, while I lift you.

Jim was lighter than a man would think, and smaller. It was the look in his eye and the smile on his face and something inside him that made him pass for a big-enough man. Lifting him, Boone could see his heart working in his throat. It was such a little piece, from being alive to being under, just the heart stopping and the breath, and then only meat left. Just the weak heart stopping, and no more smart sayings afterwards and no more fun, and something gone forever.

When he had stretched him out, Boone went to the creek again to wet the pieces of blanket. If he could get the bleeding stopped, maybe the heart would keep beating and the breath going in and out.

With night nearing, the wind had eased. The sky was a deeper gray and lay closer than ever on the land. As Boone dipped the bandages, snow began to slant out of it. By the time he stepped back to Jim the flakes were falling thick all around, cutting off the sight of timber and mountains. It was as if the gray sky had come down and closed them in.

37

There was no end to the snow. It fell all night and the next day and the night and day after and eased off as if to give the wind a chance and then closed in again and fell for another night and day. It angled down, small-flaked and dry, piling high in a rough circle around the camping place that was kept down by the heat of the fire and the crunch of their feet and the work of their hands. It sifted out of a sky as dull as lead and smoked low along the land, stinging like shot against the face and all the time piling up, piling up, so that a hunter first shuffled through it and then waded, lifting his feet high, until finally he couldn't get his moccasins above the surface of it and had to plow his way. It rolled back in his tracks after he had passed, and the sky and wind went to work on what path was left as if be damned if anything would leave a mark on what they'd done. It smothered the creek and filled its bed and smoothed it over, leaving not even the voice of it to tell that it was there. And it kept falling. Off a little piece a man wouldn't see the camp. He wouldn't spot it, it was sunk so deep, except for the smoke blowing blue out of it and the shots that Peabody fired now and then, hoping to catch somebody's ear.

Boone slid down into the circle and met Peabody's eye and shook his head while he leaned his rifle against the tree that Jim's shelter was built against. The bright, questioning look in Peabody's eyes faded. Boone plugged the muzzle of his piece with a stick and fixed a piece of blanket over the drum and tube. "How's Jim?"

Peabody gave a nod, saying by it that Jim was still alive. The want of food had taken the puff out of Peabody's face. The cheekbones showed high and wide in it now, and the bone of the chin. His eyes were opener and they seemed to look straighter, saying more than before, as if a real man was coming out of the flesh.

Boone stooped and looked inside the shelter and saw that Jim was asleep. He lay on the pine bed Boone had cut, with Boone's capote over him. One hand lay out on the capote, looking thin and weak. The freckles on the back of it stood out, as if full of life while the rest of the hand was dying. Boone could see the coat rising small and quick as Jim breathed. He backed away and faced around. "Where's Beauchamp?"

"Gathering wood. At least, I told him to."

"Son of a bitch." Boone spoke without any real purpose, saying just what had come into his head at the thought of Beauchamp.

Peabody nodded slowly as if thinking how the name fit. Then he said, "Amen." He let thought work in his mind some more. "I wonder you didn't kill him, Caudill, over the rabbit you snared."

Boone grunted, wondering himself, seeing Beauchamp snatch at the carcass that was meant for Jim alone, seeing him jerk back and hearing him whine as Boone smacked him with his open hand. Maybe it was just that he wasn't worth killing.

"I'll never forget the way he sneaked back after the Indians ran off our horses. Not if I live I won't." Peabody's eyes fixed off in space as if looking at that time again, at the fire and Jim lying by it hurt and Boone and Peabody setting up a shelter around him and the snow slanting thick in the dark. At first Boone had thought it was an animal coming up on them—a painter, maybe, or a bear out after his season—and he had laid hold on his rifle and brought it up while he watched. Then Beauchamp had called, "*Non! Non!* Me, Beauchamp, come." He shied into camp like a dog that feared the whip but feared the night more. He seemed to feel their silence and their eyes bearing on him as he squatted, warming himself over the fire. He tried a smile on them. "*Grâces à Dieu!* Me live, you live." It didn't matter to him that Zenon was dead and Jim wounded. He made a man want to spit.

Peabody's eyes came back out of space as Boone lowered himself and put his feet to the fire. They sat quiet. There wasn't anything to do, now the day was passing, but to sit and keep warm and try to hold the mind off the thought of food. Out in the snow looking for sign, a man could forget his stomach once in a while, anyhow; but just sitting by the fire he couldn't. He could hear the wind passing close over his head and feel the snow sifting into the camp hole and his feet prickling as the frost left, and all the time hunger gnawed at his guts and hunger filled his mind.

Peabody said, "I think all Jim needs is food. The wound seems to be healing."

"I got snares set. Can't be that was the only rabbit."

Beauchamp came to the brink of the circle, carrying an armload of dead branches. He dropped them and was about to climb down to the fire until Peabody said, "More! Beauchamp, more!" He floundered off then without speaking. It wasn't often he talked any more, knowing how little they prized him.

"Wood gets to be more of a problem as time goes on," Peabody said. "We've got it pretty well cleaned up close around. We need an ax."

"Might as well wish the snow would melt so's we could get to the dead fall."

"I can think of even better things to wish for."

"I done hunted this place up and down and sideways. Never seen such a country. Looks like a man would find something."

"I ought to take my turn hunting. It isn't right, your going out day after day and using up the strength that's left you while I putter around camp."

"I told you afore, it's because I'm on to it where you ain't. You tend to Jim and keep Beauchamp busy on the wood, and that's enough."

"Jim ate the final bite of rabbit this morning. I made it last as long as seemed safe."

"That was the caper."

"Tomorrow, though—?" Peabody's voice died away. He took a deep breath and let it out and looked into Boone's face. "I'll pray again tonight. Perhaps God in His mercy will answer. Don't you believe in prayer, Caudill?"

"Reckon not. Leastwise, I don't do it. Like Jim says, seems like God's going to do what He pleases regardless. I'll take this here *parfleche* off my bullet pouch and we'll soak it some and leave Jim eat it come mornin'."

"That's leather, man?"

"Buffalo hide. It's got some strength in it yet. Wisht I had a pot to boil it in. Way it is, I'll have to soak it in the powder horn."

Peabody brought his lips up tight and shook his head. "I'd think that would kill him of itself."

After a silence Boone said, "I'm thinkin' I made a mistake. I should have took out for McKenzie or Flathead House soon's we got Jim fixed. Only I didn't like to leave him hurt so bad. I figgered to down some kind of game."

"Is it too late for one of us to try? I'll take my chance."

"I do' know as I could fight the snow so far, high as it is."

"No," Peabody agreed while his eyes went over Boone. "No, I don't imagine you could—now. So I guess I'm too weak, too."

"A man 'ud have a chance with snowshoes."

Their talk tapered off and came to nothing. Hunger made a body no-account, too beat down even for talking. After a spell of it he sat back, no more than half awake, dreaming of meat while the strength leaked out of him.

Beauchamp dropped another load of wood and skidded down the bank of snow.

"Hungry," he said. "Eat snake. Eat skunk. Eat damn anything." Boone was put in mind of a dog again—a big, skulking dog that maybe might bite your face off if you closed your eyes. Beauchamp didn't show he was starving, though, as Peabody did. His face was still full and his shoulders round with flesh and when he moved it was as if he still had some power left in him.

"Go raise some meat, then, if you're up to it. Or likely you're skeered and would drop your rifle and run like you did from the Piegans."

Beauchamp let him have the corner of his eye. Afterward he reached over and took the powder horn that Boone had propped close to the fire to melt snow in. He was about to set it back, after he had drunk, but saw Boone looking at him and so got up and filled it with clean snow from the bank. Beauchamp's eyes were small and wide-set under a forehead that hardly got started before the hair bushed out on it. There wasn't any back to his head at all but just the continued line of his shoulders. Looking at him, Boone remembered Jim's saying that for a head his neck had just haired out.

The air was toning off to dark. The snow still fell, but thinner now, and a new chill was in the wind. When Boone stood, his head just cleared the bank of snow around him. He faced into the wind, feeling his skin draw up at the cheeks at the touch of it. The white world rolled away any way he looked—flats and drifts and falls and rises rolling away to where the dusk closed down. Goddam it, one thing went wrong and then all the rest did. He had been hoping for a thaw and then a freeze so as to have a crust to walk on.

Peabody sided up to him and punched a foothold in the bank in order to look out, too.

Boone asked, "Can you still hear them steam carriages clankin' across?"

Peabody stepped down, and his head gave a slow nod and then another. "I can still hear them steam carriages." He turned around while Boone squinted into the wind. Boone heard a rifle go off and looked over his shoulder and saw Peabody holding it pointed up.

"We ain't got so much powder," Boone reminded him.

"Not much time, either. And there's always a chance that some-one will hear."

Boone said, "All right." Maybe it helped keep Peabody's spirit up, thinking there was a chance a shot would be heard. Anyhow, a shot or two couldn't matter much with time running so short.

The shot roused Jim. He called out, thin-voiced, "You back, Boone?"

Boone went into the shelter. "How's that there hole?"

"Plugged up, I'm thinkin'. It don't hurt so much, only when I move."

It was almost dark inside, saving for the little flashes the fire sent in. Jim's face was a lighter spot against the dark. "I'm sorry as all hell, Jim. I couldn't raise no meat. I'll get some tomorrow for sure. Luck's bound to change."

"Sure. Can't keep on."

"Warm enough?"

"Peabody keeps the fire good." Jim lowered his thin voice so Peabody wouldn't hear. "He ain't a bad little nigger, Boone."

"Better'n some."

"I allus figgered when it came to goin' under a man 'ud put some thought to it, if he had time enough. Seems like I don't care, though. Seems like I don't give a damn."

"You ain't goin' under. Christ sake!"

"Thinkin' is too much work."

"So's talkin', Jim. Shut up now and save your strength."

"It don't make any difference. Sometimes I feel I'd as leave be lyin' out with Zenon, under the rocks and snow."

"You ain't goin' under any more'n I am myself."

"I ain't much for thanks, but if it's so I don't get a chance later on, why, I'm obliged, Boone, real obliged."

"I told you to shut up."

"If'n I hadn't begged you into it, you wouldn't be in such a fix."

"We been in worse."

"I'm light in the head, maybe, but I know you could have saved your own hide. I know it real well, Boone. I know you're huntin' every day, and the snow deep and your paunch empty, and what you git you'll give me firsts on."

"Shut up!"

Jim's smile was just a shadow across the dim spot that was his face. "Just like you say, then, hoss. I'll catch me another nap. Never knowed how good sleep was before."

Boone backed out and sat down by the fire. Peabody put wood on it, and the flames worked up, red and crackling, showing the skin drawn tight against the bones of his face. Beauchamp was slumped forward, drowsing. He was a hard case, in a way, to keep in flesh and strength with nothing for his belly to work on.

Nobody said anything. There wasn't anything to say but the one thing there wasn't any use in saying.

38

Member how Jack Clemens could play the banjo, Boone, and sing to it, and the moon hangin' low over rendezvous and a shiver inside the body that was a glad shiver and a lonesome one to boot, and whisky there for a man and purty squaws, and the heart light and who give a damn about tomorrow? 'Member, Boone? A man didn't know whether to bawl or laugh, he felt so full inside. 'Member?

It's a empty feelin' I got inside now. Seems like this damn bullet hole makes me oncommon hungry, so's I can't rightly tell whether it's chest or belly hurtin' me. Still, nothin' hurts like it did. It all seems far off, like as if a man pinched his leg when it was asleep. Ain't nothin' hurts me too bad. I'm all right. I'm comin' along. It ain't no work to talk, I tell you. Don't fret yourself, Boone. Words come out'n my mouth just like water tricklin'.

It's like a stream flowin', easy and light. We seen a sight of rivers, clear and purty rivers. We had us a whole world to play around in, with high mountains in it and buffler and beaver and fun, and no one to say it was his property and get the hell off.

You think there is a hell sure enough, Boone? It nigh made me take to God, Boone, hearing Clemens play and sing. If'n I close my eyes I can hear him plain, the nice tunes twangin' out and the voice with them and the mountains theirselves seemin' to crowd round and listen. Hi-yi. Hi-yi. Don't sound so good when I sing it, but even a Injun song was something in Clemens' mouth, like as if it brought God down from the sky. Instead of takin' to God, I took liquor and women, but God seemed all around just the same. Seems like He must have felt good, too, seein' us caper. It's ag'in nature He would be set against frolics. Sometimes, lyin' with a woman and the night thick and a wolf singing from a hill, I figgered God was close. I figgered He must be a friend, Boone, and not no stiff and proper son of a bitch puttin' my name down for hell. Sometimes when I looked out over the plains, so far and mighty it dizzied the eye, I figgered God was there, too. Who made it all and give a body an eye to see with and a heart to feel with if 'twarn't God?

I told you once I'm all right. Set down, Boone. You're nervous as a prairie goat, and your face so sharp it might be a hatchet and a frown on it like thunder. Set down. I hanker to talk.

I'm thinkin' God done it, all right, for there wasn't nobody else to. No use to think, though. A man can think his mind to a nub and not know anything about God. He's got to die, I reckon, to find out, and then, if he's dead like a dog or cow, he don't find out then. That's what frets me, Boone, maybe not even knowin' after I'm dead and so never knowin' in all my life.

Hi-yi. Hi-yi. Wisht I could sing like Clemens. Wisht I had me a banjo and knew to play it. 'Member that Taos music, Boone, and the Taos women? Best ever I seed outside of your Teal Eye. Plump they were, and soft and dressed brighter'n ary flower and their faces smart-smeared with paint. I see you steppin' with 'em in a fandango, with a new red-checked shirt on and fancy leggin's with long fringes and blue stones on your ears and your scalp knife in your belt to hold off them pore critters that passed for men there. You was some, Boone. You cut a figger. Women just naturally hankered after you, where I had to tickle 'em into it. It's true as beaver. You nee'n to shake your head.

You was a lucky nigger, Boone, getting Teal Eye. Ain't no she like her, white or red or in between, none so quiet and gentle-like and still so full of life. She ain't like a Injun, or white, either. She ain't like anybody I know of. Close my eyes and I can see her, and I can hear Clemens playin' and smell a Taos woman, all mixed up one with another, all sailin' on the old *Mandan* and Clemens pickin' his banjo and the woman dancin' and little Teal Eye lookin' out on the land with a light in her eye. Treat her nice, Boone. Ain't no punkin anywhere as good.

Reckon I could stand a bite of somethin', Boone, even if no more'n a real punkin. Would you get me a piece of liver, or some marrow, or just anything? Seems like I can't get enough to eat. Seems like I'm always hungry. Piece of that elk you shot would be slick. No meat? Thought I remembered you killin' an elk. Thought I saw you totin' it in. Thought I saw you cuttin' it up and the blood oozin' fit to make a man slobber.

It's all right. Don't look as if the devil had you. Give me a drink, then, long as we're froze for meat. It tastes good, water does, coolin' the pipe as it goes down and lyin' nice in the stomach and no sickness from it tomorrow. It calms my guts down, so's I can lie comfortable and hear Clemens again. Obliged for it, Boone. I never knowed you could be a gentle man. You was always rough and sudden and kep' a *compañero* on edge for fear of what you'd do. You was honest and true, and a body could count on you no matter if he done good or bad, but I never took you for a gentle man before.

Summers was a gentle one. Old Dick was gentle and knowin' beyant guessin' at. Wisht he was here now. How, Dick, you goddam old hoss! I didn't look for you to stay in the settlements. Me and Boone, we knowed you'd be back, with whisky in your pack and your eye twinklin'. It ain't been the same since you been gone, hoss. Drink's tasted bad and women's felt only so-so, and even the beaver holed up, waitin' for you. How!

I see him and then he's gone, Boone, my mind's so crazy-like. It comes to itself and then it goes off again, seein' things and hearin' them and gettin' all mixed up. It's clearin' now, and I see you plain and no one else in here, and outside it's cold as all hell and the snow more'n ass-deep to the tallest Injun a man ever saw. It's come to me there ain't no meat. There ain't been meat for God knows how long. It was a dream I had about the elk. Christ, you're dyin' yourself, Boone, thin as a goddam blade, you are, and your eyes big as plums and even your hands skinny.

Look, Boone, I ain't got long. When my mind's right I can see that much. I'll be under come tomorrow or next day. Ain't no use to say I'll make it. Ain't no use to try. Hear?

Me and you never et dead meat, but meat fair-killed is meat to eat. There's a swaller or two on my old ribs. Take your knife, Boone. Get it out. I ain't got long, nohow. Goddam your old skin, you hear? Boone!

Boone backed out of Jim's little lodge while Jim's voice followed after him. He turned around slow and straightened and met Peabody's eye and saw Beauchamp with his gaze fixed beyond him as if trying for a close look at Jim lying weak and crazy inside. There wasn't any reason to speak; they could hear Jim themselves; they knew he was near gone.

Boone picked up the snowshoes that his knife and awl had made out of cuttings of buckskin and limbs thawed at the fire. They were poor doings but they might last a while. He stood with them in his hands, trying for the getup to climb out of the hole and put them on. Little things had come to be work, like moving a hand or foot, so that he had to put his mind to it first and let the thought shape up.

"Another day," Peabody said, and the three of them thought his words over as if to see if they were true. Peabody's face looked all bone except for the brown beard that curled on it now, and his hands were all bone, too. Looking at him shrunk up in his long coat, Boone knew he was bone inside—bone with skin withered on it like on an old carcass the wolves hadn't found.

Even Beauchamp looked ganted up, for all that he still moved as if there was strength in him. His eyes were sunk in his head, and his brows jutted sharp over them, and the muscles of his shoulders and arms had pulled in and no longer swelled proud against his clothes. What a man noticed about him was the steady hunger in his eyes, the hunger that looked out above the black shag of his beard and left nothing else in his face. It was a different hunger from what Peabody showed, or maybe the same hunger but not mixed with thought or spirit or spunk. It was hunger as naked as a raw scalp, looking out of the deep-sunk eyes, looking at the lodge and Jim lying inside.

Peabody said, "Another day," again, as if maybe this day was the last one. The sky had cleared and over to the southeast the sun showed it was coming up. It would be a cold sun, far off and blinding-bright. A breeze ran along the snow and ducked into the hole and climbed out again, leaving the pinch of it behind.

Inside the lodge Jim was going on with his talk to Summers, to old Dick Summers who maybe might know what to do if he was around. For a flash Boone saw him, too, the keen face with the tracks of fun in it and the gray eyes glinting and the half-sad understanding. For a flash he saw him standing on the *Mandan's passe avant* above the Little Missouri, saw him pointing to a bighorn, saw him trying to talk, trying to say something, trying to come across the years with his voice. His words were a whisper lost in time, a murmuring lapped out by the water sliding along the keel. Speak up, Dick. A man can't hear you, so much has come between. How's that? How's that? It's comin' now. Go on! Go on! "They ain't a buffalo proper, nor a white antelope. . . . They keep to the high peaks, they do, the tiptop of the mountains, in the clouds and snow.. . . Come a fix in the mountains, I do believe I'd set out for one."

Beauchamp's head canted farther toward the shelter. "Die soon," he said.

Boone stepped to the bank and mounted it and stood in the breeze before he stooped to put his snowshoes on.

Out of his pinched mouth Peabody said, "You're a man, Caudill, by thunder! It's no use, though. You couldn't make it to a fort, not with good snowshoes."

"Ain't headed for a fort."

"Where?"

Boone looked up toward the peaks, white-fired by the early sun. "Yonder, huntin'."

"Come back, man. You're out of your senses."

"My medicine's strong. It brung Summers back."

Peabody gave him a long look and then lowered his head. He moved the small hands lying in his lap and brought one of them up and let his eye travel over it. "I guess it doesn't matter. Zenon was the lucky one, lying out there already under the rocks and snow."

Beauchamp's eyes still bored at the shelter.

Of a sudden it came to Boone. Of a sudden he understood. He jerked himself straight. "Watch Beauchamp, the bastard! Keep your rifle handy. You ain't no match for him."

Peabody's face turned up, with trouble and a question in it. "Come back, Caudill. We can die warm, anyhow."

"Goddam you, Beauchamp! Keep to yourself or I'll gut you alive."

Peabody got up. "It's all right, Caudill. It's all right."

"Watch him close, Peabody."

"Why?"

"On account of Jim," Boone answered and saw the question fade from Peabody's face and a slow, unbelieving horror come into it. "Zenon ain't under the rocks and snow. Not any more. Ask Beauchamp."

39

hen Boone was out a piece from camp, the sun lifted over a dip in the hills and threw its cold fire on the snow. Any way he looked, his eyes drew up and his eyeballs ached, seeing nothing but white and the shine so fierce on it that the tears came and drained through his nose and wet his upper lip, tasting salty to the tongue. He tilted his head and studied the steep lay of the mountains while the glare struck at him. Yonder, up a long gulch that led high between two peaks, maybe was a likely place. He pulled his gaze in and fixed it down in front of him where the shine was least, watching his clumsy snowshoes step and the snow pass slow under him while Peabody's last words kept running in his head. "Good luck, then! God be with you!"

The breeze wasn't more than a breath of air, but with the nip of dead of winter in it. Now and then it blew hard enough to carry a grain or so of snow; again it lay still, to wake up and lick around him as he passed. If God was with him he wished He'd tone things down. He wished He'd stop the breeze and warm the air and ease up on the shine and put meat where he could shoot it. If God was with him now, God must be almighty cold and empty-paunched. He put himself in mind of Jim, thinking about God. Let Jim figure and Peabody pray his head off; nothing would come of figuring and praying unless a man did for himself.

He watched the snowshoes shuffle ahead and bear on the snow and sink down a hand or two as he put his weight on them. They were poor doings, but they would get him there if they held out. They would get him there if he held out. He felt his heart tapping high in his chest and his breath blowing quick and shallow. A man long without meat got an idea his body wasn't his. It did things by itself that he could only watch, the poky foot coming out to set the shoe on the snow, the hand curved around the rifle and the arm carrying it, and the wind wheezing in and out and the heart pounding in his ears. Only hunger was real, the deep hunger that gnawed at the belly and deviled the guts and haunted the mind. It was the only real thing, and by and by he came to take it as a regular part of him, as he would come to take an old ache in the joints.

As Jim said, after a while nothing hurt too bad. A body could stand it. He could sit and drink snow water and let things float crazy in his head while the strength slipped from him, not feeling like so much as raising a finger to scratch an itch. By and by he up and died, being too tired to live, as maybe Jim was dying now, with his breath weak in him and his cheeks sunk and his eyes big with starving.

It was queer, not thinking of the white buffalo before, only it wasn't a white buffalo exactly or a white deer but more like a rock goat. It had taken old Dick Summers to jar his mind—old Dick Summers yelling through the years, reminding him there was game high up that a hunter hardly ever saw from below, or hardly ever hunted, either, for the going was so rough.

Boone winked his sight clear. Yan way between the peaks and over the saddle, like as not a little valley hung. Like as not the white ones played there. He held up, waiting for wind, waiting for his heart to quit hammering at his ribs, while he saw Jim lying in the shelter and Peabody sitting bony-faced by the fire and Beauchamp staring with a crazy hunger. Sneaked out, Beauchamp did, and pawed the snow off and lifted the stones away and raised himself man meat. Must be he left it out afterward and a varmint got to it, so's he didn't get all the good out of Zenon, else he wouldn't be so hungry yet and the flesh melting off him and his eyes sharp as a weasel's. Peabody would have to watch. Beauchamp was two men now, himself and Zenon chewed to one, and Peabody less than half a man.

It was too cold to breathe, almost. The air caught at a man inside as if to freeze his pipes up, and his lungs. There wasn't any good in it; there wasn't any strength to it. The chest sucked it down and blew it out and had to suck quick for more, and the knee balked before a lift and trembled at the end of it. Boone didn't know him for himself. He was like another man, far off and dim to the senses. By and by he might wake up and find himself warm and Teal Eye lying by him and meat aplenty in the pot.

He watched his feet push out. Each step was something done. Every one was one behind him and one less lying ahead. He rested again, feeling the warmth die in his clothes and the cold come creeping in. A man not on the move would freeze stiff before he knew it.

He rested again when he topped the saddle, seeing ahead a valley cupped in the rocks. A lake lay in it, probably, but it was all snow now except for one patch of twisted trees, all snow walled in by steep faces of stone. His gaze traveled high up the side until rock and sky met and the dazzle brought the tears a-running. When his heart had quieted he set out again, pointing for the timber, while he made his eyes study the ledges and come down and explore the small basin. He could look just so long into the glitter and then his eyes blurred and he had to squeeze the water out with his lids.

The timber was no more than a spot of runty trees growing toward the head of the valley, probably where snow water fed into the lake. At the far edge of it, where the wind had scoured the snow thin, he halted, for ahead of him a set of tracks stepped along, a set of split-hoof tracks not neat and pointed like the bighorn's but splayed out at the front. He sent his eyes from one print to the next, seeing them veer off to the side and lose themselves among snow-covered rocks that had broken from the cliff. He studied the rocks and the sheer face of the cliff, taking a little piece at a time but seeing nothing anywhere except stone and snow and the blinding sky arched over.

He flexed his right hand to limber his finger. He made sure of his rifle. Then he shuffled on, following the tracks, going slow and cautious as a cat on the hunt. It was movement that scared animals more than the thing itself. The tracks wound among the rocks. They led over a slanting shoulder butted up against the cliff. He saw where the snow had been pawed away and a bite of moss taken. And then he topped the shoulder and looked down, and it was like seeing two black wings up and nothing in between, two black wings thin and raised and barely moving, and then two spots as dark as coal, two spots like eyes under wings like horns. Lines swam and took shape around them, white as snow against the snow.

He heard his lips whispering. "Goddam it! Whoa, critter, whoa!" The rifle was too heavy for a man to lift. It came up hard and stubborn. He got the butt of it to his shoulder. The barrel raised and trembled so he couldn't hold an aim, close as the target was. He couldn't shoot offhand; he'd have to have a rest. He let the rifle down and lowered himself to one knee, going as slow as if he was sinking into the earth. Even so, the goat sensed danger. Its head lifted and its ears came up and its black eyes shone with looking. It was facing him, almost, but it didn't raise its gaze. It kept it lower, on the rim and cup of the valley, as if enemies always came from below.

Boone got to the other knee and started to flatten out, and the knee slipped and he half-fell forward. The black eyes lifted then and bored straight at him. He lay still as a dead man, his rifle out before him but not raised to shoot. The goat would run. It would jump in a wink. It would be gone while his hands fumbled at the rifle and his arms tried to raise it and his blind eye searched for sights. Whoa, critter, whoa!

The goat sat down on its tail like a dog, its long face dull and curious under the spiked horns, the hair hanging in a beard from its chin, hanging in an apron across its front. It wasn't a buffalo or a deer or a goat. It wasn't a creature at all. It was something grown out of the snow; it was something a crazy mind made up; it was an old spirit man from the top of the world and a bullet wouldn't hurt it and it would fade from sight directly like a puff of smoke.

The rifle sounded loud as any swivel. The crack of it went out and struck the high rock and rattled up the mountains until, far off, Boone heard the dying echo of it. The goat sat back farther on its tail, a look of slow surprise on its face. After a while it just lay down and kicked once and was still except for the long hair that the breeze played with.

Boone lay watching it, hearing his lips make words, seeing himself bringing meat to Jim and Jim tickled and his jaws working on it and strength going into him. After a while he got up and reloaded, still talking while his hands poured out powder and patched the ball and drove it home with the wiping stick.

As he started ahead he caught a flash of movement and, turning, saw another goat high on a ledge where nothing but a bird could get. He pulled out his wiping stick to use as a rest and sank in the snow and tried to get it through his sights. It moved as he aimed, going along a face of stone a man couldn't hang to, but at last he had it on the bead. It fell when he fired, coming down slow like a diver to water and making a splash in the snow.

He reloaded while his mouth kept saying, "By God! Two of 'em. By God!" The first goat was still alive, for all it lay so still. Its eye looked at him with a sad look. He put his rifle down and drew out his knife, and of a sudden the knife seemed to slash of itself and the throat lay open and the blood pumped out and his nose was in the musky hair and his mouth was drinking. When the flow was down to a bare trickle he quit sucking and sat back and licked his lips. He didn't feel sick, but all at once his stomach jumped and the blood gushed from his mouth, staining a circle in the snow. He waited until the gagging was over and then, slowly so as not to upset himself again, he began eating the snow.

A man could do so much and then no more. When all of him was spent he could only sit while the cold worked into him and sleepiness came on, and him too tired to move. With meat to shoot, his spirit lifted for a little time and strength came to him, and then the weakness took hold again and the dead tiredness. He thought about moving his hand or foot but he didn't move it. He only looked at it and thought maybe he would move it after a while.

It was as if Boone's mind watched while his body got up and his feet took him to the timber and his hands broke off branches and piled them up and started a fire with a piece of punk and powder sprinkled from his horn. He sat close to the fire, letting the heat get into him and the blood he had drunk mix with his own. A man could do so much and then no more except let weakness wash over him and sleep come on. So much and then no more, and the muscles melting away and the mind dreaming and trouble so far off it didn't matter.

He roused with a start, not knowing how long he had drowsed. The fire had burned down to ash. The sun had crossed its high divide and shone at him now from Oregon. He felt a pulse of life in him and a tired beginning of strength, felt the cold and the dying breath of the fire and hunger so sharp he couldn't hold his thought on Jim, lying sick and starved below. He got to his feet, moving easier and surer than before, and went to the nearer goat and cut out its tongue and brought it back to the fire and ate it raw, making himself take a long time at it. Each swallow was like a little swallow of power. When he had taken the last one, he lifted himself again and went out from the fire to heft the goats. One was more than a load for a man in his full strength; maybe he could tote the other. He dragged the bigger one to the timber and hollowed out the snow with his hands and drew the carcass into the hole and packed the snow back over. Afterward he piled dead branches on top. Varmints would get to the meat if there were varmints about, but they wouldn't be so quick to find it, buried as it was.

He went to the smaller animal and got it on his shoulder and straightened and started out, walking slow and careful, seeing the snowshoes sink deeper than before and the webs pull at the frames. The sun slanted low over his back, and some of the glitter was gone from the snow. His breath blew white in front of him. His nose felt plugged and stiff with the hairs in it frosted.

After a little he knew he couldn't go on with the whole carcass, even with the new strength in him, even with the going downhill now. His shoulder sank under the weight. The blade of it dug into him. He tried the other shoulder, but it sank, too, and the blade gouged him, and his whole side began to ache. He reckoned he could build a fire and eat more meat and go on and stop and eat again and so get to camp in hitches if the snowshoes held out, but a man could die waiting for him.

He halted long enough to rip open the carcass and tear the insides out. He cut the liver free and buried the rest of the entrails in the snow. Then he cut along the ribs to the backbone and broke and knifed the bone in two. He slitted the back legs and cut a stick and slung the hind quarters as high as he could on the limb of a twisted tree. The liver he tucked into the folds of his hunting shirt before lifting the forepiece to his shoulder. His load was lighter now by more than half. His back could stand it. His legs could keep moving. Maybe the snowshoes would hold together.

The sun sank behind a bank of clouds and a quick darkness came on. His feet were shadows making a riffled shadow of the snow. The breeze died with the darkness. Not a breath moved, and nothing sounded, not even the howl of a wolf. A man walked with darkness over him and the snow soft under his feet and his body tired but tough and patient now, and more than ever he came to wonder if he was real or only something dreamed.

The moon tipped over the hills. The snow shone in it and the trees stood black, and it was as if a friend had come. The world was deep and quiet as if waiting, the air still and the moon soft and not a sound on earth except the snow giving to his step. Out of the west where the clouds were banked a puff of air blew, a puff and then another and then a wind blowing warm as spring, a wind to thaw the snow and make a crust when the cold came on again. A man could walk and shoulder his load forever while the moon shone and the warm wind blew and the white land rolled away.

A yellow light rose from the snow. A voice called out, "Who's that? Who's there?" A whiff of wood smoke came to Boone's nose. He didn't answer. Let Peabody shoot if he wanted to. Let him shoot and be damned. He stood at the hole and let the goat slip from his shoulder and slide down the bank. "By thunder! come down, man! Here, I'll help." He felt Peabody plucking at the strings of his snowshoes, felt his hand on his arm, felt him easing him down the bank. He heard Beauchamp make an eager, animal noise in his throat.

"How's Jim?"

Peabody's eyes fixed on Boone's face were round as an owl's. "Alive. I think his mind's clear." Peabody stooped and threw some twigs on the fire as if to make sure Boone could see inside.

Jim's face was still and sunk in like a dead man's. Boone bent over and then he saw the eyes open and living yet. He pulled out the liver and cut a slice and held it over Jim's mouth. He saw the mouth work and heard the meat crushing and felt the lips moving against his fingers. He cut another slice and fed it in and then another while Jim's gaze never left his face.

Jim's voice said, "Obliged. Wouldn't no one do so much."

"Can't have no more now, or your stomach'll up and puke."

Jim's hand came up as if to touch Boone's arm. Boone backed away and turned from the shelter and saw Beauchamp crouched, sharp-eyed, while Peabody cut on the meat. "You'll git your share, Beauchamp," he said as if to a friend, and wondered at himself afterward. It made a man unnatural to see Jim crying.

40

Jim said, "I've et white-buffler meat until I've growed a hump on my back."

"I wouldn't say you had all you could stand, not the way you're goin' after that joint." Boone wiped his knife on his leggings.

"I could eat it from now on, for a fact. Seems like I don't more'n get filled up than my stomach asks if it ain't time to eat again."

Peabody swallowed a bite and licked his lips and paused before reaching out to cut another piece. "It's the same with all of us. I never would have thought men could eat so much. If we stayed here until spring, there would hardly be a beast of this kind left in the mountains, if Boone could keep on finding them. We've eaten four, almost, down to the hoofs and hair."

"It's part being starved," Jim explained while he chewed, "and part it's just that it's meat. Meat don't bloat a man or lie heavy in him but just sets natural."

"It must be," Peabody agreed while his gaze went over Jim. "It's amazing. I never saw an invalid recover so fast."

"Mountain doin's. You never hear tell of sores runnin', nor delicate stomachs, nor heads achin' except from whisky—not in the mountains, you don't."

"Empty belly ache," Beauchamp said, remembering, his mouth making a hole in his black tangle of whiskers. "Ache all time, by damn." It wasn't often he spoke; mostly he just looked, and you wouldn't know there was an opening in his face but for him feeding meat into it.

The sun was shining down into the camp hole. It lay with a touch of warmth on the back of Jim's head. Overhead he couldn't see a cloud; there was nothing there but the sky with its blue glitter and the sun far off and small and bright as brass. Standing up, though, where the wind could get at him, or moving out from the fire, a body knew well enough it was winter.

"Could starve still," Boone said. "It could snow deep over this here crust. For that part, it sure as hell will." His glance came over to Jim.

"Nee'n to look at me. I'm fit to travel, I am. Might be I'll have to poke, but I'll get there." Jim wasn't talking loose, or on the prairie, as they called it. His strength was growing fast as a weed. With every bite of meat and every nap he took, he felt it bigger in him, felt it rising up and reaching out into every little muscle. If only they hadn't run out of tobacco, he would be almost his old self again.

Peabody ran his fingers over the jaw he had scraped the hair from with a knife that Boone had sharpened on his stone. He was a sight different from Beauchamp; he and Boone and Jim all were, with their faces smooth now like sure-enough mountain men's. "We better go back," he said as if he wasn't sure.

Boone answered, "We been tellin' you, you're the one to say." When Peabody didn't answer right away, he added, "Me and Jim, now, we said we'd take you over." Jim knew Boone wasn't thinking about the promise so much. He was thinking about Red Horn and his old ones and the young Piegans that had run the horses off. Boone wasn't one to tuck his tail.

"But Deakins here! He needs rest and good food. It's out of the question for him to carry out his contract."

Jim said, "Out of the question, hell! Maybe I ain't a full man yet but I'm nigh to it. And babyin' won't help."

Peabody spread his hands. "We have no horses, no equipment, no supplies."

"We got two feet each," Boone reminded him. "We got two rifles and flint and steel. What you really think, Jim?"

"We got to travel, regardless. Time we get to Flathead House or McKenzie either one, I won't know I ever had a hole in me."

"Do you suppose they'll outfit us at Flathead House?"

"They'll put us up all right," Boone answered, "but maybe balk at fixin' us to go ahead."

"It isn't a matter of money. I can pay."

Jim said, "We could steal us some horses from the Flatheads, maybe, if the company acts ornery."

"I wouldn't want stolen horses. I wouldn't want that." Peabody's mouth tightened, as if honesty was a pain in him.

"No stealin', no cussin', no rollin' with women," Jim said, feeling a little smile twitch at his lips as he met Peabody's glance. "Just prayer is all. Peabody, damn if you won't torment yourself!"

Peabody smiled back, not getting his dander up as he might have earlier. "Everyone to his principles."

"We'd only borry the horses," Jim argued. "We'd only sneak us a ride, and what's a ride worth after it's took? You can't be fancy-fine about sin in the mountains."

"How far to Flathead House?" Peabody asked.

Boone answered. "Two camps, about, with Jim the way he is. Closer'n McKenzie by a far shoot."

"And all of you are willing to go on?" Peabody's eye went from Boone to Jim to Beauchamp. Beauchamp gnawed off another bite of meat.

"What kind of talk you think we been makin'?" Boone asked.

"I wouldn't want anything to happen." Peabody's voice was low as if he talked to himself. "Zenon on my conscience is enough."

"You're the damndest nigger!" Jim said, smiling again. "Got no business here, I say, with such a passel of principles and conscience. How you aim to get Oregon settled without accidents and men dyin' and all? It ain't as if you killed Zenon. The Injuns done that. Ease your mind, Peabody. There ain't nobody holds anything ag'in you, here or in heaven or hell, far as I know."

Peabody was silent. He got up after a while and climbed out of the hole. Jim could see him, gazing east first, and then west, and the wind streaming at him, and his thoughts like something you could read in his face. Already, Jim realized, he was beginning to get the look of the mountains in his eyes, the look of distance and weather and hard doings and hungers outside the stomach.

The lines in Peabody's cheeks tightened, and his small chin set. "By thunder," he said through close lips while he faced into the west, "we'll go on! We'll go on, then!"

41

Spring lay on the land, the first touch of spring, delicate as something that a breeze might break, or a sound. The sun sailed in a sky like deep water, touching the earth with a soft warmth. The pinched skin loosened in it and spread smooth over the flesh, and the muscles rested long and easy and the heart lifted, afraid, almost, to believe. Riding out of the canyon of the Medicine where flowers had begun to blow along the edges of old snowbanks, Boone saw that green had tipped the plains.

"Early," he said, "for spring. Way early."

"Can't come too quick for me," Jim answered, "not after the winter we been through." They let their horses stop after the climb. "Buffler country again. Look on it, Boone! Ain't it good for the eye?"

"Seems like my eye's been caged in by mountains and trees. Seems like it wants to run now, like a dog off a tie rope."

The plains rolled out below them, mile on mile of plains dipping away and meeting up with the sky at the edge of the world, and the air so clear and fine that the gaze ran dizzy. Not so far away a little bunch of buffalo grazed, ragged against the new green, and beyond them a band of antelopes streamed light and quick as if not bound to earth.

Jim said, "Jesus!" as he squinted into the distance, and after a pause went on, "Old Peabody wouldn't know to like this. It would drive him back on himself, being so Christly big and free."

"Wonder what he's doing now?"

"That little nigger was all right. Bet he does good. Bet he gets his chin set and his mind fixed and his mouth to making talk and does all right."

"He could talk a man out of his squaw, right enough. Look what he done at Flathead House."

"Wasn't talkin' alone. Part was just Peabody, honest and straight-speakin' and gritty, too. I can see him now, palaverin' with them British and bringin' them around to his way for all they wanted to shy from it. None could out-nabob him."

What Boone saw, though, when he thought back to the winter, was not Flathead House and the British and Peabody arguing himself into a new outfit, but Jim sick, and rock goats like scraps of cloud among the peaks and the snow so deep the tops of the young pines looked like grass above it. He called to mind the warm wind and then the cold and crust and the four of them going slow down the western slope and traveling Clark's Fork later and dropping down to the Great Plains of the Columbia and reaching the river and going on almost to where the Snake came in before Peabody allowed maybe he and Beauchamp could make it alone. He remembered Jim getting stronger and good-spirited and his red hair gleaming in the sun, and the weather fair enough, though sometimes bitter still, and he and Jim forted up, after Peabody and Beauchamp had gone on, waiting for the passes to open while the thought of Teal Eye and his young one kept working in his head.

"Nigh talked me into goin' plumb to the western ocean with him, Peabody did," Jim said. "Ain't no Teal Eye waitin' for me."

Boone turned and grinned. "I'm a growed man now. Reckon I could've made it back alone."

"Thought I best come along. Pups is quick to say they're full dogs." Jim kicked his horse as Boone's started up.

It was past the time when the great owl nested, past the moon of the big winds. Teal Eye looked for him, standing maybe at the entrance to the lodge and facing west, hoping to see, far off, the fleck that would come to be a horseman and the horseman coming to be her man. Red Horn would have seen there was meat in her tepee, and Red Horn and the young Piegans would be friendly enough. A thing done was a thing done, and no need to think more about it. He had a medicine glass for Red Horn, so's he could light his pipe from the sun, and shells for Teal Eye that had come from the sea. With his spurs he pricked his horse to a faster pace.

"Weather's so damn soft it can't go on," Jim said while he watched a bird sitting white-breasted on a bush. "Winter'll come back and nip growin' things and freeze the tail off that there early bird."

"Think so?"

"It's certain sure. Never knowed it to fail. Leave good days come, and a man better set hisself for bad. Only it's fat today, ain't it? So quiet and gentle-like, and grass shooting up and all."

"It is, now."

"If you listen, you can might' nigh hear things growing. I crave to unfork my horse and get my ass unsprung and just lie around and eat and sleep and let the sun shine on me. Hope Teal Eye'll be on the Teton, like you think, and not to hell and gone on the Judith or Musselshell or somewhere."

"She's there, all right, if only she could coax Red Horn into it."

"Same place?"

The same place, with the clear stream winding in the cotton-woods and trout feeding on the first frail-winged flies and the hills pointing up like a woman's breasts, and Teal Eye standing there again and crossing her wrists and bringing them over her heart so that the breast pushed out at the side, and Poordevil saying "Heap punkin!" through the hole in his jaw. South, the two buttes would be rising, and buffalo would be lazing down from the benches and the black birch blowing and the valley lying unspoiled and quiet between the ridges as if just waiting for a man to see. He had been a long time away, up the Marias and over the hump and down the Flathead and far along the waters of the Columbia and then back, up the River of the Road to the Buffalo and across the top of the mountains again and down the Medicine, past the sulphur springs that flowed warm and stinking from the rocks and gave the river its name. Everything seemed a long time away, Teal Eye and the Teton and all, with so much in between that it was as if he never could get remembered feelings back. Time lay between him and that other day, time and all the miles he had traveled and all he had seen and done. But once he was with her, everything would come right again. Once she lay by him, he would be himself. He could sit again and let time run on, not caring that it did, while the breeze played among the lodges and the sun shone yellow on the grass.

"Too nice to last," Jim said again, rising and stretching in his stirrups. "Enj'y it now, on account you'll have ice on your whiskers tomorrow."

"What makes you such a sorry man? You ought to take your-self a squaw, Jim, a good squaw."

"Maybe it's many squaws as has made me sorry."

"You ought to take one and stay by her, for a spell, anyhow."

"I'm thinkin' not. I won't never settle with one. Like a grass-hopper, I am, jumpin' one place and then another, and no sense to know good from bad."

"You're too choosy, maybe. One's like another."

Jim looked at Boone and then spit over the shoulder of his horse. "You'd as soon stay on with them Flathead and Nepercy women then?"

"I got me a woman a'ready."

"Sure. Can't everybody be so lucky."

Boone let Jim's words turn in his head, looking at them one way and then another without fixing his mind sharp on them. It made him proud inside to know that another set store by his woman, but it made him a little edgy, too, like a dog with a bone. It was good Jim was his friend and Teal Eye was Teal Eye, else a man might worry himself.

The mountains fell away behind them, reaching high and jagged into the sky and the blue of distance settling on them. Gophers heavy with the young ones they carried piped at the horses and dived underground, their tails whisking, as the horses came close. A badger, surprised while he chewed on a dead bird, lumbered off to one side and halted on the mound of earth he had scratched up digging a hole and watched them with a slow blaze in his eyes.

To his right Boone caught a glimpse of the westward one of the two buttes, peaceful in the low afternoon sun. They would see the valley soon, the quiet valley of the Teton, half meadow and half trees, where Teal Eye had said she would try to meet him. Maybe she had birthed the young one now and would be slimmed down. Maybe her eyes reached out and soon would see him as just a speck moving down the ridges. He hoped it was a coming man she had and not a little squaw. Squaws didn't grow up to be fighting men with scalps on their leggings and gun covers. Squaws' lives weren't much no matter what.

The benches fell away in front and curved out at the sides, and in the cup the Teton lay just like before. They let their horses come to a stop while they took it in, neither one speaking until Jim said, "Ain't it a camp I make out, Boone? Yonder, in line with the hill that pushes out?"

"Wondered if you'd spot it. Red Horn's Piegans, for sure, like Teal Eye promised."

At the foot of the slope Boone spurred his tired horse to a trot. This was coming home again. It was like doing, awake, what was left from a dream. It was like doing what he had done before, as if he was just coming to the Teton and smallpox had scattered the Piegans and silence hung over the country. If he turned, he might see Poordevil and the red horse trotting proud. It was like that other time, except now he knew she waited for him.

When they were still a half mile from the village, some Piegans jumped on horses and came galloping. One turned out to be Heavy Runner, with his hair wild and his skins dirtier than before. Boone heard Jim making palaver while he sat his horse and gazed yonder at the village. It was a fair-sized camp now, Red Horn's was. Dogs ran out from it, making a racket around the horses as the Indians led the way in. Squaws watched and went to chattering as they went by, saying Strong Arm and Red Hair had come back. An old Indian raised his eyes from a looking glass and stayed the hand that had been plucking the hair from his face, lifting it after he saw who passed. A woman came out of a lodge, her eyes wide like a watching doe and her body slim as a girl's. Boone rode to her and dismounted, seeing gladness and trouble both in the face. Jim called, "How be ye, Teal Eye? Still purty as a pet bug, you are."

Teal Eye didn't speak. She reached out, almost as if afraid to touch, and placed the palms of her hands on Boone's neck and stroked them over his chest while tears shone in her eyes.

"Later'n I thought," Boone said while his gaze took her in, "but I come back." His eyes questioned her, but still she didn't say anything. He went on in Blackfoot. "Have you given me a son? Does Strong Arm have a son?"

Her mouth said, "Yes," but something waited in her face as if she had not told him all.

"I want to see him, Teal Eye," Jim said. "Let me git a peek, too."

Her hand made a little motion toward the lodge. Boone stepped past her, inside. The lodge was thin and old and let the sun through, but still, coming from the shine, he had to wait to see. After a little he spied the baby on its holder, with a skin over its body and a hood drawn over its head so that nothing showed except a small and withered face. Boone bent over and laid the hood back.

From behind him Jim said, "Damn if it ain't got a touch of red in its hair! Maybe grow up to be purty like me."

Teal Eye breathed at Boone's side. The English words stammered on her lips. "Eyes no see. Eyes got sick. No see."

The baby stirred at her voice. The lids pulled open. Before they closed again, Boone saw the eyes swim shrunken and milky-blind.

42

When Boone had a mood on, there was nothing to do but let it wear off. He would be silent and grumpy no matter what, not answering to talk or laughing at jokes but going along with his lips tight and his eyes dark until the trouble in him eased. If a man understood, he just let him alone, knowing time would take care of him. Time would make him himself again; he would get used to his baby's being blind and so not have to take his hurt out on others as if it was their fault the young one couldn't see. Leave him be and he would get friendly sooner or later and take pleasure in things in his corked-up way. Boone never was one to let out what was in him, being a silent man, mostly, and too proud to show himself. Only it must be hard on Teal Eye, living with him now and him not speaking except to grunt and his eyes clouded and far away.

Jim flicked his horse with the tail end of his reins. He was on his way to Fort McKenzie, where he would drink himself some whisky and maybe lie around for a few days and earn a dollar or so by killing meat for the fort or interpreting for Chardon, the bourgeois. By the time he got back to Red Horn's band Boone might feel like speaking a word to him once in a while.

From the plain he could look down on the wooded valley of the lower Teton. Magpies cried from down there, and a crow called, sounding like a hoarse whisper against the wind that flowed out of the northeast. Up on the plain, ground larks flitted from under his horse's feet and jackass rabbits leaped out of hiding and went bounding away, stopping to look after a while, their front feet held up dainty and their coats already turned from snow-white to dirty gray. Spring was coming even if the weather didn't know it. A week of good weather and the cottonwoods would bust their buttons and the diamond willow run out leaves as narrow as snakes' tongues, and at sundown a man would hear the killdeer crying.

Spring made a man feel good and sad, too, and wild sometimes, wanting to howl with the wolves or strike north with the ducks or fork a horse and ride alone over the far rim of the world into new country, into a fresh life. Spring was a good hurting inside the body. It made laughter come easy, and tears if a man didn't shut them off. Come a soft night, and he could sit under the sky and watch the stars or moon and listen to running water, and he would feel a pushing inside of him, a reaching for things he couldn't single out—for a woman, maybe, who was all he ever could think up and more, for the quietness a man never seemed to have until he looked back and saw he had passed it by, never knowing. Old times came back to him then, so's he felt like crying over them, and old friends he had traveled with and parted from, never thinking that those times and those friends would come to be an aching in him. Jourdonnais and Dick Summers and Poordevil, and long days on the *Mandan* and nights on the Powder and that evening in Colter's Hell with the first people and the fine, high singing overhead and the air itself breathless, and all of them gone from him now except as pictures in the heart.

Spring made a man a little crazy. It gave him ideas he wouldn't want to own to—ideas like baying the moon or flying with ducks, sharp beginnings of ideas, like finding a certain woman willing, that he pushed quick from his mind. Anyhow, spring made some men crazy. Maybe not Boone. Maybe not a man that had a Teal Eye for his squaw and wanted nothing but to go on as he was. Maybe there was just one big hunger that other hungers grew from.

Jim rode down into the valley of the Teton where the stream turned north. He climbed the far slope and halted his horse on the high nose that separated the Teton from the Missouri. He saw Fort McKenzie below him, with only three tepees pitched about. Beyond it the Missouri flowed wide, shining silver in the sun. The valley would be green with leaf soon, and a man stopping on the nose would feel shriveled with the wind and sun and would kick his horse downhill to meet the cool breath of the valley. The breeze was still raw now, and the trees stood naked below. Cold had followed that first taste of spring along the Medicine, as Jim had said it would.

The feel of the country settled into Jim, the great emptiness and age of it, the feel of westward mountains old as time and plains wide as forever and the blue sky flung across. The country didn't give a damn about a man or any animal. It let the buffalo and the antelope feed on it and the gophers dig and the birds fly and men crawl around, but what did it care, being one with time itself? What did it care about a man or his hankerings or what happened to him? There would be other men after him and others after them, all wondering and all wishful and after a while all dead.

Jim tried to shake the miseries from his head. It was Boone being so sully that made his thoughts sorry, or the wound he had got and the long hunger. He clucked to his horse and rolled in the saddle to its downhill jolt. Where the ridge leveled off, he spurred the horse to a gallop and pulled up short before the outer gate. A Frenchman peeked through the pickets and swung the gate open to let him through and closed it tight afterwards. There wasn't an Indian in the store except for a couple of squaws that showed by fancy fixings of ribbon and red cloth that they belonged to the men in the fort.

"Where's the customers?" Jim asked.

The Frenchman gestured with his hands, saying only God knew. A clerk eyed Jim, his hands palms down on the counter. "Only customers we get these days are ugly customers," he said.

"They'll be liftin' your hair if you ain't careful, from what I hear."

The guard at the inside gate carried a good Hawken in the crook of his arm. He studied Jim as if to make sure he didn't need killing.

There wasn't much doing inside the grounds. Over by a shop three pork eaters were sorting and mending gear. They and the guard were the only men in sight except for Alexander Harvey, next man in line to Chardon, who sat in a doorway out of the wind sunning himself. The flag overhead snapped in the breeze, and the sun ran along the cannon that was kept aimed at the gate.

Jim said "How" to Harvey and slid off his horse. He rested his rifle by the door and sat down in the dust. The horse nosed off, hunting for a spear of grass on ground that the company horses had picked bare while being kept up for fear of Indians.

"I got beaver in my pockets and my pipes is dry," Jim said. "None of your pizen, either, but good drinkin' whisky with some age to it and the taste of wood."

Harvey let his squinched eyes travel over him. "Particular, ain't you? We got plenty of whisky in the store yonder."

"I said good whisky."

Harvey got up as if he didn't want to and stepped inside and came out with a jug and two cups. "Just come from the Piegans?"

"Red Horn's band, up the Teton."

Harvey poured the drinks, his strong, thick face down-turned on the jug. "What kind of medicine they makin'?"

"British, mostly. Likely they'll go to Fort de Prairie for trade. You know why."

Harvey tightened his mouth. "What's their talk?"

"They're sayin' you and Chardon ought to have your black hearts cut out. Likely right, too. Where's Chardon, anyway?"

"Out. Can't stay in this goddam fort all the time."

"Takes all hands with him, don't he?"

"Maybe needs to."

"What I hear true, that you aimed to rub out the whole bunch of Bloods? Loaded a cannon with trade balls and trained it from the blockhouse and got your riflemen set and asked the Bloods up to trade?"

Harvey said, "Red bastards! We only got five of them and no horses. Things went wrong. They run off without their furs, though."

"What was behind it?"

"'Member that nigger Reese? Friend of Chardon's?"

"That real, black-skinned nigger?"

Harvey nodded. "The Bloods killed him. Made Chardon mad as all hell. It was me told him how to get even."

"Don't see how you can expect the Piegans to come here for trade."

"Didn't do anything to them."

"Doin' it to the Bloods was the same thing, to their way of thinkin'."

Harvey drained his cup. "They'll come back," he said, and sucked a drop of whisky from his lip. "What's Caudill doin'?"

"Trappin' a little. Huntin' buffler."

"How's he feel?"

"Got other things on his mind, I'm thinkin'."

"That's good."

"It is, now. He could make things bad if he took it into his head to lead the Piegans against you. They could rub you out, dead easy, firin' down from the hill acrost the river. Only I don't guess Boone'll do that way. It ain't like him to scheme a thing. He acts quick and sudden."

"Soon kill a man as look at him."

"He's all right."

Harvey refilled the cups. "Smart squaw he's got." The thick face had a far-off, searching look. "Prettiest anywhere." He switched at his moccasin with a stem of grass. The corner of his mouth made a little dent in one cheek. "Maybe you could tell how is it."

"You're a damn fool."

"About some things, maybe. Not about that. Not about you, Deakins. You and minks are turned the same."

"She ain't that kind."

"Good Jesus! I haven't heard that kind of talk since church let out. What squaw ain't?"

"All the same, she ain't."

"Me, I would like to have a chance, with Caudill maybe a thousand miles away. There isn't a squaw but would trade, offer her enough beads or red cloth or face paint."

"You got a surprise comin' if you try."

Harvey's face showed he was already trying in his mind. For a little, Jim's thought ran away from him, seeing Teal Eye and himself with her and nothing about but the shielding willows rustling in the breeze and the grass waiting. He jerked a leg straight and got out his pipe and tobacco. A man had some wild ideas when the spring sap ran in him.

"Reminds me," Harvey said. "Got a letter for Caudill. It come with the winter express from Pierre. You want to take it to him?"

"Might as well. You want any meat raised?"

"Ought to have enough when Chardon and the rest come in."

"I'll just take the night, then, and put out tomorrow. Pour another drink. I told you I got beaver to spare. And set a bottle by for mornin', for I look to have a head."

The next morning, riding back the way he had come, he was glad he had the bottle, or what was left of it after the first drink. He felt tired and beaten down. He had a thickness in the head and a slow ache behind his eyeballs that pulsed to the jog of his horse. The wind blowing out of the north with the sting of winter still in it made his eyes stream. He pulled up and wiped the water away and took the bottle from the overlapped folds of his buckskin shirt and poured a big drink into himself. He would feel better after a while with the whisky catching hold again and the air fanning his head clear.

The sun, just raised above the eastern sky line, shone flat across the plains. The dead grass bent to the steady wind, above the green that had started up from below. A half-dozen crows raised from down in the valley and shouted after a big hawk that flapped straight ahead as if all he wanted was to get away from their noise. Tatters of clouds blew out of the north.

It was a raw and lonesome day, with nothing in it but the rush and whistle of wind and the worn land standing to it. It was a day when a man felt small and out of kilter, and hankered for people and frolics and walls to keep the weather out. It was a day when he hankered to be close to somebody, to be understood and made over, so's the weight of loneliness would be lightened. Boone, now, liked weather. He didn't seem to need man or woman to keep his spirit strong. He didn't seem to need even little Teal Eye warming his lodge, and her voice soft and her manner gentle and her big eyes quick with feeling for him. He liked wind and storm and emptiness, as if they were company enough; but not many did. Not Jim Deakins, riding along with a case of whisky sickness and a low heart.

The wind kept up all day and was still blowing as he went on again next morning after he had made a lonesome camp and suppered on a chunk of meat that Harvey had given him. Time went so slow the mind could believe it stood still. The sun rose a little way in the eastern sky, shining on Jim's back, and stopped there as if dreading to come full into the wind. The plain crawled ahead of him, making tired-like for the mountains ridged far against the western sky. His horse lagged over it, putting a few spears of grass or a sprinkle of rocks under him as he stepped, and facing, head down, to an ocean of grass and rocks enough to make a peak. Off to the side one gopher chased another—a he and a she, probably, working up to a family. By littles the shadows shortened and grew to nothing and by and by began to point the other way. The wind blew itself out except for scattered leavings that puffed along trying to catch up. By the time the sun went down, even the leavings were gone. A still twilight lay on the world, darkening slow to night.

Boone brought his lids down little by little, screening out the valley below him and the ridge that rose beyond it and at last the sun itself except for the red light that swam through. This was how it was to be blind, not to see the buttes and the mountains against the sky or the wooded line of the river, not to see the coyote trotting far off or the camp in the trees or Big Shield and Bear riding toward him, not to see even the hand held close before his face but only the red swimming and maybe not even that. Maybe only thick and steady darkness like in a cave or out on the plains at night with the clouds drawn low and not even one star peeking through. A man couldn't find a trail or sight a rifle; he would have to feel his way like a worm and hope someone would bring meat to him. He would have to learn the sun by its feel and the land by the touch of it under his feet and people by the pitch of their voices or the whispered way of their step. He would have to listen for things, as Boone listened to the soft plod of the horses that Big Shield and Bear rode.

"Strong Arm sleeps," Big Shield said, and then Boone let his eyes come open. The two Indians slid from their horses and sat down and lighted their pipes.

"The buffalo has gone away," Bear said after he had drawn deep. "Only old ones are left here—only wolves' meat. We have looked in the four directions, Big Shield and I, and the herds are far off toward the new sun. They have run before our hunters. It is time to move."

Big Shield bowed forward in the sign for yes. "We are here too long."

"Our trappers come back to the lodges without beaver."

"The beaver have been taken. The spring lift is small."

"The camp makes a bad stink because we stay too long."

Boone let them talk. They were warriors yet, but with years growing on them and a liking for slow palaver while they smoked in the sun. A blind man hearing them would wonder if the words were made by tongues and lips like his own working in faces like his hands told him his was itself. Boone shut his lids again, trying to figure what he would make out the two to be if he had only his ears to tell him. After a while he heard Bear say, "You cry inside, Strong Arm."

Bear's eyes were old and tracked around by wrinkles but still sharp as a hawk's. Boone dropped his own before them and picked up a rock and began digging at the ground with it. He was of a mind to laugh or say it wasn't so and to go on to something else, being as his feelings were nobody's business, but Indians were easier to talk to than whites and medium friends easier than close ones. He drew back from showing Jim what was inside him, as he drew back from showing Teal Eye, feeling weak and shamed for them to see, but it was different with two old Indians who wouldn't add to what he said or pry beyond for more.

He nodded slowly. "Is there medicine to make the blind eye see?"

Big Shield said, "Our medicine men make medicine, but blindness is too strong for them."

"It is better to go under," said Bear. "It is better to kill the blind."

"I cry for the blind one in my lodge."

Bear nodded. "I cry for my brother who cries. Does Red Hair cry?"

Boone nodded. "Jim cries. He is my brother, too."

Bear put more tobacco in his pipe. "It is for him to cry." His eyes went to Big Shield for a yes. "It is for Red Hair to cry."

For what seemed a long time Boone searched Bear's face, which was cut and puckered by time and thought. Bear's old lips sucked at the stem of his pipe. His breath pulled a whiff into his lungs. Then he met Boone's gaze and answered the question in it with another. "Does the black eagle father the red hawk?"

Boone heard his own voice like a crack in the long silence. "You make light talk."

Bear's gaze was roaming the valley again. "It is you that make light talk," he said. "You know. When a man knows it does not matter. I have given my wives for whisky and powder. I have given them to show I was a friend. It was all right. When a squaw sneaks out and her man does not know, then he feels blood in his eye."

Big Shield knocked the ash from his pipe and got up. "I had a wife, and she lay in secret with a man." He rested his finger above his nostrils. "I cut her hair off and her nose and put her out of my lodge. I took two buffalo horses from the man. I found other squaws. Life was good again."

They climbed on their horses and jogged down toward the village.

Teal Eye said, "Red Hair went to Fort McKenzie."

"Who told you?" Boone watched her fussing with the baby, her eyes dwelling on the blind eyes as if of a sudden they might see.

"He came to ask for you."

"For me, was it?" Boone asked and shut his mouth on what he might say next. There was puzzlement in her face, as if she couldn't make out what he aimed at. He looked at the baby and looked away and looked again. The red wasn't bright sorrel like Jim's hair, but it was red just the same—red crossed with Indian black and showing dark on the head like the bark of old spruce. Did the black eagle father the red hawk? He got up and stood for a while unseeing, feeling sick and swollen with suspecting, feeling like a man snake-bit, the pain small and sharp in the beginning and the mind numb but unbelieving, and then the bite spreading and the flesh puffing and hurt bursting the body. He would ask if he could believe the answer, but a woman that had tricked a man would lie to him.

To her back he said, "Better to kill a blind baby."

The words spun her around. She got up slow, her face showing shock over the sorrow that had been there before. "Boone!"

"He is better dead."

"You don't mean what your mouth says!"

"You heard. How long will Red Hair be gone?"

She lowered her face from his, as if she had looked for something and not found it, and turned back to the baby. Seeing her droop, he felt mean, but fierce and pleasured by meanness, too. He watched her out of the tail of his eye, wondering what secrets were in her, wondering what she kept from him. Morning, and his talk with Bear and Big Shield, seemed so long ago that he had lived a lifetime in it. There had been the pinch of pain and the unbelieving, and then the remembering, then the figuring, while the pain grew and the unbelieving littled and such a misery came in him as the spirit couldn't stand. He knew well enough that Jim was drawn by Teal Eye. He had seen a hundred things to make him know and heard a hundred more, though he hadn't believed that Jim would do him bad. It was Teal Eye he had misfigured, thinking it was no more than liking she felt. It was Teal Eye, bent over with her back to him and maybe the secret held dear in her and her body remembering the touch of Jim's.

All at once he couldn't stand to be there longer. "No tellin' when I'll be back." He threw the English of it at her. "Three or four sleeps."

She didn't answer, but he knew she followed him with her eyes as he went out. It occurred to him while he walked to his horse that maybe she was thinking that with him gone she would have a chance with Jim.

At first he rode just to ease himself, making his horse drive into the wind, feeling the good, hard lash of it against his cheeks and the honest push of it on his chest. Wind was something a man could stand to, and be goddamed to it. It was something he knew. It was something he could figure, and no doubt and no waiting and wondering about it, and no black poisoning of the blood. Later he noticed that he was making in the direction of Fort McKenzie, and a plan took shape in his head. Already Teal Eye believed he would be gone from the lodge for three or four nights. He would ride to McKenzie and make out to Jim that he would be out of the village for a time looking for buffalo and beaversetting and a likely camping place. Then he would watch, and then he would follow. He would set his trap and see what came to it and so find out quick, maybe, whether Bear was right. It stood to reason he was, the more Boone brooded on it, remembering the smiles Jim had for Teal Eye and the long, slow looks and words like posies, and her face lighting up at the sight of him and the pleasure in it at his talk. Bear and Big Shield took it for sure he shared his squaw with Jim. More than likely the whole band did, and because of things they'd seen, being wrong only in thinking the sharing was his doing. Damn himself for a fool, going along blind while they played behind his back and made sport of him! All the time he had figured Teal Eye was his alone and never to be anybody else's. He had lain with her at night and felt richer than other men to have her and so deep satisfied he couldn't talk about it, even to her, for the feeling was like a weakness in him, like a secret that had to be kept in his own skull, hidden under his own ribs.

As the sun went down he hobbled his horse in a gully where a trickle of water ran and climbed out of it afterward and made toward the three antelopes he had seen from the other side. He tied his handkerchief to the end of his wiping stick and lay down with his rifle and held the stick up so that the flag fluttered in the wind. The antelopes danced in, darting back now and then and afterward dancing closer, until he had his sights on one and let his finger bear on the trigger. The two lit out like birds after the shot, their white rumps gleaming, but the one squirmed broken in the grass. Boone made his supper from it.

The night came on so black he couldn't tell where earth left off and sky began. Lying under a buffalo robe with his saddle for a pillow, he couldn't see a wink overhead or the top of a hill round about. He might as well be blind, except for thinking the sun would rise again. He lay lost in darkness, with up and down and sideways all the same, and the torment swelling in him as his mind ran out, picking up things seen before and things heard and felt, making up things that hadn't happened yet. Jim talking. Damn if it ain't got a touch of red in its hair! Bear talking. Big Shield talking. It is for Red Hair to cry. When a man knows it does not matter. I cut off her nose and put her out of my lodge. Life was good again. Himself talking. You was nigh the only friend I had, Jim. Leastwise, I thought so. Don't see how you could treat me so, me as trapped and traveled and drunk and played with you and saved your hide to boot and trusted you with Teal Eye for all I knew you're horny. You done it, though, and now, goddam you! Himself talking. Wisht I would believe you, Teal Eye, but sayin' it ain't so don't make it not so. Wisht I could take you back like before and tell you all that was in me. I ain't been one to talk. Talkin' comes hard, but you knowed I was gone on you all along. You didn't have to go somewheres else to find a man as really wanted you. I catched you, though. No use to beg. Bear talking. Breeze talking. Night talking. Does the black eagle get the red hawk? So goddam dark tonight a man can't see a thing.

The wind woke him up, tearing at his robe. The sky had paled to a dead gray. In the east the sun showed it would be up directly. Boone ate and caught his horse and rode on.

The sun was straight overhead when he spied a horseman traveling toward him. Pointed as he was, the man would pass maybe a long rifle shot to the south of him. Boone angled his horse to the left behind a screen of willows growing along a little marsh, not trying to figure out why he did except for thinking he didn't want to talk to anybody. He dismounted and watched through the willows. It was plain the rider hadn't seen him for he kept coming straight on, sitting his horse bent-headed and letting the horse just laze along.

It could be Jim, from the looks of him, bound back to camp from McKenzie. It could be Jim, riding slumped over and off his guard and thinking about Teal Eye and all. After a while Boone saw it was Jim, sure enough.

A slick man would ride out and tell Jim he aimed to go to the fort and farther and wouldn't be back for a time. He would make double sure his trap was set. A slick man would see the red hair and smile just the same and maybe shake hands and never fear for what his hurt and hate might make him do. Boone stood and looked, and it was as if all feeling held still and tight-drawn, too, while Jim came on and passed and drew off to the west.

When Jim was a safe piece ahead, Boone climbed his horse and followed. The trap was set good enough already, and no long waiting to find about the catch.

From the top of the ridge Jim barely could make out the village. A fire or two glimmered from the wide basin that the river had cut through years stretching back farther than any man could think. The lodges were like half-seen shadows against the deeper shadow of the land.

The dogs barked as he drew close to camp, and ran out toward him, coming dim into a sight like sound taking shape. He spoke to them and yelled his name to let the Piegans know who came. A squaw stood at the entrance to a lodge, making a lump of darkness against the firelight inside, and watched him pass by. Boone's tepee glowed from a built-up fire.

From in front of it Jim called, "Boone, I got a letter for you." No answer came.

"Where's Strong Arm, Teal Eye?" He could see the shadow of her moving inside, and he dropped from his horse and poked his head in.

She straightened, standing near the baby lying on its holder. "He went to hunt. He will not come back tonight."

Jim stepped inside and set his rifle against a lodge pole and held up a little way from her. It came to him, seeing the firelight lying on her face, that he never could remember how like a girl she was, or how open her eyes were and how hurtful. She was a surprise each time he saw her. "I brought a letter for him, from Fort McKenzie."

She didn't reach for it, but took a long, slow look as if she could read it unopened in his hand. Her face lifted then to his, and he recognized the sadness in it, not sadness shown by a frown or wrinkles or the mouth turned down, but spoken from the heart. He felt his own heart fall, and swell with pity for her.

She asked, "It comes from his people?"

"I think so."

"It will take him away."

Jim fell back into English. "Hold on now, Teal Eye! And if he goes, he'll come back. He won't ever pull away from you."

Her voice wasn't much more than a whisper. "My baby blind, and Boone mad with me, and the white people's letter to take him away." Her face lifted to him. "I am afraid, Red Hair." Her head went down, and a little shudder ran over her, and she took a short, uncertain, turning step that seemed to Jim to have all of hopelessness in it. He didn't know when he went to her. He only knew his arms were around her and her head was on his chest.

Into her hair he murmured, "Now, punkin. Things'll come right."

She let him hold her, and pity ran in him and anger at Boone and at things, and then the pity and the anger drew back before something else. He felt her body against his, felt her breath hot and quick on his throat, felt her breasts on his chest and one slim leg touching his own. Harvey's words leaped before him, Harvey's words and the wild picture that had darted into his own head, and for just an instant the man in him reared, and it was as if this time, this doing, this having her was bound to happen all along and nothing and nobody on earth to stop it.

His hands came fierce to her arms and held her out while he searched her face. She was like a bird in his grasp, a caught bird that held quiet for what he would do, its heart racing inside the breast, its eyes wide and pitiful, with dark and secret waters flowing.

And then he felt her trembling and knew again the sadness in her face, and sense came to him and understanding, and the man in him melted. He bowed his head over the dark hair and held her easy, knowing he could never take her. It was the blind child that let him hold her, the child and the fear of losing Boone, and Boone so jailed inside himself she couldn't know his heart or show her heart to him.

"Teal Eye," he said while his hand patted her. "Pore Teal Eye."

Boone rounded to the south so as to approach the village against what little breeze there was. This way he wouldn't rouse the dogs. A hundred yards from the camp he dropped off his horse and went ahead on foot, picking his path and setting his feet down soft. He felt the blood beating in his head and his muscles tight and the whole of him strained and ready as if it was sure what he would find. He made himself stop and breathe deep and loosen up. He made himself remember it was just an off-chance his scheme had worked already. He tried to tell himself he could be wrong. But when he started walking again, the blood beat and the muscles tightened. Once among the tepees he stepped sure and confident, to show to anyone who watched that he was at home, but he still went quietly, not wanting the sound of his movements to reach into his own lodge. There was starlight around the tepees and dying fire-glow from inside and the sounds of sleeping.

His lodge pointed up before him. He stopped at the side of it to listen, but all he heard at first was the heavy thumping of his heart. All he saw was one shadow standing dim against the wall of skins. Then a voice spoke, low and soft as a man might speak to a woman when heat was running in him. He heard it say "Teal Eye" and didn't wait for more. He cut around to the opening and ducked and shouldered inside.

They didn't see him right away. They didn't hear the brush of his clothes against the lodge. They stood there, making one shape, making the one shadow he had seen against the wall. He knew what was doing now. He knew what he had to do. No use to talk or think or wonder. No use to ask or plan. A man's body acted for him. He said, "By God, it's like I thought."

They fell apart, and Jim said, "Boone!" and didn't say more but stood trying to smile and the firelight showing guilt on his face as plain as day and flashing on the fear in Teal Eye's eyes. Jim's arm came out, stiff and clumsy as a stick, and Jim's mouth said, "I brung a letter for you."

The pistol was better than the rifle. Jim cried, "Boone! Boone!" as he saw it coming up, and Teal Eye tried, too late, to throw herself between and so to save her secret man. Closed in by walls, the pistol sounded big.

Jim staggered back, feeling as if his whole chest was empty, feeling as if it had been sunk in by a blow. He tried to straighten. He made his legs walk him toward the door for a breath of the air he was dying for. He fell on his face. It was all he could do to turn over. He wanted to cry out. He wanted to say it wasn't so. He wanted to own up that he had a crazy minute, but no harm done and Teal Eye not to blame. The words wouldn't come; he couldn't get the wind for them.

"I ought to cut your goddam nose off!" It was Boone, turned on Teal Eye. She didn't answer. She didn't move, except that the tears came to her eyes and glimmered in the firelight and started down her cheeks in two big drops.

Things seemed a far way off, so far away the voice couldn't reach, far away and fading farther. Jim saw legs at the entrance to the lodge and followed them up and came to the faces of Indians thrust inside and nothing showing in them but the asking look of animals. One of the faces said, "Him go under."

Boone stooped and whipped up the letter, and his voice lashed at Teal Eye. "No good to cry. By God, I catched you!"

Jim sucked for air. He had to speak. He had to explain. You're a hard man, Boone, and closed in on yourself, and Teal Eye sad with the blind baby and afeared of losing you, and no one to let it out on, no one but me. No harm done, Boone, no harm at all. I wasn't no more than a chest to cry on and a hand to pat her back.

He couldn't catch air enough for talk, not more than a drop

of it before pain bore down and shut it off. He felt if he looked down he would see his chest blown open and the heart beating naked and the lungs twisting for air. He heard Boone's voice like a whip and Teal Eye trying to answer and heard the Indians grunting and saw them pushed in at the door and Teal Eye with her child's eyes wet and pleading.

It wasn't any use to try for words or breath or time; it wasn't any use but to lie quiet while the eye saw and the ear heard and the heart bled itself out. Far off, it seemed, Boone was moving, marching to the entrance with the letter unopened in his hand, marching with his head up and the braids swinging to his step while the Indians made way from him and he passed from sight. Jim brought his gaze to Teal Eye, standing as if too hurt to live and her girl's body drooping and the open, dark eyes crying as they looked the way that Boone had gone. "You no come back," she said in English, so low Jim hardly heard. "You no come back."

This was the way it was at the last. A man faced up to death alone, his sight dimming and his hearing dulling off, and he so lonesome the heart squeezed up to nothing and the mind drew back from thought. The world pulled away from him, the lodge and the air and the clouds and dark hills outside and folks that stood about, until only the ground he rested on seemed close. This was the way it was with Jim Deakins, laid out with a bullet hole in him and no one alongside to touch his hand and ease him over. This was the way it was with Deakins, who had been ready to wrong a friend and spoil a woman's life and had got hold of himself but messed things up all the same, and now no chance to set them right. He had to lie helpless and lonesome, but not much afraid any more, while over him and over the lodge that shut him in the deep sky deepened over the empty plains. He heard talk, breathed by the breath but not sounded by the voice. "I'll know about God, I reckon, now." After a while he realized that it was his lips that had spoken.

PART V

1843

43

Winter was gone from the valley of the Missouri, but spring hung back. The time was an in-between time of gray rains and angry spells of wind and a muggy chill that kept the clothes damp. Waking in the mornings, Boone felt his skin grained and stiff against the touch of his buckskins. Buffalo still hung to the shelter of the brush waiting for the sun, lunging in the mud along the shores as the pirogue startled them, staring after it with dull, bad-tempered eyes bushed about by winter hair. Overhead the mallards flew in pairs, their wings whistling, and slid down to the water and swam with their heads high as if on watch for nesting weather. Along the banks the leafless willows whipped and gray-trunked cottonwoods waited, holding bare limbs up.

"Meanest by-Jesus time of all," said Old Man Mefford while he worked the steering oar and squinted down river out of a face frosted with white stubble. "She ain't winter or summer or spring or fall or foul or fair but just, by Jesus, nothin'. Savin' a spear or so of grass, everything's dead and bare as a fresh-skinned bull. I can stand cold and hot and snow and dust and all, but this here knots my guts. Makes a man down on his luck, it does. Almost wished I'd traded these here furs at Union, 'stead of boatin' 'em down to St. Louis for the extra in it. Beaver's lower than a snake's belly anyhow. How'd you do, Caudill? Done traded yours, I s'pose?"

Boone sat with his back against Mefford's two-year catch of furs. They were covered by buffalo hide drawn tight by lashings. He glanced at Mefford and at the river and at the right-hand boatman in the bow. The boatman looked up, expecting an answer.

"Them Crows," said old Mefford after giving Boone time to speak, "they're the thievin'est bastards this side of hell, I reckon. Don't know how I ever got out with the plews I did. And sharp, too. They can spot a cache a eagle couldn't. Five seasons ago, it was, me and another cached the purtiest fur a man ever see, dug out the ground careful and laid the sod back on top and toted the extra dirt to the river. Afterwards we scared a bunch of buffalo across the place and rode away sayin' there wasn't a nose or eye in man or brute as could tell there was beaver underneath. But, by Jesus, them Crows did! Warn't a hair left, come spring. You mixed with the Crows, Caudill. Ever see the beat of them for stealin'?"

The oarsman put in, "The Assiniboines, they know to steal, too."

"Them Rocks! Piddlin' people if ever I see any. Ain't as good as plain niggers, be they, Sam?"

"Niggers is good at stealin'. They sho' is. Kin lift a hen off a roost and she never cluck." Boone shifted, seeing Sam at the left oar and his teeth flashing white in his black face. Half the time Sam sat with a sleepy smile on his mouth and the oar forgotten, thinking of hog meat, maybe, and sweet potatoes and corn bread, and maybe a black woman that waited for him. Sam was a free nigger whose five years were so near up at Fort Union that the company let him go, him and the other oarsman, a Frenchman who went by the name of Antoine. When they learned Mefford was fixing to put out from Fort Union and needed help with the two small dugouts he had hitched together and built a platform across to make a pirogue, they asked to go along, being so eager to get back to the settlements as to brave the fear of Indians.

"Piddlin' is what I say, eh, Caudill?"

Things changed in twelve years. Banks caved in, and bars and whole islands washed out, and the river gouged new beds, so that a man returning wouldn't know where he had been except for the hills lying as always and streams feeding in. He would look for a point or a growth of brush that had been fixed in his mind by something happening, but he never could be sure he saw it, the way the river ran. He never could say it was right here that such and such took place.

"Too bad your ma never l'arn't you to talk, Caudill, so's we could pass the time of day. It's a comfort, talkin' is." Mefford's faded eyes half-smiled at Boone and went on to the Frenchman. "He don't hardly hear me. He needs to be with folks. Been in the hills so long he's growed dumb like one and his tongue no good but to lick with."

Old Mefford talking day and night, talking just to hear himself, talking as if to make sure he was alive and not crazy, talking because at last there were ears to hear, old Mefford talking and sometimes the boatmen joining in, telling with a shine in their eyes what they would do back in the States, and sometimes Nigger Sam singing sad while the ragged banks streamed by and the dead land waited for spring. You couldn't stop old Mefford. A sharp look wouldn't still his tongue, or a sharp word, or anything this side of a killing.

"When was it I seen you last, Caudill? In 'thirty-seven, warn't it, on the Seeds-kee-dee there below Horse Creek? Was a redhead with you, and Dick Summers as was ready to leave the mountains. You rubbed a man out, I recollect, throwed his arm out of socket and stabbed him with his own knife. I remember that redhead for the fun in him. Where's he at, anyhow? What became of you atter 'thirty-seven? It's like you crawled in a hole."

"What if I did?"

The river looped through the long land of the Assiniboines, striking one way and another like a hurt snake that couldn't remember to make for a hole. It ran aimless and cold among the hills, leaving a muddy suds along the banks. It ran like a river lost, hunting a way to the sea, brown as old leather by day and black against the bleached slopes by night. Tied up at islands with the sun gone from the sky and the darkness thickening and the dim stars caught in the water, Boone listened to the worried mutter of it, listened to the talking-to-itself, to the sound of hunting along the shores, while Old Man Mefford clacked away and Sam and Antoine laughed and the wet wood popped in the smudge they had built. "Ain't hardly seen an Injun. Not hardly a nit, by Jesus. Safe as a church, it is. Safe as ary goddam church. Puts me in mind of a time—" Far overhead, out of sight in the dusk, Boone heard wild geese on the wing, making late for the north. Their voices carried down to him, the small honks of one to another, keeping up courage for the

340

flight in the dark. "We never sighted even a moccasin track all that spell, or I'm a nigger." The moon rolled up and threw a long shine on the water. From the shore a hoof made a sucking sound as it pulled from the mud.

A man learned things in thirteen years—and went empty and numb with the learning except for the quick angers in him. He let the sun shine on him and the wind blow him and sights come to his eye and sounds to his ear, and never thought beyond. He was like a dumb brute, with yesterday lost behind him and tomorrow dim ahead and just this here, just this now, counting with him, just the sun and the wind and the river and trees and hills. Only he could play with the notion of evening a score, like with the sheriff at Paoli. He could think to get back at people and feel his jaw setting solid and his insides reaching for the time.

The river hunted through the hills and turned sharp as if it had found the way at last and streamed south to the old country of the Mandans and the Rees, past the Knife River, the Heart, the Cannonball. The Mandans were gone now, dead of the smallpox, and the Rees had pulled out before the Sioux, and the villages of both were fallen and rotted, with bushes growing where men had sat solemn in palaver and animals feeding where the *Mandan's* hot crew had groaned over Ree squaws in the dusk. It was only the hills that remained, only the river, and it too busy to remember except sometimes at night when the sky lay quiet in it and a man looking down jerked his eyes away, not wanting to see what was pictured from before. Past the Grand the river went, past the Moreau and the Cheyenne, deep into the country of the Sioux, past old forts weathered down and pulled apart for steamer wood, past new ones, past forts going up and the sound of hammers knocking and hails from the shore, and all sliding by and being lost to sight and hearing as if they never had been.

It wasn't often they saw Indians except around the forts. "Safe as ary church, I tell ye," old Mefford said out of his brush of white beard while Sam and Antoine nodded, their faces slack with feeling safe. "Red devils won't rub you out, will they, Sam?"

"No Injun gonna git this niggah. This niggah rollin' home."

Mefford's old eyes were always watchful, running quick along the river and the shore while his hand worked the rudder. "Maybe talked too soon, yestidday and afore." His gaze was slitted against the shine of the sun on the water. "Pawnees, ain't they, Caudill, and more'n a few?"

"Sioux."

The Indians stood on a point, a dozen or so of them, and waved for the pirogue to put in.

"Sioux or Pawnee or what the hell, we won't mess with 'em."

"Ah got no business with Sioux," Sam said, for once busy with his oar.

"Wave, you red bastards, and see what it gits you!" Mefford had pointed the pirogue toward the farther bank. "No cause to be skeered," he said to the boatmen. "Red men can't shoot for shucks —not with guns, they can't."

Antoine had better leather in him and more sense than most Frenchmen. His oar moved sure and steady, and his face had the cool look of figuring the danger and counting it small.

The Indians lined up along the bank, their hands hanging straight at their sides. As the pirogue drew abreast and kept to its course, two of them raised guns. Smoke puffed in little clouds, the two balls plopped into the water short of the target, and the crack of the musket shots came after. The Indians pranced on the point. Their cries carried sharp across the river.

"Couldn't hit the ground with them old smooth bores," Mefford said. "Howl, you brown skins! Squaws, are we, and afeared to fight? Since when did dogs git to talkin'?

"Red and thievin' bastards they all are," he went on as the Indians passed from sight around a bend. "A good Injun is a dead one, I say, for all that some mountaineers say different."

Sam was grinning, now the danger had passed. "Squaws is good," he said, his eyes remembering. "Sho' is."

"Not so much. A man comes to think they're some, on account of there's no whites about. Alcohol and river water and tobacco juice tastes good if a man can't get whisky. And roots is better'n to starve. Mountain men fool theirselves, braggin' on this and that, but all the time knowin' better inside. Ain't it so, Caudill? Answer up. By the look of you you know red meat."

"Answer for yourself. Your goddam tongue ain't happy without it's waggin'."

342

"'Scuse me. By Jesus, but you're a touchy man. Must be you et a cactus by mistake and got stickers in your gizzard. What a man in a fix like yours needs, now, is to open his bowels. Ain't nothin' cheers the spirit so. If you're beat down, squat down, I say, and get the load from your breeches."

Antoine smiled as he brought the oar through. "Old men, too old for women, they think bowels."

"Lose his courage, old man do." Boone looked around, not knowing what Sam meant at first. "Kin only grunt." Sam shook his head as if the thought of his manhood gone made him sad.

"This child wouldn't know about that," Mefford answered. "Have to find someone older'n me by a damn sight. I'm fit, I am, as a young bull in rich grass. Nary ache or pain or failure nowhere." His mouth closed for a minute and his eyes fixed far off. "Know what? A nigger off by himself does a power of thinkin'. Wonders about things and builds up a sight of questions, and no answer to 'em. Why'n't the stomach feed on itself, you reckon? I was four days without meat when that p'int come up, and damn if I know yet. Why ain't it fixed so's a man feels always like he does with a good cup of whisky in him? Why's men willin' but women mostly's got to be bought, with beads or paint or promises said before parsons, dependin' on their skin? Crow Nation says it's all right to steal, but not the government, by Jesus! Gimme the why to that."

The talk went on, morning to dark, one day after another, steady like the churn of water along the banks, like the risen river that rushed the pirogue along, past the White and the Running Water, as if in a fever to be rid of its burden.

A steamboat stood to the current, her stacks pouring smoke and the wind screaming against her and the water boiling against her bow where a man worked with a pole, feeling for depth.

"*Omega*," said Mefford, watching the side wheels beat at the water, "and, by Jesus, she ain't makin' a inch. Losin' ground, be'int she? That wind'll blow her stacks down." He waved as the pirogue came on. "How there, you beavers."

From the decks men signaled back, and Boone could see their mouths round with words that wouldn't carry into the wind. It seemed as if she was there just for a flash, gleaming white in a shaft of sun that found a hole in the clouds, and then she lay astern and soon lost to sight. He said to Mefford, "Give me a keelboat any day. They'll find they wasn't so smart, goin' to steam."

The river boiled ahead, past the Jim, the Vermilion, the Big Sioux, out of buffalo country and on toward the settlements; the river and time brought them into spring. The sun lay warm and the air soft, and by night the frogs tried their voices. In a day, almost, the trees broke into leaf, not cottonwood and willow alone but trees strange to the sight after so long away. They reminded Boone of home, or what he had called home, of home and Pap and Ma and Dan. Cabin and kinfolks rose in his mind, plain as yesterday, as if he had no more than said goodbye before he started back and all the seasons since were made up in his head. He could see Ma's letter, could hear the young clerk at Union sounding out the words for him while his own eye followed the lines.

Der Boone Your pap has died and I only tolbul and likely not here long. If you get this I would like to see you before to late. The Napiers has gone away. Ma.

The tired face rose before him, and the misty eyes and the body worn from doing. She had been gone from his thoughts for many a year, except for just a flash now and then, and she was back. He saw her in his mind without wanting much to see her sure enough. A man grew away from things, and feeling died in him, and he couldn't put himself back where he was even if he tried. It was another who had said goodbye to her long ago and had sniveled in a cow barn, remembering the twitching of her nose, remembering her "Good luck to ye, Boone."

Looking out at hills set small and close and the sky pale and low overhead and the trees thick enough to smother him, he was half a mind to turn about and strike out as he had struck out long before. Only it couldn't be the same again, the life couldn't—not any more, not for a while, no matter how much he wanted the world big again and the way clear and the air blue and deep above. A hard and aimless anger edged up in him, wanting something to take itself out on. He shifted himself on the pirogue.

A settler's cabin stood in a clearing, and the settler himself hung to the handles of a plow pulled by a team of mules. He whoaed the mules when he saw the pirogue and leaned on the plow to watch, a big man dressed in ragged linsey stained with walnut. His voice boomed out, "Hello, you mud cats."

"Hello, grayback."

"Grayback maybe I be, but I ain't never seed a mud cat I couldn't handle."

"You been foolin' with minners." To Boone, Mefford said, "What gits into these damn farmers makes 'em want to mix with river men?"

The man shouted, "Pull up, if you dast, and shake the water from your pants and stand up to an honest-to-God man."

"Where's he at?"

"You're lookin' at him."

"Don't see nothin' but a pair of mules and what one dropped behind him."

"They don't call me Bull for nothin'. Shut up or pull up and goddam to you either way."

"Bull, is it? I'd take you for a steer, now."

"I kin change your mind for you. Ain't fought since yesterday, and I'm full and splashin' over."

Boone said, "Pull to!"

Mefford peered out of his old eyes. "You want a go at him?"

"Ain't a man among the four o' ye," the farmer yelled.

"Pull to!" Boone said again.

Mefford ordered, "Put 'er in!" and moved the steering oar.

Boone jumped ashore. He saw a woman with a rag tied over her head come out of the cabin door carrying a corn-shuck broom.

The man wrapped his line around the plow handle. He came to meet Boone. There was the fighter's light in his face and the fighter's loose ease in his movements. A grin came on his broad face. "Ain't many as'll stop any more. Stranger, ain't ye? Reckon it wouldn't be right to do my best."

"You want to fight or just talk?"

"Fight's my name and fight's my nature, and holdin' back this way sours my milk."

Still smiling, the man came in, his head ducked like a bull's, his thick arms out in front of him. Nigger Sam yelled, "Fix 'im, Ol' Cranky! Fix 'im!" Boone waited until the man struck, waited until he felt the blow hard and solid on his face, and then he let go, standing flat-footed and braced so as to get power in the blow. The one lick stopped the farmer. His head jerked straight and his body swung off balance. He went down hard when Boone struck again and lay on his back with his eyes only half open. After a while he grunted over on his side and looked up while Boone waited. There wasn't any grin on his face and no pleasure in his eye, but only a dull surprise. A trickle of blood ran from his broken lips.

"Get up if you want to fight."

"Don't you dast, Henry!" It was the woman, rushing between them while her mouth spouted words. "You stay right there. Hear?" Her gaze swung to Boone. "You got murder in your hands and murder in your eyes, or I don't know gee from haw. My man fights just for fun and shakes hands after and makes friends." She raised the corn-shuck broom. "You git! Git off our place, you—you murderin' white Injun, you!"

"He asked fer it."

"Git!"

Boone turned. Mefford was piling back into the pirogue, and Sam and Antoine after him. "Push 'er out, Caudill," Mefford cried, chuckling. "I can stand to men's talk but not to skirt scat." The pirogue eased out into the current. "He won't forgit that lick, by Jesus!"

The man had climbed to his feet. He stood with his arms limp and the smile broken on his mouth and the light knocked out of his face.

Boone didn't guess he would dare a mountain man again.

44

By Jesus," old Mefford said, "here's doin's. Ever see the like of that, Caudill?"

At the Independence landing a steamboat was pulled up, its smokestacks cold, and men were rolling barrels and carrying sacks from her. A couple of skiffs lay close by, rocking to the pulse of the river. On the bank other men bustled around white tilted wagons hitched to droop-eared mules or oxen standing lazy in the sun. The men pushed and lugged and lifted. They strode to the water's edge and struggled back with their loads and stuffed them through the tail holes of the wagons. They swore at the teams, their voices full-throated and strong with purpose. "Whoa, you, Bess! Whoa, Jack! I'll beat the tarnal hell out of you, you wood-headed bastards!" Downstream a piece, as if too polite to stand close to the swearing, two women watched. A small boy pulled at one of them, wanting something.

Mefford said, "Hurrah for Conestoga! I ain't ever seen movers till now."

"Crazy sons of bitches!"

"Likely so, but it ain't catchin'. We'll have a whiff of 'em." Mefford slanted the pirogue to shore. Sam jumped out and tied up, and Antoine and Mefford got out after him. "Come on, Caudill." He lifted his voice, aiming at a man walking back to the steamboat. "What you fixin' to do?"

The man stopped and spit in the dust. "Where you been anyhow?"

"Up river."

"Must have catched your head in a hole, not to know."

"We hearn a word or so, but a man can hear anything."

The man spit again while he measured Mefford. "Bound for Oregon, that's what." He walked on, as if what he said was enough to still the tongue.

Sam and Antoine and Mefford drifted off, watching as they went and stopping to talk when someone would hold up for it.

The wagons arched high over Boone in the pirogue. They stood big against the land and sky, seeming big enough to roll the country flat to a man seated low on the water. From a hill, now, or out on the plains they wouldn't be as much as a bug on a hide.

Boone wondered if Dick Summers had seen them. He wondered if Dick watched from some place now with the little smile on his mouth and the wrinkles drawn around his gray eyes. He aimed to talk to Dick, but not anyway soon. He didn't want to see him now, nor anybody else in particular.

"Passel of 'em. Hundreds. Maybe a thousand over town-way."

The man who had come idling along the bank didn't quite look at Boone. Just the tail of his eye looked, traveling from Boone's moccasins to his leggings to the red cotton shirt he had put on for summer to the handkerchief he wore on his head.

"They're buyin' and tradin' and meetin' and electin' and all."

"So?"

"There's a world of 'em, God hisself only knows how many, and all hot for Oregon." The man ran his hands into the pockets of his homespun pants. "Don't know nothin', most of 'em, about travel. I give 'em some advice. 'Take a flintlock, not a cap gun,' I says. Right, warn't I?" His eye looked for an answer and, finding none, shifted off again. "What good's a cap gun without caps, and where you gonna find caps in Oregon? 'Take a plenty of cured meat and flour and some sweetenin',' I told 'em, 'and stache the sweetenin' in the flour so's not to break the glass.' A body needs a sight of things, travelin'—pots and kittles and knives and salt and yarbs and dried stuff and beans. Can't get along with just a little old plunder bag full. Right, ain't I? I reckon they could use me, if it was so's I could go along. I done traveled a right smart in my time, maybe not as much as you, from the looks of you, but a right smart all the same."

One peg boot came out and scuffed the ground in front of him. "Wisht I could go, but a man with ten in his fambly can't light out like a bird. I done spent too much time in bed, I reckon. A man can't do everything." His eye, set in a face that had got old without growing up, went to Boone again, expecting a smile or a nod or a yes said by the mouth. It was a weak and shallow eye that drove away easy. "Got to stay hereabouts, hitched to a plow like a mule, account of my fambly. Ain't nothin' in farmin' in this country, neither, just work and sweat and no money or fun. Not like in Oregon, where things grow big and rich without hardly no trouble at all." The eye lighted, thinking of Oregon. "What you say? A man with ten children and a woman wore-down-like, you think he could make it?"

"You got no business in Oregon."

"No?"

"No more'n these others, the goddam fools! Ought to stay home and not spoil a country as wasn't meant for the likes of you."

The man's jaw sagged like a scolded boy's, and the shallow eyes rounded.

"Stick to your bed and your birthin'. It takes a sure-enough man for Oregon." Boone drove the eye away again.

The man's face had gone empty and still as if waiting for thought to come to it. He turned it toward the ground and watched one boot push out and then the other. His mouth worked as if to speak, but nothing came. He sidled off, his shoulders drooping under his worn shirt. A man might feel sorry for him except he was a fool. He might feel sorry except, by God, it did good to get him told.

Mefford said, "There she is, you niggers, old St. Louis herself, just waitin' for us. Me, I'm dry as a year-old cow chip, and I hanker for women and play and all. Get up, river! Get up, pirogue! This coon can't stand to poke."

"I'll git off yonder." Boone motioned with his thumb.

"What!"

"Yan side."

"Not gonna spree in St. Louis!"

"I told you yan side."

"By Jesus!" Mefford wagged his head while he changed course.

Antoine put in, "Caudill, he have something better, *peut-être*, that way."

"Maybe so, but there ain't nothin'll surprise me after this."

"We hurry, to put him off, Sam," Antoine said, stroking with his oar. His voice was happy with looking ahead. "The small minute of waiting seem so long."

The pirogue nosed against the shore.

"Good luck to you, Caudill, and I hope you don't get no crazier and no crankier."

As Boone went by him, Black Sam looked up, his sleepy eyes suddenly soft and deep. "Goo'bye," he said. "Goo'bye, sad man."

The stagecoach stood at the side of the trail, like a big black egg on wheels, the horses unhitched from it and tied up to trees. Two passengers were on the ground watching while two others helped the driver shape a pole to replace the doubletree that had snapped when an axle hung on a stump.

Unspeaking, Boone walked by, feeling the faces of the passengers turning with him and hearing their lips murmur after him. Out of the murmur a few words came. "Got his hair in pigtails. See? Like a wild Indian."

Farther on a priest sat on a stub, his hands folded over a book in his lap while his eyes dreamed in the trees. As Boone approached, he lifted the book and turned a page or two and then put it down and let his hands rest on it again while his lips moved silently. His eyes woke up when Boone came even with him. "Good day," he said. He was a middling man as to size, with a round face that was full and pink from good living and looked all the pinker for the white collar and black coat below it.

"How."

"Rather walk than ride?"

"Quicker if a man's used to it."

"The trees are beautiful. Such a forest!"

"Too damn thick for my likin'."

"Sit down, won't you?"

"What's on your mind?" Boone let himself down on a stump.

"You're what they call a mountain man? A fur hunter?"

"I've catched a few."

"Where?"

"Most any place you could name."

"Missouri? Yellowstone? Columbia? Colorado of the West?"

"All of them and more."

"Please excuse my questions. You see, I want to go among the Indians. I'm on my way to Bardstown and from there, I hope, to the far west." His gaze went down to the hands folded across the book. "You've had many experiences with the Indians, I'm sure."

"Some."

"Say you were in my place, where would you like to go if you had the choice? I mean, to what tribe?"

"They don't want white men's ways, none of 'em."

"You haven't heard of our mission among the Flatheads?"

"Bunch of squaws. Squaw tribe, Flatheads and Nepercies both."

"Perhaps the others think they don't want white ways, but they need God."

"They got their own god."

A small smile, not unfriendly but not shilly-shally either, came on the black robe's face. "A god, but not God."

"The ones they got do good enough—good as any, I reckon."

The priest shook his head while he held the small smile. "No god does well but God."

"Can't see much difference myself."

"It isn't what a man sees." A plump finger came up and laid itself over the heart. "It's what he knows in here."

"You think your way. I'll think mine."

The face reddened above the white collar, but the voice stayed gentle. "That's a privilege in this country even though we abuse it." It was a keen and knowing pair of eyes he had. After a little silence he added, "Men are happier, knowing God," and waited for the answer it would bring.

"I git along all right."

"I see."

Boone got off the stump the priest had motioned him to. "No use to talk. Wisht you priests and preachers would stay out of the mountains myself."

"Why?"

"Just, goddam, because."

Boone didn't wait for more talk. He lifted his rifle and went on, walking the road to Paoli.

He always had felt at home outdoors. It was as if the land and sky and wind were friendly, and no need for a pack of people about to make him easy. The wind had a voice to it, and the land lay ready for him, and the sky gave room for his eye and mind. But now he felt different, cramped by the forest that rose thick as grass over him, shutting out the sun and letting him see only a piece of sky now and then, and it faded and closed down like a roof. The wind was dead here; not even the leaves of the great poplars, rising high over all the rest, so much as trembled. It was a still, closed-in, broody world, and a man in it went empty and lost inside, as if all that he had counted on was taken away, and he without a friend or an aim or a proper place anywhere.

When he came to a town, though, it wasn't any better, with fools staring and wagging tongues and thinking as how one man ought to be like another and all knuckling under to rules and ways and work and sheriffs and judges, and calling themselves free. And all living smothered by walls and roofs, breathing air that the good was gone from, breathing each other's stinks and the stinks that the hogs made in the pens back of the houses. Even the forest was better.

Near a deadening along the trail a big blue-tick hound got up from the door of a cabin and walked out, stiff-legged, for a look at Boone. His nose spread with smelling, and a soft rumble sounded in his throat. He raised old, sad eyes to Boone's face. Someone had cut his tail off. The nubbin that was left tried a slow, asking wag.

Boone walked around him, and afterward a voice called out, "Say, you, that's my dog!"

Boone turned and saw the hound at his heels and a red-faced man standing in the door. "Don't act like it."

"Mine just the same."

"Who's sayin' he ain't?"

"You been whistlin' him off."

"You're a liar."

"Must have. He ain't never followed a stranger before. Here, Blue! Here you, Blue!"

The dog sat down, his grayed muzzle lifted toward Boone, his sad eyes seeming to flow with the question in them.

"It's them goddam leather pants has got him trailin' you. Thinks you're huntin', maybe. Chase him here, will you? I take it back about the whistlin'."

"Chase him your own self."

"All right, then, if you want to keep your dander up, mister, but I done took it back."

Boone said, "Git home, boy! Git!"

The hound didn't move, except that in the dust his piece of tail swung a slow quarter-circle.

"Good-enough hound," the man said, coming up with a stick, "but independent-minded as all hell. Has a idea he can think and do for himself. I've beat his hide off and kep' him tied and starved him and all, but like I said he's a mule-minded damn hound. If he wants to run he runs, and no holler or horn'll bring him back. Tell him to lie down and he stands up, and tell him to stand up and he squats."

"What went with his tail?"

"I got so bull-mad at him I bobbed it, thinkin' it would l'arn him some sense. Look at him, will you? Never seen him eye a man that way before, like you were God Almighty." The man raised the stick. "Go back, Blue, you ornery potlicker! Back!"

The dog stood up, his flews hanging loose and his great eyes swimming on Boone. "Back, damn you!" The club beat his hindquarters down. It knocked him half over. It made a hollow thump on the ribs. Boone saw the ribs working for breath.

"That's enough!"

"How's that?" The man stopped with the club upheld.

"You ain't fitten to own a dog."

"This here's my business."

"The hound's goin' with me."

The man let the club down. "Lookie here. That's same as robbery. I'll git the law."

"Not if he just follers, it ain't. I go for'ard and you back, and let the dog please himself."

"No, by God!"

The hound had got up again.

"It's fight, then."

"That's a top dog. Worth a piece of money, he is. Boar coon never lived that could match him. It ain't right."

"Git on! You ain't goin' to fight, and I don't aim to talk." Boone reached out with one hand and caught the man by the shoulder and swung him around.

"It ain't right, I say! It ain't right! I'll git the law!" The man shuffled toward the cabin, his red face back-twisted on his neck and his mouth running with words.

With his eye Boone pushed him toward the cabin. Then he swung around and set out, hearing the man half-whispering, "Here, Blue! Here, ol' Blue!" after his back was turned.

The trail ran like a thin, deep canyon through the trees. The forest squeezed in, dark and broody. There wasn't a sound in it, not the rustle of wind or the crack of a twig under a hoof or the chirp of a bird or anything at all unless a man listened close. Then he heard a soft padding behind him.

The tavern keeper sat in a hickory chair outside the tavern. "Bedwell?" he said, while his good eye lifted to the sky. The other was just a slitted sink in his face. "No, sir," he answered, "don't recall such a name." He swung his good eye back to Boone. "Bedwell? Sure you don't mean Bedwet or Bedwetters? Plenty of them around, no doubt." When he grinned, his good eye slitted, too. He rocked on the heels of his chair.

"I knowed him once, him and a man named Test as was a judge."

"Now you're shortenin' to my range. You'll shoot a long piece to find Test, though. He's laid his burden down, as the sayin' is. Do' know what his burden was, unless it were that big belly, but anyway he's laid it down." The tavern keeper held up one hand and counted off the fingers with the other. "Four years ago it was now, he up and died while court was settin'. Had a growth in him nothin' would tech. Went to Corydon and Tare Holt and all around where men had read medicine, but wasn't no man or no medicine could help him."

"Who's high sheriff now?"

"Had a big funeral. People from hell and gone come, some to grieve and some to guzzle. Good time for drinkin', with the weather cool and all. Biggest day I ever had, I do believe, unless maybe for elections. Never keered much for Test myself, but I declare I always felt some'at grateful to him for dyin' when he did. Yup."

The man patted his leg and looked off into space again. "Take like now, a death don't mean so much, even a big one, with the weather comin' warm." His eye left the sky and fixed on a cow that went creaking in front of his place, her tail fanning at the flies. "A man don't start a fire inside with the sun blazin' out. Leastwise, some don't. Now's for me, a swaller or so makes me forget bein' miserable hot. Trouble with cold-weather drammers, they don't take enough."

Boone leaned on his rifle. Blue shouldered his thigh and sat down by him and sized up the tavern keeper with unwinking eyes. Across the road the courthouse sat, smaller than Boone had pictured it and old with weather. No crowd moved around it, but his mind made one, himself and Bedwell and the sheriff and the people following after, poking at him with their eyes and pecking at him with their lips. Beyond the courthouse he could see the jail. He could see the big, dark figure of the sheriff in the half-dark and the hand lifting with the whip.

"Good hound you got there," the man said, "only them great big eyes knows too damn much."

"Mark York still sheriff?"

"Not here, he ain't."

"What you mean?"

"He ain't sheriff here on account of he's a corpse."

"Dead?"

"Corpses generally is."

"Kilt, I reckon."

"Nope."

"How, then?"

"Died sudden. Died sudden and sodden, as someone put it. Had a fine belly of liquor and died in bed peaceful as a baby, and I bet his blood would run a full fourth proof the way he'd fired it up. How long you been gone?"

"A spell."

"Could be long or short."

"Could be."

"Don't waste wind, do ye? All right. All right. Ain't no law about talkin' or smilin' or such. Anything I can do for you, like settin' out a bottle or anything?"

"Wanted to see York was all."

"Friend of his?"

"I aimed to kill him."

Behind him as he started off Boone heard the front legs of the chair come down.

The cabin squatted in its hollow, the two-part cabin with the dog trot connecting and the shagbark hickory close by like always, except that lightning had struck it and put a scar high on the trunk. A breath of smoke came from the chimney and lay close over the roof as if it had no place to go. A pig grunted from its pen, and out in the pasture, closed in by the worm fence, an old cow lined her head with her neck and let out a long bawl.

The sun was fading out in the west, not going down in a blaze of clouds, not leaving twilight over the land, but just pulling from sight and letting the dark come on.

A long, thin man came out of the cabin carrying two buckets and made for the pigpen, and afterward his voice floated out in a wail, calling the cow. The cow stood listening, making up her slow mind, and tried a step and then another and settled to a draggy walk.

The woodpile was down almost to nothing. A man running and grabbing for a club might come up with no more than a splinter.

For a long time Boone sat on the slope of a hill, his mind not thinking, but feeling running old and deep in him. The blue-tick hound dozed at his side, waking now and then to sniff the air and rolling his sad eyes and fixing them on Boone as if to make double sure he was still there before closing them again.

Not until a window showed yellow with light and the dark had gathered thick in the trees did Boone move. Then he got up and let his feet take him down the slope.

45

I t was the phthisic killed your pap," Ma said. She overflowed the chair she sat on, being big-hipped like an old squaw but wizened from the waist up and not strong and quick in her movements as a squaw would be.

"You told me that."

"It was his sinnin' killed him," Cora put in while she wiped a pan. "It was the Lord in His wrath."

"It ain't becomin' to talk that way, not about your man's pa."

"All the same it was."

Boone sat in the doorway, only half hearing what the two women said. It struck him again, though, that Dan's wife was a fool, laying everything to God or the devil. "If it was the Lord," he said while he watched Dan's two boys climbing a black-oak tree, "He was late gettin' around to it. He should've kilt him sooner."

"Your pap's dead, Boone," Ma said.

"That's what I heerd."

"It was the phthisic done for him."

Boone didn't say anything to that. Ma was getting old and mixed in her mind so that she didn't remember from one word to the next what it was she had said.

"It ain't for us to pass judgment on the dead," she went on. "Pap had good in him."

356

"Ought to. He never let none out."

"In a way you put me in mind of him, Boone. You're broody-like your own self, and quick to blaze out. Your pap went down to bone with the phthisic, him as was so strong and tall, and couldn't hardly make out to lift his hand to wipe his mouth after a spell of coughin'. Just bones, he was, and the skin lyin' loose, and his eye like glass with the fever. He asked about you, Boone, more'n once. You oughtn't to think hard of him." With one finger she wiped away the wet that had come to her eye.

Boone didn't bother to answer. It beat all how Ma could grieve for the likes of Pap and couldn't talk about him without a sad, rabbity look and the tears leaking. She fumbled with her knitting now, on account of the tears.

Punk had climbed almost to the top of the oak. He hung to it with one hand and waved down at the doorway while the sun shone on his wild suit of rusty hair. "Look at me, Uncle Boone! Look at me!"

Andy, being younger, couldn't climb so high, but he waved from lower down and called, "See me! See me, too!"

"Tell them boys to get out'n that tree and fetch some wood," Cora asked Boone.

Old Blue lay in the dirt, in a spot of shadow at the side of a bush. He rested his muzzle between his paws. A little circle of gnats wheeled around his lids, making him wink. When his big, sad eyes came open afterward, they were always steady on Boone.

Ma said, "Time for Nancy Litsey to git here, if she's comin'. Said she'd bring some late-bloomin' flower seed for them cabbage plants I let her ma have."

"She'll come trottin'," Cora said, "bein' as there's an extry pair of breeches in the house."

"I swear, Cora!"

"She'll have her head high and that little nose openin' and closin' and her hair flyin' loose and no eye but for Boone." Cora put her hand to the rag that was tied over her own hair.

"Purty, to my way of thinkin'," Ma answered, "and comin' eighteen. Ain't she purty, Boone?"

"Good enough, I reckon."

"Can't see why you don't take notice of a good-turned girl like her."

"I seen good-turned ones afore."

"Redskins, I'll warrant," Cora said. "Heathens, that's what." She was a strong-minded woman who never talked quite friendly but not unfriendly enough to make a ruckus about unless a body was on edge. Probably words wouldn't tame her anyway; what she needed was a good lodgepoling. "You look close to a heathen yourself," she said to Boone, "with your hair long and all."

"He don't take after an Indian so much since he took off them buckskins and put on linsey," Ma put in.

"Too hot for leather," said Boone. "Too damn hot for anything." He squirmed his back against the doorsill to stop a tickle that a tear of sweat was making. It was a low, soft, smothering country, Kentucky was, where heat lay on the skin like a wet hand. Even the tail end of the day, with the sun going down and the shadows growing, still kept a man dripping.

Cora put lettuce in a wood bowl and cut radishes into it and went over to the fire and laid slices of hog meat in the spider so's to have some grease for the green stuff. She did most of the women's work, being as Ma's joint water had dried up. Ma said boiled sassafras rubbed on hot didn't do any good, or the wild raspberry wine that Cora had put by. In her slow, creaky way, though, Ma did a fair share of work. Her hands were always busy, with knitting or mending or carding wool from the few sheep Dan had, and every day she crippled down to the garden and tended the lettuce and beans and turnips and such.

Boone looked away from inside the house and saw Nancy Litsey coming up the path. Her hair shone like new straw in the low-blazing sun, and she had a red bow ribbon at the neck of her butternut linsey-woolsey. Homespun hung on most women like a sack, but with Nancy it put a man to wondering a little what was inside. She said "Evenin'" and stepped beyond him into the cabin.

Boone heard Ma and Cora speak to her and heard her answer, without paying much mind to what they said. A body could go along like dead and keep things buried so deep in him they never came to thought, and then one day, seeing maybe a head of hair like wheat straw, he would feel a stirring in him like a finger working. He could go along like dead except sometimes at night when lonesomeness would come on him and he would listen to the small sounds of Kentucky, to crickets chirping and a mouse running in the grass and a mockingbird singing to the dark, while a hankering swelled in him for a wolf howl and the rush of mountain water.

Punk pulled at Boone's sleeve. "Git your rifle, Uncle Boone, and come and shoot a eagle for us."

"Hit's two eagles," Andy said, "nestin' in the big sycamore where the old sow beds down."

"Would you, Uncle Boone? Would you? They're big and black as anything."

"Let it cool off some."

"Promise?" Punk asked. "Promise?" When he nodded, the two of them ran off.

Cora's words sounded from inside. "Wisht I had a cucumber. This here'd be tasty with just a touch. I never took no stock in cucumber's causin' biles and chills and yellow janders."

Nancy had a voice like a small, clear bell. "Pa says wherever jack-o'-lanterns be, there's fever."

By the side of the stones that Dan had put down for a walk the marigolds were getting ready to bloom. Ma took care of them, too, and of the hollyhocks and cornflowers that were pushing up. A gourd was climbing on the palings of the fence, getting mixed up with a trumpet vine. Boone's gaze lazed along the flowers and over to Blue and up the vines and above the palings and on across Dan's tobacco patch to the trees and hills beyond. He could look without really seeing and let his mind go without really thinking. He could look yonder or look inside to where the women were and make out, on a shelf, the little gourds that Ma kept her seed in and see hanging from a roof log the strips of dried pumpkin left over from winter, and it was as if another's eye saw them and another's head took them in. Only the little stirring in him was sharp, only the little finger of hunger working.

Dan came walking from the barn, swinging his legs slow and lazy. "Heat like to done for me," he said, letting himself down on a wood block and drawing his sleeve across his forehead. "Corn's a-wiltin', it's so hot and dry."

Dan had grown to be a long, slow-moving, slow-talking man with an Adam's apple like a point of bone pushing against the skin. There was a slow smile on his face a good part of the time, as if he found a secret, sad fun in most things, even in Cora and her tongue. Dan didn't like much to work, though. He didn't do any more than he had to.

Boone said, "I gave up on my job a little spell ago. Sun's like hell let loose."

"You been doin' too much anyway, cleanin' out stumps and rocks and makin' things smack smooth. Work like a crazy man, you do." Dan picked at the ground with a stick. "Like I said, wisht you'd take a notion to go in with me. Plenty of work here for two, and land enough."

"Don't reckon I care to." The women inside had quit talking to listen.

"It don't get you anything, roamin' don't. You had your taste of it, Boone."

Ma said, loud enough for them to hear, "Humans wasn't meant to traipse around all their lives."

"What you got out of it, after all?" Dan asked. "Don't see gold hangin' to you or rich clothes or anything."

"Wasn't lookin' for gold."

"Ever see any, Boone? Ever look for it? Must be some, in all that passel of country."

"We had beaver."

"You mean you never looked back, even, to see did you kick up any gold."

"We had beaver."

Dan looked at Boone like he might look at a crazy man. Boone just let him look. There weren't any words to make Dan know how it was. After a while Dan nodded and said, "Beaver, eh?" as if letting go of something he couldn't make out. "There'll be a pile of folks in the west before you know it, Boone. It'll be just like here, only more work to get started."

"You don't know a damn thing about it, Dan."

"I know I can't hardly handle this place myself." He gave Boone a slow smile. The knot in his throat pushed up along the skin of his neck and then went back again.

"Farmin's too much like work," Boone said.

"Might be we could buy us a nigger. What you think about slaves, Boone? Some fuss over the rights of it."

"I do' know."

"A body would think you never used your head at all. You got some idea, for certain."

"Bein' free means fight, to anything."

"So niggers ain't desarvin'?"

"Fight enough, and freedom comes."

"Could be you're right, but gettin' back to farmin' and to work, what's trappin' if it ain't work? And goin' hungry and cold and your feet wet half the time and your backside stiff from a horse and fear of redskins in you steady? What's that?"

Blue snapped at a fly and then laid his muzzle back between his paws.

Boone didn't answer right away. When he did it was to say, "We never counted it work."

"Can't see fun in it myself."

Cora spoke from inside the kitchen. "Have to be kin to Injuns for such to pleasure you." She stepped past Boone, walking as if she was all business, and carrying a bucket of ashes that she dumped in the hopper outside. The hopper was full to the top. One day now she would dump water on the ashes and so make herself some soap.

Nancy said, "Maybe I'm kin, then. I feel like I'd like it."

Boone tried to picture her in a tepee, tried to picture the straw-colored hair and the pale face and the high head and the slender nostrils that had a way of widening now and then. She was like a young mare, that's what—a nervous mare watching and trying the breeze.

Dan laughed. "Reckon I'll go, Nancy, if'n you'll go along."

Boone heard Ma's voice. "Don't take no notice, Nancy. He don't mean anything. One thing about the Caudills, they's all one-woman men. Pap hisself was, till the phthisic carried him off."

Cora let her eye fix on Boone as she passed inside. It was a hard brown eye, set in a tight-held face, that seemed always on the watch for something to blame a body for. She was so set against sin, Boone thought she must have a time with it herself. Back at the table she gave a loud sniff. "What you sayin', Nancy! The west ain't a place for decent people."

"You know a hell's sight of things that ain't so," Boone said to her.

Cora went on talking to Nancy. "Can't get that Boone inside a door, hardly. Won't sleep in a bed. Has to be outside like a wild critter."

A house smothered a man, sure enough, once he had got the

smell and look and feeling of the mountains in him. A house was close and shut in and full of little stinks, and a man with a roof over him and walls around couldn't see the sky or feel the wind or even know the time of night by looking overhead. "Don't like butter, neither, nor bread," Cora went on. "Likes marrow more'n butter. Put salt on a thing and you sp'ile it for him. Just straight meat and branch water, that's what he wants."

Dan winked at Boone. Under his breath he said, "Don't mind her, Boone. What the preacher says is righteousness is set so deep in her she's got to dig at somebody."

"Don't you ever hush her?"

Dan's face went solemn and tired for a little, and then the slow smile came. "It don't fret me much, not any more. Seems I can put up with things better'n you, like with Pap. Half of livin' is just holdin' in."

The girl's carrying voice came through the door. "It don't seem to have worked him harm." Boone had an idea that her glance had slid over to him, sizing up his built and heft. He squirmed a little under his shirt, feeling not quite comfortable.

Dan winked again. "One on your side anyhow, Boone," he said, low-voiced.

"If 'tweren't for you, I'd hush Cora's mouth good."

"Don't do it, Boone. It don't matter to me, and you ain't here but a while."

Boone listened to Nancy's "I best be going," and saw her coming for the door. As she went by, she turned her face full on him and her mouth made a quick smile, showing small white teeth. She was gone then, stepping up the path like a high-blooded young mare. Boone watched her going and knew that Dan watched, too. Even Blue raised his old head. It was a soft look she had had for him. Maybe he could call it inviting. The world and all had been like make-believe lately, with nothing of real feeling in it, and now there was this sharp, beginning stirring.

46

Tell us about Injun fightin', Uncle Boone," Punk said.
"I'd ruther hear about b'ars," Andy put in. "Tell about a
b'ar fight."

"No! Injuns! Injuns!"

"Bet I could kill a b'ar some time."

"You couldn't, neither," said Punk. "Shoo, maybe I couldn't
my own self, and I got two years on you."

"It wouldn't harm ye to tell 'em a little bit of something,"
Dan said to Boone. There was a gentle scolding in his voice and
in his face. "You ain't hardly opened your mouth to 'em about
the west."

"Don't shine at storytellin'." Boone tried to get comfortable in
his chair. It was a straight-back chair made of hickory poles and
woven bark. Ma sat in one like it, except it had rockers, and Dan
was hunched up on a three-legged stool that Boone remembered
from Pap's time. The two boys were on the floor. Cora went out the
open door with a pan of slop water. When she came back in, she
said, "Nigh to bedtime, you boys."

"No, Ma! Uncle Boone's fixin' to tell a story."

"We ain't sleepy."

"Got the wide-eye, ain't ye?" Dan asked, smiling down at the
pair of them.

Cora sniffed and went to wiping off the table.

"Cat's got your Uncle Boone's tongue," Ma said, her hands
busy with her knitting needles. "Won't hardly pass the time of day
with a pretty thing like that Nancy. Don't keer how his pap went."

Outside, the day was paling off toward night, though dark
wouldn't come for an hour yet. Through the door Boone could see
the old barn and a mockingbird fluttering up from the roof of it and
settling and fluttering again and all the time singing fit to tear the
throat out.

The boys' faces were turned up to him, waiting for him to begin.
With his first finger Punk worried his rusty forelock.

"Won't hurt the boys not to get abed so soon," Dan said to
Cora. "Seems like Boone might come out of his balk." Cora put her
washrag away and perched stiff on a chair as if just waiting for the

foolishness to be done. It was her sitting that way that made up Boone's mind.

"Reckon you never seen a white bear," he said to the boys. Punk held his knees in his arms and rocked back and forth on his butt, listening.

Andy said, "Never seed ary kind of b'ar."

"A ten-footer, this one was, and heavy as a ox."

"How long would his teeth be?"

"Long as this here finger, almost."

"An' sharp? Sharp as granny's knittin' needle?"

"Sharper."

Punk said, "Leave him go on, Andy."

"Eatin' berries, he was, when Tom Quinn run into him, onexpected, high on the Little Bighorn. Good country there, Dan. You never seen the like of it, 'round here."

"What about the b'ar?" Punk asked.

"Bear riz on his hind legs sudden and made a swipe at Tom and like to tore his arm out. Muscle was all pulled from it, for a fact, and the bone showin'. Tom yelled out, and I looked up from downstream a piece and seen what was up."

Speaking of them made the time and place come back, and Tom Quinn's scream shrill in the ear and the bear standing tall and the sun white on the tips of his fur.

"Go on, Uncle Boone!" Andy said. "Don't keep stoppin'."

"I up with my old Hawken and fired quick, and that there bear let down and the bushes shook like a herd of bulls was in 'em as he made for me. And me without time to load my rifle again and only an old pistol on me."

"Did you kill him?" Punk wanted to know.

"Man has to keep his head. Has to keep steady. Has to hold his fire."

Boone was holding himself steady again while the bear came on. He was seeing him charging big and black against the graveled bank and rearing at the last with the red drip of berries on his mouth and the clawed hand ready for the slap that would tear a man's face off. He heard the grunted breath of him and heard Tom shouting.

"You kilt him, I bet," Andy said. The click of Ma's knitting needles drowned Tom out.

"A white bear on a charge allus rises at the last, to hit you a side blow with his paw. That's the slick time to shoot, when his face's struck out straight at you and a ball won't glance off his head."

Dan asked, "You wait that long, sure enough?"

"I took aim between the eyes and let go."

"What else, Uncle Boone?"

"No else to it. He went over, dead as a bone, and I stuck my knife in him."

Cora came farther to the front of her chair. "Bedtime. Hear, Punk? Andy?"

Dan said, "Y'eat b'ar, I reckon?"

"Barrin' somethin' better."

"I don't guess a man ever lacks for victuals in the mountains, what with all that game around."

"Even wolf meat suits the taste fair enough. 'Member onc't runnin' into some British over in Oregon, and we was all froze for powder, but one of them British had some almighty big fishhooks—cod hooks, he called 'em—and we tied three together and hung 'em from a tree, baited with a rabbit we snared. Mister Wolf would jump for the rabbit and get hisself hooked and so hang there till we come along, with maybe his hind legs just touchin' the ground. Mostly, they was dead, time we showed up."

"It's ag'in Scripture," Cora said.

"What's ag'in it?"

"Eatin' meat strangled in its own blood. The Book tells you to keep away from meat offered to idols and from blood and from critters strangled."

"An empty belly don't go by a book."

Cora said, "Better if it did. Git to bed, you boys."

"Ever go hungry for a long stretch?" Dan asked.

Before he thought, Boone spoke the thing that had sneaked into his head. "Rock goats saved us once."

"What's a rock goat?" Punk asked, hunching closer.

"Nothin'. I was talkin' to your Pa."

Andy's mouth was pouty. "Ain't you goin' to tell us, Uncle Boone?"

"It ain't anything."

Cora got out of her chair. "I said bedtime."

"Go on, please! We can listen, can't we, Pa?"

"No, I told you," Boone said.

Dan's voice was soft. "Looks like your Uncle Boone has done talked hisself out." As Punk got off the floor, big Dan reached out and scuffed his head with his knuckles. "Take yourself along now, Punkin Top. And you, too, Andy."

"Where'd he get that rusty hair? His mammy's side?"

It was Cora that answered Boone. "Never no redheads in our family."

Ma looked up from her knitting. "Your grandpa, now, was a little bit pinky, him that died of the milksick before ever you was born, Boone. Or was it after? I swear, I can't keep things straight in my head. Anyhow, it was the milksick, but your Pap died of the phthisic."

The slow smile was on Dan's face. "This'n just stoled into the fambly, I reckon."

"You was sayin' about them rock goats," said Punk.

Boone got up. "This here chair makes me ham-shot," he said and walked out the door.

47

She met him by the fence that cornered halfway up the hill, as she had said she would.

Sliding away from the house, keeping to the shadows so's Dan or Cora or the boys wouldn't sight him, Boone saw her standing and the light lying on her from the moon that had just got untangled from the timbered hills and was setting out to shine. She was watching the moon, watching with her hands down and her chin up, and the lines of her soft and shadowy against the slope. He stopped to look while his heart beat strong in him and the stirring grew to a purpose that made all else seem small and distant. While he halted, he heard the mockingbird singing, singing blind or to the moon or the night or to the nest it had somewhere, singing loud and steady as if it had to sing. Climbing the rise, he kept his eyes on the girl but still went so quiet that it was old Blue, snuffing along a varmint's trail, that gave her a start.

"You scare a body dead," she said after she had made him out. "You don't make sight or sound, and then, of a sudden, you're standing close."

"Didn't aim to scare you."

"I don't guess you can he'p it. It's fightin' Injuns, ain't it, that makes you go so soft?"

"That, and huntin'."

"Huntin's tame around here, so Mose Napier said. You know the Napiers?"

"Used to."

"You would, they lived so close. They was still here when Pa came to take over their place. Mose looked funny, for his face was whopperjawed."

Boone hunted for a spot to sit and cleared it of a dead limb that had blown from a wild cherry tree. "Best sit down."

Instead, she climbed the rail fence and sat facing into the moon.

"You traveled nigh everywhere, your ma says," she said while he leaned against the fence.

"A right smart."

"My pa has seen a sight of things. Been to Indiany twice. He says it's mostly hoss thieves and such in Indiany."

"I stoled a horse there, at Paoli."

"Stoled it!"

"To get even, was all."

"Oh." After a little silence she said, "I can't stay long. Ma or Pa'll skin me."

The moon was growing smaller as it climbed, smaller and brighter so that her hair caught a gleam from it and he could see her lips moving when she talked. Off a piece old Blue snuffled among the bushes, and crickets set up their thin crying. It wouldn't be so long until the katydids joined in, grieving because summer was going. What Boone heard most, though, was the mockingbird, singing as if it couldn't stop. "You ain't bothered with them mockingbirds in the mountains," he said while he studied her face.

"They don't bother me. It's nice to my ears, and brave, singing away all night."

"I'll take a painter, or a wolf."

"Sometimes I come awake at night, and there's the mockingbird singing, and it's like it was saying all was right."

"A bird don't know about that."

She might have been speaking to the moon instead of him. "Those times, I think I'll go to far places one day and wear a boughten dress and eat off plates with flowers painted on."

"West is better, where there ain't such a passel of people." He let himself down in the spot he had cleared. "Best set here."

"Chiggers torment me terrible. Salt and lard don't help me, or anything but to let them die and hold back from scratchin'."

"Too early for chiggers," he answered, but she still sat there on the fence with her face seeming to dream at the moon.

This was how it was with a white woman. She put talk in the way and made up piddling dodges, pretending all the time not to know the prime thing that brought a man and woman together. A squaw, now, would own to what was in a man's mind. It would be yes or no right off, and no play-acting about it.

"Why'n't you get down?"

She climbed from the fence then, as if his words pulled her slow, and let herself walk over and sit down a little way from him. She turned her head to his turned face and drew back a little and smiled a quick, unsure smile, and he saw the white teeth and the little flare of the nostrils. "You're a solemn man," she said on her breath. "Can't tell what to make of you." She leaned back, holding her arms straight behind her, the heels of her hands braced to hold her up. That way, the moon shone full on her face, on the delicate nose and on the lips and on the wheat-straw hair combed back from her forehead. "You reckon folks live up there, Boone?" she asked.

His hand reached for one of hers and felt it small and hard and braced against the grass. She didn't draw it away but didn't give it to him, either. It might have been that the hands touched by accident, and nothing meant by it. He took his own away and sat wondering, with an edge of anger in him, how a man went about making up to a white woman. He moved closer to her, crowding her a little, and she turned and said "Mister Caudill!" in a put-on voice and turned away again. "Can't tell what to think of you."

"Ain't any different from other men, I reckon, not in what I want."

He heard the quick catch of her breath, but when she spoke it was still in make-believe. "Mister Caudill wants the whole hill to set on, him with his eye dark and set as the hole in a rifle bar'l and his mouth never smilin'. Reckon it would hurt him to smile." She brought her face around and turned her own smile on him.

His arm bore her back, the arm that had gone out of itself squeezed her to him and bore her back while his mouth hunted on her face.

"No! Boone!" The make-believe was gone. "No! No!" Her breath panted the words. Against his mouth her cheek was hot. "No!" Her back stiffened against his pull, stiffened and gave to him, little by little, while the panting grew and the hands that had made out to push him away lay weak on his shoulders. "No, Boone." His mouth found her lips and the lips came alive and her back settled to the ground. There was the hot, fast breathing of her in his ear and the arms tightening and the body answering, and, far off, the fool mockingbird singing, until the blood in his head shut it out.

He got up afterward and straightened himself, looking down while she lowered her skirt and curled on her side and lay in the grass, her mouth still a little broken from the feeling in her and her shoulders bucking to her catchy breath.

Her voice was small and jerky but still it spoke as if of something sure. "When'll we be married, Boone?"

He had wanted this woman and now he had had her and never wanted her again. In him there was only a deadness, the numb deadness of a man sure enough about dead. He sank down in the grass.

"When, Boone?" It was her hand now that hunted for his and cuddled it in the warm palm as if it was hers for good and all.

"I ain't thought about that."

"We got to be married," she said, and he thought he heard the quick sound of scare in her tone. "We just got to be married."

Not even the stirring was in him but only the dead emptiness and, slowly, the feeling he had to go. He couldn't abide Kentucky

longer, couldn't abide the little boresome life, couldn't abide Ma
or Dan or this girl that thought she owned him. Things began to
flash in his mind, out of the dark he'd kept them buried in. He had
had this Nancy, and now he couldn't think of her for the dark,
slender face and the big eyes of another that he had sworn to put
away from all remembering.

"You ain't said when, Boone."

He had to go. His feet straightened and lifted him up. "I got
a woman."

He left her sobbing in the grass. Once he heard her cry after
him and took a glance back and saw her sitting and bowed over.
It was too bad she took it so hard, but he had to go. Under him his
feet quickened.

No light showed from the cabin. He opened the door and felt
for his buckskins and rifle behind it and closed the door and put
on his hunting shirt and leggings. Old Blue sniffed at the leather
and at the rifle and raised his head, thinking these tame days were
gone. In the moonlight Boone could see the slow switch of the nubbin that was left of his tail.

Things kept coming at Boone, up from his deep guts into his
mind, out of no-feeling into hurt. He couldn't hold them back,
couldn't keep folks and places and remembered doings out of his
head, goddam it! Goddam it! Dark eyes and blind eyes and bright
blue eyes. Black hair, red hair. "Reckon this'n just stoled into the
fambly." Goddam it! Brown plains, west wind, wide sky, pistol
sounding big inside the tepee.

He had to go. West again. Somewhere west, as in that far-off
time. Maybe to see Dick Summers on the way. Maybe to tell old
Dick.

He didn't realize he was running until he saw Blue trotting
to keep up.

48

A woman yellow with fever and heavy with the young one in her paddled to the door and stood there puffing a little, looking at Boone out of eyes that had a sick shine on them.

"No got food," she said in a high flat voice while she shook her head.

"I ain't an Injun. Dick Summers here?"

"You look like one, enough to fool a body."

"Dick Summers here?"

"He is and he ain't. If it's the house you mean, he ain't. He's yonder in the field somewhere."

"I kin wait, or look for him, one."

"Set on the step then. He'll be in directly."

Boone leaned his rifle against the cabin and sat down. The woman eyed him a little longer and then went back into the cabin, walking splayed out like a duck.

The cabin was like what Boone thought it would be, knowing Summers, neat-built and strong, with the cracks chinked tight and real glass in the windows. It made a shadow, standing against the low sun, that reached out from him as far as a man might flip a pebble. Blue lounged into the shade, turned around twice and lay down, his old head pointed toward Boone. Down from the cabin, to Boone's right, there was a barn and farther on a field that was hip-high in corn. In the pen next to the barn a pig was grunting. A dog that was all hair and bark ran from behind the house and yipped at Blue. Blue winked one eye and let a low growl out of his phlegmy throat, and the small dog backed up, still yipping. Then he lifted his leg against a bush and scratched the ground afterwards and trotted away with his head held high as if he had made a good out of it.

After a while Boone saw a man coming out of the field, driving a mule. The man had an old black hat on and a faded blue shirt and a pair of jeans that seemed about to drop off of him; he walked stooped, dragging his feet a little, but Boone knew it was Summers.

Boone sat watching and waiting while Summers went inside the barn. The mule came out and lay down and rolled up a dust, and Summers appeared and started walking toward the cabin, wiping his forehead with his shirt sleeve.

"How, Dick."

Summers stopped and squinted from under his dusty hat and then walked forward, still squinting. "I be dogged!" His hand slapped his jeans and sent out a puff of dirt. "If it ain't Boone Caudill! How be ye, boy?"

"So's to git here, anyways." Boone took the outstretched hand. The smile felt strange on his face, as if the face almost had forgotten how to smile. "The heat like to put me under."

Summers wiped his forehead again. "A man gits used to it. Wise-lookin' hound you got, but old and wore out like me. Come in and set. Where you pointin', Boone?" His voice rose. "Woman, bring that there jug."

"Outside's good enough, ain't it?"

Summers paused on the step. "This nigger's nigh forgot how a mountain man feels. Outside it is."

They sat cross-legged on the ground. Summers spun his hat toward the step, where it made a little cloud when it hit. With his hair cut off, a man might almost think Summers had been scalped. His head was white as any eagle's, and there were lines in his face that Boone didn't remember. He didn't remember that Summers' shoulders slumped, either, or that his feet dragged or that his belly sagged over his belt. Except for the gray eyes that were straight as ever and still had a twinkle in them, it was as if Summers never had been a mountain man. It was as if he had grown old holding a plow, looking at the hind end of a mule.

The woman came out of the door. She had a finger hooked in the handle of a gallon jug and carried two tin cups in the other hand. For all he was old and changed, Summers must be a man yet to put that swelling under his woman's apron.

"This here's Boone Caudill," Summers said to her. "Been with me on many a spree."

"I hope you ain't workin' up to a case of bottle fever," the woman said, "not with such a sight of things to do. I thought he were a Injun."

"He'll stay for supper."

"It's nigh done."

"I ain't hungry," Boone said. "Just got a terrible dry."

Summers splashed liquor into the cups. "Put 'er down, then." He looked at the woman again. "We kin eat any time. S'posin' you leave us be."

To Boone she said, "Liquor don't set good with him no more. Too old to drink is what I tell him, and tied up with rheumatics. I hope you won't be temptin' him to get hisself drunk."

Boone looked at the ground, feeling the blood stir in him. It wasn't right for a woman to plague a man, leave alone an honest-to-God man like Dick. She ought to leave him be, like a Blackfoot woman would know to do, like Teal Eye would know, looking at him with her big eyes, not saying anything, letting him have his way, not thinking he was right or wrong or drunk or sober but just that he was himself. Just that he was her man.

"You do look like a Injun." The woman paddled away, closing the door after her.

"Good woman, for all she ain't such a punkin," Summers explained. His eyes, fixed on the door as if he could still see her, were gentle.

Boone loaded his pipe and got it going and turned the stem for Summers after he had puffed to the earth and sky and the four directions. Summers blew out the smoke and lifted his cup and swished the whisky around in his mouth. He sat quiet then, letting talk wait on the liquor. Boone drank his drink in a gulp. Summers poured the cup full.

The frogs started singing as the day turned off toward dark. The air was moist and close like a wet shirt. Boone felt a trickle of sweat on his ribs. Up on the Teton it would be cool now, and dry, and the squaws would be playing in front of the lodges, playing and laughing and squealing sometimes while the sun sank and the west wind moved along the grass. Later the stars would come out, sharp as sparks, and coyotes would sing, and wolves, and a man warm in bed beside his squaw would hear the river whispering.

"Seven year it's been, Boone," Summers said. "What about you?"

"I'm headin' back."

"Where you been?"

"In Kentucky State, visitin' kin."

"And before?"

"With the Blackfeet, mostly, on Maria's River and the Teton and all around there."

Summers asked, "Teal Eye?"

"We hooked up." After a silence Boone added, "It wasn't her

as set the Blackfeet on the *Mandan*. They wasn't Blackfeet anyways, but Big Bellies."

"Same breed of cats."

"No."

"Where's Deakins?"

A man was coming along the path toward them, his high, heavy boots kicking up a wisp of dust with each step. He had his homespun pants tucked into the boots. He said hello with a little signal of the hand. "You wouldn't have a team to sell, would you, mister, ox or mule?"

Summers answered, "Reckon not."

"I got to find me a team."

"So?"

"I didn't plan too good, for Oregon."

"You ain't the only one."

"I got a woman and a whole mess of furniture and such down here to Independence. They tell me I won't ever make 'er with the outfit I got."

"You're too late anyway. Everybody's lit out."

The man nodded. "The woman got sick on me. I be et for a tater if a woman can't get sick at the damndest times. And besides, axle's busted and the mud it come over the hubs. Time I got to Independence there wasn't nobody left. I'm fixin' for next year."

"Be plenty of critters at Independence afore then."

"Uh-huh. Mules with forty devils in 'em and ox straight from hell, and all of 'em set at fancy figures."

The man's face was on Summers, waiting for him to agree. It was a round, open face, a face, Boone thought, that never could keep a secret.

Summers said, "Get shet of your furniture afore you start."

"Get shet of it?"

"You will by and by, regardless. Soonest done, soonest mended."

"Cherry chists and chairs and beds and all?"

"All of 'em."

The man said, "Good Lordy!" and added a question: "You ever try to throw your woman's stuff away?"

"She don't have no fixin's much, savin' what I built myself and can build again. Have a drink?"

The man shook his head slowly while his tongue came out and

slid along his lips. "Reckon not. Liquor don't make for easy goin' in my fambly."

Boone said, "Your woman, now, she must be some. It was her notion, going to Oregon, I bet."

"Come to think on it," the man said as a child might have said it, "maybe it were."

"What for you goin'?"

"What for I'm goin'! My God, man, where you been? I'm goin' for soil rich as gold and crops the like of which you never see, and weather that suits a man come winter or summer, and no fevers to shake the bones loose. That's why I'm goin'. Ain't you hearn about Oregon?"

"You been there?"

"I been told plenty."

Boone turned to Summers. "We've half-froze in Oregon. We have, now. And gone with our bellies squeezed up, livin' on wild-rose buds and damn few of them about. Ain't it so, Dick?"

"Many's the time."

The man's eyes were full of doubt as he studied them. "That ain't what I hear."

"Besides," Summers put in, "you'll be fightin' Britishers afore you know it. Britishers and Indians both."

"It's our country, by God! It's good old Americky, clean to fifty-four forty, or will be, anyway."

"You'll freeze out and starve out," Boone said, "or maybe get rubbed out, if'n ever you get there."

"What you mean, 'rubbed out'?"

"You'll go under, that's what."

"Go under?"

"Get kilt. Don't you know white man's talk?"

"I reckon maybe you got a reason to scare a man off."

Boone swallowed another cup of whisky and wiped his mouth with his knuckles. "It ain't your country, nor any greenhorn's country. Why'n't you stay to home?"

"I reckon there's room for all."

Boone got up. "There ain't. She's crowded now so's a man can't catch his breath. It belongs to them as found it and lived in it. Hear?"

"You an Injun?"

"Piegan, me!" Boone shouted and whooped a war cry and jumped for the rifle he had leaned against the cabin.

The man backed off, his eyes wide and white as onions. "All the same," he said while a look of balkiness covered the first surprise in his face, "a man's got a right to go where he wants." He turned and walked down the path, his shoulders held straight under his checkered shirt.

Boone leaned the rifle back against the cabin and sat down again. "Give me another drink, Dick. Damn greenhorns!"

A twinkle shone in Summers' eyes and then went out. "A passel of 'em's went a'ready, and more's a-comin'."

"They won't shine in Oregon. They'll come draggin' back, them as don't go under."

"I do' know, Boone. They got the bit in their teeth, some of 'em, like you just seen." Summers was quiet for a while and then went on, "I reckon they'll be trompin' over the trails we made and climbin' the passes you and me saw first and pokin' plows in along the river bottoms where we used to camp. They got a hunger, they have. This nigger don't look for the old days to come back."

They sat quiet, drinking, as the dark closed in around them. A screech owl began to whimper in a tree behind the cabin. Ma would say someone was going to die. Old Blue got up and stretched and looked at Boone as if asking his leave and went moseying away.

"Changes come on, regardless," Summers said while he poured more whisky. "Ain't nothin' in beaver—not since them Londoners took to silk."

"Beaver's sceerce."

"Not even a rendezvous any more."

"Bridger's set up a fort on Black's Fork where the free trappers aim to go."

"What you figger to do, Boone?"

Boone let his empty cup dangle from his finger. It was a long time before he felt like answering. Then he said, "There's buffler aplenty."

"You, a true mountain man, hunt coarse fur!"

"Maybe." In his mind's eye Boone could see Zeb Calloway, sitting there in the dusk by Fort Union. He heard his voice, coming through all the time since: "Another five year and there'll be naught but coarse fur, and it goin' fast."

It was as if Summers saw and heard Zeb, too, for he asked, "How long since we seen your uncle?"

"Thirteen year or so, it was."

"Thirteen. It don't seem that long, in a way, but in a way it seems so far back it wasn't even us as heard him."

"He was wrong, wrong by eight or ten years."

"Close enough to be right. What went with him?"

"He went under there at Union, went under happy, with his belly so full of whisky it kilt him."

"It's a good way, if a man's got to go."

"Good as any."

"You ain't said about Deakins and Teal Eye. You goin' back to Teal Eye?"

Summers studied Boone. He was heavier than he had been, and even stronger, as strong as a buffalo bull, by the looks of him. The muscles of his arms showed under his shirt, and the thick column of his neck spread out along his shoulders and down the swell of his chest.

"Have another."

For all his strength, though, there was trouble in him. Summers could see it in his eyes and around his mouth and in the way he drank liquor, as if apurpose to make his mind blank. He was a man with a misery eating at him—a deep misery, that would come out by and by, likely, if he kept downing whisky. Somehow Summers was reminded of a thing hunted, and no way for it to turn. Already the whisky was showing on Boone. His eyes slid slow in his head, and his mouth moved around a word as if to shape it careful before turning it loose.

"We had us some times, Boone."

"Y'ever see the upper Teton, or what they called the Tansy?"

"Where it meets up with the Marias is all. It's had more names than most. Rose was one of 'em."

"Higher up there's two buttes and the valley wide above and, where the river comes out'n the mountains, a peak like an ear on its side."

"I never seen that."

"Christ, but it's fair country, Dick! Mountains to the west, and the valley and the plains rollin' away. And buffler! Christ, I seen buffler thick as gnats. I seen 'em chased over pishkuns and lyin' kickin' below by the hunderds, and the Piegans with clubs and knives and arrers runnin' among 'em, makin' meat."

It wasn't so dark yet that Summers couldn't see. Boone brought his cup to his mouth. His eyes were set far off, seeing the Teton, Summers imagined, and the mountains and the buffalo, and seeing Teal Eye, too, though he didn't speak of her. For an instant Summers saw it all, too, and he felt himself wrench inside, wanting to be loose again, and free, wanting to trap and hunt and to know danger and good loneliness, wanting to see bucks with feathers in their hair and squaws in scarlet blankets. And then the feeling went down in him, leaving a small deep sore that didn't bother him if he just didn't pick it. He was too old now, and he had a white wife and a baby coming on, and the old days were lost, anyhow. Farming was the right caper for him, when he really thought things out.

"I know," he said, watching Boone. "Feel like eatin'?"

Boone came up on his feet and steadied himself.

"I'm goin' on, Dick."

"Better stay all night." Summers arose. Boone was rocking back and forth as if he rode the deck of the old *Mandan* in a storm.

"I got to go on."

"You ain't right to go, Boone. You had a sight of liquor."

"Maybe I'll see you."

"You'll need more whisky, come mornin'," said Summers, thinking maybe he could change Boone's mind through delay. "Come inside and I'll pour you some." He went through the door and lighted the oil lamp with a splinter held in the coals of the fireplace. He found a bottle on the shelf. "Set a spell longer."

Boone didn't seem to hear him. He stood rocking, his eyes distant and fixed and a look on his face such as Summers never had seen there.

"The world's a-comin' at me like a sea," he said, "a hill and then a holler rollin' under my feet, tryin' t'upset me. I drunk too much, Dick, but I got to go on. Got to go for'ard." His hand took hold of the latch on the half-opened door.

"Don't hurry yourself. I ain't got this bottle ready yet."

Boone looked down in his palm, at the latch his hand had broken off. "It's all sp'iled, I reckon, Dick. The whole caboodle."

"I don't guess we could help it," Summers answered, nodding.

"There was beaver for us and free country and a big way of livin', and everything we done it looks like we done against ourselves and couldn't do different if we'd knowed. We went to get away and enj'y ourselves free and easy, but folks was bound to foller and beaver to get scarce and Injuns to be killed or tamed, and all the time the country gettin' safer and better known. We ain't seen the end of it yet, Boone, not to what the mountain man does against hisself. Next thing is to hire out for guides and take parties acrost and sp'ile the country more. You must've heerd about old Tom Fitzpatrick pilotin' movers to Oregon last year, damn him! It's like we heired money and had to spend it, and now it's nigh gone."

"This here hand done it," Boone said, holding the hand before him. "This here finger pulled the trigger. I reckon I sp'iled it all, Dick." He looked at Summers, his eyes so dark and troubled the gaze of them was like a quick, deep pain in a man. "I kilt Jim."

"Kilt Jim!"

"I been tellin' myself I done right, Dick. But I don't know. I don't know for sure. Maybe I ain't honest."

"Kilt Jim!" Summers said again.

"It's like it's all sp'iled for me now, Dick—Teal Eye and the Teton and all. Don't know as I ever can go back, Dick. Goddam it! Goddam it!"

He had pushed the door clear open, and his feet shuffled and found the step and took him out. Summers followed him, forgetting to give him the bottle he held in his hand. A dog barked, townway, and another took it up and another until finally Boone's old blue-tick hound came loping from behind the cabin and stopped and pointed his nose at the sky and let loose with his deep bay. For a while Summers could see Boone, weaving big and dark into the darkness, and then he couldn't see him any more, and he turned and went back into the cabin. There was cold corn pone on the table, and cold poke greens and a ham butt and a pitcher of buttermilk. His woman had gone to bed, she tired so easy these days.